THE SNIPER'S KISS

Acclaim for Justine Saracen's Novels

Waiting for the Violins is "a thrilling, charming, and heartrending trip back in time to the early years of World War II and the active resistance enclaves...Stunning and eye-opening!"—*Rainbow Book Reviews*

"I can't think of anything more incongruous than ancient Biblical texts, scuba diving, Hollywood lesbians, and international art installations, but I do know that there's only one author talented and savvy enough to make it all work. That's just what the incomparable Justine Saracen does in her latest, *Beloved Gomorrah.*"—*Out In Print*

"Saracen blends historical and fictional characters seamlessly and brings authenticity to the story, focusing on the impacts of this time on 'regular, normal people' ... *Tyger Tyger* [is] a brilliantly written historical novel that has elements of romance, suspense, horror, pathos and it gives the reader quite a bit to think about...fast-paced...difficult to put down...an excellent book that easily blurs the line between lesfic and mainstream."—*C-Spot Reviews*

"*Sarah, Son of God* can lightly be described as the 'The Lesbian's *Da Vinci Code*' because of the somewhat common themes. At its roots, it's part mystery and part thriller. *Sarah, Son of God* is an engaging and exciting story about searching for the truth within each of us. Ms. Saracen considers the sacrifices of those who came before us, challenges us to open ourselves to a different reality than what we've been told we can have, and reminds us to be true to ourselves. Her prose and pacing rhythmically rise and fall like the tides in Venice; and her reimagined life and death of Jesus allows thoughtful readers to consider "what if?"—*Rainbow Reader*

"*Mephisto Aria* could well stand as a classic among gay and lesbian readers."—*ForeWord Reviews*

"Saracen's wonderfully descriptive writing is a joy to the eye and the ear, as scenes play out on the page, and almost audibly as well. The characters are extremely well drawn, with suave villains, and lovely heroines. There are also wonderful romances, a heart-stopping plot, and wonderful love scenes. *Mephisto Aria* is a great read."—*Just About Write*

"Justine Saracen's *Sistine Heresy* is a well-written and surprisingly poignant romp through Renaissance Rome in the age of Michelangelo...The novel entertains and titillates while it challenges, warning of the mortal dangers of trespass in any theocracy (past or present) that polices same-sex desire."—Professor Frederick Roden, University of Connecticut, Author, *Same-Sex Desire in Victorian Religious Culture*

By the Author

The Ibis Prophecy Series:

The 100th Generation

Vulture's Kiss

Sistine Heresy

Mephisto Aria

Sarah, Son of God

Tyger, Tyger, Burning Bright

Beloved Gomorrah

Waiting for the Violins

Dian's Ghost

The Witch of Stalingrad

The Sniper's Kiss

Visit us at www.boldstrokesbooks.com

THE SNIPER'S KISS

by

Justine Saracen

A Division of Bold Strokes Books

2017

THE SNIPER'S KISS

ISBN 13: 978-1-62639-839-9

THIS TRADE PAPERBACK ORIGINAL IS PUBLISHED BY
BOLD STROKES BOOKS, INC.
P.O. BOX 249
VALLEY FALLS, NY 12185

FIRST EDITION: MARCH 2017

CREDITS

EDITOR: SHELLEY THRASHER
PRODUCTION DESIGN: STACIA SEAMAN
COVER DESIGN BY SHERI (GRAPHICARTIST2020@HOTMAIL.COM)

Acknowledgments

Historical fiction is not only the creature of imagination; it also relies on professional expertise. In this respect, I am most grateful for advice and translation (from/into Russian) from Tatiana Davydova and especially from Galina Lemelman, who maintains her own brave LGBT press in Moscow. Fellow author and lawyer Carsen Taite provided me with useful legal information, and Radclyffe, in her surgeon's persona, assisted me in calculating how badly I could wound my heroine without killing her. I offer gratitude and affection to Shelley Thrasher, a friend, I hope, and stalwart editor, who has guided me through the shoals of prose writing for eleven novels. I acknowledge the brilliance of artist Sheri Halal, who conjured another eye-catching cover from the paint box of her mind, and the eagle-sharp eye of Stacia Seaman for final editing. Lastly, I again pay homage to Radclyffe the publisher, who built the edifice of Bold Strokes Books on the strength of her own imagination and industry. I wish I could share a bottle of wine, or three, with you all.

To the Soviet women who gave their lives in World War II

PROLOGUE

Major Pavlichenko rested both elbows on the table and stared down at her wineglass. "We're not like other soldiers. Yes, sometimes they send you off to knock out communication lines or machine-gun nests, and then you're just a rifleman with a good aim." She paused, turning the glass with her fingertips, and Mia knew more was coming.

"But sometimes it's personal. You're assigned to hunt a particular officer, or an enemy sniper, one of your professional colleagues, so to speak. Then the act of shooting is…a kind of intimacy and leaves a mark on you."

"Intimacy? Shooting an enemy from a long distance?"

"Yes, because the target's not anonymous anymore. You might track him for days or watch him for hours, as he moves around his subordinates. When he finally settles down and you get him in your scope, you fixate on him, on his uniform. While you're waiting for the perfect shot, you can see his rank on his cap or collar, his medals. You study the details of his face, whether he shaved that morning or has a dueling scar. Maybe he's handsome or looks like someone you know. You wait for him to turn just the right way, and when you lay your crosshairs over his face, you look into his eyes. He's perhaps five hundred meters away, but he could be in your embrace, and he's yours completely."

She stared into space and seemed to be remembering.

"You feel a surge of power but also a little sadness because you know this man has no idea he is in the last moments of his life. How many more breaths will you allow him to take? You're tempted to let him take another and another, because by now you're half in love with him. But then you remember your duty and your homeland, and so, after a farewell in your thoughts, you fire. Your shot, your touch, is directly to his head. It's a moment you never forget, and we have a name for it."

"A name, for a kill? What's that?"

"The sniper's kiss."

Chapter One

New York City, August 1942

"Patricide," the detective said, sitting across from her at the interrogation table. He pronounced the word slowly, like something he'd never said before. "Don't see much of that."

Mia Kramer remained silent.

He leaned toward her, resting on his forearms. His rolled-up sleeves revealed an unpleasant amount of hair, and he gave off an odor of old sweat in spite of the fan that whirred from a shelf behind him. "The neighbors heard you fighting on the roof of the building. What were you doing up there anyhow?"

Mia sat back against her chair, seeking a maximum distance from him. "What do you think? It's August, we live on the top floor of a tenement, and it's like an oven inside. My father was drinking. We argued awhile, and I came downstairs again. I don't know what happened after that."

He slid a file toward him from the side of the table and opened it to typewritten papers stapled at one corner. He turned the pages leisurely, though obviously he'd already read them. "It says here you threatened him, that you hated him."

"Everyone hated him. Everyone, except...that woman." She looked away. "Wanting to do something is not the same as doing it."

The detective read from the paper again. "'That woman.' You mean Agrafina Smerdjakov, otherwise known as Grushenka, the wife of Pavel Smerdjakov, the owner of the shop your father worked in. The ncighbors across the alley heard the whole argument. They claim you called him a pig for screwing his boss's wife, and in return, he said you were a pervert for doing the same thing."

He glanced up, smirking. "I've always wondered how you girls do that, with no natural equipment." He snickered. "But that must have made you pretty angry, knowing your old man was doing your girlfriend. Enough maybe to shove him off the roof." He shook his head. "What you people get up to just amazes me. Like something out of a trashy novel."

He clearly had an entire lurid scenario in his mind, half of which was correct, and she had no defense for it. She simply dropped her eyes. "Someone else was there. I heard my father talking as I went down the stairs." It was a lie. She hadn't heard anything.

"Who was he talking to?"

"I don't know. Someone from the building, I suppose. Those neighbors who were listening so carefully, they must have heard him."

The detective tapped the file with the back of his fingers. "Nope, nothing like that here." He read from the report again. "So how come your father's called Fyodor Kaminsky and you're Mia Kramer?"

"His name was Kramer, too. They made us change it when we arrived. But when he got the job at Smerdjakov's, he used his Russian name again. The customers liked that."

"And Mia? That's your real name?"

"It used to be Demetria Fyodorovna. They changed it at Ellis Island."

"And your mother?"

"Has nothing to do with the case. She died ten years ago." Mia waited for a reply, but he just stared and then stood up from the table. Another man stepped away from the wall where he'd been standing, and they conversed in undertones.

"Can I go now?" she asked.

"Yeah. Just stay away from married women." The detective snorted, then strode with the other man out of the interrogation room.

A patrolman took her by the upper arm and led her along a corridor to a public room. Grushenka stood up from a bench as she entered. The pale Slavic face was as beautiful as ever, and the voluptuous body seemed to invite embrace. But Mia felt only disgust.

"I'm sorry, Mia," Grushenka said, pressing her lovely full lips together in contrition. "I never meant to hurt you, or anyone."

Mia walked past her without replying.

❖

The tenement apartment was still sweltering in spite of the open windows. A paper bag full of trash that leaned against the wall added the odor of rotten vegetables. She lifted it gingerly by the damp bottom, laid it sideways on the shelf of the dumbwaiter, then reeled it down by its rope to the basement for the super to collect. Shutting the door cut off the fetid odor that rose through the shaft. As she turned away, the apartment door opened and Van came in.

"So, what the hell happened?" he asked, yanking open the icebox and snatching a bottle of beer. "I've just come back from the police station, and they said he fell from the roof. Or was pushed. Did you do it?"

"You expect me to say yes? I wasn't there, so it could just as easily have been you. We both know how evil he was."

He downed half of the bottle in several swallows, then wiped his mouth with the back of his wrist. "No, just a sanctimonious pig, a fanatic."

"And you don't call that evil?"

"No such thing as evil. We're all animals who piss and fuck from the same part of our bodies. Some of us just do it in a more refined way."

She grimaced. "You don't have to be so vulgar, Van. If he wasn't evil, why did you hate him so much?"

"Because he beat me once too often, especially after Mother died. And you know what he said when he beat me? That God smites us to drive out our impurities. That every blow hardens us and shapes us. Even after he started drinking and fucking every woman in sight, he was still whining remorse in front of his stupid icons." He closed his eyes and finished the rest of the beer.

"So, why didn't *you* kill him?" Mia took the bottle from his hand and set it with the other empties.

"I could have, and my conscience would have been clear. But

I made a practical decision. If I killed him for being a pig, someone might kill me tomorrow for the same thing." He reached into the icebox for a second beer.

"What a disgusting moral code." She sat down, fanning herself with the newspaper.

"Okay, sorry. Well, whoever did it, I'm responsible for the funeral arrangements after the cops release the body. You'll have to help me."

"No, you're going to have to do that yourself. Now that he's out of the way, I'm getting the hell out of this place. I'm sick of nosy neighbors, of climbing up five flights every day, of having to stay on the roof every summer night until it cools. I've got a job offer in Washington."

"Washington? What's wrong with the accounting job you've got here?"

"Bookkeeping for a shoe store? No future in that. The government's offering much better jobs for the war. This one's with the Lend-Lease program."

"Lend-Lease. What the hell's that? Sounds like they're loaning out lawnmowers."

"Oh, come on. Don't you listen to the radio? It's war supplies. We make them and lend them to the Brits. Anyhow, I was going to announce it, but then this thing with Father came up. I'm leaving tomorrow. I need a few days to find a rooming house before I start work."

He sat down, nonplussed. "You're really serious, aren't you?"

"Yes. Don't worry. I'll keep in touch, and the police will know where to find me. You can keep everything he left. The furniture, his filthy money, this cockroach-infested apartment. You're the man of the house now. Enjoy it."

CHAPTER TWO

Washington, DC, October 1943 (fourteen months later)

Mia glanced at the wall clock. Four thirty. Technically, she was supposed to be working, but she had nothing in her in-box, so she slid the new job application from her drawer and finished filling it out.

Age: Twenty-nine.
Education: Diploma—Manhattan School of Accounting.
Work experience and skills: Typist, accountant, Russian-English translation. Dictation in English or Russian.
Typing speed: Sixty words a minute. (She exaggerated only slightly.)
Mother's and Father's names: Ekatarina Kaminskaya, Fyodor Ivanovitch Kaminsky.

Her gentle mother had been gone too long to be more than a vague memory. But her father...well...her recollection of him was a mix of disappointment and fear, ending in disgust. He'd never really beaten her, the way he had Ivan, but his orders—that she dress like a drudge, that she give up her fun-loving American friends, that she be housekeeper in their tenement apartment—were absolute and tinged with threat. Her protestations simply elicited a slap from him. "Never question my authority," he'd say. "A father knows what's best for his children." It was her first small victory to be allowed to take an accounting course at the local college, though he agreed only because he knew the dreary accounting job that followed would add to the family finances. And she'd had to fight hard to be allowed out of the house to volunteer for the Roosevelt campaign.

Well, the old tyrant had been dead over a year now, and the police investigation had gone nowhere. That was a relief, though she felt a slight shame for leaving the burial in Van's hands. Well, Van, or Ivan, as his father had persisted in calling him, had inherited Fyodor's bank account and possessions, of which the only things of value were a copper samovar and some gold-painted icons. As an atheist and a cynic, Van must have found that amusing.

She did think occasionally of Grushenka, but always with embarrassment. Since that unfortunate involvement, she'd been celibate. Men had paid court to her, but she wasn't interested. And women weren't exactly beating a path to her door. Even if they were, the risk of losing her job was too great.

Sally, sitting at the desk across from her, glanced over. "You're going to leave us, aren't you? I saw the application."

"I'd like to. When I took this job last year, I didn't think it would be so dreary. It's only slightly better than the one I had before."

Sally turned the platen and yanked out her finished page. "Yeah, numbers are numbers. Nothing jazzy about them. But didn't you work for the FDR campaign in New York during the last election? Maybe something good might come from that."

"That's what I thought. Mrs. Roosevelt even thanked me for the bookkeeping I'd done for the committee. I gave my resume to the campaign headman, hoping for a little secretarial job in the administration. But everything went to the men. It's maddening."

"Hey, Mia!" The office boy stuck his head through the opening in the doorway. "Boss wants to see you."

Mia winced with vague anxiety, then followed the boy down the corridor to the door at the end. After a timid knock and a muffled "Come in," she opened the door.

Mr. Steinman sat at his desk puffing on a cigar. Another man sitting on his left stood up as she entered.

"Mia, this is Mr. Harry Hopkins. He's looking for an assistant and insisted on talking to you."

Still bewildered, she turned to face the stranger. He was tall, angular, and gaunt, and his too-large suit jacket drooped over both shoulders. His head, which jutted forward slightly, was almost cadaverous and had a receding hairline. The hand he held out to her was all bone, as if it should have held a scythe. She took it cautiously.

"I'm pleased to meet you, Miss Kramer. I'm afraid I'm in a hurry and don't have time for an official interview. I need an assistant who's good at taking notes and dictation."

"I told you, Harry. George Osborne is good at that." Steinman tapped his cigar ash into an enormous glass ashtray.

Hopkins ignored him. "It also involves the sort of Lend-Lease accounting you've been doing, but on a larger scale."

"I'm telling you, George is the best accountant we've got." Steinman was standing now. "And he's a senator's son."

"...and Russian."

"I know Russian," Mia said quietly.

Steinman sat down again, obviously defeated, and puffed on his cigar.

"Yes. That's why I've come. The First Lady gave me a copy of your resume. So, do you want the job or not?"

"Yes, of course." That was all she could manage. "When can I start?"

"Monday would be good. That will give you time to move in over the weekend."

"Move in? Where? I already have a room in town."

"No. I'll need you close at hand. For meetings, and I've got a pile of calculations already on my desk. Your office will be down the hall from me, and they'll give you a room upstairs."

Mia was flustered. This strange, cadaverous man wanted her to live in the same house as him? Suddenly she had doubts.

"Upstairs? Where exactly is your office?"

"Sorry. Didn't I mention that? In the White House. Come around to the Rose Garden entrance at eight o'clock on Monday, and someone will take you up."

Mia checked her watch as she lugged her suitcase along the path that curved around the White House South Lawn. Seven thirty. She was on time.

"Can I help you, miss?"

Startled, she turned to see a uniformed policeman.

"Um, I'm supposed to report to Mr. Hopkins. I have an appointment at ten o'clock."

"Well, the public ain't supposed to be wandering around the Rose Garden, but I'll take you to the door." He swung toward the left and began walking.

"Thank you." She grabbed her suitcase and scurried after him. The officer led her up a low flight of steps and along an arcade to the end. A door opened as they approached.

"I got a woman here says she has an appointment with Mr. Hopkins," her guide announced. His job done, he hooked his thumbs on his belt and stepped back.

Nodding, the second officer dialed something on his phone and passed the message along. Mia glanced at her watch again. Quarter till eight.

Some two minutes later, a civilian in a dark suit appeared. "Good morning, Miss Kramer. I'm George Allen, the White House butler. Mr. Hopkins is expecting you." He took her suitcase out of her hand.

Pleased to finally be acknowledged and relieved of the cumbersome baggage, she followed him without glancing back. He led her along a corridor that took them back into the main building, and they climbed a flight of stairs to the second floor. They passed closed doors, and she wondered what majestic staterooms lay behind them. He halted at the far end of the corridor where a plaque near the door read *Lincoln Suite*. The butler knocked and set her suitcase down against the wall.

The door opened to the same cadaverous man who'd hired her. "Ah, right on time. Thank you, Mr. Allen." He waved away the butler and opened the door wider to admit her.

Inside, a desk, cabinet, and side table were covered with papers, and a jacket hung over the back of a chair. "Sorry about the mess. The paperwork just overflows, which is why I've hired you."

She nodded, waiting for more explanation of her job. Would it start with housekeeping?

"I'm sure you're familiar with President Roosevelt's Lend-Lease program. I'm in charge of it, more or less. In short, I work for him, and you'll work for me. Let me show you to your office." He stepped toward the door and held it open for her. "How's your shorthand, by the way?"

"Tolerable. I can read it myself," she said, passing him.

They strode along the corridor together. "That's fine. The supply orders are constantly changing, and while the federal budget office will do the final accounting, I'll need early estimates to present to them. So you'll be my accountant, too."

They stepped through a door into another hallway and then into an elegantly furnished room.

"And the Russian?" she asked. "You said that was a requirement."

"The Russian. Yes. For the correspondence from the Soviets. The president has his official translators, of course, but I want to have my own resources."

Her mind was buzzing with the amount of responsibility he seemed to be handing her, but it was a good buzz.

"Ah, here we are." He opened the final door to a cubicle with a tiny desk, typewriter, and a gooseneck lamp. "This is your work space. On the other side of this wall is the First Lady's office. It's small, I know, but half the time, you'll be at conferences with me taking notes."

He glanced at his watch. "I have a meeting now with the president in the West Sitting Hall, so Mr. Allen will show you to your quarters. You can settle in and then meet me back at my room at ten."

Escorting her to the door, Hopkins started off down the corridor on his long legs.

The butler still waited outside the office with her suitcase, and she rejoined him, stifling a grin.

So that's it. I work for the president of the United States.

❖

"Here you are, Miss Kramer." The butler opened the door to her room and set her suitcase down just inside. "The bathroom is down the hall on the left, and you'll be taking your meals downstairs in the White House kitchen. Supper is at seven."

"Who else is up here?" she asked, noting the other doors.

"At the moment, just the housemaids and the occasional non-state guests. So, I'll leave you to your unpacking now." With the slightest hint of a bow, he backed away and closed the door gently.

She glanced around at her new quarters, in a part of the White House she hadn't even known existed. The narrow room with a sloped ceiling was sparsely furnished, with fewer amenities than her rooming-house accommodations had offered.

She laid out her few belongings: her comb and brush, toothbrush, three changes of clothing, several sets of underwear. Nervously, she checked her watch. Almost ten.

After running her brush quickly over her hair and checking that her slip didn't show, she hurried down to the main floor to the Lincoln Suite. No one replied to her knock.

Hopkins was undoubtedly still with the president, so she strolled toward the room where they were meeting. She'd only just arrived when the door opened. Hopkins stood in the doorway, his back turned, making some final remark. Curious, she looked past him to catch a glimpse of the president and caught her breath.

The president of the United States was in a wheelchair.

CHAPTER THREE

Russia, September 1943

The air raid siren over the city of Arkhangelsk began to wail for the hundredth time, and Alexia sprang into action. The Red Army was pushing back the Germans all over the Eastern Front, but the Luftwaffe persisted in bombing Arkhangelsk, trying to block the arriving arms shipments. Not only the harbor came under repeated attack; the town itself was regularly bombarded.

She rushed down the creaking wooden staircase at the back of the house and ran full-out toward the school. The first wave of bombers was overhead now, dropping their high-explosive charges. Knocked to the ground by the first concussion, she rolled behind a truck, covering her head. Her ears rang, and when she looked up she saw that the school, just in front of her, was untouched. Unfortunately, another raid would follow within minutes.

She staggered along the cratered road to where the rest of the wardens were already assembling with gloves and helmets, and Grigory was unrolling the main hose. Waving to the team leader, she rushed up the stairs to her post, cowering behind one of the walls as the next wave of planes arrived.

As usual, the second wave carried only incendiaries. Where the earlier explosions had penetrated the roofs, the incendiaries would finish the job inside the buildings, igniting fires inaccessible to the water hoses.

The incendiaries themselves were small, but very hot. Hundreds fell at once, littering the tar-and-wood roof in a network of sizzling sparks, and the wardens lurched toward one after another to snatch them up before they burned through.

Though she held them for only a second, they scorched her gloves, and the acrid smoke reddened her face, but she and the others succeeded in flinging them onto the courtyard below, where they burned out.

Then the planes were gone, and the school still stood. Exhausted, she joined the others jogging back to town, too exhausted and coughing to cheer, or even talk.

Ten minutes later, still standing in the road, she heard the rumble, and her heart sank. A third raid. And this one was in earnest, for bombs began exploding all around them. The school took a direct hit. From their position, Alexia and Grigory watched, stupefied, as the interior of the building shot up in a mass of wood and flame and fell again, battering what was left of the walls. They didn't budge from where they crouched. There was nothing left to save.

"That's it," Alexia said. "I'm joining up."

Alexia brought the glass of hot tea from the samovar and handed it on a napkin to her grandmother. "I'm sorry, Babushka, but the time has come. All the men I know are at the front already, and now that the school's destroyed, I have no job, no reason to stay at home."

"I don't want you to leave, my Alyosha. You've been the light of this house for so many years, since your mother died." She gestured toward the simple room cluttered with painted pottery and embroidered cloths. "How will I manage without you?"

"You do very well without me, Babushka. The neighbor's boys feed the goat and chickens, you're in good health, and Father Zosima will still come by every day, as he has for years."

The old woman sipped her tea. "But it is a sin to kill," she grumbled.

"I know that, Babushka, but it's not a sin to defend yourself from a murderer. And the Germans are murdering us."

"I pray to the Virgin every night that the war will end, but it never does." She glanced lovingly toward the "beautiful corner" of the room, where a cabinet draped with a silken cloth held candles and three icons.

"Babushka, you know the village headman doesn't like you keeping those."

"I don't care. No one is going to arrest an old woman for her icons. Even if you claim to be a good communist and member of the Komsomol, I know you have a soft spot for them."

There was some truth in that. The Virgin and Child image had comforted her when she'd been orphaned at the age of seven and adopted by her grandmother. Saint George's icon was appealing because he had a horse, and she liked horses.

The third, supposedly of the Annunciation, attracted her the most. Gabriel, with silver-painted wings and streams of golden hair, was suspended in the air over the Virgin, the angelic lips lightly touching the virginal ones. From her earliest notice of the icon, Alexia had assumed the angel was a woman offering a holy, life-changing kiss. It had filled her first with contentment and then with longing. Even after formally renouncing the faith upon entering school, she had fallen asleep at night imagining that the divine female Gabriel, in a robe of fluttering silk, hovered over her and pressed angelic lips on her own childish ones.

She laid a protective arm over her grandmother's back. "I'll always have a soft spot for you and this house. But I have to go. Patriarch Sergei himself said on the radio that the task of all Christians is to defend the sacred borders of the homeland against the German barbarians."

The old woman sighed and set her tea glass aside. She placed a noisy kiss on Alexia's cheek and stroked her hair. "All right. You have my blessings, Alyosha. But you must first promise to go and see Father Zosima."

Alexia braced herself. That was going to be the hard part.

The old wooden church of Arkhangelsk had been closed for years and adapted as a storage depot. But the old priest known as Father Zosima still lived in a room at the back of it. When she knocked on his door, he greeted her with an embrace and led her into the church where barrels of kasha and dried fish had replaced the holy objects.

He drew her down next to him on a bench. "You see what the communists have done to us?"

She understood his sorrow and recalled the Christmas celebrations of her childhood, but she had no time for nostalgia. She gathered her courage and blurted out the news.

"The German bombers have destroyed my school. I have no more work, no more reason to stay here, so I'm enlisting."

He took both her hands in his. "I am aggrieved to hear it, my child. I wish you would not soil yourself by killing. Even in defense. God gives us a free choice at every moment. You can choose to serve but not shoot. Perhaps you can be a medic or a guard or a mechanic."

"Mechanic? I don't know a wrench from a potato. As far as medicine is concerned, I'm afraid I'd cause more harm than good. I'll go where they send me. Besides, weren't you in the tsar's military when you were a young man? My grandmother mentioned it once."

"Yes. I was an officer. I was also a brute to my servants and a charmer to the ladies. I even fought a duel for a woman." He chuckled at her expression of astonishment.

He smiled wanly. "I was really quite dashing, in fact, and caught the eye of a certain married lady. When her husband challenged me to a duel, I could not refuse. But the night before was a particularly beautiful summer evening. Moonlight shone on the water of the park where we were to duel. I decided I could not defile such beauty by killing someone, especially a man whom I had wronged in the first place."

"So you canceled the duel?"

"No. I let him shoot me. And you know, God rewarded me for my decision by letting me be wounded but not killed. I recovered and vowed to never hurt any man. I renounced my military commission, and after a year of study I became a priest. So you see? We always do have a choice, even if it is only the choice of self-sacrifice."

"I…I don't know what to say. I suppose I will have choices, but not many."

"Then choose to serve without shooting. And pray for the salvation of those who want to harm you. Remember, the most important gift we have is our capacity to love. Do not forget to love."

Alexia sighed. She had grown up under the guidance of Zosima, but his faith didn't include defending himself, or anyone. She thought of the angelic kiss of the icon. It seemed worlds away from the bombs dropping on Arkhangelsk.

She embraced him and left him sitting in his dusty church-turned-storeroom.

❖

The commissariat was housed in an old brick building that had once been an export station for cod, snail fish, and salmon to the inland cities. The Bolsheviks had confiscated it in the 1920s and removed its processing equipment, and now the sign overhead read WORKERS' AND PEASANTS' RED ARMY. As she entered, Alexia was sure she could detect the faint odor of fish.

The commissar was short and somewhat spherical, his plump jowls blending in a smooth line with his wide neck, and the top button of his uniform collar was invisible under the rolls of his chin.

"So, you'd like to enlist," he said. It wasn't a question, so she merely nodded.

"How have you served until now?"

"In the Komsomol. I'm also a schoolteacher. Was. My school was bombed."

"Schoolteacher, I see. But what about military training? Did you follow any of the Vsevobuch courses?"

"Yes, Comrade Commissar. Driving, marching, small-arms firing, political instruction."

"Anything you particularly excelled at?"

"No, sir."

He looked her up and down, then tilted his head. "Just how tall are you?"

"One meter seventy-seven, Comrade Commissar. I was the tallest in my class."

He scribbled something on her papers. "They'll find a place for you after your training. Here, fill out the form for your identification, then take it down that corridor to the photographer." He handed her several sheets of paper as well as a pencil and pointed with his chin toward a table in the corner.

She wrote in her birth date and place, family members, Komsomol membership number, civilian profession, and list of Vsevobuch courses, then joined the line to the photographer. When she returned to the beefy sergeant and handed over her photo and questionnaire, he clipped everything together, then slid a page of military regulations toward her. "Sign here at the bottom," he said, handing her a fountain pen. Without reading any of the text, she wrote her name.

"All right, then. You're in the Red Army now. Report at eight tomorrow morning for the ride to the training center. Don't be late, or you'll be arrested."

❖

The next morning an open troop carrier transported her and sixteen other recruits to the training center at Vaskovo, where half a dozen other trucks had arrived as well. She clambered out of the carrier, shrugging inside her coat to keep away the sharp October wind, and was glad to soon be indoors in the female barracks. She and her barrack mates were herded into a central hall, where a lieutenant delivered a patriotic speech and then ordered them to the quartermaster to be issued uniforms.

With her own bundle in hand, she stepped into an assembly room and examined the parts. The trousers were baggy, wide at the hips and narrow below the knee, with the lower portion designed to slip into boots. The boots were a disappointment. She learned that leather was reserved for officers while hers were some sort of stiff rubberized material sewn over leather soles. Tying on the new footcloths, of which she was issued two pairs, she drew the boots on and found they were a size too large.

The best part was the gymnasterka, the closed tunic that would be both shirt and jacket. Buckling on the military belt, she sensed a change of attitude. More than the official welcoming speech, the uniform gave her a sense of belonging, of being part of a body of patriots defending the homeland.

"All right, stop preening," the sergeant ordered. "Put your civilian clothes in the bags provided and write your home address on the outside. We'll mail them for you. Five minutes, then fall out for roll call."

Roll call meant another hour of standing in ranks until she had been assigned to a training group. Hers was Group J, and by the time the entire group had been assigned, she was hungry.

Her first military meal, a stew of kasha and assorted vegetables, was tolerable, and if it represented what she'd be getting for the rest of the war, she was content.

"Company attention!" Benches scraped as the recruits got to their feet. Another sergeant stood at the front of the dining hall with an open notebook.

"You all know your group designations, so you will march starting from the first table and proceed in order to the last. Training assignments are posted on the walls outside. You have ten minutes to determine your assignment and to fall in at the relevant location. Dismissed!"

Alexia shoveled the remaining portion of her stew into her mouth and joined the line from her table as it waited to exit the dining hall. Full, and feeling quite smart in her new uniform, she decided the army wasn't such a bad place to be.

❖

Because they were urgently needed at the front, their basic training was brief. They practiced running in full gear, jumping and falling without breaking a limb, shooting at straw targets, and marching in step to patriotic chants. She could dig a trench in just minutes, carry a fallen colleague on her back, and bayonet a sand-filled dummy on the run. And they listened to endless political lectures reminding her of the virtues and duties of communism.

Though she had little time for socializing, she grew to respect her comrades, tough men and women of northern Russia, hardened to the cold.

Ironically, her rifle fascinated her. The 7.62 caliber Mosin Nagant, with its bayonet attached, was longer than she was tall. With concentration, she could dismantle, rebuild, and fire it in less than three minutes, and it pleased her to hit the center of the target with surprising regularity. The rifle itself was a beautiful thing, but it marked the line between being a patriot and a killer. And always the spirit of Father Zosima seemed to hover near.

"Not bad, Mazarova." her instructor said, "You'll be an asset to the infantry."

She cringed. "You think so, sir?"

"Yes, but it's not up to me. The military board will decide what to do with you, and they're full of surprises."

The day came when training was over, and the lists were posted in the corridor. Alexia searched for her name, found it, and stood ruminating in front of the board.

Standing next to her, a comrade smiled at his posting. "Tank training. Fantastic. I love those things. Talk about power." He turned toward her. "What about you?"

"*Special Purpose Division, D.O.N, Kremlin Regiment,*" she read off. "What's that?"

"That's the NKVD Honor Guard. They're elite troops that guard the leaders. They were in the military parade in Red Square when the war started. You should be very pleased they've chosen you."

"Why do you suppose they did?"

"To start, my dear, you look great in uniform. And you're the tallest woman in our class. Ash-blond hair, great cheekbones, ice-gray eyes…your face is so Russian, it belongs on a coin."

"What nonsense. Russians don't look any special way."

"The leaders don't care, and they like having handsome people like you around them in spiffy uniforms. Don't complain. You'll stay alive longer than a lot of the rest of us."

Uncertain, she returned to her barracks. Was a pretty face all she had to offer her homeland? And what did she want to do in the Red Army, anyhow? The Honor Guard, a purely ornamental regiment, would certainly please Father Zosima. But how could it be honorable to not want to fight?

CHAPTER FOUR

The White House, October 1943

Her sparse belongings unpacked and stored, Mia descended again to the main floor and Harry Hopkins's office.

Hopkins sat at his cluttered desk, cigarette in one hand. A slight haze of smoke surrounded him, and the odor of ashtray permeated the air.

"Sit down," he said, pointing with the cigarette toward a chair at his left. "Are you settled in now?"

"Yes, sir. Raring to go." She took a seat and tried to hold his gaze yet not seem to be staring. Up close, his face shocked her a bit. Hollow-cheeked and myopic, and with thinning hair, he reminded her of the pitchfork-holding farmer in the painting *American Gothic*.

"Is this where the Lend-Lease program began?" she asked.

"Yes, in fact. But soon enough the accounting became so complex, we needed other offices, like the one you were working in, to deal with Britain, China, Free France, and the two dozen smaller allies. Right now, my problem is the Soviets. Not just supply issues, but also diplomatic ones. For that I need someone to read and translate correspondence between this office and the Kremlin."

The Kremlin. The word, like a sudden dramatic chord, stirred a mix of fear, fascination, distaste. She had grown up in an immigrant family with a hatred of Bolshevism, and the Kremlin was where the neo-Bolsheviks—who now called themselves Communists—were headquartered.

"We've achieved a certain rapport," she heard, and she realized she'd lost the thread.

"Rapport?" She repeated, feeling a bit stupid.

"Yes. Stalin is a dictator and a hard pill to swallow diplomatically. But he has a huge nation to hold together and defend, and is losing thousands of men every day. I respect his position and sympathize with it a great deal. Stalin knows this and trusts me for it. Our president trusts me, too, so I've been acting as his de facto secretary of state, though we don't say that around Mr. Hull, who actually holds the office. As a result, I need a Russian-speaking person at my side to negotiate the... turbulent waters." He took a final puff and crushed the stub amidst a dozen others in his ashtray.

"Has the president already met with the Russians?"

"That's what I—"

Someone knocked at the door, and he called out, "Come in!"

For the briefest moment, Mia stared, puzzled, at the slowly opening door, waiting for a head to appear. Only when she dropped her glance did she perceive feet, then knees, and finally a man rolling into the room in a wheelchair. She stood up.

"Mr. President," Hopkins said, though he remained sitting.

"Good morning, Harry. Just thought I'd stop by and see what you're hatching."

Franklin Roosevelt looked tired, in spite of his good cheer. His long, oval face and prominent chin had always appeared amiable and paternal. But now his cheeks were sunken, his hair thin and receding. His gray-blue eyes were puffy, and he seemed to squint through his rimless glasses. It was strange to be in the presence of two men with such political power who appeared so physically feeble.

But FDR's vigorous tenor voice belied his appearance. "Oh, please sit down, Miss Kramer. No need for formalities." He maneuvered himself into place next to her. "So, you are to be our plenipotentiary to the Kremlin."

"I'll serve the White House in whatever way I can, Mr. President, but I'm still only a lowly assistant."

"Don't worry, my dear. We won't overtax you. Mr. Hopkins tells me you have the best possible skills, though I suppose you are not fond of Mr. Stalin."

She winced, not knowing what to reply, but he laid a soft hand on her forearm and leaned toward her as if confiding. "Mr. Churchill is not fond of him either, but he's on our side in this war, so we have to keep him happy."

"Thank you for your confidence, Mr. President. I'll do everything I can to live up to it."

"Good to hear you say it, my dear. Now, would you like to see our command center?"

"Command center? Really? Isn't that top secret?"

The president chuckled. "I'm not going to show you our military strategies, only our wonderful setup. Very futuristic. Hopkins, would you be so kind as to wheel me there? Saves wear and tear on my hands."

Hopkins leapt from his seat and took hold of the handlebars at the back of the wheelchair. They proceeded down the corridor to the elevator, and she strode alongside the president's chair as he explained. "It used to be a simple map room, but now it's staffed twenty-four hours a day and fitted out with...well, you'll see."

The elevator opened on the ground floor, and they turned right. The guard who stood before one of the rooms snapped to attention, then stepped in front of them to open the door.

What had been a low buzz now became a cacophony of orders, conversations, and ringing telephones. Mia felt her jaw drop slightly, and she closed it again.

The otherwise drab walls were papered with gigantic maps—of Europe, Africa, Asia, all the theaters of the war. Uniformed staff, both army and navy, stood before them, some on the floor and some on ladders, moving little markers here and there, though she was too far away to discern any patterns or identifications.

"Those markers show the progress of the armies?" she asked.

"Oh, much more than that. The staff tracks the movements of all the belligerents. The land armies, the convoys, ships' day-to-day positions, sea battles and losses. It marks the whereabouts of certain people, too. You can't see from here, but Mr. Churchill is a cigar, my marker is a cigarette holder, and Mr. Stalin is a pipe. Good thing we all smoke, eh?"

Mia let her glance sweep over the walls and the military personnel moving between them. "And that's where the information comes from?" She nodded toward a long table where a row of men and women wearing headphones sat in front of typewriters.

"Yes. That's our communication staff—smart, loyal people who can be trusted. They also transcribe and file all messages that pass between myself, Chiang Kai-shek, Churchill, and Stalin. They work in alternating teams, twenty-four hours a day, and I come in periodically with the war secretary to check on our progress."

"So this is where strategy is formulated," she murmured.

"Only to a certain degree. In fact, conferences in person are much more important. We have to coordinate with our allies."

Hopkins spoke for the first time. "Which is why we've finally arranged a meeting with Stalin."

"We'd have done it earlier, but the sonofabitch is hard to pin down," Roosevelt grumbled, then glanced up at Hopkins. "Have you told her yet about Tehran?"

"No, sir. Not yet. I was about to when you arrived."

"Well, then, let's talk about it now. If you wouldn't mind, Harry?" He tilted his head back toward the corridor.

"Oh, yes. Of course." Hopkins drew the wheelchair back from the open doorway, and the guard closed the double door.

"Tehran? That's in Iran, isn't it?" Mia asked as she hurried alongside the rolling wheelchair. "I'm sorry. I don't understand Iran's position in the war."

The president chuckled as they entered the elevator. "Neither do we, and even my advisors have trouble keeping track of who's in control there. They just inform me that Iran has oil fields that the whole world covets, but since the double invasion—of the Soviets from the north and the British from the west—the Allies now occupy them. So now we can move millions of tons of war materials across Iranian territory to the Russians. Since they're close to Russia, Stalin decided it was a good place to meet."

The elevator carried them back up to the second floor, and a moment later, they stood before the president's office in the Yellow Oval Room. The door opened from behind as they reached it, Mia followed the wheelchair inside, discreetly perusing the office.

The president's dark wooden desk stood at the center of three tall windows, all hung with velvet drapery and square valances bordered in gold. The American flag and the presidential flag flanked the desk and chair, America's stately but unglamorous version of a throne.

"This is Mr. Watson, my personal secretary," the president said, as a broad-shouldered man in a gray suit wheeled him around behind his desk. Once in place, Roosevelt took a plastic holder from his desk drawer and inserted a cigarette into it. Leaning over his shoulder, Watson lit it for him. "Please, take a seat, Miss Kramer." The president motioned to the cushioned chairs in front of his desk.

"As I was saying, we've planned a conference in Tehran next month, with Mr. Churchill and Stalin. Mr. Hopkins, as always, will assist me with some of the policy statements, and you, in turn, will assist him."

"Uh, yes, certainly. A great honor," Mia stammered. "When will the conference take place?"

Roosevelt puffed on his cigarette holder through clenched teeth. "Date's not certain, and it's a matter of security to not announce it beforehand anyhow. But you should be prepared to be out of the country late in November. If you need a passport, the State Department will see to it."

"Passport, yes, sir." She could think of nothing to add.

A butler stepped in from a side door. "Mr. President, Secretary Stimson is here."

Obviously it was the signal to leave. Hopkins was already standing, and Mia leapt up to join him.

Mia's head was spinning. Her first day on the new job and she was about to be sent into the cauldron of diplomatic negotiations with Churchill and Stalin.

Tehran. Iran. The words barely held meaning for her. And the two men she was supposed to assist were physical wrecks. She felt herself bend slightly with the weight of responsibility.

As they arrived back at Hopkins's office, Mia expected to learn some of the details of the upcoming conference, but he only handed her a folder of papers and asked her to translate them. Then the phone rang.

She nodded, although he already gave his full attention to the telephone call, and she passed quietly from his office into her own.

At least she finally had a task. Under the light of her gooseneck lamp, she opened the folder. The papers were dispatches from the People's Commissariat of Arms requesting specific items, others complaining about items that had not been delivered. Midway through the pile she came upon a telegram that seemed to leap out at her. From Molotov, the Russian foreign minister.

She found herself smiling. The political name Molotov meant "hammer" and, like Stalin, was obviously chosen to be intimidating. His language was brusque as he complained about an agreement for a certain amount of foodstuffs that had been promised and that had not arrived. Since the Red Army was sacrificing its blood daily nearly alone among nations, in defense of Europe, he pointed out, a replacement shipment needed to be sent as soon as possible. She translated the letter immediately, careful to express the right amount of anger and disdain.

❖

The sound of tapping surprised her, and Mia glanced up, confused. Only on the second rap did she realize it came from the door to the First Lady's office. She stood up and rushed to open it.

Eleanor Roosevelt stood in the doorway, hands clasped at her waist, her severe gray skirt and high-collar blouse adding to the schoolteacher image.

"Hello," the First Lady said. "Mr. Allen said you were installed in your new office. The maid has just brought in a pot of tea, and I thought it gave us a chance to chat. Or are you working on something critical?"

"Oh, no. Nothing like that."

Eleanor stepped back, and Mia entered the room hesitantly. The First Lady's office was more domestic than official. A hinged "secretary" desk provided the only writing surface. It was open at the moment and revealed stationery and a tiny vase of roses. A small round table to her right was set for three, and the porcelain teapot at its center gave off a pleasant aroma.

"I was just translating a message from Molotov, but I'm sure it can wait."

"Molotov!" Eleanor threw back her head and laughed. "That old Bolshevik can certainly wait for his answer." She gestured toward the table and Mia took a seat.

"He's a real scoundrel, that one. I take pains to keep out of my husband's business with the Soviets, but I do read the newspapers. It was Molotov who negotiated the non-aggression pact with Hitler so the Soviets could annex half of Eastern Europe. Worse, he surely had a hand in the famine in the Ukraine that killed millions of peasants." She sighed. "And now he's our ally. Would you like cream and sugar?" She poured the steaming tea into both cups.

"Both, please, if you don't mind."

Eleanor passed the cream pitcher and sugar bowl to her, and they both sipped delicately.

"He's a peasant, and it amazes me that he's survived so long in Stalin's government. He was here last year for meetings with the president and the State Department, and we all had a good laugh behind his back. Oh, he puts on a good façade, but you learn a lot about a person when you unpack their bags."

Mia set down her cup, puzzled, and Eleanor raised her hand to cover her bright, ladylike snicker. "Oh, I didn't unpack his bags, but Mr. Allen did, while Molotov was out shaking hands. It's standard practice for White House guests. Believe it or not, Allen found a sausage, a loaf of black bread, and a loaded pistol."

"A loaded pistol! In the White House? And I wonder if he thought our food might poison him."

"Who knows what the man thought? Mr. Allen placed all three objects in the same drawer as his shirts but had the good sense to remove the bullets. If Molotov was upset at that, he apparently decided not to make an issue of it."

The tale allowed Mia to relax in the First Lady's presence, and she spoke candidly. "Well, he's making an issue of some of the Lend-Lease deliveries, and it will be my job to sort it out in the accounting. But I'm delighted to hear about the sausage and bread. I'll be a little less intimidated now."

"Oh, you must not let *anybody* intimidate you, my dear."

"Who is intimidating whom?" a rich contralto voice said, and Mia glanced up, startled.

A woman in her fifties entered uninvited. She was portly, plain-faced, and wore a mannish jacket over a long skirt. She dragged a chair over to the table and sat down by the third teacup.

"So you're Harry's new assistant. Is Eleanor giving you the pep talk?"

Eleanor glanced up through her eyebrows. "Hicks, do try to behave."

"What? I'm just here to meet the new recruit." She held out her hand. "Lorena Hickok at your service."

Mia took it, found it meaty, warm, her grip firm. "I'm…uh… pleased to meet you." Who was this drab, avuncular woman who could enter the First Lady's office without knocking?

As if hearing her thoughts, Eleanor explained. "Lorena is head of the women's division of the Democratic National Committee. In fact, she has rooms upstairs not far from you."

"I see." Mia smiled, though she didn't see. Hickok's job title explained little about either her residency at the White House or her familiarity.

Lorena reached past her and poured herself a cup of tea. "So, what's this I hear about intimidation?"

"Miss Kramer was just saying that she was a bit alarmed by Molotov's tone in his telegraphs. You know what he's like."

Hickok snorted. "He's a bully. They all are." She leaned toward Mia. "Don't ever let them cow you. If I'd let big-shot politicos, domestic or foreign, browbeat me, I'd never have made it as a journalist. And Eleanor would never have stood up to the Daughters of the American Revolution." She glanced toward Mia. "You must know what she did for Marian Anderson when the DAR refused to let her sing in Constitution Hall."

"I know that she arranged an outdoor concert for her at the Lincoln Memorial. I heard it on the radio."

Eleanor was more conciliatory. "The Daughters of the American Revolution has always been an all-white patriotic association. And then, of course, Washington was still very segregated in 1939. I'd hoped that Anderson's fame—and pressure from the press, other artists, and politicians—would create an exception for her, but the DAR stood fast in their refusal."

"But you *did* create a scandal, didn't you?" Lorena beamed with wicked pleasure over the top of her cup.

"You mean by resigning? Yes, I suppose I did. But my real ally was the Secretary of the Interior, who helped me arrange the concert at the Lincoln Memorial. On Easter Sunday, no less. And the park estimated that seventy-five thousand people showed up."

"I remember being thrilled by it, for her, for you, and for a government that had crossed the color line. And it *has* to cross that line. We can't claim to be the bastion of freedom when we discriminate against our own citizens."

Hickok tilted her head admiringly. "Oh, looks like we have a live wire here, Eleanor. We're going to have to keep an eye on this one." She bumped elbows with Mia.

Mia smiled weakly at the compliment. She would never have used the term "live wire" for herself.

The teapot was empty now and Eleanor was folding her napkin, a polite but unmistakable gesture. "It was lovely chatting with you, my dear," Eleanor said.

Mia pushed back her chair. "A pleasure for me, too, and now I have Russian complaints to translate. Thank you so much for the tea, Mrs. Roosevelt."

She edged toward the door leading to her own tiny space.

"Quite all right. Do let us know if the boys make too many demands on you."

Mia smiled at the word "boys" and stepped through into her cubicle.

She sat down at her desk, no larger than that of the First Lady, and stared at the dispatches. Two realities seemed to run in parallel at the White House, the political and the personal. The men were dealing with armaments, international diplomatic confrontations, posturing, and the clash of armies, while the women worked with polite letters and pots of tea for democracy at home. Two forms of politics, the global and the intimate.

This was going to be interesting.

CHAPTER FIVE

On the way to Tehran, November 1943

Mia was slightly disoriented by the rapidly changing locations, time zones, and events.

The voyage on the *Battleship Iowa* on the surging Atlantic had already been a test of endurance, and the days in Cairo, where they'd picked up Prime Minister Churchill, had brought little rest. She'd been on duty eighteen hours every day, taking notes and the occasional dictation from Hopkins. To her great regret, the schedule had left no time for her to make the trip to Giza to see the pyramids.

But against all odds—polluted water, strange food, sleepless nights—she was in good physical shape, and it took only the most casual glance to see that both Hopkins and the president were not. Hopkins, who sat in the aisle seat beside her so as to stretch out his long legs, had been plagued with stomach problems for the entire trip.

The president, spread out over two seats a few rows behind them in discussion with Churchill, was also subdued. The prime minister's brusque voice dominated the discussion, as the smell of his cigar dominated the air of the plane.

She respected Churchill, even admired him for his ability to bolster the British during catastrophic times, but she couldn't say she liked him. He was dismissive of her, a bit seedy in dress and manner, prone to outbursts, and he smelled of tobacco.

Hopkins suddenly leaned past her and peered through the porthole of the plane.

"Look down there. See that long row of what looks like ants?

That truck convoy is *us*. Along with the Trans-Iranian Railroad, they're transporting our Lend-Lease supplies to Basra and on to the USSR."

It was a revelation. "Oh, my. What a difference between reading the lists on a ledger sheet and seeing the actual supply convoys making their way to Russia. Makes me proud."

Half an hour later, as the plane began to lose altitude, Hopkins peered out the window again.

"Looks like we're almost at Qaleh Morgi." He snickered, and when he surrendered the window, she glanced down to see why. An enormous red star was painted across the runway.

"I guess Stalin wants to make sure everyone knows who's in charge, eh?" she remarked.

"Yes, and that's going to be half the battle here," Hopkins said.

"Do you think Mr. Roosevelt can handle Stalin?"

Hopkins straightened his tie. "That's why we're here. To make sure he can."

❖

A cold wind hit them as they made their way down the stairs from the plane at Qaleh Morgi airport. Though some two dozen Soviet soldiers were lined up to form a corridor leading to the terminal, only one man walked out onto the field to meet them.

The Russian bowed in a hint of a military salute. "Dmitri Arkadiev," he said with a slight nod, first to her, then to Hopkins. "Marshal Stalin arrived yesterday evening and has arranged for you to have Soviet security." His English was heavily accented but clear and correct.

"That's very kind of Marshal Stalin," Hopkins said. "But the president has his own security staff, headed by Mr. Reilly."

Arkadiev ignored the remark and simply moved aside as others came down the stairway. In fact, Michael Reilly was the next person to step off the metal steps, and he offered his hand, in turn, to the Russian security man. Their handshake was stiff, perfunctory, and Mia smiled inwardly at the image of the two security forces in competition. More of the delegation poured out of the aircraft: the president's doctor, US ambassador to Russia Averell Harriman, the chief of staff, and finally, two burly men carrying the president carefully down the stairs in a chair.

Arkadiev was stone-faced, and Mia was certain that he and everyone else waiting at the airfield was stunned to see the president of the United States carried across the tarmac and lifted into an American car.

After the unmarked presidential car took off, carrying only Roosevelt and his bodyguard, Hopkins, Mia, and Reilly followed in one of the other vehicles. As they rode through the city, she glanced through the window at the land called Persia, disappointed.

The main streets were paved, but the sidewalks were not, and the dust stirred up by people walking seemed to cover the house fronts. Most of the street traffic seemed to consist of horse-drawn wagons and carriages, and she caught sight of only one bus, a wretched, rickety thing, full to bursting and without a door. Through the closed windows, she could still detect the smell of sewage.

At the American Embassy, an escort led them into a reception room where the US ambassador to Iran was already sitting with the president. When the entire delegation had arrived, the ambassador gave a brief welcoming speech. While porters led the other guests in order of rank and importance to their respective accommodations, the ambassador drew Hopkins, Harriman, and Roosevelt to one side.

"Mr. President, the Soviets have some very disquieting news."

As if on cue, the door to the anteroom opened, and a bland little man with a mustache strode in. He was slightly pudgy, and his wide head swelled above a receding hairline. Rimless glasses, similar to those the president wore, gave him a benign headmaster look, but Mia recognized him from newspaper photos. Molotov, the thug Eleanor Roosevelt had described. Had he brought his private pistol to Tehran?

The man stopped before Roosevelt and offered his hand. "Welcome, Mr. President. Forgive me for this intrusion, but our head of security informs us that German agents are plotting to capture or kill any of the three leaders of the conference. They've already parachute-dropped automatic rifles and grenades at locations around the city."

Molotov had addressed the president, but Reilly responded. "Have any of these agents been captured?"

"Yes, most. But it appears that perhaps half a dozen are still at large, and they have radio transmitters. The Soviet and British embassies are across from one another in the city and can be cordoned off together, but your embassy is far outside of Tehran."

"Your solution?" Reilly was succinct.

Molotov smiled a kindly, schoolmaster smile. "That Mr. Roosevelt move to the Soviet Embassy. You'd have some measure of independence yet still be well protected. The rest of the delegation, both political and military, can remain here."

"That's fine with me," the president said, preempting his security chief. "Thank you, Mr. Molotov. Please convey our acceptance of Marshal Stalin's offer."

When the transfer was finally executed, it was pure theater. A cavalcade of US and Soviet troops marched out to accompany the presidential car along the main thoroughfare into Tehran. Inside the car, an American security agent posed as Roosevelt, complete with cigarette holder clenched in his teeth. Wearing the president's felt hat he waved presidentially through the window, while in a dusty, unmarked car, accompanied by a single jeep, Roosevelt himself bumped along dusty back streets.

Mia sat between two men in the rear of one of the "official" cars, listening to the remarks of the president's protectors.

"You know that every room, sofa, and toilet will be bugged in that place," Hopkins grumbled. "It's going to be nigh-on impossible to have a private conversation."

"I'm sure you're right," Reilly said. "If the president needs to discuss matters away from Stalin's ears, he'll have to do it at the British Embassy."

"Do you think they'll find the agents still on the loose?" Mia peered out at the countless dark alleyways.

Hopkins nodded. "If I know the Russians, Tehran will be teeming with NKVD and Soviet troops. Stalin doesn't go anywhere outside Moscow without an army of protection, and now it covers us as well. I'm sure that's why the president accepted their offer."

Reilly agreed. "It was probably wise. I've hardly more than a dozen men under my authority while the Soviets can offer hundreds. Besides, if anything happens to the president in the Soviet compound, our secret service will lose their jobs, but the Russian secret-service men will be dead before nightfall."

They pulled into the compound and were directed toward a building at the far end where an entire floor of rooms was turned over to the US visitors. Mia deposited her suitcase in a cubbyhole room down the hall from the more stately one assigned to Hopkins. A suite with sitting room and private bath had been set aside for the president.

After an ad hoc lunch prepared by the embassy cook, Roosevelt and his immediate entourage met in the president's sitting room to discuss scheduling, and the lack of strategy surprised Mia. It seemed that the president planned to use goodwill and charm to win Stalin over rather than an agreed-upon discussion schedule.

But before anyone could speak, a Soviet officer entered, followed by ten uniformed guards and Joseph Stalin. The guards, both male and female, took up positions along the wall on both sides of the door, automatic rifles across their chests.

Stalin ambled toward the president, obviously in an excellent mood, perhaps because the installation of the Roosevelt party in the Soviet Embassy was a show of strength for him. The "father of the Russians" could spread his protective cloak around the American president, too.

He was shorter than the press photos had led her to believe. His coarse square face was heavily lined and pockmarked, but his wide mustache and full, thick hair combed straight back gave him an air of bullish virility glaringly absent in both Hopkins and the president. Thank God that, in the twentieth century, it took more than bullish virility to hold power.

Stalin bent forward and shook Roosevelt's hand vigorously. "I am so glad to finally meet you," he said through his interpreter, who stood at his side.

He drew up a chair and began a lighthearted banter, about flying and the unpleasantness of having to travel far from home. His Georgian accent was conspicuous. Roosevelt omitted mentioning that his host had flown fifteen hundred miles while he himself, in a wheelchair, had traveled over six thousand.

Instead he politely asked how the Soviet troops were faring, and Stalin admitted candidly that the Red Army was bogged down on most fronts. Roosevelt said the United States was doing its best to draw off some of the Wehrmacht into Italy and North Africa, though Stalin's cool expression made it clear that the strategy was not enough. Not nearly enough.

Sitting behind Hopkins, Mia scribbled notes as inconspicuously as possible, glad for the delay that using an interpreter caused in the dialogue. Once she'd slipped into the flow of the conversation and used initials and symbols in place of words, it went quickly, and she had the leisure to look up occasionally at the dictator and his guards. The Russians seemed to glower across the room at Roosevelt's guards, who, in turn, glowered back at them. Even the plain-clothes security forces watched each other with suspicion. Never were two world leaders better guarded than in that room on that day.

The Russian guards who stood with their automatic rifles across their chests had surely been chosen for their beauty as much as for their prowess. The eight broad-chested men, with distinct Slavic faces, were as virile as their leader, and the two women were tall and handsome.

One of them, in fact, was stunning. A pale blonde with full lips, wide cheekbones, and slightly hooded eyes seemed familiar, and with a jolt Mia realized why. It could have been the sister of Grushenka, a taller, nobler, fully armed Grushenka.

She tore her eyes away, realizing she had missed a remark by Stalin, and hoped it was something trivial. But just then he stood up, and it was clear that his visit had been a courtesy, a way to show camaraderie with Roosevelt before Churchill entered the mix. With another series of handshakes, he left, once again followed by the splendid beasts of his military guard.

❖

At ten o'clock, the first official meeting of the Big Three leaders began in the main part of the Soviet Embassy. Roosevelt sat with Hopkins, the admiral who headed the Joint Chiefs of Staff, and representatives of the navy and air force. She made a note to learn all their names.

Winston Churchill entered, having just come from the British Embassy across the street. As he passed her, Mia noted the familiar odors of cigars and whiskey. He took his place, along with Foreign Minister Eden, an admiral, and an RAF officer.

The door opened again and Stalin entered, followed by Molotov and the guards, and the room fell silent. As if compelled by some vast magnet, all those who were sitting stood up. Only Roosevelt, in his wheelchair, remained seated, and his sly smile suggested he enjoyed being exempt from the general obeisance.

Mia readied her fountain pen for note-taking but allowed herself a final lingering look at Stalin's personal guard. The men, she supposed, were the same as before, but all Mia really cared about was…ah, yes, she was there, second from the end, the splendid "Grushenka" guard.

Mia's attention was drawn back to her work as Stalin welcomed everyone with general pleasantries. Churchill followed, reminding his audience they were the greatest concentration of power the world had ever seen and that together they directed armies of some twenty million men.

Mia scribbled for the next two hours, then after a break, for two hours more, recording the discussions, agreements, and disagreements about the running of the war. By the end of the afternoon, all she could think of were her slowly cramping fingers and dinner.

In fact, the Americans hosted the first formal dinner of the conference. The presidential cook, together with kitchen staff from the US Embassy, produced a banquet that ought to have impressed their Russian hosts, although the endless obligatory toasts were made with bourbon rather than vodka.

Off duty, Mia could observe Stalin's guards at her leisure. Once it even seemed the "Grushenka" guard glanced back at her, but it was probably her imagination. Her foolish, lonely, starved imagination.

❖

The second day of the conference began as intense and wearying as the first, with negotiations over Poland's postwar boundaries, the dividing up of Germany, and the formation of a United Nations Assembly.

Inevitably, Stalin brought the discussion around to the demand that the Western allies open a second front to draw off some of the German force in the East. Roosevelt announced a rough date for an invasion, called Operation Overlord. It would be headed by Dwight Eisenhower and would occur—and here both Molotov and Stalin scowled—in the spring of 1944.

"Why not sooner?" Stalin demanded to know. "Every day you wait, a river of Russian blood is being shed."

Churchill reiterated, "The English Channel, with its winds, storms, and currents, is simply unsuitable for military operations before May. It's much too dangerous for our landing craft."

Stalin leaned forward and pointed with the stem of his pipe. "The Red Army has weathered far worse conditions for two years, and we have just lost nearly a million men at Stalingrad."

The truth of the remark brought a tense silence to the room. It was mercifully alleviated when Churchill signaled someone at the door, and a British honor guard entered wheeling a large wooden case on a handcart.

Churchill stood up from the table, strode toward the mysterious case, and opened it. With a flourish, he withdrew a huge, jewel-encrusted Crusader's sword in a scarlet scabbard and presented it to Stalin. "We in the West acknowledge the tragedy of Stalingrad. Therefore, in the name of our King, George VI, we offer this Sword of Stalingrad in recognition of the bravery of the men fallen in defense of that great city."

Obviously surprised, and with much of his anger assuaged, Stalin took the sword, kissed the blade, and handed it to Voroshilov, who stood next to him. It was perhaps a bad omen that Voroshilov took hold of it so clumsily that the blade slipped out of the scabbard and fell to the floor.

❖

Dinner on the second evening was at the British Embassy, and at seven o'clock, the Soviets arrived in force. Stalin was accompanied by Molotov, Voroshilov, and the man whom she now recognized was Beria, head of the NKVD. Pale, pasty men, lacking completely the statuesque beauty of the honor guard that followed directly behind them.

Another contingent—it must have been fifty—of ordinary soldiers streamed in behind them and took up position at every door and window within sight and, presumably, within the entire building. The only way the leader of the Soviet Union could have been attacked that evening would have been by bombardment from above. The Grushenka guard didn't glance her way this time, but Mia seemed to sense an awareness radiating from her.

Dinner once again was awash in liquor, and she shared in the toasts saluting the various armies, air forces, navies, cultures, ancestors, courage, and miscellaneous manly virtues. The alcohol made her dizzy, but it also fueled her courage. At the end of the dinner, she threaded her way among the British guests toward the Russian security chief who stood a few feet from Stalin. She tugged on his sleeve and he turned around, startled.

"Excuse me, but can you tell me the names of the honor guard?"

He seemed as surprised to hear Russian from an American as he was puzzled by the question. "Why do you want to know? Have they behaved badly?"

"Oh, no. Mr. Hopkins, the president's aide, wants me to record the events of the evening, and I was so impressed by the guard detachment I thought it would be nice to record their names. For posterity."

It sounded lame, she knew, and she could see by his frown that, even if he knew them, he would not tell her. She searched for a way to backpedal.

"Perhaps just the two women. We have no such women in our military, and I personally admire their inclusion. But if it is contrary to protocol, I apologize for asking."

He seemed to weigh the risk of giving personal information against the requirements of hospitality. "I do not know their full names," he said. "But the dark-haired one is Tatyana, and the blonde is Alexia. Will that be enough for your report?"

"Yes, thank you."

Mia backed away, pacing carefully and gripping the backs of chairs to keep her equilibrium. *Alexia.* She pronounced the name as she walked. It seemed as splendidly Russian as the woman herself.

The next day, though slightly hung over, she joined Hopkins as they filed into the conference room for the summation meeting. When it was adjourned and she gathered her notes, Stalin announced that there would be a photo session outside of the embassy.

"Newspaper photographers?" she asked Hopkins. "I thought the entire conference was a secret."

"Military photographers. The president will announce the results of the conference when he returns, and we'll use the photographs then."

He wheeled Roosevelt out before the portico and helped him onto a chair. Churchill sat, slouched and grumpy, at his left in the tunic of an air commodore of the RAF. Stalin took his seat at the president's right, looking dour in his usual military tunic, with a single decoration, the gold star of the Hero of the Soviet Union. Roosevelt twisted slightly toward him and crossed one leg over the other. Only someone who looked very closely could see the outline of steel braces under his black socks.

The army photographers took a series of photos, with various military and political retinues in the background, and then the show was over. As soon as the cameras were out of sight, Roosevelt's personal assistants helped him onto his wheelchair, and the final handshakes, bons mots, backslaps, half lies, and promises marked the end of the conference.

Departure the next morning at Qaleh Morgi airport was anticlimactic. Stalin accompanied the president to his plane, striding alongside the wheelchair. His heavily armed guards marching in two lines, flanked them both.

When the departure formalities were done and the president was safely inside the Air Force C 54 transport, Mia mounted the steps behind Hopkins. Before entering the plane, she glanced back at the Russians, not at Stalin, the Man of Steel, but at the splendid woman of flesh and blood standing at attention.

CHAPTER SIX

After the excitement of Tehran, the December days seemed long and dreary. Mia spent her workdays monitoring the Lend-Lease orders to Russia and the United Kingdom, and only the memory of the trains and truck convoys traveling through Iran toward Russia reminded her they were real.

But the sky was bleak, and her tiny cubicle never seemed quite warm enough. It was also Christmas Eve, and she was slightly grumpy that she had to work. She had allowed herself to doze slightly over her ledger, when the sound of a polite cough woke her.

"Oh, I'm terribly sorry, Mr. Hopkins. I guess I nodded off."

"Quite all right. It's Christmas Eve, anyhow. Why don't you close up shop and come over for a holiday drink."

"Sounds great." She closed her ledger, clicked off the goosenecked lamp, and followed him into his office. While he poured two small glasses of bourbon, she drew up a chair and sat across from him.

"What's the news from the front? Or have you been in the Map Room lately?"

"The Russians are advancing slowly in the Ukraine, or at least not retreating." He took a sip of his bourbon. "Anything interesting in the cables?"

"Molotov is still complaining about discrepancies between what we promise and what is delivered and demanding duplicates. Our agents in Arkhangelsk, Murmansk, and Basra have sent cargo lists back to us, so the materials make it that far, but some of them don't get any farther. Molotov is convinced we're shortchanging them."

Hopkins closed his eyes, either from fatigue or exasperation, she couldn't tell which. "In any case, we have to investigate."

"Who should we call?"

"I mean face-to-face meetings. I'm overdue to meet with several of the big players in Moscow anyhow: Molotov, Ustinov, our Ambassador Harriman, a few others."

"Another trip overseas." She felt a wave of sympathy. Traveling was hard on him. "When will you have to leave?"

"Not just me. I need you to accompany me, for the same reasons you came along to Tehran. You know the inside workings of the program, can do the accounting if necessary, and most of all, you speak Russian."

"Oh!" She straightened. She hadn't anticipated that. "Well, then, when will *we* have to leave?"

"Right after New Year's. January 3, to be exact. It'll just be the two of us, so we won't have the circus we had in Tehran. Ambassador Harriman will meet us in Moscow. With any luck, we can resolve the various problems in a couple of days and then have a day to relax. You can look around and see what you remember of Moscow."

"Actually, I'm from St. Petersburg. I mean Leningrad. Obviously I won't be able to go there."

"No, of course not. The siege is still on. Poor devils. Starving to death, and we can't get any of our stuff through to them. You still have relatives there?"

"No one I'm in contact with. Moscow should be interesting, though."

"I was there last year, and it was in pretty bad shape. Nightly blackouts, food and fuel shortages, long lines in front of the shops. Pretty tough people, the Russians."

"True, but they seem so...overwrought...so melodramatic about everything. Worse than the Italians." She snickered.

Hopkins sat back and crossed his legs, his bony knees outlined through his trousers. "Maybe that's what appeals to me. They've suffered throughout their history. First the tsars, then the revolution, now the Nazis. And even if Stalin is a brutal dictator, I appreciate what they're trying to do with communism. Not that I'm a communist. Good grief, no. But, like the president, I think government has a responsibility to take care of its people, to see that everyone gets a fair shake."

"That was the New Deal, wasn't it? And you worked on that with him." She sipped her bourbon.

"Yeah. We've both been lefties from way back. And I *like* the melodramatic part of Russian culture. Mussorgsky, Tchaikovsky, Rachmaninoff. I'm fond of their literature, too. Well, as much of it as I've read—Tolstoy, Dostoyevsky."

Mia laughed again. "I agree about the music. And their ballet is pretty terrific, too, but spare me Tolstoy and Dostoyevsky. My father made me read them. Too obsessed with God for me."

Hopkins took another mouthful of whiskey and let it swirl around in his mouth for a moment. "Passionate about God, maybe, but not Christian in the usual sense. Tolstoy ridiculed the miracles and superstitions in the Bible and saw value only in the Sermon on the Mount. He even wrote his own *Gospel in Brief* with no miracles and no resurrection."

"Still, every Russian drama is connected with God. Seems silly to me."

"Well, it's Christmas Eve, so let's leave a little room for Him, shall we? You're coming to the White House celebration later, aren't you?"

She tossed back the last of the bourbon and stood up. "Definitely. Carols and party food. That's the kind of theology I like."

"Bah, humbug, eh?" He chuckled as he closed the door behind her.

When Mia arrived in the East Room, the First Lady was already sitting by the Steinway piano in an armchair. Lorena Hickok stood behind her. A musician in a tuxedo was playing Christmas carols. The Christmas tree, in keeping with wartime austerity, was of modest height and decorated with simple red glass balls and tinsel. Some thirty identical boxes wrapped in red and green paper lay in a ring around its base.

At the conclusion of "Oh, Come, All Ye Faithful," Edwin Watson wheeled in the president. He carried his beloved Scottish terrier Fala on his lap and chanted "Ho ho ho" as Watson parked him next to the tree. Eleanor rose from her armchair and went to stand by him for the official

Christmas photo of the first family. Then she returned to her armchair and to Lorena.

Roosevelt gave a brief welcoming speech full of platitudes about tradition and family Christmas, then gestured toward the black-suited man who stood next to him.

"In keeping with the religious meaning behind this lovely evening, I've invited Pastor Bainbridge to give us a little inspirational talk. Pastor Bainbridge? You have the floor."

The pastor cleared his throat and glanced around the room. "The president and Mrs. Roosevelt have asked me to bring a Christian message to this event, and rather than read the usual story from Luke, I've decided to break with tradition a bit and perhaps find another meaning for faith. Please bear with me as we explore the thoughts of a great Russian mind." He held up a thin, red paperback book entitled *The Grand Inquisitor*.

"This is a short work that appears as a chapter in one of the novels of Fyodor Dostoyevsky. In this scene, Christ returns during the Inquisition and performs a few miracles but is arrested by the inquisitor and cast into a dark cell. But then..." The pastor began reading from his booklet.

> *In the pitch darkness the iron door of the prison suddenly opened and the Grand Inquisitor came in. "Why art Thou come to hinder us? Tomorrow I shall burn Thee at the stake as the worst of heretics. For Thou mayest not add to what has been said of old, and mayest not take from men the freedom which Thou didst exalt when Thou wast on earth with thy three temptations. For fifteen centuries men have been wrestling with Thy freedom, but finally, they have brought their freedom to us, the Church, and laid it humbly at our feet.*

The pastor glanced up from his book. "To refresh your memory, Satan offers Jesus three temptations. One, give everyone bread, and they will follow you. Two, jump from a high place without injury to prove you are divine. And three, become ruler of the earth to compel people to do good. Jesus refuses. And why? For the sake of free will, so that men can choose faith or not. But the inquisitor claims that free will is a curse and that, fortunately, the Church has removed it and comforts mankind by claiming absolute authority over human behavior. Believers, he says, 'crawl to us and lick our feet' for liberating them from that freedom. And when they ask wherefore comes our knowledge of what God wants, we call it *Mystery*."

He looked up at his audience and seemed to catch Mia's eye before continuing. "But here is the lesson, my friends. Christ never replies. He simply kisses the old inquisitor on the lips in the Russian manner. That is his answer: the kiss, the embrace of the denier, irrespective of the power of his argument. What's more, the entire tale of the inquisitor is told by Ivan, the atheist in the novel, and when he tells it to his pious younger brother who quarrels with him, the boy kisses him in the same way."

He closed his little red book slowly, as if it were scripture, and tucked it under his arm. "Here endeth the Christmas lesson, my friends. It concludes with the command to love one another, to counter heartless reason with God's greatest gift, the kiss."

He bowed his head to polite applause and did not seem to notice that his listeners were exchanging bewildered glances. "I wish you all Merry Christmas," he said, and stepped away.

"What the hell was that all about?" Lorena Hickok had wandered over to where Mia stood.

Mia frowned. "Beats me. He couldn't have picked a worse author than Dostoyevsky. I read that chapter in school. It's much much longer, and much more boring. And the whole notion of kissing away logic is…well, insulting."

Harry Hopkins joined them. "I think you're being a little hard on poor old Dostoyevsky. He was doing the best he could for the time. He saw suffering all around him and used his characters to act out the arguments going on in his head."

"Don't all novelists do that?" Mia asked.

Lorena snorted. "The boring ones do. The good ones give you the romance in the first chapter."

Hopkins laid a thin hand very lightly on her shoulder, urging her toward the bowls of potato salad, plates of toast triangles covered with cheese or cold cuts, and a platters of cakes and cookies. "I say we stop worrying about Russian literature and enjoy the party treats."

Mia loaded her plate and joined the line to the punch bowl, where one of the kitchen staff ladled out hot mulled cider. While she shuffled forward holding her plate, she had a sudden recollection of the Crusader's sword Churchill had presented to Joseph Stalin and Stalin's response of kissing the blade. Not what Dostoyevsky intended, she thought, smiling to herself. Obviously, there were kisses, and *kisses—* but all of them silenced speech.

❖

Christmas morning Mia ambled leisurely down the hall from the White House cafeteria where the staff had just enjoyed a breakfast of pancakes and waffles. She clutched her gifts, the box of chocolate the Roosevelts gave to every staff member and the new fountain pen Harry Hopkins had bought her. A Schaeffer White Dot, in tortoise shell. Now she was headed toward the library to fill it with ink. As she reached the stairs, a bulky figure blocked her way.

"Merry Christmas!" Lorena Hickok said with robust cheer. "Have you looked out the window? It's started to snow, and I was just searching for someone to stroll through the Rose Garden with me."

Mia was still intimidated by the gruff woman with the deep voice, but she didn't relish spending the rest of Christmas Day in her tiny upstairs chamber with only her radio as a companion. "Sure. Just let me get my coat."

Reaching her room, she deposited her gifts on the bed, snatched up her wool coat and hat, and hurried down again to the door leading to the Rose Garden.

The snow now fell in thick flakes, and their footprints whitened again behind them. Mia drew her scarf tighter, wondering what they'd talk about.

"So, how was the Tehran conference?" Lorena began the conversation. "I know it was ages ago, but I was away on business all of December, and we haven't talked since you left. Did you meet the big man himself?"

"Stalin? Of course I didn't *meet* him, but I did see him up close. He's rather ugly but has a certain magnetism, and everyone's afraid of him. He has a Georgian accent, too."

Lorena guffawed. "That's right. Eleanor told me you're Russian, so you can understand him. When did your family come over?" She swatted a bush, knocking off the powdery snow.

"Back in 1918, from St. Petersburg, during the civil war. I was ten."

"Do you get nostalgic when you hear the language?"

Mia thought for a moment. "Yes, I suppose it has a certain warmth that reminds me of childhood. But what about you? Where do you call home? And what brings you to the White House? If I may ask."

Lorena raised her collar to cover her neck and closed the last button. "I'm from Wisconsin and was damned glad to get away from the place when I went to work for the Associated Press."

"Journalism must be exciting."

"It was. I met great people—actresses, musicians, opera singers. And in '32, I covered the campaign of a certain Franklin Delano Roosevelt, where I met Eleanor. She got me a position working on the New Deal programs. Then, just before the war, I was hired by the Democratic National Committee."

"Sounds like you're very important to the Roosevelts." The snow wafted into her face, and she tugged her hat lower on her forehead.

"I like to think so. But I'm a little jealous of your travels. I mean, you've just been in Iran with the leaders of the Western world."

"Yes, it *was* amazing to listen to those men discuss the fate of all of Europe, how they planned to divide Germany and Poland, and so forth. And at the dinners, they drank like fish."

Lorena laughed again. "Yes, they do that, those politicos. Some sort of test of manliness. Even if it kills them."

Mia felt a certain warmth from Lorena, a certain trust. Spontaneously, she added, "And you should have seen the Russian honor guards. Exotic uniforms, Slavic faces, the kind you don't often see here. Some of them really beautiful. There was one, a blonde…"

"A boy? They have that kind of ash-blond look. A bit rough, but appealing."

"No. This one was a girl. A young woman. Her name was Alexia."

"Ah, you even learned her name. Well done."

They made a circuit of the White House and returned to the portal. Mia glanced back over the grounds, watching their footprints in the white carpet gradually disappear. She smiled at the fantasy landscape, vaguely recalling innocent winters in St. Petersburg.

As they entered, a man waited next to a security guard, and her heart sank. "It's all right to admit him," she said to the guard. "It's my brother." She waved good-bye to Lorena and drew him to the side, scowling. "For God's sake, what are you doing here?"

"I had a hell of a time finding you. I knew you were in Washington, working on the war in some way, but I never thought you'd be here. Wow. Nice going."

She drew him to a quiet corner. "You still haven't told me why you're here."

He pursed his lips, as if reluctant to speak. "The police have reopened the case of Father's death."

"What? Why? It's been over a year now, and they found no evidence of a crime."

Van shrugged helplessly. "Apparently Smerdjakov, you know, his boss, found a letter that you'd sent his wife saying how much you wanted to get rid of him."

"But that's nonsense."

"You never wrote a letter?" Van crossed his arms.

Mia found herself stammering. "Well, I did, but it was just some silly love letter written in a fever of infatuation. I mentioned something about having big plans once I was free of him, but I just meant after I'd moved out. She knew I'd applied for a better job and planned to leave."

She winced, recalling her reckless trust in someone so shallow. "So now I'm a suspect again?"

"Not officially. I mean, the police have the letter, and they've questioned Grushenka. I just wanted to let you know what's going on so you could, well, get away if you need to. I mean, they can pick you up at any moment here."

"Van, I'm not going to run away from my job at the White House just because the police found an old love letter from me that said I was unhappy at home. You were, too. We both hated his hypocrisy, the way he ruined God for us."

"Yeah, he did, didn't he? Certainly as an explanation for the whole wretched world. The war, the suffering, the guilt and obligations that have nothing to do with reality. It's like a train ride I don't want to be on."

"So you're an atheist now?"

He shrugged. "It's not God that I don't accept, Mia, only I most respectfully return Him the ticket." He buttoned up his coat. "Take care of yourself," he said, and strode toward the door.

She watched him pass the security guard and disappear across the Rose Garden. Typical cynical Van. But she was inclined to agree with him.

CHAPTER SEVEN

Alexia snapped to attention in the guard station at the Kremlin Palace. "At ease, soldier." Nikolai Vlasik, head of Stalin's bodyguards, passed by with a slight nod. She resumed her guard position holding her ceremonial rifle across her chest.

She hoped he hadn't noticed how bored she was. The Special Purpose Regiment had an important function, of course, guarding the heads of government. But it didn't feel like service to the motherland.

Perhaps it was the cold that crept into her from the concrete floor of the station. Outside the station it was twenty below zero, and though she kept the door shut and wore a thick wool coat, her shiny leather boots seemed to conduct the cold right up her back.

The already dark afternoon and evening dragged by, and finally, at eighteen hours, her relief came. She stepped out, saluted, stepped to the side, and marched stiffly away while the new guard took up position.

Her ice-cold feet ached as she crunched through the snow along the northern corner of the Kremlin. She passed the rows of antique French cannons mounted in front as trophies and fast-marched to the end of the barracks, where the women of the regiment were housed.

She yanked the door closed behind her, breathing in the warm interior air and stamping life back into her feet. Only Ainur, a dark-eyed woman from Kazakhstan, was off duty and slouched on her bunk reading *The Red Star*, the army newspaper.

"If only they let us stand guard in valenki," Alexia moaned, dropping onto her bunk and drawing off her boot. She untied her footcloth and rubbed icy toes.

"Then you'd look like some peasant from the *kolkhoz*." Ainur snorted. "But it's only because I'm your best friend that I say that."

Alexia snorted back. "My feet are my best friends, and they hate you." She tied on clean footcloths that were at least room temperature and padded over to her friend's bunk. "So, what's the news?" she asked, nodding toward the newspaper.

Ainur glanced back down at the article. "Leningrad. The Volkhov and Leningrad fronts are just starting a new offensive to break the encirclement south of Lake Ladoga. This might be the breakthrough."

"I wish I was there helping out."

"I thought you had an aversion to those kinds of bloody battles."

"You make me sound like a coward. I'm not. I'm a good patriot and willing to die for the homeland. But I was raised by a priest, who told me that killing is sin."

"Priests are traitors. So, now you're reconsidering? About killing, I mean."

"I might. Frankly…" Alexia glanced around to make sure no one was within earshot. "I'm a little tired of the backbiting among the officers and others coming and going at the Kremlin. When you stand guard around them, they forget you're there, listening to the nasty little conspiracies they come up with. Always trying to undermine each other and curry favor with the boss they're all terrified of. It doesn't feel like you're helping the war at all." She sighed and leaned over Ainur's shoulder toward the paper.

"So what else is in the news? Anything more cheerful?"

"A nice report about our snipers. Zaitsev, of course. Everyone loves him. But this says they already have heroes from the Women's Sniper Training School in Podolsk. Look here. They even have pictures. Very attractive. But of course the big name is Pavlichenko, with a score of over three hundred."

Alexia took the paper out of her hands and perused the article. Half a dozen women were named and their "kill" scores listed. The largest photo showed Lyudmila Pavlichenko, a round-faced woman with an appealing sisterly face but dreadfully cut hair who posed stiffly with her sniper's rifle across her chest.

"They look good, posing with their rifles, don't they?" Ainur said. "I bet they get a lot of respect from their comrades."

Alexia shrugged. "We get plenty of respect, too, and we don't have to fire our guns."

"Yeah, maybe standing at the wall or by Lenin's tomb. But no one looks at us when we're freezing in our guard boxes."

"I was thinking more of state occasions. When Tatyana and I stood guard at the conference in Tehran, I could feel the foreigners staring at us."

Ainur snickered. "They were staring at you because you're pretty and look so fine in your uniforms. Vlasik also seems to think so. Have you noticed the way he watches you?"

Alexia gave another dismissive shrug. "If that gets me service at the foreign conferences, he can ogle me all he wants. That was the best assignment I ever had. I like traveling outside of Russia, meeting foreigners."

"Be careful. If anyone hears you talking like that, you could get in trouble."

"As long as you don't betray me, I'm fine. Now let's go to the mess hall. I have to go back on duty soon, and I need something hot in my stomach."

Alexia drew on her boots again, and as they marched together down the corridor toward the mess hall, she bumped elbows with Ainur. "So, tell me more about the women's sniper school."

As if to underline Ainur's assessment of him, Nicolai Vlasik summoned Alexia to his office the next day. Alarmed that he had somehow learned of their conversation, which could easily land her in Lubyanka Prison, Alexia hurried to his door. She tugged down her tunic, checked that her boots were free of mud or snow, and knocked.

A gruff voice called out, and she entered, closed the door behind her, and saluted smartly.

Vlasik sat upright behind his desk, his hands clasped under his impressive array of high-powered medals. She disliked looking at his squarish, slightly jowly face and stared at a spot directly over his head. His long silence made her certain he had gotten word of her remarks. Her mouth went dry.

"How long have you served in the Kremlin Special Purpose Regiment?"

"Five months, sir." Her heart fluttered. So short a career, now come to an end.

"Interesting. In such a short time, you have already come to the notice of Comrade Stalin."

Alexia dropped her glance to look at him directly. The word Stalin had her full attention. "Come to his notice? How?"

"Marshal Stalin approved your performance in Tehran and has specifically recommended you for a task."

So, obviously no Lubyanka. Now if he would only get to the point.

"In a few days time, two Americans from the White House will be visiting the Kremlin, and a private guard will be assigned to each one for security. You will escort them to meetings, remain in attendance unless directed otherwise, escort them to their hotel afterward, and then report back to me each evening. Is that clear?"

"Uh, yes, sir. If I may ask, who are the persons in question?"

"We will inform you before you're sent out. You'll be personally representing the Soviet Union so you must be on your best behavior."

She snapped to attention. "Will that be all, sir?"

"Yes, for the moment. You are dismissed."

As she hurried back to her barracks to tell Ainur, she could barely stifle a grin. Escorting American visitors from the White House. Suddenly being a guard was interesting again.

CHAPTER EIGHT

January 1944

After an international flight to RAF Kinloss Airport and a train ride to Invergorden, Scotland, Mia stood wearily on the dock next to Harry Hopkins. They both stared mournfully at the Catalina flying boat rocking in the icy water in front of them. Much wider than any plane she'd ever seen, its propeller engines hung from the wings over the fuselage, and it reminded her of some vast bird of prey.

"So this is what you get when you're not entitled to presidential treatment."

"Afraid so. Since we don't have air-force escort, we have to travel around North Cape, Norway, to Arkhangelsk. Worse, they're already carrying cargo, so we're being shoved into the machine gunner's station in the tail."

As soon as the hatch opened, they climbed inside. They crammed their baggage into the Plexiglas blister and crouched below the machine gun, which Mia fervently hoped would not be needed on this trip. They wore padded flight suits, but she already felt the chill of the unheated craft.

"How long is this flight?" she called out to the navigator, knowing the answer would not be welcome.

"About twenty-one hours, and most of that will be in darkness. We're fully loaded so can't fly at top speed. Best to sleep through the trip."

"Sleep, sure thing," she muttered, and stretched out the best she could, tucking her hands into her armpits and using her luggage as a pillow. The hours passed and she tried to doze, but the cold and the roar of the engines made it impossible.

Consequently, when they arrived in Moscow and landed on the Moscow River, she was dizzy with exhaustion. They clambered out onto the dock into the shock of frigid winter air.

The US ambassador to Russia, Averell Harriman, strode toward them. "Welcome to Russia. You both look like you could use a warm-up and some rest. Come on. We'll do our best to make you comfortable at the embassy."

While they walked toward the ambassador's car, Mia studied the man through sleep-deprived eyes. She'd corresponded with him several times on Lend-Lease matters, and he'd been one of the president's allies moving in the background at Tehran. Now, up close, he was rather handsome, and his robustness contrasted radically with Hopkins's bony frailty.

"How's the embassy managing, Averell?" Hopkins asked.

"Only just. We're down to a staff of six but still get the work done. Spaso House was damaged by bombs in '41, and the repairs are ongoing. Fortunately, we still have telephone lines and a telegraph, and can do basic business."

He opened the car door for her and she dropped into the rear, much relieved. Soon she could wash and eat and sleep. For once, she was glad to be only an assistant, allowed to doze in the warmth of the backseat while in the front the men talked strategy.

Spaso House, in the New Empire style, with its central portico, was a bit like a White House in miniature. Inside, the main hall and soaring domed ceiling were impressive, even to her foggy mind. Harriman noticed her perusal of the ceiling and smiled.

"Not bad, eh? It was built just before World War One for a fabulously rich merchant. Back in those tsarist days, you *could* be fabulously rich. You should have seen it before they took down the chandelier."

Mia nodded appreciatively. "Is it always so chilly?"

"Unfortunately, yes. The air raids broke a lot of windows, and we can't get glass for them. We've had to cover them with wooden boards, and the cold seeps through the cracks. The furnace doesn't always work either, so we've installed oil stoves in the sleeping rooms. It's a little unsightly, but we still manage to provide a luxury that is rare in Moscow these days, hot water."

Once in her room, Mia lit her stove immediately, then unpacked her suitcase. Though the hot water in the bathroom down the hall was not sufficient for a full bath, she managed a warm wash, then hurried back to her room. The bed was fresh, and as soon as she warmed it with her body, she fell asleep.

❖

Harriman and Hopkins were already at the table when she came downstairs, and the cook brought her breakfast. The scrambled eggs, though a bit watery, were from real eggs, but the bread was gritty and dry. The coffee was the real thing, but the absence of bacon, or any meat at all, was disappointing.

"Who are you meeting with first?" Harriman asked.

"Dmitriy Ustinov, Arms Minister." Hopkins warmed his hands around his coffee cup.

"Oh yes, at the People's Commissariat of Armaments, over on Gorky Street. I'd planned for Mr. Dornwend to drive you in the embassy car, but the Kremlin wants to send one over with their minders. They call it 'security,' as if someone might assassinate you if you were alone, but they simply want to monitor you."

"Really? It's gotten that bad?" Hopkins set his cup aside and lit a cigarette.

"Yes. The Kremlin is very suspicious of foreigners. But it's not so bad. You can go most places in Moscow. You just always have a babysitter." He glanced at his watch. "They should be here any minute."

"I suppose we can regard them as guides," Mia said, chewing her resistant toast.

Harriman glanced past her toward the sound of a door opening. "Ah, that must be them. Early, of course." He downed the last of his coffee and stood up.

Two uniformed guards stood in the entryway. One was a dashing fellow over six feet tall, and the other was a stately blond woman. Mia halted in mid-step. It was the Grushenka guard she'd seen in Tehran.

"We escort you to Kremlin," the young man said in thickly accented English.

Mia regained her composure. "It's quite all right. You can speak Russian," she assured him. "May I ask your name?"

"Kiril Yegorov." Obviously relieved, the young man tipped his head in the hint of a bow. Mia turned to the young woman.

"And you are Alexia."

The woman's surprise was disciplined, merely a slight lifting of the brows. "How do you know that?" she asked in Russian.

"You were one of Stalin's guards in Tehran. They told me your name."

Alexia seemed perplexed but did not reply, and Kiril continued. "We have an official car outside, and of course we do not want to keep the Commissar for Armaments waiting." He gestured toward the door.

❖

Kiril sat in the front with the Kremlin driver, while Alexia, to Mia's delight, squeezed into the rear with Hopkins and her. After a short ride in which Kiril identified the historic buildings, and Mia translated for Hopkins, the driver deposited them at the People's Commissariat of Armaments. A single contingent of guardians recognized the Kremlin guards and let them pass. At the relevant office, the two minders waited in the corridor.

Ustinov was in full uniform, in a smartly fitting tunic with ornamented collar and three stars on his shoulder boards. Under a Hero of the Soviet Union star, he wore a row of other medals. His thick head of hair was typically Russian, as were his wide face and large mouth.

Another man stood nearby, portly and of some lower rank. "This is Major Leonid Nazarov, my assistant," Ustinov said. "Please sit down." He indicated the two chairs placed directly in front of his desk.

A stack of ledgers already lay there, suggesting he'd done some research. He got right to business.

"Thank you for coming to Moscow," he said. "Rather than force you to read our Russian accounting, let me just explain the areas that are deficient."

He pointed out the list of discrepancies, verifying them with copies of the lists his office had submitted and various ledgers that revealed what had in fact been delivered.

"We are not so obtuse that we do not recognize that men and goods are lost at sea and on the road. Our problem is that your agents at the delivery stations provide lists that do not correspond with what arrives in our factories."

After an hour of comparing lists and figures, Hopkins drew the discussion to an end. "There is only so much we can explain here, sir. If you could provide me with a copy of your records, we can study them at greater leisure and come back to you with some sort of clarification."

"Yes, of course. Mr. Nazarov has such copies, for both you and for the Foreign Ministry, which shares our interest."

"No doubt. We have a meeting later today with Molotov," Hopkins said.

Nazarov produced a notebook from a shelf and presented it without speaking to Hopkins, and while all four exchanged courtesies, Ustinov led his visitors to the door.

Their two minders snapped to attention as the door opened. After a final shaking of hands, Hopkins and Mia pulled on their coats and ventured into the Russian winter again.

❖

The much shorter meeting with Foreign Minister Molotov was not nearly so amicable. Molotov made many of the same complaints and Hopkins the same provisional explanations. Unlike his colleague, Molotov insisted the only solution was to have duplicate shipments sent for those deemed lost. "In most cases, the lost items are not vehicles or large weaponry, but smaller items: clothing, foodstuffs, medications. These are easier to ship in duplicate immediately after a claim is made."

Hopkins's voice was becoming hoarse. "Mr. Molotov, at the moment, I cannot provide a definitive explanation for the discrepancies. We already have the ledger from the Commissariat of Armaments to study, and if you can provide us with similar copies, from the other distribution points, we will be happy to study them as well."

"Of course we have copies." He snapped his fingers, and an orderly appeared with several bulging folders. Mia winced. She was going to have to read all of them.

"The missing items are critical to the war effort. Irrespective of how you explain the deficiencies, they need to be compensated for and the original number provided immediately. Is that clear?"

Mia translated his demands without softening his tone. Hopkins stiffened in reaction, though his reply was impeccable. "Thank you for your time, Foreign Minister. In keeping with Mr. Roosevelt's wishes, we shall endeavor to supply the Red Army with whatever it needs to fight an *enemy it once trusted.* You will be hearing from us at the appropriate time." He offered his hand for a cold handshake and turned away, leading Mia from the room.

In the corridor she couldn't resist a smirk. "Well done, Mr. Hopkins, reminding him of his own blunder in negotiating a pact with Hitler."

Hopkins snorted faintly and tugged on his winter coat. "It was the least I could do to the little tyrant," he murmured.

Kiril and Alexia stepped toward them, and together they marched along the corridor to the portal.

"Shall we escort you back to your embassy now?" Kiril asked.

"I suppose so," Hopkins said. "I'm bushed." He looked mournfully at the still-closed door, apparently not keen to venture out into the painful winter air.

"But it's January 6," Mia reminded him. "Orthodox Christmas Eve on the Julian calendar."

"Is that so? I had no idea you were religious, Miss Kramer."

"Oh, I'm not at all. But I have childhood memories of Christmas services." She turned to Alexia. "Is it true that Christmas is now forbidden?"

"No, not at all. Communists consider religion the opiate of the people, but Stalin hasn't forbidden it," she said defensively.

Hopkins was not convinced. "I thought Stalin ordered all the churches closed and even destroyed the great cathedral."

Alexia shook her head. "He did in the beginning, but last September, he met with the bishops of the church, and in return for their support he gave permission for them to open the Moscow Theological Seminary and to elect a new patriarch. After that, some other churches opened again, too."

"So where do the Muscovites go on Christmas?" Mia got to the point. "I'd love to see a Christmas service, or part of one. I remember they were long."

Alexia's reaction was guarded. "All the big religious events are in the Yelokhovo Cathedral now."

"And is there a service today?" Mia was suddenly determined.

Kiril shook his head. "There is a mass, but it's late now. The church will be full, and you won't find a place to stand."

"What about tomorrow? Surely on Christmas morning…"

Hopkins tugged his fur hat down over his brow and wrapped his wool scarf twice around his face. Only his eyes were visible, and his voice seemed to come from far away. "Out of the question. We have a dinner engagement tomorrow, with Stalin and his ministers."

Mia would not give up. "That's in the evening. We have the morning free. If you're not interested, I'll go alone and be back hours before the dinner."

Alexia was obviously not thrilled. "It starts at nine, but I don't think my commander will agree to one of his guards attending a church service."

"Fine. Tell him that we're sentimental capitalist Christians, that we'll take the embassy car and that you'll wait outside."

Hopkins nodded toward Kiril to finally open the portal to the icy exterior. "Do what you wish. Just take me back to the embassy now so I can warm up."

"Are we agreed, then?" Mia looked toward Alexia. "You'll pick me up at eight thirty?"

Alexia glanced away, then sighed. "Yes. All right."

"Wonderful. *S razhdestvom!*" Mia exclaimed. "Merry Christmas."

CHAPTER NINE

The next morning, Mia ate breakfast alone. Hopkins had made it clear he saw no reason to join her in a freezing orthodox church listening to Old Slavonic chanting and so remained in bed. Ambassador Harriman, on the other hand, thought it was a good way to get to know another side of Russia and agreed to provide the embassy car and driver.

At eight thirty she was at the portal drawing on her coat as a military troop carrier dropped off her "security" for the day.

Ambassador Harriman appeared just as she was preparing to leave. "Enjoy your hour of nostalgia. Robert's bringing the car around now. He'll drop you off, and you can tell him when to return." He patted her gently on her well-insulated back as he opened the door for her. "Merry Christmas."

"Merry Christmas to you, sir."

Alexia stood by the side of the embassy car, as before, in a sheepskin coat and furred ushanka. The ear-flap hat suited her perfectly. Well, everything suited her perfectly. The driver climbed from the car to assist them, but Alexia had already opened the rear door for them both, so he waved and sat back down at the steering wheel.

As the car moved away from the embassy, the tires crunching on the crusted snow, Mia felt a childish joy. It was Christmas morning, the *real* Christmas, not the American version, and she would celebrate it with the lovely Alexia. Now, if she could just get her to go one step farther.

"Alexia, today it's just you and me. Kiril's not here to keep an eye on you. Will you come inside the church with me? No one has to know.

Besides, Robert's going to drop us off and come back later, so you would have to stand outside in the frigid air the whole time."

Alexia seemed to consider. "You make a good point. Well, maybe I'll just stand inside the portal, away from the cold."

Mia smirked. Inside the door was as good as inside the church. "Good. That's settled."

❖

In the snowy setting, the Epiphany Cathedral at Yelokhovo, with its central dome, bell tower, and four corner domes, looked like a postcard picture. Its neoclassical exterior was a bit shabby and in need of paint, but considering the war that raged even at that moment, it was a beautiful sight. Hundreds of people, bundled in bulky clothing, formed a line along the street, shuffling toward the wide main entrance.

"I'll come back in an hour and a half," Robert said. "Is that enough time?"

"Yes, and I promise we'll be here so you don't have to wait," Mia assured him. "Thank you for taking the time to drive us."

Mia and Alexia joined the line, polite enough not to crowd in at the front, but rude enough to use Alexia's military uniform to step in somewhere before the end. Their place guaranteed they'd get through the door but would not be trapped too far inside where they could not leave without disruption.

Fifteen minutes later they were inside, where the sheer density of bodies raised the air temperature twenty degrees. Mia removed her wool hat and loosened her collar. Remembering the correct protocol, she drew a cotton scarf from her pocket and draped it loosely over her head and shoulders.

"Surely you don't believe in all this." Alexia glanced toward the ceiling, suggesting the entire ceremony.

"No, I don't, but before I was Mia Kramer, I was little Demetria Fyodorovna Kaminskaya, and I did believe. I just want to see if it still has the power to move me."

With Alexia shuffling alongside her, they arrived within sight of the center of the church. They would have to stand throughout their visit, for no one but the elderly and infirm could sit. Mia gazed around the interior, so completely different from the elongated Western cathedrals she'd studied.

The entryway, with its comparatively low ceilings and archways, was more like a crypt. The massive square piers that supported the wide vaults were heavily carved with gold filigree and at their centers held glass-covered icons in black and gold. Icons—somber haloed images of Christ—also hung in filigreed frames from the tops of the pillars. Farther in, the crypt-like entry opened abruptly to a central space that rose up high, but the heavy baroque ornament and iconography continued, filling every bit of space up to the dome far overhead. It seemed as if all the riches of the world were being offered up.

The congregants, with few exceptions, were elderly, though a few held young children in their arms. She swept her gaze across the old women, bent and haggard in their fringed scarves, and the old men, many of whom resembled her father before he shaved his beard upon arriving in America.

The deep voices of a male choir rumbled, as if from the very belly of the earth, and the service began. The first to arrive were the regular priests, deacons, if her memory served correctly. All wore brocade gold silk that fell to the floor and covered their feet, and capes that rose high behind their necks, a strange display of opulence in a wretched war-strained city, but she supposed church vestments were a holdover from tsarist times. Carrying tall, narrow tapers in pairs, tied together at the top, they chanted as they entered. The patriarch followed in white brocade silk and a high, bulbous miter. All the men had full beards, though the patriarch's was longer and whiter than the others, and gave him an unmistakable Father Christmas look. He swung his silver censer, to chase away evil spirits, she supposed, and even from a distance, she could smell the fragrant incense.

She could make no sense of what they chanted in recitation and response, then remembered it was Church Slavonic, not meant to be understood. Still, it was pleasing to hear, a deeply soothing, otherworldly sound.

But their beards, the rich bass of their choir, and the complete absence of women in the celebration reminded her how very male the orthodox church was. God was male, his earthly representatives and celebrants were male, and women were there to simply worship.

Her thoughts returned to Alexia, who stood next to her, in uniform but inconspicuous in the tightly packed crowd. What did she think? What did it mean that she'd been raised by a priest? Was that any different from being raised by the pious and fanatical Fyodor Kaminsky?

One of the priests appeared bearing a tome with an ornate jewel-encrusted cover. He held it up before the patriarch, who kissed it, then opened it to the first page. The choir stopped for a moment, allowing the patriarch to recite the text, then responded in intervals. The story of the nativity, she guessed.

Losing interest in the recitation, she studied the cathedral interior again, the holy opulence that meant to lift the spirits of the congregation into the ethereal. At the same time she felt the pressure of Alexia's shoulder against her in the crowd and smiled inwardly. The Divine Spirit being summoned by the celebrants would surely disapprove of the forbidden animal pleasure that lifted her heart just then.

She was startled by hot breath on her ear as Alexia leaned near and whispered, "It's time to go." Obediently she followed Alexia's lead as they wormed their way back through the crowd. At the entrance, which was as packed full as the rest of the church, they fastened their coats and drew on scarfs and hats.

Prying open the huge church doors, they stepped out into the icy wind.

The embassy car was not in sight, so they huddled by the church door exhaling columns of steam and clapping their upper arms for warmth.

"What did you think of our orthodox ceremony?" Alexia asked.

"Pure theater, of course, but I have to admit, the child in me loved it. I remembered Easter at the great Church of the Resurrection in St. Petersburg with my parents and my little brother."

"You don't believe in the Divine Father?"

"In fact, I get along just fine with no father at all, divine or earthly. Still, I'm sentimental about big holidays."

"It's the same for me. I don't remember my father, and the local priest was the only male presence for me. I loved him, but I began to doubt when I went to school, and by the time I joined the Komsomol, I rejected faith completely. Only the moral part of it remained, and that's what has held me back from fighting. At least so far."

"You sound like you're having doubts about that, too."

"Yes. I think faith, even that tiny remainder, has caused me to stay a child, if not a coward, when Russia really needs me to be an adult, at the front."

Just then, the embassy car came into view, and they waved it over. Once they were seated in the warm interior, Mia continued. "Does that mean you're going into active service?"

"I think so. I have to apply for training. My commandant won't like it, but he won't refuse."

"What do you want to train for?"

"Apparently, I'm a good shot, so I'll go where I can do the most good. I want to be a rifleman. A sniper."

In the late afternoon, still warmed by the memory of the morning in church, Mia crunched across the snow toward the Grand Kremlin Palace. Taciturn as always, Hopkins strode alongside her. Kiril and Alexia marched a few steps behind them, still doing their job.

"Ironic, isn't it, that Stalin the atheist has invited us to dinner on Christmas Day? Do you suppose he harbors a tiny bit of sentimentality?"

Hopkins shook his head. "I doubt it. The communists got rid of all the church 'fathers,' but they replaced them with the likes of Stalin and Molotov. Same obedience, just no ceremony."

She gazed up at the imposing façade of the Grand Palace, a vast block of a building with three ranks of windows, though she knew from reading that the upper floor had a double row of windows and that the palace had only two floors. The upper one held the vast spaces of the five great halls, named after the Russian saints: George, Vladimir, Alexander, Andrew, and Catherine.

The Dining Hall of Catherine the Great where they ended up dazzled with gold. She stared, stupefied, at the ceiling. Apparently noticing her awe, Hopkins leaned toward her and whispered, "It was Catherine the Great's throne room."

The hall had a vaulted ceiling, like the church she'd just been in, though this one was supported by massive pylons with bronze capitals and malachite mosaics, and the carved doors held an elaborate coat of arms. The chandelier hanging over the center of the room astonished her, given the German bombing. But there it was, in all its tsarist splendor.

Dinner was served in a semicircular reception hall adjacent to the Great Hall, but it, too, was staggeringly ornate, with floral paintings and walls upholstered in gold-green brocade, matching that of the chairs.

The table was set for eight, though the guests milled about until Stalin himself arrived and all were seated. As the only woman at the table, Mia was thoroughly intimidated and was glad that her function would largely be as Hopkins's interpreter. Stalin's other guests were former foreign minister Litvinov, acting as interpreter, then Molotov, Beria, Voroshilov, armaments minister Ustinov still looking splendid in his uniform, and finally Nicolai Vlasik, head of the Kremlin Guard.

The right side of the table held Harriman, Hopkins, herself, and Ustinov's placid assistant, Leonid Nazarov.

The food offered was plentiful and varied: wild birds, fish dishes, borscht, potato dumplings, pirozhki, red and black caviar. Dinner began, as always, with a series of vodka toasts.

To her surprise, the conversation touched only very lightly, almost flippantly, on the issues addressed at Tehran and soon migrated to generalities. Stalin continued toasting and urging his guests to empty their entire glasses. Mia realized it was his way of loosening men's tongues and getting his opponents to reveal themselves.

She was confident that such a primitive ruse could not trap Hopkins. He had nothing to hide, was at the core guileless, and had no agenda other than to keep Stalin happy without being servile to him. Moreover, alcohol appeared to make him even more amiable than sobriety.

But by the second hour, he was clearly not holding up. His persistent stomach problems obviously could not cope with the heavily salted fish, the cream, and the river of vodka. He excused himself momentarily to use the facilities, and when he rose from the table, his face became splotchy and discolored. Harriman stood up quickly and guided him from the dining room.

The dinner conversation continued, with Stalin recounting a tale of his early Bolshevik days. It soon took a bawdy turn, and he began to use Moscow slang, which escaped her. Everyone laughed.

Eventually Harriman returned, alone. "Please excuse us, Marshal Stalin. With thanks for your great hospitality, Mr. Hopkins has unfortunately taken sick, and I must escort him back to the embassy."

Stalin stood up. "I am sorry to learn that we have overtaxed Mr.

Hopkins's digestion. Would you like some assistance to help him to the car?"

Harriman raised a hand. "No, thank you. We can find our way out and do not want to disrupt your dinner. Miss Kramer, would you…?"

Nazarov also got up from his seat. "Oh, please. Do not deprive us of the one pretty face at the table."

Ustinov added, "Yes, if Miss Kramer finds our Kremlin diet tolerable, we would love to continue our visit with her. I am sure she has tales to tell about the White House."

Stalin extended a meaty hand in her direction. "What do you think, Miss Kramer? Will you do us the honor?"

Mia stared at Harriman, pleading with her eyes to be rescued. But the ambassador had only Hopkins on his mind and effectively abandoned her. "It's quite all right with us. We'll send the car back in two hours," he said, and with a final wave to the table, he left the dining room.

She went slightly limp. She was stuck with a table full of Kremlin big shots and way out of her depth. Was it better, or worse, that all of them were intoxicated?

As it turned out, it was better. Stalin signaled for dessert to be served with wine, which he pointed out was Georgian, so if anyone complained about it, he'd be shot. He chuckled, and everyone at the table chuckled nervously with him. But following Stalin's lead, Ustinov talked of bagging elk and bear in the snow, Molotov of escaping Siberian exile during the tsarist regime, and after each tale, the table drank to the teller, or the bears, or Bolshevik heroism.

"So, Miss Kramer." Stalin slammed his empty glass down on the table. "It's your turn. Tell us something about life in the White House."

One did not refuse the dictator of all the Russians, so Mia searched her memory for a story that would not compromise anyone. Roosevelt himself was forbidden territory, and so was Hopkins. Who could she expose to Kremlin judgment? She could think of only one thing.

"I will tell you about a great prize the White House has. That is the wife of the president, Eleanor Roosevelt. A great lady. I think you would like her, Marshal Stalin, as much as you like our president."

"Oh, would I?" Stalin took a pipe from one pocket and an envelope of tobacco from another. What makes you think so?" He tapped a quantity of tobacco into the bowl and pressed it down with his thumb.

"Because she's a friend of American workers and of the American people of all colors."

"How many colors do you have?" Molotov snickered, leaning toward Stalin to light his pipe for him.

Stalin puffed until the tobacco glowed bright orange and he sucked in smoke. "Don't be rude, Vyacheslav Mikhailovich. Let the woman talk." He blew out smoke in a thin stream. "So, tell us the story of Yeleanor Roosevelt," he commanded.

"It concerns another great woman, a Negro opera singer named Marian Anderson. Miss Anderson wished to sing a concert in a hall owned by a patriotic group called the Daughters of the American Revolution."

"Hmm. Revolution. That's a good thing."

"Not in this case, sir. These women refused to allow it because, although Miss Anderson is a magnificent opera singer, she is a Negro."

"And Yeleanor Roosevelt's role in this?"

"Mrs. Roosevelt arranged for her to sing outdoors in front of the Lincoln Memorial and at the same time for it to be broadcast on the radio. So in the end, Miss Anderson sang not for three hundred people in a hall, but many thousands in Washington and millions across the nation."

Stalin nodded. "Excellent story. And that deserves a toast, too. To Yeleanor Roosevelt and opera singer Median Enderson." Everyone at the table stood up and emptied their vodka glasses, and with Stalin's eyes on her, Mia could not avoid downing another dose of the brain-scalding liquid.

She dropped down onto her chair and breathed deeply, wondering how much longer she could last. Could she keep her wits about her? She was confident of not saying anything improper to her hosts, but would she be able to find her way through the Kremlin Palace back out to the embassy car in... She peered at her watch until her eyes focused on the tiny numbers. In half an hour.

The stories continued around the table, and as the men became drunker, they became more vulgar. When she was no longer the center of attention, she faked drinking each toast to keep from losing consciousness.

Finally the hour of her liberation came and she stood up, massaged her mouth to prepare the muscles for speech, and said, "Marshal Stalin,

I wish to thank you for your great hospitality, which only increases my admiration for the Russian people. Unfortunately, I have obligations to my own government and have to return to my embassy now, with great regret."

Did all that come out all right? She thought so. As she turned around, she was struck by a wave of dizziness and found walking difficult. Fortunately, a butler came and led her outside the Great Hall, where, to her enormous relief, Alexia waited.

Without comment, Alexia helped her into her coat and guided her to the palace courtyard. The ice-cold air hitting her face sobered her a little, but not enough to dampen her high spirits. She'd been tipsy before, but never quite as drunk as this, and was enjoying it. Plus, she realized, it was still Christmas. The thought made her philosophical and affectionate.

She halted and took Alexia's arm. "Look how clear the sky is." She swayed slightly as she tilted her head. "You can see millions of stars. Millions and millions and millions." She found the idea thrilling.

Alexia scanned the sky, blowing little clouds of steam, perhaps humoring her. "The priest who raised me always said the stars were proof of God's existence."

Mia chuckled. "Funny, scientists would say the stars are proof God *doesn't* exist. In any case, when you see this many, you can't help but feel connected. Even the ancients gave them identities. Right up there is Orion, for example." She pointed upward more or less in the right direction, gripping Alexia's shoulder to keep her balance.

"You can identify the constellations?"

"Na, just showing off. Orion's easy because of the three stars that make his belt. Then you can look for the stars that make his shoulders and feet."

Alexia held her collar up under her chin. "I don't see a man in the sky. I see—I don't know—some great force, unfathomably vast and wholly indifferent, that has no face. There's a majesty in that."

"I know what you mean. It has no interest in comforting us, yet we are comforted. As by the sunrise." Mia smiled, pleased to have produced such poetry from an alcohol-soaked brain.

The embassy car pulled up in front of them, and she tumbled into it. Once inside, she rambled on about the mysteries of the universe and the beauty of the human spirit. Alexia agreed in each case, seemingly amused.

When they reached the embassy, Mia realized that her Russian Christmas was over and in just a few minutes she would be alone.

"Will you guard me all the way to my room?" She snickered. "You know, so that I don't do something anti-Soviet on the way."

Alexia laughed softly. "All right, I'll go, to protect the motherland from you until the very last moment." The embassy guard admitted them both, and, gripping Mia's arm, Alexia strode beside her up the stairs and along the corridor.

Mia fumbled for her key and opened the door to her room, then drew Alexia by the arm in with her, delaying separation. "A shame I have to leave tomorrow. A shame there's a war. A shame you'll be on the battlefield soon and I'll never see you again. Here we've just met, and now...poof! Gone to fight for the motherland."

"I'll think of you while I'm fighting." Alexia laughed and brushed Mia's hair out of her face, her first intimate touch. "And if I survive the war, and you return to Russia, perhaps you can find me. I am Alexia Vassilievna Mazarova. My grandmother lives in Arkhangelsk, and the priest Father Zosima will know how to find her, if he, too, is still alive."

"Those are a lot of 'ifs,' my dear Alexia. I don't think I will ever be able to remember enough to follow that trail. But I will always remember this."

She grasped Alexia's head with both hands, and pausing just long enough to look into the startled gray eyes, she pressed her lips hard against Alexia's mouth.

Alexia stood rigid in her grip but did not pull away, and the awkward kiss lasted scarcely more than a few seconds. Then Mia herself stepped back, realizing the magnitude of what she had done. Surely it was an offense: against diplomatic protocol, against the decorum of the United States Embassy, and against the innocent person of the guard herself.

It was the worst mistake she'd made since arriving in the Soviet Union.

"I...I'm sorry. It was the vodka and...well..."

Alexia's face showed no expression at all. "Good night, Demetria Fyodorovna Kaminskaya," she said, and let herself out.

❖

The next morning Mia was awakened by a firm rap on the door. Struggling up to full consciousness, she called out, "What is it?"

A man's voice sounded through the closed door. "Mr. Harriman requests your presence at breakfast."

"Yes, yes, of course. I'll be down right away," she stammered, noting that it was already ten o'clock. God, what a headache she had.

She dressed quickly, brushed her teeth to lose the foul taste in her mouth, combed her hair, and rushed down to the breakfast room. Harriman and Hopkins both sat over coffee cups, though only the ambassador looked alert. Hopkins slouched in his chair, his skin an odd gray color.

"How are you feeling, sir?" she asked, in spite of her own malaise. Someone from the kitchen set down a cup of coffee in front of her, and she warmed her hands on it before taking the first comforting swallow.

"Better, thank you," Hopkins said, "but I don't think I'll be doing many more of Mr. Stalin's dinners. What about you?"

"I held up pretty well, in spite of half a dozen more toasts. However, they forced me to tell a White House story."

A shadow passed over his face, and Harriman set down his cup. "Good heavens, what?"

"I told them about the First Lady and the Marian Anderson concert at the Lincoln Memorial. I thought since several million Americans knew the story, it wouldn't hurt if the Kremlin did, too. Did I overstep?"

Hopkins waved feebly. "No, not if that's all you said. As long as you didn't make Mr. Roosevelt seem weak."

"Oh, I'd never do that." She noticed a few triangles of cold toast on a rack near her cup and helped herself to one. "I'm aware of the delicate position we're in. Which brings up the question, do we have all the documents we need for the investigation of the lost goods?"

"Yes, they're packed, and I've given all the parties our assurances. I believe we've left them with a good impression. Don't you think, Miss Kramer?"

Mia recalled her awkward molestation of a Kremlin guard.

"Uh, yes. I think so."

CHAPTER TEN

Washington, DC, Winter 1944

Mia continued to plow through the documentation of deliveries via the Arctic and the Persian routes, trying to determine where the losses were occurring. Nothing stood out enough to account for the Russian complaint. Nonetheless, at Hopkins's behest, she sent out orders for duplicate shipments of the small arms, clothing, fuel, and foodstuffs that had mysteriously disappeared.

A month passed, then another, rainy blustery days and nights in Washington, DC, and she tried to keep track of where the front line in the East was. The last news on the radio was that the Leningrad siege was lifted, which removed the vague guilt of knowing she had relatives there whom she could not help. A great battle still raged at Narva, in what was once Estonia, but that was far from Moscow, which Hitler's troops would never see again.

And Alexia Vassilievna Mazarova? Was she still standing statuesque guard at the Kremlin? Or had she in fact transferred and was slogging through the snow and mud of the Eastern Front?

The Washington winter made Mia lethargic, and even the comings and goings of high-ranking military in the White House halls did nothing to excite her. Until one morning at the beginning of March, a light, ladylike rap came from the First Lady's study. Mia called out "Come in!" and Mrs. Roosevelt entered. She wore a wool business suit and hat, and held small leather gloves in one hand.

"How have you been, dear?" she asked. "I've been on the lecture trail for the president and never seem to have any time these days. I'm afraid I've neglected you. I thought I'd catch you before I went out again."

"How kind of you to say that, but I haven't felt at all neglected."

"I'm glad. But I confess, I'm here because I have a little request."

"Anything you wish, Mrs. Roosevelt?" Mia said, pushing her papers aside.

The First Lady drew on one of the gloves. "You see, the president and I have invited someone to the White House, both as a good-will gesture and to increase public support for our entry into Europe."

"Yes, ma'am?"

"But we need someone who speaks Russian, and the president is loath to use his official interpreter."

"I'll be happy to help, but who is the guest?" Mia imagined one of the pasty men she'd met in Moscow and wondered if this one too would travel with a sausage and a pistol.

"Major Lyudmila Pavlichenko. A female sniper who has just received the Hero of the Soviet Union medal and whom the Kremlin is quite keen for the West to meet."

"Oh, that sounds intriguing. When does she arrive?"

The First Lady clasped her hands, her gesture of satisfaction. "Tomorrow afternoon. I shall ask Mr. Hopkins to give you the day off to join the welcoming committee."

According to the printed biography forwarded by the Soviet Press Department, Lyudmila Pavlichenko was twenty-five years old and already a major. A photo that had come with the press material showed a dark-haired woman with a simple, open face and slightly heavy brows, in a three-quarter pose. She held a rifle across her chest, of which only the scope and the bolt handle were visible. What stood out was her atrociously cut hair, for a large, straight tuft of it jutted out from under her field cap as if it had been blunt cut in a hurry with a bayonet.

When she arrived at the White House, President and Mrs. Roosevelt met her at the entrance while Mia acted as interpreter. After certain pleasantries, the Roosevelts invited their guest to luncheon along with the Russian ambassador and his wife, and while the group ate chicken à la king, Mia had a chance to study her.

She looked older than her years, though at certain angles she was attractive in a matronly sort of way. When she removed her enormous officer's cap, she revealed a slightly tidier though still uninspired haircut, but her eyes seemed kind, and the fact that she had no feminine vanity was in its way appealing. Most importantly, she spoke intelligently, a welcome but unnecessary skill for a sniper. She was also adept at concealing what surely must have been shock at seeing the president of the United States in a wheelchair.

"You must be glad to get away from the battlefield," Eleanor said, cutting her chicken into tiny pieces that needed only a few nibbles before they could be swallowed.

Pavlichenko ingested the big chunks with no reservation and wiped her mouth. "I hate to leave my colleagues in the struggle, but my visit here was also a military duty."

"Where were you engaged for the most part?" Roosevelt asked.

"In the Crimea, defending Sebastopol," she said with obvious pride.

The president frowned slightly with paternal concern. "Where you ever wounded? It seems so much more terrible for a young woman."

Pavlichenko straightened slightly. "Twice, in fact. Shrapnel wounds from shells exploding close by. Sometimes the Fritzes would put up so much noise blasting away at me, it was a real concert. Bullets whistling over me and hitting all around me." She swept her fork in imaginary trajectories past her head. "Wounded or not, all I could do was stay down and not move for three hours."

"How dreadful for you," Eleanor exclaimed, with polite horror.

The luncheon conversation continued in such fashion for an hour, and at its conclusion, the president announced, "Miss Kramer will take you on a brief tour around the White House. After that, the press will arrive for some photographs, and then at four, we'll have a reception. Miss Kramer, would you also be so kind as to escort Major Pavlichenko to her hotel after the reception?"

"I'll be happy to," Mia replied, pleased to be away from her cubicle for a couple of hours.

While President and Mrs. Roosevelt returned to their duties,

Mia guided the guest through the main staterooms, explaining what little she knew about their functions. As they strolled, Mia noted that Pavlichenko was slightly plump, as a woman would be who simply did not care about her appearance. Her indifference to style was also evident in the way she wore her uniform. The man's tunic, amply decorated with medals, was cinched with a Sam Browne belt high over her rounded hips and directly under her breasts. She wore a skirt that hung in a formless column to mid-calf over leather boots.

"I understand you were in Moscow," Pavlichenko said as they left the last of the staterooms.

"Yes, in January. Bitter cold, of course, but I got to see the Grand Kremlin Palace. I was tremendously impressed, as you can imagine."

"Yes, it is impressive. But the tsars built their palaces on the blood and toil of the people."

Their arrival at the press conference removed the need for Mia to reply to such cynicism. A butler stepped in front of them and opened the door to a room full of reporters. Camera bulbs flashed and shutters clicked as they entered and took seats behind a lectern.

Eleanor Roosevelt spoke first, lauding the courage and forbearance of the female Russian soldiers and the importance of the alliance between the United States and the Soviet Union in fighting for freedom.

"We have American women in all branches of our military service, I am pleased to say. WACs, WAVEs, air force service pilots called WASPs, and women serve even in the marines and coast guard. We can be proud of these, our sisters, wives, and daughters, but we cannot say, and I dearly hope we never have to say, that our women give their lives in the trenches."

Polite applause followed the mention of patriotic women.

"However, it has been the fate of the Soviet Union to be invaded by a ruthless foreign force, and thus it has mobilized *all* its citizenry, its women, too, even on the front lines. I am honored to present one of their bravest…" She paused dramatically. "And most deadly. Major Lyudmila Pavlichenko, you have the floor."

Mia repeated the First Lady's introduction in Russian, for the major's benefit, and during the renewed applause, Pavlichenko strode to the podium.

Obviously unaccustomed to public speaking, she unfolded a piece of paper and addressed the room of reporters haltingly. After a few remarks about the kindness of the Americans to receive her, and her hopes that the Americans would soon join the European struggle, she simply asked for questions.

"How many men have you killed?" some young reporter shouted from the rear.

Pavlichenko seemed unfazed by the crudeness of the question. "Over three hundred."

"Did you miss shampoo and pretty dresses and makeup on the front?" another called out.

"Some of my comrades do. Perhaps the way you would miss your shiny shoes and neckties and clean white shirts."

"Do romances happen on the battlefield?" A few reporters snickered.

Pavlichenko exhaled in obvious exasperation. "In blood and filth and snow, with comrades dying or mutilated every day under fire and bombardment? Rarely."

The questions continued in the same trivial vein until Pavlichenko lost patience. She leaned forward with her elbows on the podium and seemed to stare at those in the back row. "Gentlemen, millions... *millions*...of Soviets have died defending their homeland, while only a few thousand Americans have fallen in North Africa, Italy, and the Pacific. No one has come to our aid on the Eastern Front. I am twenty-five years old, and I have already killed 309 invaders. Do you not think, gentlemen, that you have been hiding behind my back for too long?"

After a moment of stunned silence, the reporters applauded.

❖

The reception was both pleasant and tedious. It was another occasion to eat festive food a cut above what the White House cafeteria usually served, but tedious because the people that came along the reception line to greet the guest asked the same dreary questions again and again. How did she like the United States? How did she like American food? How did she like American clothes, cars, jazz, and all things American? Pavlichenko's answers became briefer and briefer.

When the last person passed them, Lyudmila broke away to chat a bit with Eleanor Roosevelt and Harriman, who spoke enough Russian to act as interpreter. Mia relaxed where she stood, sipping her fruit juice.

A reporter sidled up next to her. "I wonder if they all look like that," he muttered.

"What do you mean?" Mia was sure she knew but wanted him to say it.

"Well, frankly, she's a little frumpy, don't you think? Not like our women."

Mia felt her cheeks redden. Without facing him, she asked with forced neutrality, "You think so?"

"Well, it's obvious, isn't it? I mean, what kind of fellow would want to romance someone who shot people and looked like that?" She could hear now the slight slur in his words that suggested he'd drunk too much White House wine.

He went on with his theory of femininity. "They make a good pair, don't they, the sharpshooter and the president's wife. Two homely women who found another way to advance themselves in a man's world."

Mia turned slowly toward him and hoped her contempt was as obvious on her face as in her words.

"You may be judging all women by what you feel in your groin, but not all women care about your sexual approval. One of those 'frumpy' women has published more than you and has influence on the domestic policy of your country. The other one, in case you hadn't heard, has personally felled, with a single shot, over three hundred better men than you. So I think this would be a good time to shut your pie hole."

She turned her back on him and wandered over to where Pavlichenko was in conversation with the president and Harriman.

"Thank you for agreeing to this tour, Miss Pavlichenko," the president said, looking up at her from his wheelchair. "Unlike in your own country, a good many Americans are unwilling to fight for Europe. Even the attack on Pearl Harbor has not convinced them that this is a global war. I am hoping your courage will set an example."

"I hope so, too, Mr. President, for you are well aware how urgent it is that you open up a western front and draw off some of the German force from our cities."

Roosevelt reached up as if to take her hand, then apparently changed his mind, and the hand dropped awkwardly back onto the armrest of his wheelchair. "I assure you, we are doing everything in our power to prepare a spring invasion, as I promised Marshal Stalin. It will be soon. Very soon."

Pavlichenko nodded, and if she was disappointed, she did not show it. What showed was fatigue. The president had the sensitivity to notice.

"I think we've worn you down enough, Miss Pavlichenko. Miss Kramer, will you escort the major back to her hotel? Mr. Watson will call a car around for you."

❖

As they made their way from the White House to the Mayflower Hotel in the car, Major Pavlichenko suddenly turned to Mia. "You know, you are the only woman in this country I have been able to talk to without an interpreter, and it's been a very long day. Why don't you join me in the hotel bar for a...for whatever it is Americans drink?"

Mia remembered the Russian propensity to celebrate all things with vodka, even the end of a day of diplomacy. "This American drinks a little wine now and then, after a long day, and I'll be happy to join you."

The Mayflower bar was typical of its genre. On one side, a half dozen two-person tables stood along the wall, and on the other, a faux mahogany bar with a double row of glasses hanging upside down on an overhead rack. They took seats at one of the tables, and Pavlichenko removed her enormous officer's cap, releasing once again her formless hair.

"A glass of your house red wine," Mia said to the waiter.

"Please tell him I'll have the same as you," Pavlichenko said.

"No vodka?" Mia asked.

"No sense in reinforcing a stereotype."

When the drinks arrived, they toasted, took the ceremonial swallow, and Pavlichenko unbuttoned the top button of her tunic. "I don't know why they make the collars on these things so high."

Mia smiled at the fact that the major had just acted out two clichés, letting down her hair and unbuttoning her collar. "I have to tell you, frankly, that I'm happy Russia has sent us a woman sniper and not a man. The American public is barely aware of the Red Army, let alone that women fight in it. Can you tell me how many there are?"

Pavlichenko took another large swallow. "In the military in general? Several hundred thousand. As for snipers, that number grows monthly, and the schools are graduating them even now. I would say maybe two thousand."

"Do snipers generally know about each other?"

"They do if they come from the same schools, and some become known if they attain high scores."

"I have a friend," Mia said, conceding inwardly that molestation might not constitute friendship. "Someone I met while I was in Moscow named Alexia Vassilievna, but her friends called her Alyosha. Anyhow, she's currently in an honor regiment but wants to become a sniper, and I wonder how she would do that."

"If your friend is a party member and has superior visual ability, she could qualify, and if she does, she'd probably go to the Central Women's Sniper Training School near Podolsk."

"I guess I don't really know what a sniper does. How is it different from the shooting by ordinary soldiers?"

Pavlichenko leaned forward onto her elbows, her eyes bloodshot. "Well, sometimes they send you off to knock out communication lines or machine-gun nests, and then you're just a soldier with a good aim." She paused, formulating the rest of her answer, turning her wineglass on the table.

"But often you have to hunt a particular officer, or even an enemy sniper, one of your professional colleagues, so to speak. Then it's personal, and the act of shooting is a moment of intimacy that leaves a mark on you."

"Intimacy? Shooting someone from a long distance? How can that be?"

"Yes, because the target's not anonymous anymore. You track him or watch him, sometimes for hours, and when you finally get him in your scope, you fixate on him, on his uniform. You can even see his rank on his cap or collar, his medals. While you're waiting for the perfect shot, you see the details of his face, whether he shaved that morning or has a dueling scar. Maybe he's handsome or looks like a man you know. You wait for him to turn just the right way, and when you lay your crosshairs over his face you find yourself looking into his eyes. He's perhaps five hundred meters away, but he could be in your embrace, and he's yours completely."

Mia simply nodded, not wanting to interrupt the narrative.

"You feel a surge of power but also sadness because you know this man is in the last moments of his life, but he has no idea. How many more breaths will you allow him to take? You're tempted to let him take another and another, because by now you're half in love with him. But then you remember your duty, and finally you fire. Your shot, your touch, is always to his head, usually to his face. When it is, we have a name for it."

"What's that?"

"We call that the sniper's kiss." She emptied her glass and wiped her mouth with her fist.

Mia chuckled softly. "Rather the opposite of the Jesus kiss," she muttered.

"Jesus kiss? I don't understand."

"Oh, sorry. It just reminded me of something a pastor said at the White House Christmas party. He quoted Dostoyevsky, whose Grand Inquisitor challenges Jesus, and all Jesus does in reply is kiss him. A sort of 'love is the answer' answer."

Pavlichenko snorted. "Dostoyevsky! A nineteenth-century intellectual who wallowed in personal soul-searching. He has nothing to say to a people struggling against an invader." With a swallow of wine, she changed the subject.

"By the way, Miss Kramer. I got a letter from Georgetown University inviting me to teach as a guest lecturer in the Russian language and history. Perhaps they did not realize I was here only for a short visit. When I return home, I will thank them formally, of course, but would you be so kind as to let them know immediately that my travel schedule is very tight, and I will not be able to do anything that is not on the scheduled tour?"

"I'll be happy to do so, though that would be a real coup, wouldn't it?"

"A coup for your university or for Russia?"

"I suppose for both. The best sort of international relations." Mia finished her wine. "Would you like another? Courtesy of the White House."

Pavlichenko shook her head. "Thank you, no. I'm really ready for bed now." She rose from the table, set her officer's cap on, and tugged on her tunic that had ridden up over her hips.

Mia left an adequate number of bills on the table and escorted the guest as far as the elevator. "I believe someone will arrive tomorrow morning to escort you to the train for Chicago. I think it's wonderful what you're doing, and I wish you good luck on your tour."

"Thank you for your service and your companionship, Miss Kramer. And who knows? If this war can bring me to the White House, perhaps it will lead you again to the Kremlin." After a light hug, Pavlichenko stepped into the elevator.

With a curious feeling of solidarity with the cynical sharpshooter, Mia strode toward the hotel exit and the White House car.

❖

At the White House, one of the security men met her at the door. "Miss Kramer, you have a visitor. Says she knows you. She's waiting in the visitors' foyer."

Searching her memory for who might be visiting her, she hurried down the corridor and opened the door. It was the last person she wanted to see.

The woman was wearing her fox-fur coat, which Mia had once thought elegant but now found as vulgar as the too-large earrings, the too-high heeled shoes, and the too-red lipstick.

"Grushenka. What the hell are you doing here?"

"Well, there you are, finally, my dear Demetria. You've kept me waiting, but I'll forgive you." Grushenka gave her a peck on the cheek. "You're looking well. Working at the White House has done you good."

"Answer my question."

"Aren't you going to ask how I am? I'll tell you how I am. Not very well. Pavel found one of your letters, and like the fool that he is, he took it to the police. I suppose he wanted to implicate you. You know how much he hates you now. But the police said it was not strong enough evidence to arrest you."

"Well, that's good news. The whole disaster happened over a year ago, and I'd like to forget about it, and you too, for that matter. What do you want?"

They were still standing in the middle of the room, but Mia had no intention of offering her a seat for a cozy chat.

"You want to forget me? How can you be so cruel? We were so good together."

Mia felt her lips harden. "You took advantage of me, though I still can't figure out why. Was it boredom? It certainly wasn't passion, because a month later, you were doing it with my father." She looked away. "It makes me sick to think about it."

"It wasn't like that. I really did care for you. But one evening, after I'd drunk too much, Fyodor caught me off guard and…well…nature just took over. You know how stormy Russian men can be. It didn't last very long."

"You came all the way to Washington to tell me this crap? I don't want to hear it."

"Well, no. You see, Pavel has had a few problems in the business. Frankly, we're broke. So I thought in the meantime, with your White House salary and all, you could help us out. Just…say…two thousand dollars, and I'll disappear completely and never speak a word to anyone here of what happened."

Mia stared at her, stunned. "You've come here to blackmail me. Is that it? If I don't pay you two thousand dollars, you'll get me fired."

"Actually, I was thinking more of the president than of you. Mr. Roosevelt is campaigning for reelection. This kind of slander about his staff whispered to the conservative newspapers would be very embarrassing."

Mia was paralyzed with outrage. Bad enough to have her own career ruined, but to compromise President Roosevelt…She suddenly felt nauseous.

"You have to give me time," she said, beaten. "I simply don't have two thousand dollars. I'll need a few days to figure out how to get it."

"You have lots of rich friends here in your new life, so I'm sure you can borrow it. I'll give you until Saturday. After that, I'm going to *The New York Times*."

CHAPTER ELEVEN

January 8, 1944

Alexia leaned against the wall of the oven that heated her barracks room, pressing as much of her back as possible against the tiles. The tall ceramic ovens were fueled only in the evenings, when most of the guard came off duty, and now, just before supper, she savored the first firing. She let her mind drift into pleasurable thoughts, the sound of chanting in Old Slavonic, the smell of incense, and the kiss of an American woman.

"What are you smiling about?" her comrade Olga asked.

Alexia was startled out of her reverie. "Oh, just enjoying the warmth. If only I could get it to spread down to my feet."

"Take off your boots and heat your footcloths," Olga advised. "You'll have warm feet at dinner."

"Even better with clean ones." Alexia strode to her locker, took her last clean footcloths, and marched back to the oven. Draping them over her back, she flattened herself once again against the oven wall. The fresh fire warmed deliciously, and after only a few minutes, she was able to wrap her feet in the heated cloths. Sliding her boots back on, she sighed with pleasure.

She stood up to join the other women hurrying toward the mess hall when a young private stopped her. "Major Vlasik orders you to report to him. Right now."

Frowning in a mix of anxiety and annoyance at missing dinner, she followed him back down the corridor to the commander's office.

Vlasik sat relaxed, his arms crossed, but she saluted and stood at attention until his "At ease" order.

"Two things," he began, as if to prepare her for a list. "Your escorting of the American diplomats was satisfactory. I have already commended Lieutenant Yegorov. However…"

Alexia's lips tightened. She hated the word "however."

"I understand that you accompanied Miss Kramer to church services."

"Yes, sir. It was Christmas morning, sir. She explained she was raised Orthodox and requested to see such a service."

"Do you not appreciate how inappropriate that was for a member of the Kremlin regiment?"

"Yes, sir. But I assumed I was obliged to grant her request, since she was Marshal Stalin's personal guest."

"'Personal guest' is an exaggeration. She was the secretary to a White House emissary. If she attended a dinner with Comrade Stalin, it was as an interpreter."

"Yes, sir. But Metropolitan Sergei has expressly allied the Church with the nation in defense of the motherland, so I thought it would not be offensive on this one occasion—"

"It is not your place to make such judgments. But I will let it pass this once."

Alexia was too much of a soldier to reveal her feelings and remained neutral. "Thank you, sir. But you said 'two things,' sir. What was the other one?"

"Your dissatisfaction. I understand you feel your role as Kremlin guard is a way to avoid active service. Perhaps you think we are a regiment of cowards."

Alexia was momentarily speechless. How could he have known her thoughts? She had not fully resolved the issue in her head, so how could she explain it to him?

"Not at all, sir. I am very satisfied, in fact, deeply honored, to serve in this way. At the same time, I think of my brothers and sisters at the front who offer their bodies in the defense of the motherland and wonder sometimes if I don't have a moral obligation to do the same."

He closed his eyes for a moment, as if in paternal concern. "Alexia," he said, and it was the first time he'd ever called her by her first name.

"Am I in trouble, sir?"

"You should be. If anyone else were sitting here, you would be. But I know you're a patriot and a good party member. If you don't want to continue in the Kremlin regiment, we have hundreds of qualified recruits who will happily take your spot. You must think seriously about this."

His reaction was unexpected. She had not yet decided, but now a decision was thrust upon her. If she stayed, she would be guarding and ceremonially marching until her retirement from the service. Father Zosima would certainly approve, but her conscience would not.

She took a breath. "I would like to serve at the front, sir." There, she'd crossed the line.

He drummed his fingers on his desk. Was it in impatience at her naïveté? "In what capacity? Medical? Communications? If you do not request specific training, the army will assign you to cooking or laundry. I don't think that's what you had in mind."

"I…um…well, during training, I was superior in marksmanship."

"I see. Well, the army always needs marksmen, it's true." He sat up, terminating the interview. "All right. I will recommend you for sniper school. You are dismissed."

Stunned at how quickly it all went, she snapped to attention and saluted. "Yes, sir, Comrade Major!"

❖

Duties at the Central Woman's School of Sniper Training in Podolsk were decidedly less glamorous than those of a Kremlin guard.

The barracks, built only months before by the women themselves, were basic and, in the January weather, even colder than her quarters in the Kremlin. And the call to duty was even more rigid. Each morning, she had five minutes to wash, dress, and fall into line before the mess hall.

Breakfast—of black bread, sausage, and tea—had to be collected, consumed, and cleaned up within twenty minutes. The recruits were still strangers, all afraid to speak, so the main sound in the mess hall was the clank of the metal mess kits.

At seven o'clock, the recruits fast-marched to the quartermaster, where they lined up to receive their uniforms. Alosha's gymnasterka was simpler than her guard's tunic and had collar tabs with an enamel and brass insignia of crossed rifles over a target. Her breeches hung on her, but their bagginess was useful for kneeling and squatting, which she'd never done as a guard. The bottoms tucked into boots of imitation leather, though for winter training on icy ground, she was also issued the dense felt valenki.

At eight o'clock they filed into a small auditorium for political instruction, ensuring they were all motivated by the highest communist principles. Alexia glanced discreetly at the other women, wondering if they were as bored as she was listening to the principles that she'd heard reiterated endless times since joining the Komsomol.

Nine o'clock brought them to the gymnasium, where they were lined up in two squads, each with four rows of five women abreast. "You will memorize your place in the lineup," the sergeant ordered, and Alexia noted that she was the second woman in the second row in the second squad. That was convenient.

"The rules for discipline and for service of the garrison are posted in each barracks, and you will learn them by heart tonight."

The next order was to drop to the floor for calisthenics, which proved more rigorous than she expected. At the end of the hour, she stood in place once again, dry-mouthed and panting. But if that was the worst they had to throw at her, she'd do fine.

The women stood in formation for several minutes, watching the platform at the front. Finally, a door opened and the major emerged, a large robust man with a Cossack mustache.

The fifty recruits came to attention. This, they all knew, was Major Kulikov, who had fought alongside the famous Vassily Zaitsev at Stalingrad. The two associations, Zaitsev and Stalingrad, gave him an aura of greatness.

Two men came directly behind him wheeling a long cart. "At ease," Kulikov said, and at his signal, one of the men opened the cart lid and lifted out a rifle. An unmistakable murmur of approval rippled through the ranks.

The men handed rifles in armloads of five to the woman at the end of each row, and she passed them along until each recruit held one. Alexia hefted hers. It was longer but a bit lighter than the ceremonial rifle she'd held at the Kremlin. She was used to rifles, but obviously most of her classmates were not.

Major Kulikov laid his fists on his hips and shook his head. "Look at you," he snorted. "You're cradling those things like babies. They are deadly weapons, which you are going to use to kill people. When in tight formation, hold them upright and vertical, at your right shoulder. When in the field, grasp them like this." He held one diagonally in front of him, one hand midway up the barrel and the other around the stock with the index finger flat against, though not around, the trigger.

"This is the Mosin Model 1891/30, your friend and savior. You will always know how many rounds are in the clip and how many clips are left on your bandolier. You will know every part of your rifle and keep it spotlessly clean and oiled. To do so, you will disassemble it in this manner, using the bayonet as a screwdriver."

He lowered the lid of the cart, making a tabletop of it, and recited a stream of instructions as, with a few deft movements, he broke the rifle down to its component parts. Within a minute, it lay in pieces in front of him.

The young recruits watched, and Alexia's sideward glance saw their expressions of both anxiety and determination. She knew those emotions, for she'd had them the day she learned to assemble her guardsman's rifle. If she could learn one, she could learn another, and so could they.

"You will learn the disassembly, and by tomorrow, you will be able to do it blindfolded. In the meantime, first squadron will march to the firing range with Sergeant Gryaznov, and second squadron will follow me to the slope. Dismissed."

In the corridor outside the gymnasium, they received the next items of their kit: cartridge pouches holding forty rounds of ammunition and a canvas bandolier with fourteen five-round clips. Over it all, each wore a thick padded jacket that fell to her hips.

Most interesting, Alexia found, were the sniper gloves divided into thumbs, index finger, and mitten for the last three fingers. Logical, of course.

The outdoor air was frigid, but by the standards of the Russian winter, which they all knew, was tolerable. So they marched cheerfully along the path that took them to a wooded slope.

As they came near, they passed a bin from which each of them took a white camouflage outfit, and Alexia drew hers on, snickering to herself. They called it a suit, presumably because it had sleeves, trousers, and a hood, but it would have fitted no one less than a giant. Drawstrings held it closed around the face and waist, but otherwise it billowed in the wind as she jogged.

Major Kulikov paced in front of them as they lined up near the training woods. "You will learn two lessons today: concealment and endurance," he said. "We'll start with endurance. If you're impatient, angry, hungry, cold, or have to piss, you're useless. Then you're just another rifle in the infantry. So, how do we avoid those things?" He paused for a moment, then answered his own questions.

"Carry food, wear extra layers, pee before you take position. But sometimes you're stuck in place for four hours. Or six. Or eight. And the enemy is waiting at the other end of the field for you to lift your head just a few centimeters. And your bladder is full."

No one spoke.

"You use this." He tapped the tiny spade strapped to his upper arm. "When you arrive to set up your 'hide,' you dig a slight cavity in the ground below where your hips are going to be. When the time comes, you have to develop the skill to open your clothing and let go without wetting yourself. Now, I know that's a little harder for girls to do, but you'd better find a way, because that can save your life."

"So will you show us how to build a hide?"

"That's what we're here for." He led them over to one of the larger trees. "You see how the snow wafts up on one side of the tree? That's what your hide should look like. You just move the top layer aside, dig a pit with that extra hole in the bottom, then lay a support over the cavity—a few branches and a cloth—and cover the whole thing with a snow roof. You scatter branches and dead leaves over the top as camouflage, and you're done."

At his instruction, they set up little igloos, and if they passed muster, he nodded. If not, he kicked the faulty structure apart and they had to start again.

"All right. Now that you can make a nest, you have to shoot from it, so you've got to move the rifle nozzle from side to side without being seen. You do that by covering the tip with a white cloth."

"Don't we also work in twos?" Alexia asked.

"Only if you're working from a trench instead of a single nest. If conditions allow, your spotter can use binoculars to locate the target, but the target may also be looking for you, so now you have two people to hide."

"What about when there's no snow?"

"Same principles. Different strategies. You'll need rag capes, face covers, other equipment. I'll show you those tomorrow. Any questions before we do target practice from your nests?"

One of the braver women raised a hand. "Just one, Comrade Major."

"What is it?"

"That thing about digging an extra cavity for urinating. What about taking care of the other thing?"

He snorted derisively. "You better pray you don't have to. You still have to do it lying down and staying almost motionless in your hiding place. Then you either have to stay with it or find a way to dump it without revealing your position. And of course you'll stink when you get back to base."

"Can't you just toss it behind you or over the top?"

"A big motion like that will give you away. I once spotted a German sniper who'd relieved himself in his mess kit and then tried to lob it away from him. To do that, he had to lift his head just a little bit."

"Did you shoot him?"

"I did. It was the last shit of his life."

The day was long, very long, but at eighteen hours the shivering recruits were ordered to the mess hall for supper. When Alexia had her mess tin full of steaming soup, she spotted her squad mates at one of the tables. She sat down and nodded a greeting to all of them.

"Well, that was fun," a dark-haired woman with pixie-like eyes said, holding her hands over her hot soup. "I can't bend my fingers and I can't feel my toes."

"Is that all? Just your toes?" A muscular woman with a very short haircut sneered. "Imagine having to lie in the snow for four hours on these." She glanced down at her enormous breasts.

Both giggled, and the first one glanced toward Alexia. "What about you? Anything frozen off you?"

Alexia mimicked superiority. "The Russian patriot does not freeze, and nothing must ever fall off."

"Oh, yes. I forgot." Pixie-eyes held out her hand. "Aleksandra 'Sasha' Yekimova."

Short hair and large bosom held out hers. "Kaleriya Petrova. Call me Kalya."

A short, swarthy woman with heavy eyebrows leaned toward them. "Fatima Mironova, from Kazakhstan and Leningrad."

Alexia added a fourth hand to the group clasp. "Alexia Mazarova. Alyosha to my friends. I feel lucky to be here, don't you?"

The swarthy one shook her head. "I don't feel so lucky. I was at the aviation academy, but they wouldn't let me fly and sent me to manufacture planes instead. So I applied for sniper school. Anything was better than a factory."

"I definitely do," the one called Kalya answered with vehemence. She spooned up a portion of soup and sucked it in noisily. "I joined up with a friend from the *kolkhoz*, and they put her in laundry service. I was afraid I'd get that, too, but fortunately, my eyesight was better than hers. Poor kid. All she does all day is wash mud, blood, and lice out of soldiers' underwear."

Sasha wrinkled her nose in disgust. "I wanted to be in the Red Army chorus, but it's all men." She also spooned up her soup, though with delicacy.

Kalya looked surprised. "Chorus? What made you want to do that?"

"I was studying to be an opera singer when the war started. My father sang in the Bolshoi chorus, and we always had music in our house. I really miss it." She looked glum for a moment, then turned her attention to Alexia. "What about you? What did you do before?"

Alexia wiped her mouth. "Well, there's 'before' and 'before-before.' Before-before, I was a schoolteacher in Arkhangelsk. But after I enlisted, I was posted to the Kremlin guard. I guess because I'm tall."

"And good-looking," Kalya added admiringly. "Did you guard anyone interesting, like Stalin?"

"All soldiers in the garrison end up guarding Stalin one time or another. That's part of the duty. But I also guarded the delegation that went to Tehran. That was exciting. Then in Moscow, I had to guard some Americans."

"Wow. You met Americans," Sasha exclaimed. "Who were they?"

"Assistants to President Roosevelt. A man, very quiet, odd looking, and a woman."

"A woman, too? What was she like?" Fatima asked.

Alexia stared into the distance for a moment. "Probably the most interesting woman I ever met. She spoke Russian, so we could talk."

"Gosh. What does one talk about with an American?"

"Oh, this and that," Alexia replied vaguely, and was saved from more interrogation by the bell terminating the mess. "But now I have to memorize all the rules posted on my barracks wall."

By the second week of training Alexia knew her Mozin-Nagant rifle better than the fancy automatic she'd carried at the Kremlin. She could dismantle and reassemble it in minutes, with her eyes closed. She also knew to carry a cloth to conceal the muzzle—white in the snow, gray otherwise.

And now, gazing out over the target range, she felt the comfort of its wooden stock against her cheek. Heavy boots crunched through the snow, behind her.

The gunnery sergeant's voice was bright in the cold air. "It is critical to be able to judge distance in order to set the range-finder on your scope. Account for wind, rain, or snowfall. Look for smoke for wind strength and direction."

The snow crunched again as he trod to the next recruit. "If you just want to take out an ordinary soldier, aim for the body. It's a larger target and will tie up the enemy with wounded. But if it's a high-value target—officers, machine gunners, radio operators—shoot for the head."

More crunching, farther away. "And remember to cover your muzzle flash whenever possible. If you don't get your man, you'll give your position away and the next shot will be for you."

He stepped away from the line of women lying on the snow. "All right. Commence firing."

She waited for the moving silhouettes to come into sight, various German helmets and caps drawn on a string at the other end of the range. The simple soldiers were obvious and easy, but the high-value targets worth double points appeared for only an instant. She focused her attention on the area enclosed in her scope and moved the muzzle in a slight arc.

There was one. Bang. Another. Bang. She held back as the flat infantryman helmets passed, letting the other women dispatch them. Again, a high-peaked cap. Bang.

By the end of the session, she'd scored half a dozen officers, three machine gunners, and four ordinary Wehrmacht. Her high score won her a small bar of chocolate with her supper.

The next day they worked in teams, and Fatima was her spotter. Fatima swept the horizon with her binoculars. "Officer approaching from right. About two o'clock."

"I see him."

The cardboard figure stopped, then backed away to be replaced by two bucket helmets. "Crap, lost him. No, wait. I see the tip of a machine gun. It's a nest. Take them out."

Alexia fired twice and the cardboard figures fell over.

In the three hours, a long series of figures danced along the rim of the target trench, some slowly, some rapidly, their hats or guns or postures identifying them. When the instructor blew his whistle to end the exercise, Alexia's team scored the highest.

"I wonder why officers wear tall, pointy caps," Fatima mused. "If I was one, I'd want a nice flat one."

"Swagger surpasses safety, I suppose," Alexia murmured.

Nikolai Kulikov waited for them in the mess hall, his arms folded. His status as a survivor of Stalingrad and a student of the great marksman Vassily Zaitsev himself had earned him deference and respect, and some of the women were in awe of him. Alexia was more curious about Zaitsev, who was all but the patron saint of snipers, and after their ration of vodka had been passed around, she approached him.

"Comrade Sergeant. If I may. We want to be ready on that day when the first shots are real. What was it like for you?"

He poured himself a second vodka, to which, as an instructor, he was entitled, and stared at it as he swirled it around in the glass.

"My dear comrade. I hope you do not have the same experience. *My* first great battle was Stalingrad, and I can recall that first day, in September 1942, as if it were yesterday. We marched overland to the Volga, and already from afar we could see the city had a crimson sky over it, like an erupting volcano. Tiny black things swarmed in circles over it, and those were German planes dropping bombs, stoking the fire."

He ran his finger around the rim of his vodka glass. "It was like we were marching toward hell. In an hour or so, when we actually were crossing the Volga, the burnt-out buildings were glowing inside, like monsters eating up our men. This time the little black figures running back and forth across the glow were soldiers, but we couldn't tell if they were ours or theirs." He stared into space for a moment.

"When we reached the shore, we dashed forward screaming 'uh rah!' to give ourselves courage, but a petrol storage tank nearby took a hit, exploded, and drenched us in fuel as we ran. We caught fire but kept running while we tore off our flaming hats and coats. The fact that we were already at full speed and reacted instantly saved us from burning to death. That's your answer. My first hour in battle was running with screaming naked men into the inferno of Stalingrad." He swallowed the rest of his vodka.

The women sat speechless at the tale, but Kulikov was obviously warmed up and had another one to tell.

"Every day, if we weren't killed, we got better at our job. Once Zaitsev and I and two others were on Mamayev Hill. It was covered with corpses. Our job was to keep the Fritzes pinned down away from a spring, so they'd run out of water. But they beat us back so we couldn't reach the spring either. Anytime someone, Soviet or German, crawled down to the spring with a bucket, he'd get shot. For three days we lay there parched, and it was unbearable."

He paused for dramatic effect.

"Then Zaitsev remembered that the corpses all around us had canteens. We crawled out under cover and brought back a dozen of them. The water was old and not great, but it kept us going. The Germans never thought of it and kept trying to get to the spring, where we knocked them off one by one."

"A good lesson, Comrade Major," someone said. "To use our brains and not just our eyes."

"Yeah, and to start out with a full canteen." He snorted and strode from the mess hall.

Kalya watched him leave. "They keep telling us about Zaitsev, but my hero is Comrade Pavlichenko. She's one of us."

"Do you suppose the British and Americans have women snipers?" Sasha asked. "Or are they softer than we are?"

Alexia gave a faint shrug. "Could be. I only met that one American. Kind of soft, but with a spirit tough as any man's."

"Really? How do you know?"

"She partied all night with Stalin, and then she kissed me."

❖

On April 1, 1944, the Central Women's School of Sniper Training graduated its second class of snipers, and fifty women carrying their Mozin-Nagant rifles fitted with PU scopes of 3.5 magnification marched past the reviewing stand.

Their instructors and senior government officials sat in a row before a huge red banner that the Supreme Council of the Soviet Union had presented to the school.

The parading women halted and the speeches began. Alexia barely listened and was already thinking of the next morning when she would be deployed to the 1st Belorussian Front Army under the command of General Rokossovsky. She would pack her small kit and march with the others with the same orders to the station to board a train to Novgorod.

There, at some point, she would be called upon to use her newly acquired skills, not to shoot holes through a painted cardboard cap, but to kill a living German point-blank. Father Zosima would be appalled.

CHAPTER TWELVE

April 1944

"Come in." Hopkins's somewhat bored voice came through the door, and Mia let herself in.

"I'm sorry to bother you, but I won't take long." She held out an envelope. "It's my letter of resignation."

He frowned consternation. "Good grief. Whatever for?" He took the envelope but held it in front of him without opening it. "Has anyone mistreated you? Is there some problem?"

"In fact, the problem is mine, sir. Not the job. I love it."

"Then what's the reason for this?" He laid the letter on his desk. "Unless it's for a very grave matter, I can't let you leave. You're too important to the program, especially now, when I have to accompany the president on the campaign."

Mia took a step back, unprepared for his reception. "Well, it's precisely because of the campaign that I have to leave. You see, I was involved in an...um...indiscretion a year or so ago, before being hired. I thought it was all behind me, but it's come back to haunt me."

"An indiscretion. Has this anything to do with the death of your father? I thought the police had closed the case. Are you implicated in any way?"

Mia took a breath. "Not in the death. At least I don't think so. It's been months since my brother said the case had reopened, and no one from the police has contacted me. No, it's a personal indiscretion." She paused, gathering her courage. "With a woman."

"A woman? I see." A frown passed quickly over his face and disappeared. "But how does that affect your work here, or the campaign?"

Mia pressed her forehead, as if to push away a headache. "She's blackmailing me, threatening to go to the newspapers. And her revelations could prove an embarrassment to the White House, particularly now."

"Did you commit a crime?"

"No sir. Nothing like that."

"Did you do anything violent?"

"Not at all. Quite the opposite."

"Then the issue is your fear of public opinion?"

"Public opinion that could taint the president, yes sir."

He leaned back and lit up a cigarette, a trick he always used to give himself a moment to think. He inhaled and blew out smoke.

"The president is more resilient than you might think. We have a number of people of your…uh…disposition on the presidential staff, and it has so far never been an issue. But if she's threatening to make the information public, we'll have to separate you from the White House."

"Exactly, sir. That's the reason for my resignation."

"No, no. Nothing as radical as that. We need only relocate you where you will be irrelevant to the campaign. To Moscow, for example."

She was taken aback. "Moscow? On what pretense? Weren't we just there two months ago?"

"Yes, but it wouldn't be a pretense. As you know, inventory is still disappearing mysteriously, and I'm convinced the problem is in the Russian distribution."

"So, you want to post me to Moscow, alone, to deal again with Mr. Molotov and his complaints?"

"You wouldn't be alone. Mr. Harriman would meet you and fill you in on the status quo. The State Department will not mind issuing another air ticket, and you already have credentials with the Kremlin and the Ministry of Armaments. You have as much expertise to deal with them as anyone."

"And you think that'll work. I mean, to protect the president?"

"I'm certain it will. The heads of the major newspapers aren't interested in embarrassing Mr. Roosevelt. They've downplayed his paralysis for three terms, so if your blackmailing friend shows up in their offices with such accusations, the editors will come to us for confirmation, and we'll say we have no such person working in the White House."

It was, in fact, an elegant solution. "Thank you, sir. I hope to live up to your trust in me."

"Never mind. Just prepare to leave in the next few days. I'll inform Mr. Harriman of your arrival and formally request meetings with Molotov and Ustinov. I expect you to accomplish something while you're there."

"Understood, sir. Thank you."

"Yeah, yeah," Hopkins said, and dropped the unopened envelope into his trash bin. Turning back to his desk, he flicked off the long ash of the cigarette that had lain in his glass ashtray.

"The White House has been negotiating the fate of all of Europe. Does this stupid woman think we'd be thrown by a bit of sordid gossip?" He spat out a bit of air to show his contempt.

The map-room staff reported that since February, the Axis powers had lost superiority in the airspace over the Baltic through to Leningrad, and that Allied traffic had a 90 percent chance of getting through. Mia didn't care for the remaining 10 percent, but it was the only deal on the table.

Fortunately, the Douglas DC-3 carrying Lend-Lease radio equipment encountered no enemy presence and dropped safely to a lower altitude over Leningrad, now relieved of its two-year siege. She peered through the airplane window, trying to spot anything recognizable of the city of her childhood, but could make out only the two island districts that sheltered it from the sea and the Neva River that curved north and then south into the Baltic. She searched her feelings for homesickness but found only faint nostalgia for the happy family of her early years.

It had all changed with her mother's death from diphtheria, as if it were only his wife who had kept Fyodor's baser nature in check. His moral squalor that alternated with religious fervor had confused and tainted her and Van.

And her involvement with Grushenka, which at first blush had seemed like romance, had been no better. Mia winced at the memory. The beautiful Grushenka, who threatened to blackmail her now, and—the irony was excruciating—who looked much too much like Alexia.

Alexia Vassilievna Mazarova. Was she still standing guard at the Kremlin, handsome and safe from the war? Or had she joined the infantry and was now slogging through mud?

The first rough bump as the aircraft touched down at Moscow Airport broke her reverie. Time to go to work. She gathered her scant luggage, the greater weight of which was created by copies of the Lend-Lease books she brought to compare with local accounts. The aircraft door slid open, and as the Russian spring air blew inside as a sort of welcome, she followed the other passengers down the stairs onto the tarmac.

Though it was April, snow had obviously fallen, and the tarmac was wet with slush.

She glanced around, searching for Averell Harriman, but saw no one. She halted, perplexed and slightly alarmed. What now?

Finally, a man broke away from the crowd and approached her, and she recognized the chauffer from the embassy. He tipped his hat and held out a hand to take her suitcase.

"Hello, Mr....Oh, I'm sorry. I've forgotten your name."

"Dornwend," he said, touching his cap again. "You can call me Robert. Important thing is, I know who *you* are. Mr. Harriman is in Kuibyshev today and asked me to pick you up. But don't worry. Your room is ready, and the ambassador will return tomorrow or the next day."

Mia was struck by a moment of panic at the thought of approaching Molotov alone. But she reminded herself that she was only a telegram away from Harry Hopkins. Besides, most of the people she'd have to deal with at the Kremlin were familiar with her. For heaven's sake, they'd gotten drunk together. How difficult could it be?

❖

The next morning, the ambassador had not yet returned from Kuibyshev, and all she had for support was Robert the chauffeur. He cheerfully dropped her off at the Spasskaya Tower entrance of the Kremlin, but she was no better prepared than when she'd left Washington.

"Thanks, Robert," she said as he held the rear door open for her. "I don't suppose I'll need to go back to the embassy until later this afternoon. Say, about four? And do you have any last words of advice, by the way?"

"Well, I *have* had success getting in good with the Russians by offering them American cigarettes. That's not going to work with Molotov, of course, but maybe a guard or two. You never know."

She patted her empty coat pocket. "But I don't smoke and so I don't carry any around."

"Here. I've got a pack of Lucky Strikes and I've only smoked one. Take it, courtesy of the US government." He drew it from his shirt pocket and tucked it into her hand. Touching one finger to his cap, he climbed back into the car and started off through the slushy snow.

With cigarettes or without, Molotov kept her waiting, as she knew he would. A cheap exercise of power, she thought, though, to be fair, the foreign minister probably had other matters to deal with. In any case, she put on her best face when he admitted her.

"So, you finally have located your miscalculations?" he asked coldly. Clearly, he did not view the search for discrepancies to be a collaborative effort, and she'd have to humor him.

She laid her several loose-leaf notebooks carefully on the edge of his desk, though his cold glance down at the invasive books told her she was trespassing on his space. "I've returned because we feel the problem arises on this side, and I'd like to sit down with various agents along the lines of distribution to pinpoint the leaks."

"You imply theft on the part of our transport agents?" He seemed affronted. Yet it was exactly what she was implying, and she would have to choose her words carefully.

"I suggest nothing, Mr. Molotov. But our search indicates a reliable accounting of items shipped to your ports, subtracting those lost at sea. What remains now is to examine the manifestos and receipts at each step here."

"I understood that is what you were doing the last time you

visited." He held his cigarette to the side of his face, a foppish gesture at odds with his bullying manner. It was an American cigarette, she noted.

She maintained her tight smile. "It was only a preliminary judgment. Now that we've examined our own records, I need to compare them with the receipts your agents have signed."

"I'm afraid such receipts do not reside with me. For that you must refer to the relevant agencies. You could start with Dmitriy Ustinov at the Commissariat of Armaments." He stubbed out his cigarette, leaving a one-inch butt in the ashtray. She wondered which of his lackeys would fish it out and reclaim the remaining tobacco. "Will that be all?"

He was dismissing her after only five minutes. You bastard, she thought, but retained her composure.

"I'm sorry to have wasted your time, sir. I'll leave you to your more important affairs and wish you good day." She took up her loose-leaf notebooks, and as she turned away, she had the unmistakable impression that he brushed off the corner of the desk where they had lain, polluting it.

She trudged back through the wet snow toward the offices of the Commissariat of Armaments, cold moisture seeping into her boots. *Grushenka, you bitch. If not for you, I'd be home in Washington doing my job.*

The unexpected sight of the changing guard at the Kremlin Palace brought her to a halt. She watched as the sentries marched toward one another, saluted, executed an elaborate double about-face, and separated. Only when the relieved sentry began the return march did she recognize him. The handsome, amiable Kiril.

He marched stiffly and in step with his colleague toward the Arsenal, his ceremonial rifle on his shoulder. She couldn't interfere with the ritual so she discreetly followed him all the way to the entrance of his barracks. Only when he relaxed his guard and signaled good-bye to his mate did she run to intercept him.

"Kiril, stop," she called out, and caught up with him on the steps. "Do you remember me?"

He smiled warmly. "Yes, of course I do, Miss Kramer. The American lady who wanted to go to church. It's nice to see you again. What brings you to the Kremlin? You are without escort this time."

"Yes. This time I'm not a guest of Marshal Stalin, only an

annoying secretary of Mr. Hopkins trying to get information. But I was wondering, is Alexia Vassilievna still with the Kremlin Guard? I'd love to see her again."

"No. She was transferred shortly after you left in January. To the sniper's school at Podolsk." He counted on his fingers, calculating the time elapsed. "I'm sure she's graduated by now."

"Ah, I see. Do you know where they go after graduation?"

"I can't say for certain, but the last report in *The Red Star* was that female snipers were very successful on the Novgorod front. She's probably based somewhere around there."

"Have you heard from her?"

"No, but she wouldn't write to me. Her grandmother, maybe."

"Well, thank you, Kiril. I won't keep you any longer. Take care of yourself." She exchanged a warm handshake and turned, twice defeated, toward the Commissariat of Armaments.

Dmitriy Ustinov was more welcoming than Molotov had been and even made room for her books on his desk. "I see you've been hard at work," he said, running his finger down the summary inventory page. "Have you pinpointed where the discrepancies begin in the delivery chain?"

"Not yet, but I'm much better prepared now. I've spent the last two and a half months making parallel lists of the items that seem to have disappeared, and at this point, I need to see the receipts from each distribution spot."

"Receipts. Yes, of course," he muttered. At the sound of a door opening, he glanced up. "Oh, there you are. Miss Kramer, you remember Colonel Nazarov, my deputy?"

The stocky man she remembered from her last visit shook her hand warmly. "So glad to see you again," he said. "I haven't forgotten our very jolly dinner last January with the boss."

Mia instantly liked this man. "That's an evening I will never forget. Marshal Stalin was in top form all evening, wasn't he?"

"He surely was." Nazarov hooked his thumbs in his belt like some jovial grandfather.

"Colonel Nazarov has just come from a tour of various factories," Ustinov said. "Have you found everything in order, Nazarov?"

"I was just about to make a report on that subject exactly. Yes, within normal parameters, the distribution matches the inventory given to me. If deficiencies exist, we must look elsewhere."

"What sort of factories do you refer to, Colonel Nazarov?" Mia asked.

"The Tankograd tank factory in Chelyabinsk, another in Kovrov assembling field telephones, and the Tula rifle factory."

"Has the food arrived as well?" Mia asked. "I mean the tons of canned meat sent along with the shipments of arms. We know that an army marches on its stomach. And so do the workers who produce their weapons."

"Oh, yes. Plenty of Spam on hand in all three factories. Our workers are very grateful for that."

"And front-line supplies?"

"I'm checking on them the day after tomorrow when the next supply plane goes to Novgorod."

The door to the office opened, and all three of them turned as an adjutant stepped into the opening. "Excuse me, Colonel Nazarov. A telephone call. From General Molotov."

"Ah, yes. Will you excuse me? A good man never finds rest, eh?" He saluted Ustinov, offered a quick handshake to Mia, and marched from the room.

Mia had a sudden idea. "General Ustinov. I'll take your lists with me and study them this evening, but would I be able perhaps to visit the rifle factory Colonel Nazarov mentioned?"

Ustinov hesitated. "Arms factories are usually off-limits to foreigners."

"Yes, sir. But I do represent the agency that supplies so many of your weapons and so don't fall into the category of 'ordinary foreigner.' I think you could make a case that Mr. Hopkins and I are *part* of the Soviet munitions production."

He scratched in front of his ear. "I see your point, Miss Kramer. All right. I'll write a pass authorizing your visit. Fortunately, the train from Moscow passes near the factory."

"Thank you, Commissar Ustinov." She held out little hope that the visit would produce anything, but it would at least show Hopkins that she'd gone all the way to the end of the distribution line.

And it would certainly be interesting to see how rifles were made.

❖

Upon her return to the embassy, she discovered Ambassador Harriman had arrived, and she joined him in the dining room.

"How did it go?" he asked, pouring her a glass of wine. Another benefit of living at the embassy, however cold and windowless it was.

"Good and bad. Molotov is still being uncooperative. He complains but does nothing to assist us. He's such an—" She stopped as he raised a finger to his lips, and she remembered all the eavesdropping bugs.

"Soo…let me say that my main problem all day was wet feet." She drew a pencil from her pocket and wrote on a napkin.

Losses seem to occur between depots and factory. I think it's either Molotov or Ustinov.

"Wet feet all day is dangerous. So what do you plan to do?" he replied to her small talk.

"I suppose I'll have to look around for some rubber boots, won't I?" She scribbled another line on the napkin.

Going to an arms plant in Tula tomorrow, with Ustinov's permission. Maybe I'll find the scoundrels there.

"Well, be careful in the meantime. We don't want you getting sick," he said, but, taking her pencil, he wrote on the other side of the napkin.

Tread lightly. Corruption and backstabbing everywhere.

"Thank you for that advice. You're right, of course. Um, would you pass the wine?"

❖

The Tula Arms Plant, Mia learned, had transported its primary manufacturing beyond the Urals during the German invasion and left only one division in local operation. Nonetheless, when she arrived at its single remaining factory, she found a storm of activity.

The plant foreman met her at the entry gate, presumably after a telephone call from Ustinov. A haggard man in need of a shave, he could have been anything between forty and sixty. He was friendly and garrulous, and seemed to relish the idea of showing her around.

"So, what do you mostly do here?"

"*Everything for the front, everything for victory* is our motto, though in fact, our larger guns are produced in the east. This plant makes and refurbishes small arms, that is, the SVT-40 self-loading rifle, Nagant revolvers, Tokarev pistols, and the Mosin-Nagant 91/30 sniper rifle."

"I understand you receive many of the parts from the United States."

"Yes. A lot of the steel comes from there, as well as the metal jackets for the shells."

"Are you well supplied? I mean, do you ever have to slow production for lack of materials or a late delivery?"

"No, the parts deliveries are always sufficient and on time. The factory operates twenty-four hours a day, in three shifts, so if we ran out of a part, it would bring the whole operation to a halt. You are welcome to visit the factory floor, if you wish."

The "floor" consisted of a seemingly endless row of tables set end-to-end, with workers on both sides assembling parts drawn from wooden crates behind them. Almost all were women and old men. The clatter of metal against metal set up a sort of white noise, pierced occasionally by someone shouting.

She approached closer and peered over the shoulder of a woman as she oiled and fitted a spring into a magazine clip for one of the rifles. The woman's hands were bony and weathered, and every crease and fingernail was black. Mia could not see her face, but even from the rear it was obvious how gaunt the woman was. Her work smock was filthy, too, though cleanliness was probably of a very low priority in such a factory. Not to mention the scarcity of soap. Still, it made her cringe.

She returned to the foreman, who waited for her at some distance. "May I see the end of the production line, too?"

"Of course. That will be at the far side of the hall, where they attach the scope."

Two other women, equally malnourished, worked on the scope, one attaching it and the other measuring its accuracy. She held it up to her eye and pointed it toward a cardboard grid, then handed it back for adjustment. After two or three of such adjustments, number-one woman passed it to the final table, where an old man attached a cloth strap to rings on the nozzle and stock. Then he laid the rifle in a wheeled crate next to others. When the crate was full, a young boy wheeled it away.

"It all seems very efficient, though I'm sure it's exhausting."

"Everything for the front, everything for victory," he repeated. "That's what keeps us going."

Mia couldn't tell how much of his reaction was genuine patriotism and how much propaganda. She knew about the sacrifices on the battlefield but had never imagined how hard life also could be in the factories.

"Can you show me the canteen?"

"If you wish," he said, and led her along a corridor and down the stairs to a basement. She checked her watch, seven in the evening. "When do the workers get dinner?"

"A hot meal is served every eight hours, at five thirty, thirteen thirty, and twenty-one thirty. That is, at the beginning of the shift for some people and at the end of the shift for others. The food is whatever the commissariat has provided that week."

"What does the commissariat usually provide?" She recalled an enormous shipment of Spam, powdered eggs, and sugar on the list from the depot at Arkhangelsk. It had been signed for ten days before.

"Kasha, mostly. And bread. Though the delivery is late this month. And the last delivery of flour was only half. Nobody explained why. We've had to cut the rations for the last three months."

"Do you have meat?"

"A little horse sausage, but that was last month."

"I mean the American Spam. Recently."

"No. No. Nothing like that. Not since I've worked here."

"I see. Well, thank you for taking the time to show me around. I won't bother you any longer. I have a train to catch, so I'd better start for the station. Please, take these as a token of my thanks for your help." She tapped out four cigarettes from her pack and presented them. For the first time, he smiled.

They shook hands and she left, suspicion crackling in her head.

❖

Mia sat fretting on the return train to Moscow, not only about the information she had just obtained and which would surely have ramifications, but about her arrival. Robert had agreed to be at the Moscow station when the train from Tula arrived, but they had been sidelined twice while a troop train and an industrial train had claimed track priority, and now they were pulling into Moscow station over two hours late. Would he wait?

But as she descended from the train into the cold mist of the station platform, a different figure came forward to greet her.

"Colonel Nazarov? What a coincidence." She accepted his gloved handshake and tried to look past him. "I was just about to search for my driver."

"No need for that, Miss Kramer. The embassy car arrived some time ago, just before I did. I explained to the chauffeur that for this trip, you were under my protection and that I would see to your safe return. My car is waiting to take you to Spaso House."

"Ah, I see," she said, nonplussed, and followed him through the station to the street outside. It was only eight in the evening, and not yet dark, but the heavy skies had blocked sunlight all day, and the early evening atmosphere was morose.

Nazarov joined her in the backseat of the car and turned amiably toward her. "I hope you found your journey worthwhile. Did the workings of the Tula factory meet your expectations? It's one of our more important recipients of military hardware, so we are most anxious to see they are supplied adequately."

"Yes, it seemed so. The foreman made it clear that the parts are delivered on time and in the right quantity. Obviously, that would be critical, since a single deficiency would disrupt the whole manufacture, and the Kremlin would be involved."

"Yes, quite so. I'm pleased you were satisfied that we're doing our best to move the American goods along. The gaps you believe to have found are most likely bad bookkeeping at the depots in Arkhangelsk and Murmansk."

"Yes, that's possible. In any case, thank you for your assistance. I'll put that in my report to Mr. Hopkins."

Upon reaching the embassy, she shook his hand once again and hurried through the dark back into what passed for American territory.

❖

The next morning, before breakfast, she composed the text of her cable to Harry Hopkins.

Met w Ustinov and Nazarov stop even cajoled inspection of Tula arms plant stop workers malnourished canteen not receiving shipments stop mechanical materials and parts arriving but not food and possibly clothing stop workers are in rags stop theft somewhere betw Ustinov and factory presumably to divert to black market stop not sure who to inform stop anyone in the delivery train could be guilty stop please advise soonest full stop.

The wording seemed a bit strong. Maybe she should check with Ambassador Harriman before going on record. He'd already warned her to tread lightly.

She slid the draft to the side and realized she was hungry. All she'd gotten the night before was a quick sandwich from the embassy kitchen. A hot breakfast would do her good, and it would give her the opportunity to catch Harriman before he disappeared into his office.

As she emerged from her room into the corridor, she passed the cleaning lady, a woman whose name she didn't know. "Good morning," she said in passing, and let her mind drift to the thought of a cup of the embassy coffee.

❖

"No, you can't make direct accusations," Harriman said. "Pilfering at that level is a major offense, and people are executed for less. I suggest you simply report what you saw, and what people said to you, and leave it to Hopkins or the White House to decide what action to take."

Mia shrugged. "That seems to defeat the purpose of my coming, but I'll do what you suggest. So what should I report to Molotov? He's the one who's always complaining about being cheated."

"But he's not complaining about problems at the Tula factory, is he? It was for a wide range of things that he was demanding double delivery. Missing Spam from the Tula plant was not one of his concerns."

"But it should be one of his concerns. The Tula plant makes sniper rifles, among other things. If the workers are malnourished, they can't be expected to produce precision weapons. Depriving them of food amounts to sabotage."

"Perhaps so, but that's not for you to judge."

"It's frustrating. This is the first theft I've been able to track down and have hard evidence for. The signed manifesto from the depot shows the food was shipped out. Leather, too, incidentally, for the shoulder straps, though the ones I saw were cotton. I've got to start someplace and show Molotov we're taking his complaints seriously."

"I see your point. So, why don't you tell him verbally that the food shipment seems to have been diverted? He'll have something to go on, assuming he wants to 'go' there at all, but you won't incriminate anyone."

"What about Hopkins? I'd like to clearly state my suspicions to him, at least. I wrote a telegram this morning that…well…named names. Cables from the embassy are secret, aren't they?"

Harriman nodded. "Yes, once we transcribe them into code. Otherwise, I suggest you continue to gather your information without treading on toes, and then report verbally to the relevant parties. Do not leave a paper trail."

"Yes, I suppose you're right." She reached for the marmalade, but it had lost its taste.

❖

As if things could not get any worse, Molotov was not even available. At the Commissariat of Foreign Affairs, his secretary announced the foreign minister was in a meeting with Marshal Stalin and had no opening during the rest of the day. Would she like to request an appointment for the next morning?

Resigned, Mia agreed. Yes, she would. In the meantime, perhaps the foreign minister might want to read her report. She handed over the slender envelope with her observations, expressed as objectively as possible, letting him draw his own conclusions.

Then she left the commissariat at a lingering pace, stopping at the Spasskaya Tower before wandering over to the corner where Robert had agreed to pick her up in two hours. What could she do in the meantime?

She hadn't waited for more than two minutes when a GAZ-Ford limousine pulled up in front of her, and two bulky men in uniform leapt out. As they came toward her from two directions she realized, from the color on their caps, they were NKVD police. The smaller of the two laid one hand on his holster and said, "Please come with us."

CHAPTER THIRTEEN

April 1944

Alexia clambered down from the train at Novgorod. Since the Germans had been expelled in January, the station was in full operation, transporting troops to reinforce the follow-on offensive against the German army north. On this day, it received the 109th Rifle Division under the command of Major Bershansky, along with its separate sniper unit of twenty-four women.

The euphoria of the January liberation of Leningrad had subsided, and the Soviet troops found themselves in a hard struggle pushing the Wehrmacht westward. The addition of the 109th Rifle Division, including its snipers, was to add reinforcement to the slowing advance.

"These are our quarters?" Sasha glanced around at the cracked plaster and broken windows of the room they would bivouac in for the night. The remains of a blackboard on one wall revealed it had been a classroom, and Alexia felt a twinge of sorrow thinking about the school she had taught in and seen destroyed in Arkhangelsk.

"At least they're going to feed us," Alexia said, pointing with her chin toward a field kitchen just outside the school. A soldier fed wood into the small stove at the center while smoke rose from the chimney. The copper kettles on both sides already gave off steam, so it was clear the meal was ready to be served. By the aroma that drifted toward them, she could tell it was borscht.

In fact, they had just unloaded their packs against the wall when Major Bershansky arrived and ordered a lineup. They snatched their mess tins from their packs and ran to join the others. The cook, a grizzled, portly fellow, obviously had drawn some advantage from his proximity to food. He whistled softly as he ladled out the beet stew and twinkled at the line of women who held out their tins.

A few minutes later, they sat on their bedrolls with the steaming stew and a thick slice of larded black bread. Hardly had they finished their portions when the cook passed by the women's corner with a canister of remaining stew.

"They told me you're all snipers, so I wanted to make sure we take good care of you." He ladled the canister's contents into the tins held out to him.

"Thank you, Cook. But you've got a lot of mouths to feed tonight."

"That's a *good* thing. Lots of mouths means lots of soldiers." He squatted down next to them, his captive audience. "We cooks can always tell how the army's doing, even if the officers don't tell you nothing. We know the casualty number same as the medics. Coupla times the field kitchen behind the line cooked up a hot dinner for some thirty men, but when the battle ended, no one made it back. All dead or wounded. We'd cooked all that food for no one."

He glanced around, perhaps realizing that this was defeatist talk that could land him in prison. But when Commander Bershansky stood in the doorway, he seemed not to hear it and ordered everyone into the central courtyard of the school.

A microphone and speaker had been set up on a small platform at one end of the yard, and anticipating the usual political speech, Alexia and her friends lingered toward the back.

She was surprised, however, when a woman came to stand by Major Bershansky, and he announced, "Hero of the Soviet Union, Major Lyudmila Pavlichenko, has a few words to say to you."

The troops cheered, for every man and woman in the Red Army knew her from *The Red Star* articles, and Alexia cursed herself for not moving closer to the front of the group.

The hero sniper began to speak. "I have just returned from a tour in the United States, as the guest of President and Mrs. Roosevelt, and I did nothing but boast about the courage and determination of the Red Army. I know you will continue to prove these boasts true."

Another round of cheering came from the crowd and took a moment to subside.

"But please keep in mind that we are an advancing army now.

You are no longer defending our cities but winning them back from the enemy. They are less arrogant now, but more desperate, and they will use every trick they know to draw you into their fire. As a sniper, I know these tricks."

More cheering, which she quieted with a raised hand. "Snipers are defensive. We lurk in fixed position and watch for advancing, over-confident soldiers. But now, *you* will be those advancing soldiers, and I caution you to be ever watchful. Be suspicious of areas that saw fighting but have fallen still. That is where the enemy will be lurking. Your own marksmen must use new tricks to lure them into revealing themselves."

Kalya jabbed Alexia with her elbow and whispered, unnecessarily, "She means us," but Alexia said, "Shhh."

"The soldier who wins, the soldier who survives, is the one who uses his head and works with his comrades to draw the fascists out of their holes. I know you will make me, and the motherland, proud. That's all I have to say."

When the cheering stopped and the troops began to filter back to their respective bivouacs, Alexia elbowed her way forward to the platform. A circle of men was already around the major, and it seemed they would monopolize her forever, but finally Pavlichenko caught sight of her and turned her head.

"I'm a sniper, too, Comrade Major," Alexia announced, instantly regretting the outburst. It sounded childish.

As if to underscore the foolishness of the remark, Pavlichenko reached between the men, shook her hand, and asked, "What is your count?"

"My count? I...uh. Well, I've just graduated from the Central Women's School, so at the moment..."

"I see. Zero. Well, it's where we all start. Tomorrow, you can put your skill to the test, and I'm sure you'll do well. What's your name, Corporal?"

"Alexia Vassilievna Mazarova, Comrade Major. Though I'm called Alyosha. A boy's name, I know, but my father named me after a character in a book, and..." She fell silent, suddenly aware of how much nonsense she was chattering.

"I see. Well, just remember to follow your training, and..." Pavlichenko also paused for a moment. "Did you say Alexia Vassilievna?"

She nodded. "Yes, Comrade Major."

"I believe you have a friend at the White House. Unless there's another sniper named Alyosha."

Kalya piped up. "No, she's the only one."

Alexia felt her face flush, she wasn't sure from what. "That must be Miss Kramer, a diplomat whom I guarded in Moscow."

"Well, you'll be glad to know she remembers you, too."

Her face warmed even more. The woman she'd kissed had not forgotten her. She dropped her glance.

At that moment, Commander Bershansky returned, bringing the small talk to an end. Pavlichenko patted her on the shoulder. "I wish you all courage and success tomorrow." With that, she marched away beside the commander.

Sasha jabbed Alexia with her elbow. "I had no idea you had friends in high places."

Alexia strode away, suddenly protective of the memory and the woman, who had disappeared but now seemed real again. As she lay down for her last full night of sleep before going into battle, she relived the sensation of the sudden forceful lips, over and over again.

❖

They awoke before dawn and scrambled into a line of troop carriers for their first engagement south of Novgorod. As they rumbled along the crater-pitted road, German planes flew overhead but dropped no bombs. She guessed they were reconnaissance flights and hoped the absence of bombardment meant the Luftwaffe was short on bombs.

But the retreating Wehrmacht found other ways to kill. The first houses the advancing army encountered were smoldering ruins, and in the village behind them, the Wehrmacht was still entrenched. Major Bershansky distributed his troops in a curve around the village, interspersing his snipers where they might be useful. Alexia and Kalya reported to him for their assignment.

The major set down his field phone that had linked him with his forward rangers. "Reconnaissance says most of the Fritzes have moved to the west of the village, but they've left a machine gunner behind the wall of the first house. Looks like it's just him and another man, probably a spotter. We don't have any artillery, and he's too far for a hand grenade, but there's a long gully about three hundred meters from the building. You'll have to take him out from there."

"Yes, sir," both of them said, though Alexia heard how high and tight her voice sounded. "He has an overview of the field, so you can't let him spot you."

"Understood," Kalya said, sounding confident. At least one of them was.

As they crept away toward the enemy, Kalya took charge. "Look, we should take position about ten meters apart but where we can see each other. When we have him in our sights, we both shoot, and if we don't get him, at least he won't know where to return fire."

"I understand," Alexia said, and they slipped along the gully. When Kalya signaled "stop," Alexia scraped a shallow trough at the rim with her bayonet and laid the muzzle of her rifle into it. While she waited for the next signal, she studied the window where the machine gunner was set up.

She could see him intermittently, peering out from under his helmet, though the tripod and the protective armor of his machine gun made it difficult to aim at him.

She set her scope for a distance of three hundred meters, and when she brought it into focus, she could see amazing details. He was young and had a scrappy beard, and was obviously talking to his comrade, for she could see his lips moving. Something even made him laugh, which seemed so incongruous to the mortal danger he was in. She wished she could laugh with him. She slid her finger gently alongside the trigger, and her hand began to tremble.

Just then Kalya whispered, "Now," and Alexia suppressed her tremor enough to caress the trigger. The two gunshots were the loudest sounds she'd ever heard.

Through the scope she could see the machine gun jerk into the air and the gunner topple forward. She convinced herself it was the gun barrel she'd hit and Kalya's bullet had killed the man. She drew back the bolt and knocked another bullet into the chamber.

At that moment, the spotter lunged into sight, grasping the machine gun, and she fired off another shot. He, too, toppled forward. No doubt this time. It was her bullet.

She dropped her head onto her arm and broke into tears.
Father Zosima. Forgive me.

❖

The battle continued for the rest of the morning, but Alexia simply shot wildly in the direction of the enemy. German soldiers fell, but she never knew whose bullets killed them. Within a few hours, the division overran the village, and she could already sense what it meant to be battle-hardened. At the end of the day, as she marched back to the troop carriers, stretcher bearers were bringing in the dead and wounded from all directions. Anxiously she checked their faces and saw to her relief that none of them were her friends. So this is victory, she thought. It felt nearly the same as defeat.

Reaching the field where the troops were once again mustered, she watched with mixed feelings as the medical vehicles turned north to return to the Novgorod station. The troops would continue south on foot. The field kitchen had followed them, and the exhausted victors received a mess tin of steaming kasha for their labor. Then they were ordered again to march.

At that moment, she realized how easy they'd had it before, sleeping in a schoolroom and being transported by truck. Now they were genuine infantry, foot soldiers, slogging along the roads marked by charred houses, barns, corpses. The Wehrmacht collected its dead and wounded, as did the Red Army, but no one collected the dead peasants.

The April rains had started, but only lightly, and the roads were still intact. They could march with some speed in pursuit of the retreating Germans, until the next locus of confrontation, though no one told them where it would be. Marching wearily, she located Sasha and Kalya and fitted herself between them.

"How did you feel, Kalya? I mean after you killed your first man?"

Kalya snorted. "I felt just fine. I have no sympathy for the bastards. Men just like them killed my family."

"What about you, Sasha? Was it hard?"

Sasha glanced sideways at her with her pixie eyes. "What? Oh, yeah, sort of. It's different when it's so personal. But that's our job now, isn't it?" She scratched her head. "Damn. I could really use a shampoo."

Alexia laughed. "Maybe our next battle will be in a town that still has hot water, and as a reward for your shooting a German officer, they'll let you take a bath."

But the next battle was at Tolstikovo where the Red Army drove the Wehrmacht from the town. The troops were allowed to rest for a night, but baths were not on offer.

Borki was more of a challenge, for they first had to ford a stream, and shots that felled two of their scouts told them snipers were holed up on the far side. Reconnaissance reported that the riflemen were hidden somewhere on the ground near a mill, apparently guarding a radio visible in the upper floor. Someone had to take out both the rifles and the radio.

"Corporal Mazarova, that will be you," Major Bershansky said, pointing at Alexia. "Yekimova, you'll be spotter." Sasha nodded agreement. The *rat-a-tat* of machine-gun fire had been ongoing, and they crouched low, scuttling from cover to cover toward the designated house. They spotted a depression and crawled along it until it deepened and they could crouch unseen. The machine-gun fire stopped.

"Do you think they've retreated?" Alexia asked.

"I'm sure they haven't. This is just what Major Pavlichenko warned us about. Let me take a look." Laying her rifle aside, she extended her small periscope and surveyed the field. "So many places he could be," she muttered. She passed the periscope to Alexia, who saw the same half dozen rocks, broken walls, wrecked vehicles, the blasted remains of a tree trunk. Behind the tree stump something sparkled. A reflection on metal, perhaps?

"I think he's behind the stump," Alexia whispered. "How can we force him to shoot first so we can see his muzzle flash?"

"Well, you can try that old trick of raising your cap, while I watch through the periscope," Sasha said. "Just be sure to keep your head out of it."

With a grunt, Alexia belly-crawled farther along the gully. Splinters of wood lay about from a blasted fence, and she propped one up with her woolen *pilotka* at its top, rising only a centimeter above the rim of the depression. No sooner had she crawled out of the way than a shot rang out and the cap flew off the wood.

"He's there, all right," Sasha announced. "He thinks he's got you. Now let me raise *mine*, and when he moves out to shoot, you get him."

Alexia was already in place, her eye glued to her scope as Sasha lifted her cap on the post in the same way. The sniper fell for it again. Alexia could see him clearly as he raised himself just high enough to take aim.

Two shots sounded simultaneously, his shot and hers. His hit the mark harmlessly, knocking away Sasha's pilotka. Alexia's shot was fatal.

❖

In the next ten days the division pounded its way southwest through a string of burnt-out villages, until finally it took Menyusha. A third of the sniper unit was lost during the battles, but the surviving women gained the privilege of sleeping in a barn along with the wounded. The medics hung a lantern overhead from one of the beams so they wouldn't be in total darkness.

While the medics, also mostly women, saw to the needs of the wounded, the sixteen remaining snipers scattered through the barn collecting straw to sleep on.

Alexia leaned against a stall wall across from Sasha, Kalya, and Fatima, and drew off her boots. "Oof. That feels good," she said, rubbing her toes. "Be nice to have some water to wash off the grit."

Sasha yanked her boots off as well. "Why stop there? How about wishing for a hot bath and a hair wash?"

Kalya stretched out on the dry straw. "You're still going on about that shampoo. Well, I'm just glad to be able to get a night's sleep without worrying about attack or groping hands."

"What hands have been groping you?" Alexia asked. "It can't be the men in our division. They're like our brothers."

"Not all of them. Some of them can't seem to keep their hands off these." Kalya cupped one of her own ample breasts.

Sasha untied her foot cloths and shook them out. "Kalya's right. On the battlefield, they're good comrades, but afterward, after a little vodka, they sometimes forget to be 'brothers.' The other day, one of them, a lieutenant, believe it or not, tried to kiss me. Said he'd been away from his wife for over a year and had forgotten what a woman's lips were like. I told him to try a sheep."

Another woman spoke up. "I've never been kissed at all. If the man's young, and not too dirty, I wouldn't mind a kiss. We could be dead tomorrow. Who wants to die without ever being kissed?"

Kalya folded her arm back behind her neck as a pillow. "Well, there are kisses and *kisses*. I got nice kisses from my babushka, and once from a pretty boy in school. Nothing to be excited about. But the serious ones, I think you get only a few of them in life."

"My sister said a good kiss starts on your lips and then goes all the way down to your groin." Sasha stretched out and rested on one elbow. "What about you, Alexia? Have you ever had a kiss like that?"

Alexia stared into the distance at the lantern, remembering the kiss that had shaken her. "No. Nothing like that."

"Well, I've kissed a few Germans," Fatima said, chuckling. "Not on the lips, though. More like between the eyes." She snorted and rolled over, pulling her field blanket up over her shoulder.

Kalya chuckled. "Yeah. A kiss from Stalin." Then she also turned away and curled up for the night.

Alexia stared into the darkness for a few moments before dropping off. She dreamt of the icon on her grandmother's wall, of the long-haired angel, swathed in silk, kissing the Virgin's mouth.

❖

After two weeks of nearly constant fighting, they reached Medved, and the spring rains finally arrived in full force. The troops were drenched all the time, and advancement along the roads of deep mud was excruciating.

When the storm tapered off to mere rainfall, Major Bershansky called in two of his favorite snipers.

"Mazarova, Petrova, our scouts spotted some German brass over that hill. Go take a look and see if you can knock off someone of value."

"Understood, Comrade Major," Alexia and Kalya said almost in unison.

They crept to where the officers had been spotted and crouched behind some cover, both in capes of tattered rags painted the color of dead leaves. They waited for hours but could see no sign of life. Meanwhile the gray sky darkened even more. Then thunder cracked and a wall of rain fell, and they soon lay shivering in a pool of mud. This was surely a waste of time.

Overhead Alexia heard what sounded like a Tupolev transport. What was it doing here? Supplies usually arrived in Novgorod and were trucked to the lines. Maybe the storm had blown it off course.

She let her mind wander on what it could be carrying. Ammunition almost certainly, but also warm clothing and new boots? Spam maybe?

Another sound filled her with dread. The *rat-a-tat* of a fighter plane attacking.

She rolled onto her back and looked up, though by now the battle was nearly over. The fighter had shot off half of one of the Tupolev wings and now circled around it, trying for a second shot.

Mortally wounded, the Tupolev managed a wide, curved descent and disappeared behind a distant farmhouse. The absence of explosion told her it had managed a crash landing, and that meant wounded men. Someone had to get to them.

But the moment she stood up, she'd be shot, and so she waited, and waited, watching through her periscope for the slightest movement.

Was it her imagination? No. Something did move at the top of the wall, just a spot, but it wasn't enough to shoot. If she could just get him to raise his head to aim. For that, she needed to give him a reason to shoot.

She focused on the tiny spot and held it in her sight with a steady hand, compensating for the force of the wind. "Kalya," she hissed to the other mound under the rag cape a few meters away. "Keep your head down but fire into the air. Let him see your flash."

Kalya lay flat and out of range but raised the tip of her rifle over her head and fired blindly toward the wall.

As she'd hoped, the dark spot rose to take aim, revealing a paleness beneath it. Alexia fired, and it dropped backward. "Got 'im."

From her position, facedown in her trench, Kalya chuckled. "Number nineteen. I'll vouch for you."

"Good," Alexia said, collecting the shell from the deadly bullet and dropping it into her pocket. It would rest in her pack alongside the previous eighteen.

❖

With the enemy sniper eliminated, Alexia and Kalya crept slowly forward until they came within sight of an enemy jeep partially obscured by bushes. A driver sat at the wheel while an officer radioed from the rear.

"This one's mine," Kalya murmured as they slid ever closer. Still some five hundred meters away, they stopped.

"Can you do it from here?" Alexia whispered.

"Like giving you a drink," Kalya said.

Alexia smiled to herself. *Da voobsche kak pit' dat'!* She hadn't heard that expression since childhood. "All right, Miss Show-off. You do him and I'll get the driver."

Kalya squirmed into a good firing position, and a short distance away, Alexia did the same. Kalya's shot had priority, so she did the count. "One…two…three."

A fraction of a second after Kalya's gun detonated, Alexia shot.

The two men slumped over in their jeep.

Wasting no time, they sloshed through mud and water back to the 109th Rifle Division headquarters in the largest of the remaining farmhouses. They stood dripping in the doorway and saluted. "Reporting mission successful, Comrade Major," Kalya said.

"Well done, soldiers. What did you get?"

"Alexia had two clean shots, a driver and a Kraut sniper. Me? I got the officer on his radio. I believe his last radio report was '*Oh, Scheisse.*'"

The major snickered slightly at the German profanity that every man in the Red Army knew.

"Request permission to investigate the plane crash just north of here," Alexia said more seriously. "It looked like one of our transports."

"Don't worry about that, Senior Corporal. I've already sent out a squad and a couple of snipers to check on it. In the meantime, reconnaissance has just informed me of a machine-gun nest south of here, near the river. We'll need to take it out before we can cross. Dry out for a few minutes and get some tea from the field kitchen. We'll send you both out with Sergeant Sumarov, who spotted them."

"Yes, Comrade Major," Kalya replied for both of them. "Will that be all, Comrade Major?"

"Yes. Dismissed."

They did an about-face and strode from the room. Just before stepping outside, Kalya swept off her pilotka cap and wrung out a thin stream of rainwater over the threshold. "Do you think it was the supply plane?"

"A Tupolev. Had to be. The storm must have blown it south. Damn. I thought the Luftwaffe was down to bare bones now, but obviously not."

Kalya was more hopeful. "They didn't explode, though, so that's a good sign. C'mon. Let's grab our tea and then look for Sumarov."

CHAPTER FOURTEEN

Mia hunched in her coat on a steel bench in a Russian transport plane, her knees drawn up to her chin. In front of her lay bales of telephone wire, crates of guns and ammunition, and other boxes whose contents she couldn't identify. Only the massive burlap sacks on both sides of her were marked RUBBER BOOTS MEN'S LARGE. Lend-Lease supplies, being delivered to the Novgorod front.

The moment she'd been picked up, she demanded to know if she was under arrest. "I have diplomatic immunity," she'd insisted.

But they had ignored her until they reached the office of Lavrentiy Beria, Commissar of State Security, and he informed her, "No, no. Of course you are not under arrest. We simply feel that your investigation would profit greatly if you take part in one of our Lend-Lease delivery transports. As it happens, one is going out just today, and you will have the opportunity to see how efficiently it is done. We will of course inform Ambassador Harriman of your departure."

"But I don't wish to go, Commissar Beria," she'd said. "Not on such short notice."

"Oh, come, come. What kind of investigator does not jump at an opportunity such as this? The next flight is not scheduled for some time, so it is imperative that you accompany this one. We also feel it is a matter of honor to show you our work."

He paused, evidently enjoying his mastery of the argument. "Besides, your message is already on its way to the embassy." He turned to the two agents who had brought her in.

"Please escort Miss Kramer to the airport."

The two goons had delivered her to the airport and handed her off to two others. The whole story was strange, and she didn't like it one bit, especially not the coercive part. Was she being kidnapped? If so, what was Beria's reason?

Presumably it had something to do with Nazarov's fraud. Was Molotov involved? It was bewildering. If the Lend-Lease theft was at the core of her forced removal, and they feared exposure, how did sending her to Novgorod solve their problem? If her suspicions were correct, she could not be permitted to return. What did that imply?

She tried to reassure herself. Molotov and Beria knew her personally, had sat with her at the negotiating table and at the dinner table in the presence of Stalin. Would they actually go so far as to… she forced herself to think the terrible word…to *murder* her to conceal the crime?

Then she recalled that, following the Bolshevik program, Molotov had left millions of his countrymen to die of famine by seizing most of the grain of the Ukraine, had condemned thousands more to labor camps, and had played an active part in hundreds of purge-executions. Making her disappear would be like brushing away a fly.

She was free to move around on the plane, but it did her little good. It wasn't like she could hijack it. She'd sized up the two men accompanying her and knew one was called Ilya and the other Yevgeny. They both smoked the usual crude mahorka tobacco.

She turned to Ilya, who sat closest to her. "We send millions of cigarettes to you, but you're still smoking that horrible tobacco? Who gets the good ones?"

He scowled at her and turned away.

She persisted. "No, seriously. I've got a pack of American cigarettes. Here. Have one on me." She slid the pack of Lucky Strikes from her jacket pocket and tapped one out into his hand. He glanced toward his colleague for approval, but Yevgeny looked away.

Once Ilya was well into his smoke, Mia brought her voice down to its softest, most casual level, as if they were all old friends simply stuck in a bad place together. "So, c'mon now, Ilya. Level with me. Are we really going to Novgorod?"

Yevgeny interrupted. "Of course we are. You think all this cargo is fake?" He kicked one of the bales of boots, and his foot bounced back.

"And what are you going to do with me? Leave me there to find my own way back to Moscow? That won't go down well with the American State Department."

"Leave you there? No, not like that." Ilya snickered, and the dreadful thought crossed her mind that leaving her there free was not the plan.

Yevgeny picked his fingernails with a tiny pocketknife and glowered at him.

A sick feeling grew in the pit of her stomach. Her heart pounded, and with a dry mouth, she said, "Tell me the truth. What have you got to lose? Are you supposed to dispose of me?"

"Shut up, Ilya. Just shut up!" Yevgeny snarled.

"Why should I shut up? What's the secret? She's going know what's happening sooner or later. You think if she knows now, she's going to run away? Ha, that's a good one!" He took another long toke on his cigarette, then leaned forward with his elbows on his knees.

"I am sorry to inform you that you will be leaving us just before we land at Novgorod. You understand?" He turned away and resumed smoking, no longer interested in the conversation.

"You mean…you're going to throw me out of the plane?" She couldn't believe the words that came from her own mouth.

He didn't reply, and she closed her eyes in silent desperation.

Suddenly the plane seemed to halt in midair, then tilt and drop, and she was sure now they'd run into a storm. The wind threw the plane violently up and down, and rocked it from side to side. Now the terror of crashing overshadowed the dread of being murdered.

Twenty minutes of such violence made her nauseous, and she feared vomiting. How grotesque, to vomit just before dying.

Yevgeny and Ilya were doing no better. Worse, even, for Ilya unbuckled his strap and lurched toward the toilet cubicle to empty his stomach. Only the roar of the airplane engine kept her from hearing the repulsive sounds of regurgitation, which surely would have set off her own.

He re-emerged, clawing his way along the crates as he staggered back to his seat, when suddenly another threat struck. The plane seemed to turn on its axis, raising one wing and lowering the other, as if to bank away from something. Then she heard it. The boom and crash of explosive fire.

Dear God. Why were they being attacked? The storm must have blown them into enemy air space.

Though her stomach rebelled and her mouth was dry with terror, a tiny, lucid part of her grasped the absurdity of being threatened with death by the NKVD, then a storm, and then the Luftwaffe. Something like panicked laughter erupted from her.

Then panic overtook her completely as the plane swerved in a wide curve, losing altitude, and she knew she was falling to her death. It was so unjust. For a brief moment she mourned that no one would miss her.

More explosions detonated outside the plane, though they seemed not to affect the wide spiral that took them inexorably to the ground. She curled up, sobbing, in the middle of a hundred pairs of men's rubber boots and, upon impact, blacked out.

Her next sensation was of cold and blackness and a terrific headache. Rough hands dragging her. Shouting. Choking oily smoke. The sudden terror of burning made her realize she was alive, and she tried to open her eyes. She couldn't. Something was wrong. Bits of color and light struck her, but no images formed, and something warm and wet sealed one eye shut. Hands slid her onto some kind of cloth and dragged her over slippery ground. Then she blacked out again.

She came to again on a wooden floor lying on her face, her head pounding. Still sightless, she tried to make sense of the sounds around her. Heavy footfall. Voices, and this time she could hear they were German. She was captured.

And the others? What had happened to the others?

"Ja ja," someone said. Funny how Germans always said Ja ja. Three men? Four men? A chair being dragged. Shouting again. "Ruskie!" Did they mean her? No. They had someone in the chair. An interrogation. Who was it? The pilot? A crewman? Or one of the NKVD men? Fully conscious now, she listened.

"Heh, Ruskie," the voice said again. A low moaning followed. The interrogator appeared to know a few words of Russian. "Where from? How many boom-boom planes?"

Now she understood. The retreating Germans wanted to know if more planes were on their way. They had probably already figured out that the Tupolev was merely transporting supplies but worried that bombers were to follow.

More shouting and the thumping of the chair legs told her the prisoner was being knocked about. He gave no information, though. And when he finally said in clear Russian, "Go fuck your mother's ass," she recognized the voice of Yevgeny.

Whether or not they understood him, the Germans resumed battering him, and his cries of pain told her their blows had become more brutal.

The torture continued for what seemed hours, and his reply to all of their shouts was a simple "*Nyet.*" Each Nyet was followed by a cry of pain, and each one was weaker. Yet his interrogators were getting nothing from him. He had been prepared to kill her, but at this moment, Mia felt a certain admiration for him, along with the terror of knowing she was next.

A final gunshot ended the interrogation, and another set of hands hauled her up into the same chair, her feet hitting the dead Russian as she fell back. Her eyes still didn't seem to work, so she couldn't see the tormentors, and her cringe was deep, animal-like.

One of them grabbed her hair and shook her, puzzled perhaps by her civilian clothing. Did he assume she was a politico of some sort? "Ruskie Kommissar?" he shouted into her face, and she could smell his foul breath. "*Mit amerikanischen Zigaretten.*" She heard the crumpling of paper and assumed he held up her pack of Lucky Strikes. Obviously they had searched her pockets.

Even if she could communicate with them, was there any point in trying to explain she was an American? Would that increase her chances of survival?

The question became moot when a distant shot sounded and her interrogator collapsed onto her lap and slid to the floor. The others, two or three, she couldn't tell, scattered, she guessed to the windows to return fire.

She dropped to the floor between the two bodies, and it was another sort of purgatory to lie there, blind and helpless, waiting for the outcome of the gun battle.

It seemed to take hours, but after the first man, and then the second, grunted and thudded to the floor, she realized that the attackers were expert marksmen and had picked off the Germans one by one.

The victors had to be Russians, so she sat up, waiting for rescue, but when it came, she was amazed to hear female voices. Once again, someone tried to lift her to her feet, but from shock, exhaustion, and the head trauma, she lost consciousness again.

❖

She awoke lying on her back on something soft. She still couldn't see and her head pounded, and when she lifted one hand to her face, she found half her head and one eye bandaged. "Hello?" she called out in Russian.

A soft hand touched her shoulder. "Hello. I'm Galina, one of the medics here. Can you understand me? How do you feel?"

"Yes, I can understand. Head hurts like hell, and I can't see. But I seem to be able to move my fingers and toes."

"We washed all the cuts on your head, but it looks like you have a concussion. You had a deep gash through your left eyebrow so your eye socket was full of blood. We stitched the gash together and bandaged you up. You can't see me with the other eye? That's probably the concussion. We'll have to wait to see what happens."

Suddenly the events before her rescue came back to her. "Those Germans who captured me, someone shot them one by one. You must have a damned good sniper."

The medic laughed. "We have several of them. The ones that saved you were Sasha and Fatima, but some of the lads were helping."

"Sasha. Fatima. Can I talk to them? I want to thank them."

"Of course. They'll want to meet you, too. And so will our commander, Major Bershansky. He'll have a lot of questions."

Of course he will, Mia thought, and wondered what she would answer. Could she tell a field commander that his government had tried to murder her?

She had only a few moments to brood before another hand touched her on the arm. "Hello there. Sasha here. Glad to see you're awake. You're looking better than when we found you."

"I'm feeling better, too. So you're the expert shot that picked off my captors. You must be awfully good. Hearing them fall dead on the floor was very satisfying."

"Thank you. I'm one of them. Fatima's also here. She knocked off two."

A voice spoke over her other shoulder. "It helped that the hut they dragged you into had so many holes. Those guys didn't have a lot of wall to hide behind. The hard part was aiming at them through the rain."

"Yes, the storm. Then the Germans shot us down. I don't know much else."

"Well, try to remember. Major Bershansky will want to know who you are and what the plane was doing in this sector. Oh, he's just arrived. Good-bye for now. Perhaps we can talk to you later." Hands pressed her shoulders from both sides.

The two friendly presences were replaced by one that sat down on her right. "How is our mystery woman?" a baritone voice asked.

"Doing much better, Major. Thanks to Sasha and Fatima."

"It seems the storm blew you over into this air space, and your pilot was able to make a crash landing. Some of us saw it come down. Apparently the Germans pulled out only you and the NKVD man they killed. So can you tell me what the plane was doing and what you were doing in it?"

"It was a transport supposed to deliver supplies to Novgorod, but got caught by the storm. Then the fighter planes spotted us and shot us down."

"And you? Who are you?"

She'd already decided the best lie was one that was 90 percent true. "My name is Mia Kramer. I'm the assistant to the head of the Lend-Lease program that supplies so much of your material and food. We make occasional visits to Moscow to monitor the program, and this time I…uh…came alone to talk to your foreign minister, Mr. Molotov. He thought it useful for me to accompany one of the deliveries. The rest you know. If it didn't burn up, the cargo could be very useful to you, too. I saw crates of rifles and lots of rubber boots. I think maybe the rubber boots saved my life."

"I've already sent out a squad to see what's salvageable. I'll report to STAVKA that we found you, and they'll decide what to do with the cargo. In the meantime, we'll move you back with the other wounded to our field hospital in Novgorod. From there they'll transport you by train to Moscow, where you can contact your embassy and arrange passage home."

"Moscow? Uh, yes, I understand," she said, but her mind buzzed trying to find a way to escape the wrath of Molotov. If she were to suddenly reappear, he would surely see to it that some new accident, perhaps even in the hospital, would get her out of the way. And as long as she was sightless, she was at his mercy.

"The medic says my blindness, at least in my good eye, is from the concussion. If I can stay here and rest a day or so, it may improve. Already I can see light and shadows."

"I'm sorry. We've just taken this town but will advance as soon as our sappers clear away the mines and my men are rested. We can't carry wounded with us."

Someone called him so he stood up and marched away. She needed to think. Would she be able to contact the embassy from Novgorod? Her head began to pound again and she lay back, defeated.

❖

Exhausted, caked in mud, but with several more "hit" cartridges in their pockets, Alexia and Kalya reported to their commander. "The riverbank is cleared, Comrade Major. Some of their infantry is still scattered around, but most seem to have retreated."

"Thank you, Senior Corporal. I'll have the sappers go out in the morning to look for mines, and you can cover them while they search. If the Fritzes have any snipers left, that's where they'll be."

"Yes, Comrade Major. Will that be all, Comrade Major?"

"For the time being, yes. Report to the quartermaster and see if he has any dry uniforms left. You look like hell."

"Thank you, Comrade Major." Both saluted and did an about-face.

The quartermaster's truck had caught up with the advancing rifle division only that morning and had set up close to headquarters in one of the other still-intact farmhouses. To remain mobile, the sergeant was careful to unload only those supplies that were needed immediately. That would be ammunition, hand grenades, gun oil, upon request by the men, food as requested by the cook, footwear, clothing, soap, and additional weaponry, only upon order by the major.

As Kalya and Alexia entered, Sasha was already in discussion with the quartermaster sergeant. Alexia clapped her on the back. "Well, look at you, all shiny and dry while the rest of us are drenched. How'd you manage that?"

Sasha turned sideways and laid a hand on her hip in mock petulance. "For your information, it's a hero's reward. Fatima and I just dispatched four Fritzes and saved a hostage, and the major sent me here. But now I'm trying to convince the sergeant to grant me a little extra soap." She ran her fingers through her pixie hair. "I can't stand the way this feels."

Kalya poked the sergeant on one arm. "Come on, comrade. You can spare just a little for a hero to wash her hair, can't you?"

At that moment, three men barged in carrying crates. "Look what we've got," they said, setting them on the floor and prying off the lids. One of them held hundreds of cardboard boxes of rifle shells, and the other, dozens of liter-sized square tins. She couldn't read the writing, but the picture on the label was of meat. Spam.

"Where did all this come from?" Alexia asked.

Sasha scrutinized one of the tins. "From the plane that crashed just north of here. The same place where I knocked off those Germans and saved their hostage."

"Hostage? Who did they capture? One of our men?" the sergeant asked.

"No, a woman. An American. The Germans pulled her and another man out and tried to interrogate them, that is, until we got there. They shot the man, and she's in the infirmary with some kind of head injury."

"What are you talking about? How can it be an American?" Alexia frowned in disbelief.

"I'm telling you, it was an American woman. Galina overheard her talking to the major. Go check for yourself. She speaks Russian."

CHAPTER FIFTEEN

The medics' station at Medved was in a barn across from headquarters, close to the road and thus accessible to ambulances. The 109th Rifle Division had one chief medical officer in charge of triage, two nurses, and three field medics/stretcher bearers. A fourth had been killed in the battle to take the town.

As Alexia entered, it was quiet. She'd noticed wounded men only cried out if they were in pain or needed water, but if the staff was able to tend them, they lay quietly, sleeping if they were lucky, staring at the empty air in fear if they were not. The two nurses, Tasha and Nina, saw to their needs all day and all night, even sleeping in the medical tent until the ambulances arrived to transport the ones who survived the wait.

At the entryway, next to the boxes of clean bandages and tins of disinfectant, Nina was pouring water from a pitcher into a mess cup.

"Can you tell me where the American woman is?" Alexia asked. "They brought her in yesterday from the crash just north of here."

"She's over there in the corner." Nina pointed with her chin and carried her water in the opposite direction.

Alexia stepped carefully around the wounded lying on bundles of straw. A couple of them, the less seriously injured, said hello, obviously just wanting someone to talk to, and she glanced down, smiling. But she continued on, drawn toward the form on the floor in the corner.

Finally she stood over the woman. The swollen face was half covered by a makeshift bandage. Visible beneath the blanket that covered most of her was the winter coat of a civilian, but not the one she remembered. Even her hair—disheveled, bloodstained, of uncertain color in the dark—didn't help.

Alexia knelt down next to her.

"Mia?" she said softly.

The woman turned toward the sound. "Who's that? Are you the medic? Can you give me some water, please? I'm so thirsty."

Alexia almost toppled back. It was Mia's voice. Weak and trembling, but unmistakable. She stood up, joyful, confused, with a thousand questions. Without speaking, she returned to the front of the station and poured water from the nurse's pitcher into one of the cups. Wending her way back, she knelt down, lifted Mia's head, and tipped the cup carefully into her mouth.

Mia allowed herself several long swallows, then turned her head slightly, signaling "enough." "Thank you, whoever you are."

"You can't see anything at all?" Alexia asked.

"Your voice," Mia said weakly. "You sound just like someone I know."

"Mia, it's me, Alexia. Remember me? From Moscow? The church at Christmas?"

Mia groped to the side until she felt her hand. "Of course I remember you. I've thought about you for months. I can't believe it's you." She chuckled weakly. "So you made it to the infantry after all."

"Yes. I'm a sniper, in fact. But what are *you* doing here? What brought you back to Russia?"

Mia grasped Alexia's hand in both her own. "A mission for the White House. To investigate missing shipments."

"But how did you end up in an airplane over Belarus?"

"It's a long story. I'd rather tell you in a more private place."

"All right, tell me later." Alexia's grasp tightened on her hand. "But you know a German fighter shot you down. It's a miracle you weren't killed in the crash."

Mia chuckled softly. "I'm sure I was saved by a bale of rubber boots. I held on to it like it was my mother. One other man survived, and the Germans pulled us both out. They shot him, though, because he wouldn't talk. And then your people rescued me."

"Unbelievable. Are you in much pain?"

"Just my head. I'm sure I have a concussion, and I can't see much.

What I see has holes in it, empty spots, mostly on one side. But that's from my good eye. The other one is covered by a bandage."

Alexia stroked the exposed cheek with the back of her fingers. "Still, those are lucky wounds. You can walk, and the hospital in Novgorod will take care of your eye."

"I don't *want* to go to Novgorod."

"I don't understand. Why—?"

"Senior Corporal Mazarova." A soldier stood in the doorway of the barn and called out to her. "You are ordered to report to headquarters. Immediately."

"I'm sorry. I'll come back as soon as I can, dear Mia," Alexia said breathlessly and kissed her quickly on the cheek before hurrying after the messenger.

Mia lay dazed on her straw. The joy at her reunion with her Grushenka guard was overwhelmed by the knowledge of being hunted and, worse, the sense of being physically helpless.

The sudden noise and activity around her told her more wounded were coming in. She sat up, tried to make sense of the fragmented images in her good eye, but could discern only two blurry figures carrying a stretcher and laying another wounded soldier next to her. The patient was apparently unconscious.

Moments later, Major Bershansky reappeared. "I've just sent a report to STAVKA of your presence here, so my superiors, and eventually yours, will know you're alive. Once you're in Moscow, you can contact your embassy. In the meantime, rest, and let the nurses take care of you until the ambulances arrive in the morning." With that, he disappeared again, and she was left alone with her thoughts.

She lay for a long while, struggling to analyze her predicament. Just how trapped was she? She felt along both her arms and shoulders and realized she had complete use of them. She could bend her knees, was sure she could even walk with a little help. She simply had a crashing headache and couldn't see clearly.

The soldier who had just been placed next to her was regaining consciousness and now moaned weakly. "Water," the soldier gasped. "Please, water." It was a woman's voice.

Mia remembered her own frantic thirst and reached across to touch the woman's shoulder. "I'll try to get you some, but be patient. I can't see."

"Please," the wounded woman gasped. "Take my mess tin, in my pack."

Mia groped for the pack, rummaged inside for the tin, and found it. "So far, so good," she muttered in English, then struggled to her feet. She peered with her one unfocused eye toward the only spot of light, the daylight at the entrance. She took a single step, then bumped a shoulder against a post. A jolt of pain shot through her already throbbing head. Shit. It was intolerable not to be able to see.

Angrily, she began unwrapping the bandage that was loosely wound around her head. The gauze stuck where the blood had dried on it over her eyebrow, but she pulled it away carefully. Finally it was off and the bloody eye was exposed. Unfortunately, it was glued shut with more blood that had oozed down from her wound.

She tottered for a moment, furious at herself and at everything that blocked her. Then, cursing, she continued forward, creeping inch by inch, groping at the air in front of her.

When she reached the entrance, it was unattended. The nurses, she assumed, were tending other wounded. "Shit," she muttered again and fumbled around the table till she touched a metal pitcher with a hinged top. It was cool, and when she dipped a finger in, she confirmed it was water. *Oh, thank God.*

She splashed some on her blood-caked eye until it ran down her face into her collar. The sensation of cool water reaching her eyeball was pleasant, though the eyelid was still glued shut. She cupped her hand full of water and simply held it against her eye.

Little by little, the blood liquefied to a goo, and the hole between her eyelids enlarged until finally it opened completely. She still only perceived fragments interspersed with emptiness, but now the field was much wider. It was an improvement.

Hoping she hadn't contaminated the drinking water with bloody hands, she filled the mess tin from the pitcher largely by touch. Now came the real task, of finding her way back.

Again she hobbled, encountering arms and legs, and she shuffled around them, holding a hand out in front of her. Finally she reached her corner. She knelt and lifted the woman's head and held the tin to her lips as Alexia had done for her a few hours earlier.

The woman drank greedily and sighed. "Thank you, whoever you are."

"I'm…a visitor." She set the mess tin to the side, within reach of the woman.

"I'm Marina Zhurova, a sniper. They just promoted me to staff sergeant and now this. I think my legs are damaged really bad, but I can't feel anything."

"The major said the ambulances are coming in the morning to take us all to the hospital in Novgorod, so I'm sure they'll take care of you there." They were the same words the others had said to her, and Mia heard now how empty they sounded. "And then you'll be able to go home to your family. Where are you from?" Surely the magic word "family" would be a comfort.

"I'm from Moscow but don't have family anymore. They're all gone. It's just me now."

Mia didn't know what to say. For all the loneliness she sometimes felt, at least she had Van.

"Try to rest now," Mia said. Another one of the empty phrases that people said to the wounded. Then she herself lay back and waited for Alexia to return.

❖

To her sorrow and confusion, Alexia didn't return, and so, the next morning, no one prevented the stretcher bearers from carrying her out with twenty-six others and setting her on a rack in one of the three ambulances.

The headache had subsided and her vision was improved, though that was both a comfort and a sort of cruelty. She looked longingly for Alexia, her chest heavy with the sense of abandonment.

Marina was alert, and at least they would be transported in the same ambulance, so they could talk. With clearer vision, Mia now could make out the horror of Marina's legs, strangely misshapen and bandaged from hip to foot. No amount of morphine could have blocked the pain of so much damage if a severed spine didn't already do so. Marina must have guessed that herself.

The nurses folded their medical records, such as they were, with name, description of injury, and treatment administered, and slid them under their tunics. Mia could feel the folded paper brushing against her chest.

"Is my pay book still in my pocket?" Marina asked weakly. "If I don't make it, I want them to at least know who I am."

"Yes, it's there," the nurse reassured her. "Don't worry. They'll take good care of you, and you'll make it for sure."

Pay book. A soldier's identification. That's what she needed.

The trucks pulled away from the camp and rumbled onto the road. The morphine the nurse had given her, together with her concussion, made her light-headed. But after about an hour, the pain returned and she felt the need to talk. "How are you doing, my friend?" she asked Marina, who lay next to her.

"Not so good. They're going to amputate my legs in Novgorod."

"No, they won't," Mia lied. "They can fix you up. It's a big hospital with good doctors." She had no idea what she was talking about.

Marina's sigh was half sob. "I wish everyone would stop lying to me. If I even live, I'll be a cripple in a bed, and I have no one to take care of me."

Mia groped to the side until she felt Marina's hand. "Please, don't give up hope. Not until a real doctor sees you. I'll ask to have a bed next to yours, and we can keep each other company."

It seemed such a flimsy comfort, but Marina seemed to respond.

"Yes, talk to me. Tell me about yourself. I don't even know your name."

"I didn't tell you because I'm running away from someone. I don't want anyone to know my name, or I'll be in trouble."

Marina gave a small, faint grunt, though if it had been stronger, it would have been a chuckle. "Do you think you'll be in any more trouble than you are now?"

"Well, you have a point. I never thought—"

The sound of careening dive-bombers sent terror through her. "Stukas!" one of the wounded men screamed.

The ambulance careened to the side and stopped suddenly as two shells tore through the forward part of the vehicle, killing the driver and the wounded who lay close to the front.

The few who could walk leapt from the ambulances and stumbled into the ditches. The rear door hung open, and Mia was about to also lurch through it when she glanced back at Marina lying helpless on her stretcher, her eyes wide with terror.

Mia swung back and curled up on the floor in the smallest ball she could manage, with one hand reaching up to Marina. "I won't leave you."

The planes strafed back and forth, sending down a carpet of fire raking across all three ambulances and on the wounded lying in the ditches. One of the ambulances blew up. Another curtain of shells cut like a blade through the roof of the ambulance, kicking up tiny spurts of blood as they sliced through the remaining wounded and Marina's pelvis. Already paralyzed, Marina made no sound of pain. Instead, she gripped Mia's hand and pushed it away.

"No. Run for it. You still have a chance," she choked.

Mia rose up on her knees and touched Marina's face. "I promised not to leave you. They might not come back a third time."

"I'm done for," Marina said between breaths. "Don't want to live…as a cripple. I have no one. Only you. Take my pay book." She laid her hand over the top of her tunic. "If you can't be yourself, then… be me." She took a difficult breath. "A kind of…resurrection."

Mia bent over the mortally wounded Marina and slid the pay book out of the pocket. "Yes, it is. I'll try to live up to your name." She kissed the dying woman gently on the forehead, then turned away and dropped from the rear of the ambulance.

Her head spinning from the exertion, she threw herself into the ditch and lay, face pressed into the dirt, when the Stukas swept by a third time and sent down another trail of projectiles. The remaining ambulances blew up with a deafening sound.

Thinking only of survival, Mia staggered away aimlessly, perpendicular to the road and out of sight of the Stukas. Finally she dropped to the ground to catch her breath.

Where were they anyhow? She calculated the ambulance had traveled about an hour, but over the pitted roads, they'd moved slowly. Following the road back to Medved, she supposed she could cover the same distance in two hours, perhaps less, if her strength held up. She had plenty of daylight.

The headache still plagued her, though more weakly, and her field of vision still had a blank spot on one side. The slacks and coat she'd been wearing since the day of her arrest were soiled and torn but kept her warm enough. She could make it.

As she struggled through the underbrush that grew alongside the road, she considered her alternatives. The destruction of all three ambulances, once the news got back to Moscow—and it would, eventually—would suggest to Molotov that she was dead. That could take days, a week. Assuming Soviet troops rescued her, what then?

Another trip to another hospital? She had to avoid contact with Major Bershansky and, with others, never use her real identity. No. She had no alternative but to be Marina Zhurova's reincarnation.

And in that case, she needed to know who she was.

She still clutched the crumpled pay book in her right hand. Crouching by the side of the road, she tried to read it. She had to hold it close and slightly to the side to get a partial image, and she could focus on the print only by squinting hard.

"All right, then," she said out loud, and read the first page. "Marina Mikhailovna Zhurova, staff sergeant in the 184th Battalion. Personnel number 6290586."

She studied the grimy photo next to the signature. It bore a faint resemblance to her, at least in hair color and head shape, but after a few months at war, even Marina no longer looked like her own photo, so it seemed unlikely anyone would notice the difference.

The second page listed her specialty, sniper, of course, and more interestingly, her education. She'd completed three years at Moscow State University studying literature, plus a number of practical courses in the paramilitary training schools.

The next page gave a Moscow home address, but parents, listed with their full names, were deceased. Facing that was a list of her military campaigns—at Moscow and later Kharkov—with dates and awards. She'd received medals, but obviously they were lost or they'd burned up with her. Mia felt a new wave of sadness at the thought. Brief glory and a terrible death.

The remaining pages simply listed the clothing and equipment she'd been issued, together with, of all things, a column for their date of return. She snorted. Marina had nothing to return at all, and neither did her incarnation. In fact, she'd have to find an infantry uniform. A rifle might be good, too. But God help her if she had to shoot it. And all that without coming to the attention of Major Bershansky.

She tucked the tiny gray booklet into her shirt pocket, and already she felt the spirit of the dead woman settling into her. "How do you like your new body, Marina?" she said into the air. "I promise to make you proud."

The sound of a vehicle approaching caused her to throw herself into the ditch beside the road. Too late. She'd been seen. But the order of "Show yourself, or we'll shoot" was in Russian, so she clambered out with her hands raised.

Two men were in a battered troop carrier, and one held his rifle pointed at her.

"I'm Marina Zhurova," she called out, hoping the pay book would convince them in spite of her being out of uniform. She had only the most flimsy explanation for that.

She handed him the book, and he glanced only at the first page. "Were you in the ambulances?" he asked. "They sent us out after the attack, but we found them burning and everyone dead."

"Yes. I think I'm the only one who got out. The others who jumped out were all strafed."

He returned the precious booklet but squinted with suspicion. "Why aren't you in uniform?"

"I…uh…was on fire, so I tore everything off. These clothes were in a pack that flew out from the explosion." Would he fall for it? It was pretty far-fetched.

"All right. Get in. We'll take you back to what's left of the camp. It was probably the same attack that got you. They wiped out headquarters and killed Major Bershansky. Captain Goretsky is in charge now."

Goretsky, she thought. She'd never heard of him. And if he'd never heard of *her*, she had a chance.

They followed the road back to the camp, which was in ruins. The house that had been headquarters was blasted, and so were the medical station and the quartermaster's truck.

"You should report in to Captain Goretsky. He's over there in that tent," the sergeant said.

"Thanks. I'll do that right now," she said as she jumped from the carrier. It pulled away and she stood, uncertain how to proceed. She needed to find Alexia, if she was still alive.

Someone called her from behind. Was she recognized? Alarmed, she spun around.

"Sasha. Thank God! It's me, the one you pulled from the plane. Please tell me Alexia is still alive."

"I'm pretty sure she is. Right before the air attack, she and Kalya were sent out on a mission. Lucky for them. The Germans made a massive counterattack with artillery and fighter planes. Caught us completely off guard. Headquarters would have Major Bershansky shot for letting it happen, except the Germans beat them to it."

"Yes, I heard. It looks like the attack wiped out most of the camp."

"It did. The whole 109th is decimated. A few dozen of us are just regrouping and waiting for orders. I'm glad to see you're on your feet again. Ironic, eh?"

"Listen, I'm stuck here the same as you. And I'm in no hurry to go back to Moscow, hospital or otherwise. I have a new identification, and I'll stay and fight alongside you, but I need a gun and a uniform."

"New identification? What's wrong with being yourself?"

"It's a long story, and I would endanger you if I told you. Surely you can't object if I want to fight beside you as a soldier."

"I think it may be a crime to impersonate a soldier, but after all, it's your head."

Mia sniffed. "You have no idea. Anyhow, do you think anyone's going to object to my fighting for the Red Army?"

Sasha shrugged. "I guess you're right. And if you're that crazy, I'll see what I can do." She took Mia by the arm. "The Fritzes have nearly wiped us out, but there may be a few crates left in the quartermaster's truck. Let's take a look."

The still-smoking truck lay on its side, its cargo of boxes and crates spilled out onto the ground. They rummaged through the wreckage until they came across a partially singed crate with a serial number. Sasha pried it open with her bayonet. "Look at that. All the new Mosin-Nagants you could want. Take your pick."

Mia lifted one out of the crate and blew off the dust. It felt alien in her hand, but she thought it unwise to mention she'd never shot a rifle. "So far, so good." She set it aside. "What about a uniform?"

"Hmm. Uniform boxes are usually green." She continued to rummage and uncovered a jumble of cardboard boxes. They were crushed, but the labels were still visible: small, medium, and large.

"I'm guessing small. It's what we all wear." Sasha tore away part of one box and pulled out a folded tunic. They weren't so lucky with the box that held the pants. They were large.

Mia tore off her coat and soiled sweater and drew on the tunic that fit her loosely, but adequately. The trousers, however, were enormous. "Do I look like a clown?"

"No one cares on the battlefield. Anyhow, they'll be warm, and you have plenty of room to sit down."

It was true. The loose rear of the pants was faintly comical but also allowed her to kneel, squat, and bend with ease, and the tunic covered the baggiest part of them. Once both parts of the uniform were on her, and buckled at the waist, she felt curiously empowered. As a final thought, she slid the pay book that identified her as Marina Zhurova into the same breast pocket Marina had kept it in.

"You'll need the shoulder boards, too," Sasha pointed out, holding out two of them. "Crimson with black edges. Just like mine." She buttoned them onto the shoulders of the tunic. "What rank are you claiming to be?"

"Staff sergeant. What does that require?"

"Oh, how ambitious. That's three chevrons." She rifled through a large box of insignias. "Ah, got 'em. You'll have to pin them on for now and sew them later."

Together they attached the chevrons, point down, in the correct position on the sleeve.

"Don't forget one of these. Otherwise that rifle will be pretty useless." Sasha lifted up what looked like a heavy double canvas strap and draped it over her head and one shoulder. Mia ran her fingers down the length, feeling the individual squares that ran along it, and realized it was the ammunition bandolier. It was heavier than she'd imagined, but it did make her look like an infantryman.

Sasha stepped back and studied her. "You'll do. Technically, this counts as looting, and we both could be shot. But the camp is disbanding, and we're leaving it all anyhow, except the rifles. I'll report that we've found them. By the way, if you're going to join us, you'd better tell me your name?"

"Marina Zhurova. Sniper and sergeant." She reached for her rifle and held it across her chest the way she'd seen Alexia do it. Then she took a deep breath.

"I guess it's time to report in. Who'd you say is in charge?"

❖

Captain Goretzky, to her relief, had no time for her. He was frantically gathering papers into a leather satchel and barking orders to subordinates, preparing to withdraw.

He glanced up briefly. "So you're the only survivor?"

"Yes, sir. They strafed us and then blew everything up."

He looked her up and down. "You look fit to me. Why were you in an ambulance?"

"I had a concussion and this head wound." She pointed to the bright red ridge that ran diagonally through her right eyebrow. It still oozed a thin trickle of blood that she had to wipe away periodically. "The concussion affected my vision, but it's better now. So I'm reporting back for duty, sir. I was in the same unit as Corporals Mazarova and Yekimova."

Goretzky sniffed. "Bershansky always did coddle his soldiers. All right. Return to your unit until further notice. At the moment, STAVKA has ordered us to withdraw to Menyusha, to the brickworks to wait for reinforcements."

"Yes, Comrade Captain," she said.

"By the way, sir," Sasha added. "The quartermaster's truck still has some rifles. Shall I make arrangements to bring them along?"

"Do that. I'll send over one of our carriers for them. See if there's anything else worth saving. If not, I want the rest destroyed."

"Yes, sir." She saluted, and Mia saluted a second later with as much snap as she was able. She was going to have to remember to do that.

Outside, Sasha clapped her on the back. "Before the carrier arrives, let's go collect everything else you're going to need on the march."

They jogged back to the jumble of boxes and found that the basic field items were still available, though not necessarily in the correct size: padded jacket, water flask, mess kit, *pilotka* cap, underwear, boots, and a backpack to carry it all in. "A shame we can't find a scope for you. But you'll need more ammunition." Sasha hooked a cartridge belt around Mia's waist. "This should do it."

"Jesus, you march with all this on?" Mia grumbled. "I sure hope Menyusha's not far."

Just then a troop carrier pulled up next to them. The sergeant who had rescued her eyed her new uniform and smiled. "Much better," he said, and joined Sasha in hauling out the rifle crate as well as others full of ammunition.

When the work was done and the remaining supplies set ablaze, Mia and Sasha joined the stragglers who marched eastward toward Menyusha. After only an hour on the road, she already hated everything in her pack, and she knew that Menyusha would be very, very far.

❖

With her entire body aching, Mia plodded along behind Sasha and the others heading eastward. It was nightfall when they reached the Menyusha brickworks and joined the other defenders. "Who's in charge?" Sasha asked as they entered the heavily guarded building.

"I am." A tall gangly man in a soiled uniform stepped toward them. "Captain Pletchev. 145th Armored Division. Who are you, Corporal?"

"Aleksandra Yekimova, Marina Zhurova, 109th Rifle Division, reporting for duty, Comrade Captain." They both saluted.

"I see. A few other women from your division are here as well, down at the far end of the building," he said. "Go join them until further orders. I'm waiting to hear from STAVKA about reinforcements."

"Yes, Comrade Captain." Sasha saluted again, and Mia snapped to attention as well.

Surprised at how easy it had been to take on a new identity, Mia strode beside Sasha down the corridor to the far end of the station. She almost laughed at the idea of what she was now, a soldier who couldn't see clearly and had never fired a gun.

CHAPTER SIXTEEN

May 1944

Silence came with nightfall, and only a few kerosene field lanterns illuminated the cavernous workshop. Sasha and Mia moved cautiously down the center of the hall, stepping over feet and equipment while they looked for familiar faces. Finally they spotted Klavdia and Fatima, and threaded their way through the resting soldiers to join them.

Fatima glanced up and smiled. "My, my. Last time we saw you, you were bandaged and blind. You've changed, my friend." She tugged on the side of Mia's uniform pants.

Mia let her pack fall, savoring the relief to her back. Now the damned thing could serve as a cushion. With her feet, her neck, and every muscle in her back aching, she dropped onto her knees and found a tolerable position on her side. "Long story," she said, punching a groove in her pack for her shoulder. "I'll tell it later." With a quiet sigh, she laid her head on the pack and started to doze.

A hand touched her shoulder, and she sat up. "Alexia! Kalya! I'm so glad to see you two."

Alexia laid down her rifle and settled in beside her, making a backrest from her own pack. "I'm glad to see you, too, but a little confused. Sasha said you managed to come back, that you could see again, and that you wanted to stay with us. I'm sure there's a lot more to the story."

Kalya slid in closer to listen. "I want to hear this, too. Why the new outfit? And the gun?"

Mia rubbed her face, wondering whether to jeopardize her new friends. "Look, it's a complicated story but also dangerous. If I tell you, you might get in trouble for not reporting me."

Kalya beamed. "Oh, that sounds much too interesting to resist. I'll take my chances. Talk."

"Well, you'll have to slide over closer where no one can hear us. And you must swear not to betray me. It could cost me my life."

All four of the snipers nodded energetically and slid some distance away from the others to make a rough circle around Mia.

She leaned forward and began her narrative in a whisper. "You know that the plane I was on was shot down, but you don't know that I was a prisoner. I was guarded by two NKVD men who were about to dump me out over German territory. Only the attack by the fighter planes saved me, although the crash gave me a concussion."

Fatima scowled. "Dump you out? That can't be true."

"It *is* true. One of the NKVD men even admitted they were ordered to. It just never got that far."

The explanation was met with incredulous silence.

"Look, I don't care whether you believe me. Just know I'm here to fight with you against the fascists and take the same risks. Can we leave it at that?"

Fatima shrugged. "I suppose if she's willing to dodge bullets the same as us, she's not a spy, eh?"

"Fair enough," Kalya said. "So, how's your poor head, anyhow?" She touched Mia's forehead lightly.

"Much better, thanks. The crash jarred my vision, but by the next day, it began to improve. I still have trouble focusing, but I can manage."

Klavdia persisted. "That still doesn't explain why you decided to join up with us."

"It ought to be obvious. There I was, in your medical station. Major Bershansky notified STAVKA that I was here and then wanted to ship me back with the other wounded. But sending me to Moscow would put me back at the mercy of Molotov. He'd just find another way to kill me."

Fatima scratched the back of her neck. "I still don't understand. Why would Molotov want to kill you?"

"Because I uncovered something that may incriminate him. When he found out I knew, he had me kidnapped and ordered his men to kill me."

Alexia nodded, as if slowly accepting the possibility.

"Anyhow, as it happened, one of the wounded on the ambulance the Germans hit was Sergeant Marina Zhurova. Just before she died, she offered me her identification." Mia reached inside her tunic and held up the pay book. "And then Sasha helped me get a uniform and a gun. So, here I am."

Kalya brushed dirt from the sleeve of Mia's tunic. "This is all much too complicated for me, and anyhow, what our leaders do doesn't concern me. Just one question." She nodded toward the rifle. "Can you shoot that thing?"

"Uh, no. I was hoping one of you could teach me. You don't have to make me an expert marksman. Just tell me how to load and fire the damned thing. But you'll have to wait until it's light. I still can't see very well."

Kalya threw her head back. "Oh, wonderful. You want to join a snipers' team and you can't shoot."

"Yeah. Something like that."

"I'll teach you to shoot," Alexia said. "Come sit here next to me, and I'll explain."

Alexia laid the rifle across Mia's knees and placed her hand on the cartridge chamber. "This is the Mosin Nagant that we all use, and it fires five cartridges from a clip. It's no good for rapid firing, like the machine gun, but if you're stationary and protected, its range is pretty good. Of course, you have to be able to see your target."

"My eyes are better than they were yesterday. Maybe they'll keep improving."

"Just try to stay under cover until they do. Now, your rifle is currently not loaded, in case you didn't notice. Do you have cartridges or clips?"

"Uh, you must mean these things." She slid a clip out of her bandolier.

"Very good. Well, you simply slide the clip into the chamber and pull out the metal strip that holds the cartridges. If you want to empty the chamber, you have to open it from the bottom, here under the trigger box."

"What if I have only individual cartridges?"

"Simple. You press them in with your thumb. Like this. Now, show me you understood by removing the cartridges and then inserting them again."

So it went for Mia's crash course in the Mosin-Nagant rifle, which distilled three months' instruction into an hour. She listened carefully, felt along the various parts of the weapon, and tried to memorize the name for each part.

By the time they all curled up to sleep next to the wall of the station, she had learned, actually, very little.

Enemy fire was sporadic the next morning, and Mia had the impression that, in spite of the damage they had done, the German forces had exhausted themselves in their attack the day before.

As word spread of the fortified position being held by the survivors of the 109th and the 145th divisions, scores of others from decimated units migrated toward the station as if to an oasis.

And while they waited for the promised reinforcements, Mia learned how to shoot her rifle. With vision that improved each day, she missed the target with ever-increasing proximity and even managed to graze it finally.

"You're doing everything right, and you have a steady hand. You should be doing better."

"It's my eyes. I can see you quite well now, but I don't have a scope, and when I stare through the rifle sight, the target gets blurry."

"Maybe it's just a matter of time." Alexia encouraged her, but she didn't sound convinced.

On the third afternoon the remnants of the 62nd Armored Division arrived, along with Colonel Borodin, its commander, and Captain Natasha Semenova, a political commissar, who immediately reminded them of Stalin's "Not one step back" policy.

The accumulation of stray units in the Menyusha brickworks did not count as a retreat, she said, but rather as a strategic regrouping. And henceforth, there would be no retreat from any position without permission from STAVKA, and under no circumstances was surrender permitted. "We have no prisoners, only traitors," she declared, echoing

Stalin's policy of abandonment of any captured Soviets. As word spread, everyone waiting in the brickworks knew they were now under Colonel Borodin's command, and they would go on the offense the following morning, no matter the cost.

❖

At five o'clock the next morning, the commissar brought the orders. Medical units would remain at the brickworks until the new base was secured, while artillery and armored units would advance, followed by infantry.

After Mia loaded her pack, hauled it up onto her back, and went to stand next to her friends, Commissar Semenova called out to her.

"You there, you're with the 4th Rifle Platoon. Fall in over there." She pointed toward the men gathering some distance away outside the building.

"But I'm…" She looked helplessly at Alexia and realized that saying she was "with the snipers" carried no weight. A dozen people had watched her learn to shoot the night before and knew she was no sniper. She could do nothing but obey.

She fell in with the mud-splattered riflemen of the 4th platoon and hoped for the best. The men seemed friendly enough. One or two of them nodded at her, apparently pleased to have a woman in the ranks, though most were indifferent. Her main perception, other than anxiety, was the smell of unwashed male bodies.

The march in the predawn light wasn't long, and by full daylight they were within sight of Ostrov. The four tanks and six mobile guns assumed attack formation, and the infantrymen marched behind them in two lines. Mia's slowly improving vision had a setback from the dust burning her eyes, though maintaining a permanent squint brought some relief.

The armored vehicles began to fire shells at the enemy positions, and Mia realized she was about to experience her first battle. Curiously, she wasn't afraid, though perhaps it was because they were on the attack. If any men fell, their cries of pain, if they uttered them, were drowned out by the sounds of the shelling and the "uuurrrahh" that swelled up from the charging soldiers.

It was a heady experience running amidst the charging soldiers, and for a moment she felt invincible. It almost seemed the Germans were holding fire.

When tanks came within a few hundred yards of the first houses, she saw she was right. The Germans had simply waited until they were within range. Now they opened fire and men fell on all sides of her. Fear invaded her, and she tried to stay behind the tank. But others had the same idea, and as they pressed in for cover, they nudged her sideways into the open again. She fired wildly as she ran, with no idea of whether she hit anything useful.

Then they reached the first houses, and the tanks pushed into the streets. One of the men threw a hand grenade and blasted the interior of the first building. She was jogging now, as close behind the tank as possible.

A figure in green in a doorway shot at them, hitting the man next to her. In spontaneous fury, she fired back and the German collapsed. She hardly had time to grasp she'd killed a man when the comrades behind her lobbed grenades into each of the houses they passed, eliminating fire on their flank.

The rest of the battle was a blur. She shot at anything green that moved and at least twice managed to insert a new clip on the run and carry on. The detonation of the tank shells, the popping of rifle fire, the shouts and screams of the men all became a sort of white noise, and her mind focused on a single task, to run and shoot until someone ordered her to stop.

The order came late in the afternoon, when the return fire ceased and the captain reappeared, ordering them to the town square.

With men and light artillery guarding all the entrances to the square, Mia's platoon and several others lined up. A lieutenant appeared, who sent scouting teams and sappers to examine all the buildings around the square, and by nightfall, they were cleared of mines. It was now safe to allocate quarters for the night.

Mia found herself in one of the grenade-blasted shops, a bakery, it seemed, though the few bits of bread they found were all charred. She dropped down alongside a group of men she didn't know, took a long pull from her canteen, and opened her provender sack to eat the field rations she'd been issued the night before.

She was spent, but as Commissar Semenova passed by she

struggled to her feet. "Comrade Captain, how can I find the snipers of the 109th," she asked.

"You mean the women? They're across the square."

"Request permission to leave and speak to them, Comrade Captain."

The commissar screwed up her face, as if searching for a reason to refuse and finding none. "All right, but report back before dawn when the new orders come. If you're not here, you'll be charged with desertion."

❖

She spotted them in a corner, by the light of an artillery shell hammered together at the top and with a wick protruding from a pool of kerosene. They nodded greeting as she sat down quietly next to them.

"So, how was your first day on the job?" Kalya asked, play-punching her shoulder.

"It went pretty well. I ran and shot, and didn't fall down or die. Considering my level of expertise, I think that counts as damned near miraculous."

"How are your eyes?" Sasha asked her in a more serious tone. "Can you actually shoot *at* anything yet?"

"Yes, in fact. As long as it's big and standing right in front of me."

"What about the headache?" Sasha asked again, with the same sincerity.

"Gosh. I hadn't thought about that. With bullets and shrapnel flying all around killing people, you never think about a headache. But much better, thanks."

"I'm glad you're here," Alexia said softly. "I was worried about you."

Mia looked, perhaps a moment too long, at Alexia's red-rimmed eyes. "Were you? That's nice to know."

They fell silent then, and Mia knew they were as exhausted as she was. For her it had been a baptism of fire, but for them, it was just another grueling day, and she was grateful to be among them. She leaned back on her elbow and studied them.

The corner where the five snipers squatted around the flame of their field lantern was a study in oranges and browns. Their uniforms, the wooden stocks of their rifles leaning against the grimy wall behind them, ranged from mahogany to russet to the color of dirty potato skins. Fatima, the black-eyed Kazakh, who sat directly across from her, seemed the most foreign, probably because she spoke so little. Mia knew little about her other than that she'd lived through the Leningrad siege.

Klavdia Kalugina, the youngest, had a round, sad face and a high voice, like an adolescent, and it was hard to imagine her killing even a chicken. Sasha Yekimova, one of her saviors from the German torturers, was boyishly pretty. Her brunette hair feathered around her slightly Asiatic eyes and offset the androgyny of her male uniform with femininity. With just a slight bit of makeup and slightly longer hair, she would be doll-like and adorable. She seemed a bit spoiled and would certainly lead any future husband around by the nose.

Next to her, Kalya Petrova rolled a cigarette out of the harsh mahorka tobacco provided to the troops. Her wide shoulders, haircut, and gruff manner made her seem masculine, but her expression was often soft, even as she blinked away the harsh cigarette smoke. With a plain square face and wide nose, she reminded Mia a bit of Lorena Hickok and, like Lorena, inspired trust.

The palest, even in the orange light of the flickering flame, was Alexia. She had the ice-blond hair and slightly hooded steel-gray eyes Mia had only ever seen in Russians and was almost archetypally Slavic. Even disheveled from the day's fighting, she was stunning, or would be after a hot bath and shampoo. The only thing that diminished her power over Mia was her resemblance to Grushenka.

Alexia caught her glance and smiled. Embarrassed, Mia smiled in return, then lay back and stared at the ceiling, trying to get her mind around the events of the last few days.

It was all but unimaginable. She was an American bookkeeper, whom fate had plucked out of a banal existence and sent on a bizarre misadventure. That same capricious fate had saved her from a death sentence, but now she was in a war zone in the company of Soviet snipers.

Kalya's lighter clicked, and a moment later she coughed.

"That stuff is going to kill you, even if a German bullet doesn't," Mia said amiably.

Kalya chuckled. "Na. Neither. Lungs tough as an ox and eyes like an eagle. You'll see. One day I'll be running a kolkhoz with ten children all just as tough as me."

Close by, one of the infantrymen who'd overheard called out, "Not a chance, Kalya. No man's going to have the guts to marry any of you. You've all been trained to kill, and the first time you have a marriage quarrel and throw a plate at him, it'll be lethal."

"Oh, go to sleep, old fool," she called back at him. "No one's going to marry you either, with that face of yours." They both laughed, and Mia could see the easy camaraderie that existed between the men and women.

"Why did you join up, anyhow?" Mia asked her. "If that's not too personal."

"Not personal at all. I enrolled in a course given by my district that taught us to shoot a rifle, and I liked the way that felt. I never thought the war would actually happen. Then, suddenly, the Krauts were rampaging across the Ukraine. It turned out I was a very good shot, so when I enlisted, I was assigned here. It was an easy transition."

"It wasn't for me," Sasha added. "I was a music student with dreams of singing in the opera chorus. I also enlisted when the Germans invaded but had no idea it would make me so different. And that's even before they discovered my perfect eyesight and put me in sniper school."

"Fighting is different for all of us, I think. No one plans to kill people."

"Yes, but most are tougher than I was. I was a little princess. I went into the recruitment office as a girl in a pretty dress and with hair down to my hips, and came out as a boy, in pants and a field jacket. Instead of hair, I had a pilotka cap, and that night, instead of a soft bed, I was on a freight train sleeping on hay."

"What about you, Alexia?" That was the story Mia wanted to hear most. But Alexia shook her head. "A long story, and I don't want to tell it tonight. They're going to wake us tomorrow at five, so I think we should all go to sleep."

Mia nodded. "You're right. And I have to go back to my quarters or risk being charged with desertion. Take care of yourselves, my dears. I'll come looking for you every day."

CHAPTER SEVENTEEN

Unusually, STAVKA allowed the newly formed division to remain a day at Ostrov to permit supplies, the medical station, and the field kitchen to catch up. Mia's relief was tainted by the discovery that her period had started.

It was a problem she should have anticipated and felt stupid that she hadn't. As soon as she was able, she got permission to cross the square to the snipers' quarters again.

"How do you deal with this," she asked Alexia. "Surely every woman in the Red Army has the same problem."

"Not all," Sasha interjected. "I stopped months ago, when my weight dropped. It's probably because of the constant hardship. As long as it's not permanent, I'm glad about it. Just one thing less to worry about when you're in the field."

"That's nice for you, Sasha, but Mia's not so lucky," Alexia chided her. "Come on. I'll take you to the medics. They'll have bandages or rags you can use."

"Bandages or rags. Charming," Mia said, following her.

"Don't complain, my friend," Alexia said. "It used to be worse. Some of the women who've been here longer tell stories about marching for hours with blood running down their legs. If they could, they cut off the sleeves of their winter underwear and rolled them up. It seems the Red Army, along with having no small uniforms for women, also never thought of that detail. Ah, here we are."

The medical station was another slightly less damaged shop front on the square of Ostrov. It had some ten canvas folding cots laid out side by side, all holding wounded, and another dozen men sat on the floor leaning against the wall. Two nurses in regular field uniforms but with white armbands were moving among them tending to their needs. A third woman, in a white smock, dried her hands and marched past them into another room.

One of the medics who was bandaging a stump at the end of a soldier's hand looked up as they came in.

"Galina, hello," Alexia said. "We won't stay long. Can you spare some bandages for my friend Mia? She is having her days and never got a woman's field kit."

"You can take some of those. Over there, in the crate next to the alcohol bottles," Galina said, pointing with her head. "But no more than one package. We're short ourselves, and even those have been reboiled and used several times."

Alexia lifted out one of the bundles of grayish-yellow gauze and handed it to Mia. "Thanks, Galina. When do you get off duty? Can you come by later for a smoke? We're in the building with the wagon in front."

Galina replied without looking up from her work. "Tonight, maybe. After the ambulances come and cart these guys to the rear." A scream of pain came from the other room. "Can't talk now, though. They're tying down one of the men for an amputation, and I have to help with the surgery." She pinned the end of the bandage, helped the soldier lie down again, and hurried past them into the back room.

Mia was glad to escape the purgatory of the medical station and deal with her own trivial problem. She glanced down at the bundle in her hand. "So, how do you manage with just this?"

"Cut it in half. Use one until it's dirty, and then change and rinse out the soiled one."

"That makes sense, but what do you do when the washed one isn't dry?"

Alexia shrugged, and her silence was the answer.

The snipers' quarters had the additional luxury of a sheltered toilet that still flushed, though the pipe that fed in water to the overhead tank had broken. "Easy solution," Kalya said, and fetched in a bucket of water, which she poured into the tank. "Now you can flush to your heart's content. But only once."

"Once will do," Mia said, and closed the door, enjoying her first moment of privacy in weeks. She quickly tore the strip of yellowish bandage in two, wondering whose blood still remained embedded in the gauze she was about to clean herself with. She hoped the person had survived the wound. Surely it would be bad luck to walk around wearing the blood of a dead man.

She wiped herself clean with one half and tied the other inside her underwear, the last vestige of her American civilian clothing. She washed the now-soiled half in the bucket, squeezed out the water, and left the toilet cubicle with the damp bundle in her hand.

"This is going to be awkward," she said. "Where do I hang this to dry?"

Kalya laughed. "Don't go all fussy on us. This is a battlefield and there's blood everywhere. No one's going to know where yours came from."

Mia joined the women in the corner they had claimed and, like them, began to clean her rifle. She had no idea how to dismantle the weapon but watched the others and saw how logical the process was.

They had no sooner finished than a young corporal announced from the doorway, "4th platoon, you're up." They all grabbed their mess tins and hurried out to line up next to the field kitchen.

Breakfast was bread, a thick cereal of various grains boiled in water, and tea. It was at least filling and significantly superior to the hard bread they'd had to consume the previous night. With her mess tin and cup filled, Mia returned to her friends.

"Hmm. Could use a little sugar," Mia remarked.

Kalya laughed. "And butter, and caviar, and meat, come to think of it. And some of my grandmother's marmalade."

"All right. I know I'm spoiled."

"We're spoiled, too, actually," Sasha said sympathetically. "I always had marmalade at home, from apples and pears. I didn't realize how bad most people ate until I became a soldier."

"Is that what you miss? The food?" Mia asked. She liked Sasha and could so easily imagine her in civilian life: coquettish, flirtatious, effervescent.

"I miss ordinariness. Cooking, setting my hair in curlers, singing, putting on dresses and heels, falling in love."

"Did you have an admirer? A gentleman, I mean?"

Kalya snorted. "I bet she had a dozen of them, didn't you, Sasha?"

"Don't be silly, Kalya. It wasn't like that. Okay. Maybe a couple of boys at school. Okay, maybe a lot of boys at school. But what about you, Marina? What was life like for you back in America?"

Mia blinked first at being called Marina. She felt certain she could trust these women but had had probably already divulged too much information about her past.

"I worked in an office, doing accounting. Yes, I liked the dresses, but the more daring women already wore pants, fashionable ones, not like these." She tugged at the knees of her baggy trousers. "But we had lots of marmalade."

"Do you still have family? Are they worried about you?" Fatima asked, and Mia remembered that Fatima had lost everyone in Leningrad.

"Um, well, I have only a brother, but I think my boss worries more about me than he does." She thought of Harry Hopkins, who surely imagined she was dead.

"Alexia said you worked in Washington, with the government. Did you ever see President Roosevelt?"

Mia wasn't sure what to reply. She'd already told them enough to endanger them.

Alexia came to her rescue. "I think it's best not to ask Marina too many questions. You know what they say. Ears are everywhere."

"Yes, and besides, I have to report back to my unit or the commissar will have my hide. She seems to hold some sort of grudge against me. That's all I need."

Mia stood up, collected her rifle and mess kit, and, with a small wave, threaded her way among the groups of soldiers to the door.

❖

The next morning at five, the order came to fall in. Sitnya was eight kilometers due south, and they were ordered to take it before nightfall. The commissar reminded the infantrymen of the "not one step back" policy that prohibited surrender or retreat, and the troops nodded silently to an order they hated.

Mia let her gaze sweep around the square of Ostrov but saw no sign of her friends.

After the morning ration of porridge, the troops began the march. The land was uncontested for most of the way, and the abandoned artillery pieces they passed told them that the Germans were in full retreat. Nonetheless, a cornered beast is most dangerous, and Mia, trudging in their midst, knew not to be cocky.

And indeed, outside of Sitnya, the Germans had dug in and set up a formidable defense. Indifferent to the cost, the colonel ordered them to attack, and once again Mia charged amidst a group of men, firing her rifle blindly ahead of her. The roaring of the Russian troops around her was soon drowned out by the sounds of exploding grenades. The Germans were throwing them just ahead of their own advancing troops, creating a line of pits between the armies. But soon the space between them closed.

Just ahead of her, the bright light of a grenade explosion revealed two silhouettes thrown into the pit, one from the German side, and the other—oh God—was Sasha.

Mia screamed "Medic," ran toward the still-smoking pit, and slid down into it.

Sasha lay on her back, blood pouring from the ragged hole that once had been her lower right arm. On the other side of the pit was the German, who had also been struck by the blast and had slid upright into the hole. He too bled profusely, from the stump below his knee. Spontaneously, both Mia and the German aimed their rifles at each other, but the German was too weak to hold his upright, and it dropped to the side. Mia turned her attention to Sasha, called out "Medic" a second time, and seized the mutilated arm, squeezing it above the hemorrhaging wound. "Medic, Medic!" she kept screaming, glancing over her shoulder.

The German was still alive, and now he simply moaned, in a German that even she could understand, *"Hilf mir, O Gott. Hilf mir."* She saw now that the front of his tunic was sodden with blood, so he must have also had a stomach wound. He stared at her and lifted one hand weakly, pointing a limp finger toward his pistol, still in its holster at his belt. *"Hilf mir,"* he repeated. *"Töte mich, Kamarad. Bitte."*

But at that moment she cared only about Sasha, who was panting through clenched teeth, obviously in agony. She stared at Mia with huge eyes, as if she knew something terrible.

"Medic!" Mia screamed again, watching the blood still trickle from the ruined arm that she could not grip tightly enough. It poured in a constant stream to the bottom of the pit and joined the pool of blood from the hemorrhaging German. Even in the terror and excitement of the moment, she saw the irony of the two bloods mixing.

"Hang on, my friend. Just a little longer." Just then the medic arrived and crawled in next to her to tie off Sasha's arm. "Help me lift her onto the stretcher," the medic ordered, and Mia obeyed, clambering next to her with the quivering form of Sasha between them. When they slid her onto the stretcher, she went limp.

Behind Mia the German had begun to sob. "*Hilf mir, Mama, bitte.*"

As she stood up to sprint with the stretcher bearers to the rear, she still heard him behind her in the pit. "*Mama...Mama...*"

❖

Deeply shaken, holding Sasha's good hand, Mia ran with the stretcher some fifty yards until the captain-commissar blocked her and aimed her pistol squarely at Mia's chest. "Get back on the line, right now."

Mia came to her senses, and with a last look at Sasha, she spun around and jogged back to the front line that still advanced under fire into the town.

She charged forward with renewed frenzy, sensing her comrades around her. They stormed past the remains of buildings, and she crouched sometimes, taking aim and picking off soldiers in green. The battle raged, it seemed, for hours, and she had just leaped up for another sprint when an enemy shell hit behind her, blasting mountains of dirt and debris into the air. The dust stung her eyes, and she coughed as she glanced over her shoulder toward the comrades coming up behind her.

All she could see in the smoke was the heap of rubble that had just fallen behind her and something pale that jutted out from the bottom of it. A hand that scratched the ground.

She scrambled toward it, tore away dirt and powdered brick, clawed doglike at the suffocating pile. An arm became visible, the sleeve torn but bloodless. Then a shoulder, and finally a head, a dirt-smeared face that gasped for air and coughed out filthy mucus.

"Comrade Commissar? Are you all right?" Mia continued brushing away debris.

Captain Semenova sat up panting and wiped dirt from her eyes. Then she seemed to remember something and twisted away from Mia to claw through the rubble. "My pouch! We must find my pouch. My party membership card…" A leather strap appeared close by her hand, and she snatched it up, pulling the pouch out from under the dirt. "I'm fine now," she finally answered, staggering to her feet. "Continue the attack, soldier."

The rescue had taken only a few minutes, and in that time, the front line had moved into the town. She caught up to them, advancing cautiously, although the defending Germans seemed to have melted away. Skirmishes took place in front of her as clusters of men were uncovered, but it was clear, the main group had retreated. They had taken the town.

By early evening, the troops amassed in an open square, each platoon reporting to its leader, waiting for the sappers to search for mines and traps. It had started to rain, and Mia crouched, somber, with her own group, her arms around herself. Her only thought was Sasha.

Her mind drifted to the mortally wounded German, injured by the same grenade that struck Sasha. Was he still alive in his pit, still calling for his mother while the rain poured down on him? The thought made her physically sick.

She squatted under a tarp with the men until, two hours later, they were assigned buildings to quarter in. Field rations were only dry biscuits, so she postponed eating. She needed to find out about Sasha. And about the others, for that matter.

She approached the platoon leader. "Request permission to look for a friend, Comrade Sergeant."

But Commissar Semenova, who seemed to be everywhere, had overheard. "No one's to leave their assigned bivouac. Understood?"

Cowed, she backed away and returned to her spot. She sat, frustrated and worried, but finally exhaustion overcame anxiety, and she dropped off to sleep leaning against her pack. But a few hours later, someone shook her by the shoulder.

"You, Zhurova, are you wounded?" The platoon leader pointed to her left leg that was soaked with blood. She realized with disgust that her blood had seeped down into her trousers.

"Do you need to go to the medical station?" he asked impatiently.

Medical station. A way to find out about Sasha. "Yes, Comrade Sergeant. Shrapnel wound."

"Go on over then, and get yourself bandaged. It's the building at the corner, where the lights are. Then report back here for orders."

"Yes, Comrade Sergeant." Still carrying her rifle, she lurched toward the spot where lanterns were hanging, the first floor of a building whose upper floor had been blasted by artillery. Stretcher bearers were plodding toward it carrying a wounded man between them.

As she strode into the medical station a figure turned around to face her. It was Alexia. And just behind her, Kalya. The relief she felt seeing them drained when she registered their drawn expressions.

"Sasha?"

"Dead. Fatima, too." Alexia pulled her out of the way of the stretcher bearers.

The two women who'd saved her from torture and death. Gone. The news hit her like a stone. She stood awhile with her friends, staring vacantly at the medics, nurses, stretcher bearers, moving in and out of the station. There was no point in asking what happened. War happened.

"Where are you quartered?" she asked the others numbly, not wanting to leave them.

"Never mind that," Alexia said. "Are you wounded?" Like the captain, she pointed at Mia's pant leg.

"No. Menstrual blood. I need to wash, but how? Where?"

Obviously relieved to have another task to tend to, Kalya took her by the arm and pivoted her around. "There's a well over there. Come on. We'll get some water, and you can clean up in the latrine." She snatched up a bucket from outside the medics' station.

It was a good solution that took their minds off their dead comrades. Setting her full bucket on the ground in a corner of the latrine, with her friends standing guard, Mia wiped down the top of her trousers, then dropped them to wash herself. The second half of the original bandage was still in her pocket and she tied it in place, rinsing out the blood-soaked portion with the last of the water. She would have found the whole procedure disgusting at home, but she recalled the blood pool in the grenade pit, the blood of the dying. This, at least was "living" blood, and cleaning it was a mere inconvenience.

"Come back with us for a while. Your sergeant won't be looking for you just yet."

"Yeah, I'd like that." She followed them to a shed close by the medical station. They leaned their three rifles against the wall and squatted on the ground. Kalya began to roll another cigarette, and Mia now understood the value of the habit. It might scorch your throat, but it soothed the mind to have something to do.

"At least the Fritzes have cleared out," Mia said weakly, just to break the silence.

"Yeah, but they make us pay for every kilometer they concede," Alexia said.

A woman came through the door and dropped down onto the floor next to them.

"Galina, finally off duty?" Kalya asked, and offered her a puff of her cigarette.

"Just for a few minutes." She took a long draw and handed it back. "Sorry about your sniper friends. If it's any comfort, Sasha went right after they brought her in, and Fatima was gone when she came in. Not much pain for either one. Be glad of that. I've also got a couple of burn patients. They're not going to make it either, but they've got some bad hours ahead before they're free."

"Yes. I guess I should be glad for small things. Burning. Uff. My worst fear." Kalya winced. "Anything but that."

Galina nodded. "Goes for animals, too. A few weeks ago, we'd set up a first-aid station next to some stables. The attack planes dropped incendiaries, and everything caught fire. The medics, even the walking wounded, ran to the stables to pull out the horses. Bad enough to watch our men die, but it seemed even worse to hear the screaming of the horses. Anyhow, we got 'em out. Every one of them."

Mia was faintly cheered by the story. Some small rescue of the innocent. A temporary one, of course.

Galina stood up. "Time to go back on duty. I'm also going to give blood. It gets you an extra ration of sugar and meat. Did you know that?" Without waiting for an answer, she strode from the room.

Mia stood up as well. "I'd better return to my unit," she said glumly. "The commissar is watching me, and I have to be in place when the orders come. Bye, then."

"Yeah, bye. See you in the next shit spot on the map," Kalya said.

Mia wandered back across the square to her own bivouac, brooding, feeling the warmth of her own blood between her legs, hoping her flow would taper off the next day.

Blood. Given and lost. Galina's, hers, Sasha's, Fatima's and the dying German's. The war in microcosm.

CHAPTER EIGHTEEN

The next shit spot on the map was a village whose name Mia didn't learn. She only knew that a stream blocked their access to it and her platoon was holed up with the colonel in a house at the foot of the only bridge. The rest of the division spread out behind them, waiting for the way to be cleared.

The colonel peered from the window through binoculars and cursed. "According to the map, that's supposed to only be a stream. And if this were July instead of May, I suppose it would be."

Mia could see what he meant. The constant rain had caused it to rise and flow quickly, and there was no telling its depth. An old stone bridge had somehow remained intact, but the retreating Germans held it.

A machine-gun team was set up behind sandbags right at the bridgehead, providing an effective block. Even she knew they couldn't advance without artillery, and they no longer had artillery.

The colonel cursed again and spoke into his field telephone. "Send up one of the snipers." And while they waited, she peered from the corner of the window along the sight of her own rifle. She could see the two piles of sandbags and the muzzle of the machine gun protruding from the split between them, but nothing more. No sense in wasting her ammunition.

Some ten minutes later, Kalya crept up behind them. "Reporting, Comrade Colonel."

"Good. I need you to take out that machine gunner. Can you do it?"

"Yes, Comrade Colonel," she said automatically, and crouched below the window. She squinted into her rifle scope. "I can see between the sandbags, but he's careful to stay out of the way. I'll have to wait him out."

"Take as long as you need."

But at that moment two men emerged rolling a mortar across the bridge and setting it up next to the machine gun behind the sandbag piles. Only the tip and a hand that dropped a projectile into it were visible. A moment later, the mortar bomb struck the building they were in, and part of the wall to their right collapsed. Kalya fell back, struck on one side by brick and shrapnel, and her rifle flew out of her hand.

Mia dropped her own rifle and rushed to her side. Kalya raised a hand. "It's my shoulder. I can't feel anything in my arm. Shit. I'm useless."

Without thinking, Mia grabbed the fallen rifle and scrambled back to the window. Peering through the scope, she was astonished how clear everything was. She saw the enemy in bits and pieces, a green cap here, a helmet there, but all was beautifully in focus.

The German mortar team shouted triumphantly, and a pale hand dropped in a second projectile. It fired, rose in a short arc, and struck in much the same place as the first one had, pulverizing the remaining bricks. But through the scope, Mia could see the mortar man raise his head above the sandbags for a split second to see where his missile struck.

With unthinking calm, she caressed the trigger and the gun fired, jolting her slightly with its backward thrust. With her eye glued to the scope, she could see the soldier fall forward over his mortar. His companion lifted him off and shoved him to the side, but that gave her enough time to draw back the bolt and aim once again. The second man raised the projectile to drop it in, and she struck it, causing it to explode in his hand.

Just then she felt someone press in beside her. Alexia also took aim and fired through the split between the sandbags, killing the machine gunner as well. With the two heavy guns now silent, the Russian troops charged, and setting up a storm of fire, they streamed over the bridge.

❖

Another day, another village, another setting up of quarters for the night. The road sign, which miraculously had remained standing through all the years of the war, said KARMAYSHEVO, but since the Germans had torched the houses, the place was little more than a church and a scattering of barns. The medical station and the officers laid claim to all of them.

Mia was assigned with her infantry squad to a patch of ground that had been a pasture. Now it was an expanse of mud, and they sheltered from the constant rain under a series of tarpaulins stretched over a framework of wood. Without dry wood, a fire was impossible, so the men huddled together for warmth. Mia unashamedly leaned against a man whose name she didn't know.

She was sorry she didn't smoke, for the men seemed to draw some comfort from their foul-smelling cigarettes and warmed one hand over the glowing ash when they weren't puffing on them.

"Comrade Zhurova," someone said, and it took a moment for her to react. Glancing up, she saw it was Colonel Borodin, and she struggled to her feet. She saluted as smartly as she could while shivering, noticing a moment later that he was accompanied by Alexia.

"Congratulations for your sharpshooting today. You and Senior Corporal Mazarova made it possible for us to move one village farther west. Keep that up, and we'll end up in Berlin."

"Yes, Comrade Colonel. It took me by surprise, too."

"I see that you still have Senior Corporal Petrova's weapon. Well, if you can shoot that well with a sniper's rifle, I'm assigning it to you until she returns to duty. Then we'll see about another one for you. In the meantime, we're transferring you to the sniper squad. Senior Corporal Mazarova has requested you as her spotter."

Mia saluted again. "Thank you, Comrade Colonel. Request permission to visit Corporal Petrova in the medical station."

"Permission granted." The colonel saluted quickly and strode away from them.

Alexia embraced her awkwardly, impeded by their heavy coats and rifles. "Well done, you. Who would have thought, eh?"

"Certainly not me. How's Kalya? Have you seen her?"

"Not yet, but one of the stretcher bearers said she was sitting up and smoking, so she's not dead yet. Come on. The med station's over there in the church. Lucky devils have a roof over their heads."

The church was dry, but that was all it was. The folding beds they'd had in the previous village had not been brought over yet, so the two dozen wounded lay on blankets on the floor.

A few wooden benches, odd remainders of those used years before by parishioners, were piled up in the rear, though some of the soldiers were smashing them to fuel the fire that burned just outside the door. The altar, such as it was, had long ago been cleared of religious objects and now held bundles of bandages and bottles of disinfectant.

They walked along the rows of wounded on the floor until they found Kalya, leaning against her backpack and trying with one hand to roll a cigarette. Alexia knelt beside her.

"Let me do that for you. You're making a mess of it." She took hold of Kalya's tiny sack of mahorka tobacco and shook a line of it into the folded paper. She rolled it slowly, and her trembling hands revealed she was more worried than her banter suggested.

Mia squatted next to her. "So what the hell happened? I wasn't paying attention, and suddenly you were on the ground. Are they going to ship you back?"

Kalya accepted Alexia's somewhat uneven cigarette roll and held it in her mouth while she lit it. She inhaled, blinking from the harsh smoke, and sighed. "Not sure. Something hit my arm and broke it. Shrapnel, maybe, because it hurts like hell. They'll send me to the nearest surgical unit to clean it up. I should be back in two weeks, with luck."

Alexia shook her head. "With *luck*, you'll be sent home for a good rest. In the meantime, Marina here has surprised us all by being a crack shot. She'll take your place until you're ready to come back."

Mia laid a hand lightly on Kalya's good shoulder. "They gave me your rifle, but don't worry. I promise I'll take good care of it. I'll oil it, keep it dry, all the things they tell you."

"You better, because I'm coming back for it. You're not going to Berlin without me."

"Wouldn't think of it."

The assurance had come from Mia spontaneously, but the word Berlin caught her up short. She hadn't thought of that. She hadn't thought of the future at all and now had to consider the possibility of being trapped in the Red Army until victory, whenever that would be.

"All right, you two. Clear out. You can't hole up here all night just to stay out of the rain." It was one of the nurses, and she was serious.

"Yes, comrade. Just give us a minute." Alexia rolled another cigarette and slipped it into Kalya's shirt pocket. "We'll check on you tomorrow if they haven't moved you out." She kissed Kalya on the forehead. Mia would like to have done so, too, but it seemed presumptuous. Instead, she once again touched Kalya's good shoulder. "Think of us while you're in your clean bed eating hot food. And hurry back."

Kalya stared up at them, wan, as the nurse returned and hustled them out of the church.

As they stood on the stone steps outside, a private rushed up to them. "Comrades, have you heard the news? The Americans landed this morning in France."

"Hurrah!" Alexia hugged her suddenly, a long, tight, wonderful hug.

When she released her hold, Mia beamed. "Thank God! Finally I'm not the only American fighting north of Italy."

She thought of President Roosevelt poring over his maps, of Churchill, grumbling about the lack of landing craft, of Stalin's endless reproaches. And now, in the fourth year of the war, the Western allies had finally come through.

"Better late than never."

CHAPTER NINETEEN

June 1944

As the weeks rolled by, marked by small and costly victories, Mia realized she liked being a sniper, if for no other reason than that they were privileged. They were too valuable to be used as cannon fodder, and the colonel kept them in reserve until after the initial attack. When the enemy dug in and set their own best marksmen on their pursuers, they were called up. Then it was a contest between experts, countering skill with skill, guile with guile. So far, she'd come out each time on top and now had her own collection of spent shells.

This evening, she slouched on her pack in the hovel they'd been bivouacked in outside of Pskov, and before she fell asleep she glanced around at the comrades who, through skill or just plain luck, still remained.

Curiously, they didn't swagger or try to outdo each other in prowess, other than the implicit competition of scorekeeping. And there was nothing masculine in their demeanor. When they were off duty, sitting among themselves, most talked of girlish things: parents; fiancés or flirtations; the dresses, makeup, hair styles they would wear again when the war was over.

And since the mortar elimination at the bridge, when she'd gained her sniper stripes, something had changed in her. Or changed again, since the dull-witted accountant who had accepted a job at the White House had fallen away in stages. She had been a victim multiple times— of her father's abuse, of Grushenka's deception, of a false accusation of murder, of blackmail, of Molotov's attempted murder. The injustices had piled up and could have crushed her. But now she had recovered her vision and a rifle, and it seemed nothing could hurt her.

And then there was Alexia.

The original attraction had been her striking Slavic beauty, an idealized symbol of a past Mia could scarcely remember. But unlike Grushenka, who had merely aroused her in the most vulgar manner, Alexia had an elegance and a restraint. Over the weeks of shared hardship, something wonderful had evolved that she couldn't quite define. She watched Alexia, sleeping a few feet away. She desired her, of that she was certain, but more than that, she felt profound allegiance to her. She understood now that soldiers did not die for the homeland, but for each other.

The door to the hovel flew open, and at least four of the women reached for their rifles.

"Hey, hey! Take it easy, girls. It's me. Doesn't anyone recognize me, or have I gotten too fat on my mother's cooking?"

"Kalya, you vixen! How are you?"

Mia leapt to her feet, along with most of the other women, and hugged her. "Why did they let you come back so soon?"

"What a question. They brought me back because I'm a damned fine shot, and the rest of you are just not up to snuff."

Klavdia pounded her back. "But your score is way behind now, old girl." She laughed. "Come on, sit down. Tell us about home and we'll tell you about the war."

Even in the darkness of the hovel, lit only by a few shell-case lamps, Mia could see that Kalya was flushed with happiness. They sat down in a circle leaning on their packs and began to talk like sisters. Focused on the new arrival, Mia was surprised to feel the pressure of another shoulder against hers.

"Alexia," she said, pleased at the touch. "It's good to have her back, isn't it?"

"Yes, it is. I wonder if they'll pair us up again."

Only then did Mia remember that Kalya was Alexia's spotter, and her joy faded to resentment.

❖

At three in the morning, Col. Borodin ordered his officers, and the half dozen snipers who remained, to his headquarters. He was somber.

"Comrades. As most of you know, Pskov is at least a thousand years old and has been in Russian hands since Alexander Nevsky took it back from the German knights in the thirteenth century. Today we face the Germans again, but the blood of Alexander Nevsky runs in our veins. The enemy has blockaded himself behind the walls of the old Kremlin of Pskov, and we do not have the luxury of being able to lure him out onto a frozen lake." Soft laughter rippled through the room from those who had seen the Eisenstein film of Nevsky's icy victory set to Prokofiev's music.

The colonel unfolded a map on his table that held a rough outline of the city and tapped the relevant part. "The citadel where they have their own marksmen posted has six towers, and I'm assigning a sniper team under each one, to knock them out. Mazarova, you're on the big tower and Zhurova will be your spotter. Petrova and Yefremovna are on tower two." He continued down the list of assignments.

It took Mia a moment to realize she'd been paired with Alexia, while Kalya, for reasons known only to the colonel, was working— with a new rifle—with Klavdia.

The colonel's voice drew her back. "It's important for all of you to take up position before daylight, so you should start out now."

"Understood, Comrade Colonel." All of the snipers saluted and made an about-face.

As they marched from the headquarters, they passed Commissar Semenova. She eyed them, as if to make sure they understood their duty. Mia stared back at her with puzzlement. Semenova had never acknowledged being saved from suffocation and harped obsessively on the "not one step back" policy. Perhaps because it was in the rear of the charge that she had been buried alive.

The snipers lined up first at the quartermaster's, who issued them rag capes. Drawing them over their heads, they looked like marching mounds of detritus.

Separating from the other teams, Mia and Alexia made their way to the designated spot below the first tower. The moonless sky concealed them but also made it necessary for them to grope their way along the ground.

The towers themselves loomed up, black against the pale, predawn sky, remainders of an age when only a handful of precision archers, the medieval version of snipers, could repel ground forces by shooting through a single long slit high on the wall.

Alexia and Mia crawled to a spot some two hundred meters from the tower, which afforded a good shooting angle.

Under one of the clusters of low bushes below the tower, they dug a T-shaped trench and covered it with brush. Alexia took position along the mid-line of the T, while Mia leaned against the ridge at the rear of the trench.

By the time they finished, the sky was peach-colored and stained at the horizon by reds and oranges. The first bird sounded, and some small dark thing zipped past them on the wing. Mia smiled. *Stupid bird doesn't know there's a war on.*

Confident of their invisibility, she leaned her head back and savored the quiet June morning. As the sun rose, it illuminated the top of the tower, changing its black to a warm earth tone.

In the increasing light, they both studied the archer's slot. Alexia drew back one side of the hood of her camouflage cape. "He's well-protected," she observed in a low voice. "But he has very little range unless he stands at the center of the opening, and then we can get him."

"Theoretically yes, the distance is manageable. But we'll have only a split second to hit him, and he knows it."

They settled in, trying to rest and stay alert at the same time. The damp earth was cold but would warm under the June sun. Mia peered up at the sniper's slot through her binoculars, Alexia through her rifle scope, and though they both focused elsewhere, Mia sensed the intimacy of their first time alone together. "I love the quiet, don't you?" she murmured, keeping her eyes fixed on the tower.

Alexia remained immobile, her eye two centimeters from her scope. "I do, too. No gunfire yet. A perfect spring morning. A shame we can't all have a picnic. We could invite our friend up there."

"Except he's under the same orders we are." Mia let a minute pass in silence. Then, "Do you sometimes resent having to choose the lesser of two evils and follow someone you don't respect? I don't mean the colonel. I mean the top leaders."

"It's treason to talk that way, you know." More silence. "But, yes. I thought I knew what to respect. All the things a priest once taught me.

But now I don't anymore. I sometimes don't care about anyone. What about you?"

"I care about you."

Alexia did not respond, and Mia realized she'd taken a step too far. "Look. I've been meaning to tell you. That time in Moscow, when you helped me back to the embassy and I grabbed you. I'm sorry I forced myself on you. It was pretty crude, and I'm embarrassed by it now. It was the alcohol."

Alexia glanced sideways. "Don't apologize. It gave me a lot to think about."

"Really? You weren't shocked?"

"Of course I was shocked. I always wondered how it would have been if I *wasn't* surprised."

Mia stifled a snicker. The solution was obvious. She took a breath and ignored her pounding heart. "I can kiss you again like that, and then you'll know."

A faint sound of steel on stone interrupted their banter, and Alexia instantly set her eye against her scope. "Our mark. He's up there."

Mia peered through her binoculars up at the archer's vent. All she could see was the tip of a rifle, pointed downward and moving slowly from side to side, scanning the land.

"He's looking for us, but the vent is too narrow for him to get a real sweep unless he leans right up against it." Mia kept her voice low, though it was nearly impossible for them to be heard high in the tower.

"Frustrating," Alexia muttered against her rifle stock. "I keep catching glimpses of his hand, but that's all. If he would only lean forward a bit, just for a second."

Mia still sat against the rear of the pit, knees supporting her forearms that held the binoculars. She was more exposed and depended completely on her camouflage. If he spotted her, he'd have a clear shot to her chest.

"Damn. He's pulled back," Alexia grumbled. "He can't be leaving his position."

"No, look. There's his hand again. He's holding a mirror to the side of the vent so he can get a good look without exposing himself. Very clever."

"You're right. When he turns it a certain way, I can see his reflection."

Peering through her binoculars until he turned the mirror to just the right angle, Mia studied his face. He was a beauty. "He's clean shaven," she said quietly. "And young. His skin must be soft. And look at those lips," she murmured, resuming the game. "He must kiss beautifully."

"Not as good as you," Alexia said without moving her head. The remark hung deliciously in the air.

"So, you did like my kiss, in spite of the surprise." Mia kept her eye glued to the target. Under the magnification, it almost seemed the German marksman could look back at her and hear her talking.

"Yes," Alexia murmured. "Quite a lot."

Mia let another moment pass, examining the implications. "I have better kisses than that." Up in the tower window, the German marksman licked his lips, as if he'd heard the remark, then lifted his cap to wipe his forehead with his cuff. "Look at him. He's blond, too, like you. A real Übermensch."

"I see him." Alexia's voice was muffled by the stock of her own rifle pressed close to her cheek. "Are there better and worse kisses?"

The German kept repositioning himself, and Mia had to keep bringing him into focus again. It was making her eyes water. "Of course. Sweet or passionate, rough or tender. But you know that, surely."

"I do. I just want to hear you say it. Looking at our handsome major up there, I'd say he likes the rough ones."

"You don't?"

"No, not usually." Alexia drew back from the scope and wiped the tearing from her eyes. "Not at the beginning."

"Good point." Mia rotated her shoulders to keep from stiffening. "Besides, on certain places one would want to be tender. Look. He's put down the mirror. All I see now is the rifle barrel and occasionally a sliver of yellow just above it. But he keeps moving, never leaves enough time to get a shot off. Damn. This could go on for hours."

"We'll just wait until he gets careless. Tell me more about your kisses. Have you kissed many women? In those tender places?"

The German's rifle nozzle made another sweep, this time lower. Impossible that he could detect them, but he seemed to be aiming at them. Mia kept her binoculars focused on him, waiting.

"A few." Mia thought of Grushenka and the several women before her. "But none of them was important. Kissing you was important, and it should have been tender."

The German sniper disappeared again and reappeared, and his rifle nozzle repeated its sweep. Alexia shifted slightly, flexing her fingers. "Yes. I'd have liked that better."

Mia's face warmed at the turn the conversation was taking, but she didn't dare set down the binoculars. Up in the tower window, the German rifle suddenly pointed downward, as if he'd heard the last remark. "Has he spotted us?" Mia whispered.

"No. He's just trying to draw fire, to watch for a flash." Alexia's voice was muffled by the stock of her own rifle pressed close to her cheek."

"Would you? The next kiss will be tender, I promise."

"You plan on another one?"

"Fervently. Oh yes. I want so much to get to know you that way. To explore you."

The sun was higher now and shone directly on the tower so that the tiny, constantly moving fleck of blond hair seemed larger and brighter.

Alexia saw it, too. "It's like he knows we're here and he's teasing us, isn't it?" She sniffed. "Explore me. With kisses? How would you do that?"

"I'd search all over you with my lips, if you let me. Would you? Look, the rifle stock is visible now. He's leaning farther out."

"No. He moved back again. We waited too long."

Squinting through the field glasses, Mia felt her pulse pound. Blood rushed down her arms to her hands, and the magnified image she held in her sight twitched slightly with each heartbeat. "I've waited too long, too. I want to be with you, intimately. I could lose you at any moment in this war and want to know you and give you pleasure before that happens."

She tensed with arousal, or was it at the sight of the rifle sliding ever farther out of the tower vent? The marksman would be fully visible again any second.

"Feel me, darling. Feel my kiss on you." Mia whispered into the air.

Two shots rang out, and an iron-hot blow crashed through her shoulder. She gasped, unable to catch her breath.

Swooning, she sensed a wet warmth spreading over her chest, then someone's hands grasping her under her arms and pulling her farther into the brush. Pain struck in fierce radiations, like fire through her back and chest, and she suddenly could not get enough air. More shots, it seemed from all directions, but her pain-seared and oxygen-starved brain made no sense of it. She fainted, then came to as she was dragged along the ground. Finally, she was lifted onto a stretcher, and she passed out again.

❖

She came to in the medical tent as someone cut up through the center of her tunic. She recognized Galina. "What happened?" she wheezed, glancing down at her blood-soaked undershirt. Alexia stood on the other side of the cot holding her hand, but breathing took up more of Mia's attention. She could feel her chest rise and fall, but each breath took in only part of the air she needed.

Galina poked around the wound, causing Mia to scream with pain. "Looks like a broken clavicle and maybe a fractured scapula. Your shortness of breath means you've also got a collapsed lung. You're lucky, though. The bullet exited again, so we don't have to dig for it. Unfortunately, the pneumothorax means we can't give you any morphine for the ambulance ride tomorrow morning. All I can do in the meantime is immobilize your shoulder."

"Ambulance ride?" She gasped and took another shallow breath. "Where?"

"The hospital at Novgorod. It's a long trip, but they have an X-ray machine and can see if they need to intervene surgically. They'll tube you to help the pneumothorax, too. You just have to hang on."

Galina cut away the undershirt, washed the area around the wound, and wrapped the shoulder in gauze, though every touch was excruciating. A dozen other wounded men called out to her, so she gently squeezed Mia's good arm as a brief comfort, then turned away to the next soldier.

Alexia knelt on the ground next to her cot holding her hand. "It's best if you try to sleep."

"They're going…to send…me back to Moscow," she said, taking a shallow breath after every few words.

"They can't hurt you, darling." She held Mia's hand up to her lips. "You have another identity. And when you get well, tell them who you are so you can contact your embassy."

"But you…I'll lose you." Pain was clouding her mind and reducing her to the most primitive of needs.

"The army's moving fast, and in a few months the war should be over. I'll find you through the embassy. I'll find you no matter what, I promise. And tomorrow, I'll come back here before they send me out on duty."

"I love you, Alexia." Mia tried to lift Alexia's hand to her chest, but every movement was agony.

"Believe me, I—"

"Senior Corporal Mazarova!" The commissar and two other officers in NKVD uniforms marched toward them. "You are under arrest for deserting your post."

CHAPTER TWENTY

Ferocious pain from her ruined shoulder, despair for Alexia, and shortness of air kept Mia awake all night. She kept trying to recall what had happened to bring down such multiple disasters but couldn't piece together the fragments. At the first glimmer of morning, the nurse came to help her to the toilet, then left her to tend to the ones more gravely injured.

She lay in a stupor, concentrating on taking each breath, trying to shut out the pain and the questions, until a figure loomed over her.

"Kalya. Thank God…Tell me…what happened. Alexia, desertion? Not possible. Must be…mistake."

"Klavdia and I couldn't really tell what was going on. We got our targets on tower two right away and came to back you up at tower one. It took us a while to crawl close to your position because we could see a hand with a mirror and were afraid he might spot us in it."

"The mirror…yes."

"From what we could see, you exchanged fire with the German, and you were hit. Alexia dragged you out of range, and that was the problem. We got the sniper, but it should have been Alexia. That tower was her job."

"But…who…reported it? Not you!" The thought of their betrayal horrified her.

"Of course not. How can you ask? No, Commissar Semenova was watching, to see if we carried out the order."

"Semenova. Bitch…And I saved her life. So…what's…the punishment?"

Ominously, Kalya did not answer.

Galina appeared behind her. "Sorry, Kalya. You'll have to leave. The ambulances are here."

❖

The vehicle rocked along the pitted roads toward Novgorod, and she recalled her first ambulance ride with Marina. This time German Stukas were not going to save her. She stared at the metal roof, body and soul in purgatory. The lack of morphine meant ferocious pain rushed through her at every jolt in the road. In moments of lucidity, all she could think of was that she'd found Alexia and lost her again, perhaps to execution. And she was the cause of it.

Injustice rang through her pounding brain. Her torment, the moaning of the others in the ambulance, Alexia's condemnation, Sasha's death, Marina's death, the countless other deaths along the Soviet advance. This, surely, was purgatory. Ivan's words came back to her. "It's not God that I don't accept. Only I most respectfully return him the ticket."

It made no difference now whether she got home or Molotov found her and finished her off. In the middle of the Eastern Front, she had found the love of her life, and all was taken away.

She longed suddenly to talk to Harry Hopkins, or Lorena, or even the First Lady. They seemed so wise. Abruptly, she recalled the happy Christmas celebration at the White House and the pious little speech the visiting pastor had given. What was his name? Pastor Bain... something. It made no difference. The man was a fool.

He'd insisted that free will was the cause of suffering, that people inevitably made bad choices. How facile that was. People didn't choose war; their leaders did. The Christmas lesson, he'd said, was to love one another, to counter argument with a kiss.

If every movement and breath didn't hurt, she would have laughed out loud. A kiss, the mere talk of a kiss, had gotten her shot and Alexia, possibly, condemned to death.

She fell into a haze as close to sleep as she would experience for the next several bleak days.

❖

The diagnosis at the hospital in Novgorod was no surprise: pneumothorax caused by penetration at the shoulder. Air entering the thoracic cavity caused a partial collapse of the top right lobe. The Moscow surgeon inserted a tube between the second and third ribs to draw out the air that prevented the full inflation of the right lung.

The surgeon, a gray-haired woman, came to visit her briefly when she regained consciousness. "How do you feel?"

"Breathing's a little better, but not a lot. I still can't take a deep breath. Will it ever get any better?"

"It should. We've relieved some of the pressure." She indicated the loop of clear plastic that rose from a hole over Mia's right breast. "But it will take a while for the lung to reattach itself, and in this case, you have other damage from the bullet to that area, so it will go very slowly."

"Other damage? It feels like someone's hammering on an anvil inside my shoulder."

"We had to clean out a lot of debris from the wound—bits of bone from the broken clavicle, fibers from your uniform, a little dirt as well. Any of those can cause an infection. The X-ray also revealed that your shoulder blade is fractured, so we've bandaged you tight to keep the shoulder immobilized. As soon as the pneumothorax begins to heal, we'll put you in a cast and move you back to a facility near Moscow. Your pay book shows that Moscow's your home, so you should be glad."

"Home? Uh, yes. Moscow. Right. So how long before that happens?"

"A week, ten days? Depends on you. Sorry. I've got to leave now. Call the nurse if you need anything." With a reassuring tap on her good shoulder, the doctor strode away.

❖

Having at least a slight improvement of air intake, and the knowledge that her broken bones would eventually heal, Mia could move on to the next source of anxiety, Alexia.

Desperate to find out what had happened to her, Mia sought any source of information about events at the front, even asking the nurse for a copy of *The Red Star*.

But the Red Army newspaper held only propaganda and news of advances, medals awarded for heroism, and an endless stream of victories. No mention of courts-martial, desertions, or executions. Of course not. What was she thinking?

She sent a field post to Kalya asking what had happened to Alexia but never received an answer. The following week a letter to Klavdia met the same silence. If Alexia had been executed, would they even have dared to contact her?

For lack of news about Alexia, she concentrated on being Marina Zhurova. From Marina's pay book, she'd long ago learned the details of her life. She reviewed every entry, built up a life from it, and could almost imagine Marina's childhood. It was probably not much different from her own, although Marina had joined the Young Pioneers at the age of twelve, while Mia was on her way to America.

After a week, she could indeed breathe better but had to return to surgery for another cleaning of the wound, which simply refused to heal. Perhaps her lethargy was the cause. Why recover? Who would she be recovering for?

But ten days after that, the hospital made it clear she was no longer in danger and more gravely injured soldiers needed her bed. So they encased her shoulder in a cast that held her bent right arm out from her body and ordered her removed to a recuperation facility outside Moscow.

Transport was by hospital train, though, as an ambulatory patient, she enjoyed no benefits. A nurse simply helped her up the steps into a normal second-class railroad car, ushered her to a seat, and handed her sausage and bread wrapped in newspaper for the five-hundred-kilometer ride to Moscow.

The men and few women around her talked and smoked cheerfully, knowing they were on their way home and that almost no chance remained of their train being strafed en route. She smiled when smiled at, replied in desultory fashion when spoken to, but she was so very weary of the war.

Sixteen hours later, the train pulled into Belorussky Station north of Moscow, and nurses helped her down from the car. She lined up with the others on crutches and shuffled along to the square outside, where trucks waited to take them to a convalescent facility. She briefly contemplated fleeing but simply lacked the strength.

Only when she was assigned a bed in a large ward did she learn the name, Botkin Hospital, where a wing had been adapted as a rehabilitation center, with the intention of returning lightly injured soldiers to the front.

She sat for a long while on the edge of her bed before a nurse came to assist her. The nurse perused the shoulder cast, then ensured that the side table held a pitcher of water and that her belongings were stowed in a straw bin under the bed. "Looks like you're pretty much able to take care of yourself," she observed.

"How long will I be here?"

"Until the army decides you can go back to the front," the nurse said, scribbling something on her chart.

"You mean rejoin the unit I was in?" How could that be? She couldn't hold a rifle. She could barely get her pants on and off to use the toilet.

"I don't know. They may just reassign you where they can use you. That's up to the army to decide." She helped Mia lift her feet and lie back on the bed. "The toilet's over there." She pointed toward the end of the ward on the right and strode off.

Mia glanced around. The ward held some forty other patients, and they seemed to range from mobile patients with damaged limbs or faces to others who appeared comatose.

Mia herself lay back, morose and defeated, until she dozed off. She was awakened by the distant sound of a telephone ringing. Somewhere on the floor was a telephone. Could she get to it at some point and call the embassy? If she could reach Harriman, he could send Robert with the embassy car, and once she was out of the control of the military, under the protection of Harriman, Molotov wouldn't be able to touch her.

But she had never needed to call the ambassador on her visits to Moscow and would have to locate a telephone book for the number.

When the nurse came again at the end of the day, she asked innocently, "I heard a phone ringing. Is there a phone on this floor?"

"Yes, the internal line, between the nurses' stations."

"Can the nurses call outside the hospital?"

"Heavens, no. That would never be permitted. The only line to the outside is through the director's office. Why do you ask?"

Mia thought fast. "Oh, I thought if I can't shoot my rifle any more, I might volunteer as a telephonist. But I have to learn more about telephones first."

The nurse patted her hand. "You have plenty of time to think about that, my dear. So just rest and let your shoulder get better. The men in charge will know what to do with you."

That's exactly what I fear.

What about simply revealing her true identity and asking the hospital to contact the embassy? But the doctor in charge would certainly notify the military authorities of the false identity—a serious military crime—long before contacting the embassy. By the time word got to Harriman, if it ever did, she would again be in the hands of the NKVD.

As she lay brooding for another night, she wondered how far Botkin Hospital was from the embassy. She knew it was somewhere in the north of Moscow, but even if she could figure out the route, could she walk the distance? Certainly not in the next days. But maybe in a week? She touched the plaster cast that fixed her shoulder in place, with her elbow awkwardly elevated. That would be the main problem. Her uniform trousers and boots were under the bed in her original pack, which had followed her from the medical station in Pskov, but her tunic, which she'd kept, was cut from waist to armpit, and she wore a hospital gown. Her coat was also in the kit, but she could slide it on only over one arm, and the rest hung down her back. Even if she didn't chill in the breezy September weather, it would be impossible to walk along Moscow streets without attracting attention.

She was trapped.

❖

A day passed, and then another, and the monotony made them all seem the same. She knew the dates only when *The Red Star* was passed around. Only the patient population changed. It was a convalescent hospital, so most were reposted to the front, as the man next to her had been.

But a few souls belonged in intensive care and not convalescence, having obviously arrived by mistake. One such man was installed in the neighboring bed during the night. One of his arms was amputated at the shoulder, and bandages covered his eyes and the top of his head. He was unconscious.

The nurse came by to check on him, and when she noticed Mia watching, she shook her head mournfully. This one wouldn't last long.

But during the night, he gained consciousness, and his moaning woke Mia from her own troubled sleep. "Where am I? My arm hurts so much, and my head. Why can't I see?"

Mia sat up and faced him, then bent forward to touch him. "You're in a hospital in Moscow, and they're taking good care of you. They'll take off the bandages soon, and you can go home." She was amazed at how easily the lie came.

To her shock, he reached up with his good hand. "Olga, is that you?"

With only the briefest hesitation, she clasped his hand with her own good one. "Yes, it's Olga."

"Oh, I *knew* you'd come. I've missed you so much. I had to leave for the front without ever kissing you. But we're together again. Can I kiss you now?"

She was struck by a sudden flood of affection and sorrow for the man who was going to die without ever having loved. "Yes, of course." Keeping his hand in hers, so that he couldn't reach up and feel her plaster cast, she bent over him and pressed her lips against his.

It was a gentle, timid kiss, but it seemed to make him happy. "Oh, Olga," he said feebly. Do you still want me after all this?"

She didn't even know the poor man's name and so just whispered, "Yes, I do."

He clutched her hand again, and his head dropped back. She watched his chest rise and fall a few times in labored breathing, and then he fell still.

She lay back on her bed and broke into quiet sobs.

❖

Another week went by, and she followed the course of the war in *The Red Star*, allowing for the fact that it was mostly propaganda. Still, while the paper always glossed over losses, it did report that Paris had been liberated in August. The first great victory of the Western Allies.

She felt a rush of joy imagining American troops parading down the Champs-Élysées.

The new battle reports made vague references to "rapid advances" through Latvia and Romania, and she could more or less guess the location of Col. Borodin and his patchwork division. The Romanian army had just capitulated, abandoning its alliance with Germany to fight alongside the Soviets, and that, too, seemed a good sign, though she wondered how that worked out in real terms on the battlefield. Did the local commanders call their troops together and announce that henceforth they were to shoot only at the green uniforms and not at the brown ones?

She wished she could laugh but was too deep in ennui and despair.

"Good news!" the nurse chirped as she made one of her rare appearances by Mia's bed. "We have a visitor. Someone to cheer us all up."

"Really? Who is that?" The sudden thought it might be someone from the Kremlin caused her to panic. It would be the end of the charade. Could she hide in the toilet the whole time he was present?

"A great hero, and she's coming especially to see the infantrymen." The nurse brushed smooth the sheet at the end of Mia's bed.

She? The word took away some of the fear, and Mia searched her mind to find someone who fit the description. One of the ace pilots, perhaps? They were in the headlines a lot. Her attention was suddenly drawn to the far end of the ward by the mix of voices and footsteps. The double doors of the ward opened, and the hero strode in.

"Major Lyudmila Pavlichenko," the nurse announced.

CHAPTER TWENTY-ONE

Mia cursed to herself and tried uselessly to slip farther down under her bed covering. The irony was excruciating. After months of fighting on the front and some four weeks in various hospitals, she was about to be exposed by someone she knew and liked.

Like friendly fire, identification by a cheerful comrade could be just as lethal as by the enemy. In the few seconds that passed as the major strode down the central aisle of the ward, a half dozen thoughts zipped through Mia's mind.

Would she be arrested? Almost certainly. Would Pavlichenko vouch for her? Why would she? All explanations would lead back to Molotov. Would she notify the ambassador and embroil the State Department in a charge of spying? That line of thought was bleak indeed.

The inner debate ended when Pavlichenko stepped up to the foot of her bed, ready to be introduced to "our own sniper, Marina Zhurova."

The hero of the Soviet Union must have been weary of introductions and of shaking hands and muttering encouragement, for she scarcely glanced up. Even after Mia held out her own good hand to shake, and they exchanged pleasantries, Pavlichenko looked at her for several long seconds before confusion clouded her expression.

Mia's hand shook, and she withdrew it while the nurse chattered on about what an honor it was, surely, for a beginner to meet the most famous woman sniper in all of Russia. Pavlichenko's face seemed to dull, and Mia dared not take her eyes from her.

After what seemed like hours, Pavlichenko nodded blandly and wished her a good recovery.

As the star sniper stepped back and resumed her circuit from bed to bed, Mia dropped back onto her pillow and released a long exhalation. Had the visitor recognized her? In the context of the hospital, apparently not. As the major disappeared through the door of the ward in the company of the hospital administrator and a coterie of military officers, Mia lay embittered by her helplessness.

She had to get out. Soon, perhaps within days, someone would come from the army, check her medical chart, and realize she was fit for duty of some sort. The next day, they'd send her off to some unit, where she would be trapped indefinitely. Alone. No. She returned to her escape plan. Not a good plan. A dreadful plan, in fact, but the only plan she had.

During the night, she would simply leave and walk as far south as possible. Judging by the way the light passed from one side of the ward to the other, she could roughly guess which way was south. Her field canteen was still in her pack under her bed, and she could fill it from the hospital pitcher. Food? Well, she could do without food for a couple of days. Without sleep, too, if necessary. And she would keep walking, asking directions judiciously, from children perhaps, and she would continue walking. At some point, she would reach Red Square, where the large hotels were, which were filled with Western journalists. And one of them would help her get to the embassy.

There, that was settled. Encouraged at finally having made a decision, she allowed herself to doze off.

Someone shook her foot, awakening her. She opened her eyes to Lyudmila Pavlichenko.

"You have one minute to tell me what the hell you are doing here and why I shouldn't denounce you. Start talking."

Mia took a breath, clearing her head, forming her thoughts to a sixty-second summary. "I came to Moscow for the White House, to investigate the theft of Lend-Lease materials. I found the thieves, a chain of command starting, I'm pretty sure, with Molotov. But when I tried to report them to the ambassador, Molotov had me arrested and put on a plane to be killed. But the plane was shot down, and I survived by joining a Red Army unit fighting in the area. I actually fought as a sniper, which you'll find ironic, and I'm here because I was wounded in action."

Pavlichenko blinked in disbelief at the fantastic tale. "Who is Marina Zhurova?"

"A comrade killed in the ambulance carrying us both to the hospital." She opened her mouth to add more detail, then realized it was unnecessary. "And I'm desperate to get back to the embassy."

Pavlichenko frowned as some of the narrative sank in. "Molotov? Theft? Are you sure?"

"Yes. You *have* to believe me and help me get out of here."

Pavlichenko shook her head. Nonetheless, she leaned forward and spoke softly. "Whatever the truth of your story, you see those men standing in the doorway at the end of the ward? That is Major General Kovpak and three officers from STAVKA. They are watching me talk to you, so I have to denounce you."

"What? I thought…" Mia stammered.

"Hush, and listen. So you have to act quickly. In about three hours, when I get back to my quarters, I will send someone with a motorcycle to the laundry exit on the south side of the hospital. You must be there at, say, ten o'clock. If you are not, he will leave again. At ten o'clock, I'll telephone my superior officer and say I saw you here, and after a lot of thought, I finally remembered who you were, and I'll give him your real name. After that, I have no idea what will happen, but by then you should be at your embassy. That's all I can do for you. Do you understand?"

Without waiting for an answer, she turned and marched back to the officers at the door.

Mia had no watch and so asked the nurse the time when she came by with the usual soupy stew that was supper. Seven o'clock. When the activity on the ward died down and it seemed like more than two hours had passed, she slipped on her boots, gathered up her coat and field pack in her good arm, and slipped through the doorway toward the toilets. There, she changed out of her hospital gown and back into her military trousers and boots. The tunic that had been cut open under the right arm up to the armpit hung like a shawl on one side of her, but her belt held it shut.

She had no idea where the laundry was but had at least determined north from south, and pressed on toward the south side of the hospital. She wandered endlessly along corridors, stepping out of sight whenever she heard someone approach.

Finally, on one of the lower levels, the smell of disinfectant and the creaking of cylinders turning told her she'd found the laundry. She waited as long as she dared, hoping for a chance to slip through the room unseen, but each time she peeked around the edge of the doorway, she saw women working. Finally, she simply stepped inside and strode past them.

The four haggard women with red hands and faces tending the machines glanced quizzically at her as she marched past them, but apparently they cared only about their duty to sterilize laundry and bandages. Security was outside their purview, and while they would certainly report seeing a woman in a shoulder cast pass through, they had no interest in stopping her.

Then she was outside. Because her coat covered only one shoulder and half of her chest, she shivered in the cool night air. It was also the first time in weeks she had walked any distance, let alone hurried, and she trembled with the exertion.

She waited, with no idea of the time. Surely she wasn't late, but would her rescuer be? She dared not pace, for fear of attracting attention, and so she huddled near the closed door, shifting from one foot to the other. How, she wondered, would she fit on the back of a motorcycle with her awkwardly protruding elbow?

Finally he arrived. Without stopping his motor, he turned off the headlight and glanced around, obviously searching for her. Relieved, she stepped out where he could see her.

He putted toward her and stopped. "Get in, quickly."

With a silent *thanks* to Major Pavlichenko, she saw it was a sturdy old M-72 motorcycle with a sidecar. She'd seen them at the front, usually with some sort of gun mounted on the sidecar, but this one was bare. All she had to do was clutch her coat and pack around her and step in.

The backward lurch as he took off jolted her shoulder, and she grunted. He careened around the corner in the darkness, and only when they were some distance from the hospital grounds did he turn on his headlight.

He was silent most of the way and she assumed he knew the route, but as they came close to the inner city of Moscow, he asked over his shoulder, "Where do you want to go?"

"The American Embassy, please," she replied, as if to a taxi driver. "Where's that?"

"Um..." She searched her mind for something to guide him. "It's called Spaso House, on Spasopeskovskaya Square, in the Arbat District." That's all she could remember.

"Ah, the Arbat. Of course," he said. "Nice place for the rich capitalists."

She wasn't sure what to reply, since a discussion of capitalism was, as the Americans said, beyond her pay grade. Whoever the driver was, he was almost certainly some poor sod struggling to keep body and soul together in wartime. And he was saving her life, so he was, at that moment, her best friend. "I guess so," she said vaguely, and bent forward against the cold.

Her open coat was all but useless, and the night air rushed across her, catching her hair and finding its way around her midriff. She shivered and her teeth chattered.

Finally, to her relief, Spaso House came into sight. He stopped near the front entrance, waited only until she clambered out of the sidecar, and then took off again. She stood alone, in her ragged, blood-soaked uniform, a coat that half covered her, a filthy knapsack, and a block of plaster of paris that held her right elbow in the air. Still shivering, she marched to the front door under the columned portico.

She banged on the door for a long time, until a uniformed guard, a corporal by his insignia, opened it. He gawked at her for a moment, and she realized what a sight she must have presented.

"What do you want, soldier?" the guard asked in English in spite of her uniform. Obviously he hadn't been assigned to the post on the basis of intelligence. She answered him in English.

"My name is Mia Kramer. Ambassador Harriman will know me. Would you please tell him I'm here and need his help?"

"I'm sorry, but the ambassador's not here. I'll be happy to announce you to the deputy ambassador, but he's asleep right now. Please come back tomorrow morning."

She was cold and losing patience. "Look, even if the deputy ambassador has retired early with his chocolate milk, there must be

other staff members still awake who can identify me." She searched
her memory. Who had been present at the brief breakfasts? No one.

"Wait. The ambassador's driver. Robert something." The corporal
remained unmoved. "Robert...Dunham? No, Dornwend. Robert
Dornwend. He'll know me."

"Mr. Dornwend is off duty now and in his quarters. You can talk
to him tomorrow morning." He was about to close the door when she
stepped forward and blocked it with her good hand. Immediately he
drew his sidearm and pointed it at her. "Take your hand off the door or
I'll shoot."

That was the last straw. "Look, you stupid shit. I work for Harry
Hopkins and the White House and have important business with your
ambassador. You can see what kind of shape I'm in. If you don't let me
in, I'll have your sorry ass busted to civilian, and you'll spend time in
Leavenworth for obstructing White House business. Now, if you won't
wake your candy-assed deputy ambassador, then at least go get Robert
Dornwend. Surely you're not afraid of *him*."

Stunned, he lowered his pistol but still held the door three-quarters
shut and seemed to consider the remote possibility she was right. "Stay
here while I check if Mr. Dornwend is available."

"Tell him it's Kramer," she called through the closing door. "Mia
Kramer!"

She waited again, stamping one foot and then the other, for
warmth. She was close, so close. Five minutes passed. Ten minutes.
She couldn't measure them except by the throbbing in her shoulder.
Twenty throbs per minute. She grew ever more furious. And then the
door opened again.

"Miss Kramer?" The kindly face that greeted her was puffy with
sleep, and his hair was still disheveled from bed. No matter, she would
have hugged him, if her shoulder cast didn't prevent it. "Dear Lord,
come in."

He drew her by her good arm into the lobby, still dimly lit and
unheated for the night. But it was legally American soil, and she was
now, definitively, home again.

"We wondered for so long what happened to you. I'm sure you
have a long and shocking story to tell, but for now, come in and have
something warm to drink." He urged her past the guard, who stood,

aloof, staring over their heads, his demeanor announcing *I just followed orders*. Yes, he had, the prick.

Robert led her to the kitchen, flicked on the lights, and set a kettle of water on the stove. "Ambassador Harriman is spending this evening with Mr. Molotov. Something part business and part social. You know how the Russians are. A Kremlin car will bring him back here, but I'm sure it won't be until the early morning hours. And then he'll sleep. In the meantime, after your little cup of tea, I'll take you to one of the guest rooms, and you can also enjoy a good night's sleep on home soil, as it were."

"You're so kind, Mr...uh, Robert. It's really a great relief. And I'm sure Molotov is filling Mr. Harriman's head with all kinds of crap I'll have to undo when we talk."

"I have no doubt of that, my dear," he said, pouring hot water over a little gauze tea sack. "I won't ask you anything tonight except for your assurances that you are all right. I mean, the bloody uniform and the cast *are* a little alarming."

"I'm fine now, Robert. The cast is for a broken shoulder and thereby hangs a tale. I'm afraid I can tell it only once, though, to Mr. Harriman." She added sugar and sipped, comforted by the familiar taste yet slightly amused at how bland American tea tasted compared with the Russian brew she'd been drinking at the front. "What's the news of the war? I've only see one side of it in *The Red Star*."

"Oh, that is a bit complicated to tell. Some business is happening in Warsaw, an uprising against the Nazis that the Russians refuse to support. The ambassador can presumably explain that. And our troops have reached the city of Arnhem, in the Netherlands. The reports are vague, so it's probably not going well."

She finished her tea. "With the liberation of Paris, we all thought the war was nearly over, didn't we? But defeating the Germans is an uphill battle. The Russians are paying for every mile of advance, too." She thought of Sasha and Fatima.

He took the empty cup out of her hand and carried it to the sink. "It's a terrible thing the world has gotten itself into. We can only pray we've learned something from it. Come on. I'll show you to your room."

CHAPTER TWENTY-TWO

I must say, I'm stupefied." Ambassador Harriman stood up as she entered his office late the next morning. "Although I should have been ready for anything." He shook her hand warmly and guided her to a chair next to his desk. "According to Mr. Molotov, you were dead, then possibly alive, then dead again. Possibly."

She sat down as comfortably as her protruding cast would allow. "What *did* he tell you? I'm curious to know. And then I'll tell you the truth."

"He said at first that you had identified some suspects in the theft, and that you decided—on very short notice and without informing me—to go with one of the distribution planes to the front. I found that hard to believe but was not in a position to call him a liar. Then he announced that the plane had gone off course and been shot down. You were presumed lost, along with the crew and cargo."

"That was it? I was dead?"

"No, a few days later he reported that you'd survived the crash, that the cargo had arrived in Soviet hands, and that as soon as you recovered from your injuries, you would be sent back to Moscow, where he would see to your safety."

She scratched along her neck where the cast was itching. "And then?"

"And then they seem to have lost you again. I got a call for a meeting about a month ago in which Mr. Molotov was in rather good spirits, considering his final report was that you had been killed by enemy fire on the way to the hospital at Novgorod. Of course I informed

Mr. Hopkins." He sat back and clapped his hands on the armrests of his chair. "And yet, out of the blue, you reappear, alive, though slightly dented."

He stood up and gestured toward the door. "So now we will take a little walk outside. It's rather nice today, so all you'll need is this." He tossed her a woolen scarf that could serve as a shawl.

They stepped outside into the late-morning sunshine. The garden surrounding Spaso House was a bit sad. In the October air, the leaves had dropped from the trees and shrubbery, and lay in piles here and there. The embassy presumably had no staff to rake them up. Nonetheless, the autumn air was clear, and after weeks in the hospital, Mia savored the simple pleasure of strolling, unaided and unthreatened.

She took a deep inhalation. "Well, I have to admit, Molotov is a crafty politician, and certain shards of his stories are true. You'll recall I had some suspects, but he was one of them, along with Ustinov and his assistant Nazarov. Nazarov, for sure, because I caught him in an outright lie. But Molotov had to be involved since he was willing to have me killed to cover the story."

"Killed? But how?"

"Well…" And during the leisurely amble over the lawns, she told the story of her last five months.

Harriman was silent throughout except for an occasional grunt of surprise.

"So that's it." She concluded her story.

He slowed his pace. "I wonder how Molotov found out what you knew and that you were about to report your suspicions to the White House."

Slightly chilled, Mia pulled the scarf over her exposed shoulder. "I think I know. I had all my suspicions laid out in a draft letter, the one you advised me not to send, and I didn't. But it was lying on my night table that morning, uncoded, of course, and when I left my room to see you, I passed your cleaning woman. I didn't think about it at the time, but it's possible she photographed it. Or memorized it."

"Cleaning woman? That would have been Svetlana, who has keys to all the guest rooms. Curious. She never misses a day, but today she didn't show up for work."

"That could mean she's the Kremlin's eyes in the embassy, while their bugs do the listening. So, where do we go from here?"

"I don't know, frankly. Offhand, my advice is still to not burden the White House with the accusation, given the negotiations going on about world issues. Not to mention that the president is campaigning for reelection. Molotov is a very big fish, and much too close to Stalin." They walked in silence another twenty paces.

"I think you should go ahead and make out your report to Harry, but not treat it as a demand for justice. I believe you, and Harry will believe you, but—at least for the kidnapping and murder attempt—you have no proof. I suspect Harry will set it aside, since his primary concern is keeping communication open between the president and Stalin. A scandal of this magnitude would be a serious embarrassment to Stalin, but also a major problem for us."

"For Molotov, too, wouldn't it? I mean, wouldn't Stalin solve it by eliminating him? He's done that to men for far less."

"That's a good possibility. And knowing that gives you an advantage."

Mia halted and let the morning sun warm her face, then refocused her thoughts. "Speaking of the bugs in the house, do you suppose word has gotten back to the Kremlin that I'm here? By now most of the staff knows it, including Svetlana."

"I'd say it's a near certainty," Harriman said. "Are you ready to go back inside and talk about more trivial things?"

"You mean our chat for the Kremlin? Yes, I am. Then we'll see who telephones and wants to talk."

❖

Back in the ambassador's office, they took up the positions they'd left shortly before. The walk had been refreshing, but Mia was glad to be sitting again. She resumed scratching the back of her neck where the plaster cast chafed.

"How's the shoulder? Sorry. I should have asked sooner. Do you need further treatment? I can get a doctor in, if you want."

"No. The cast seems adequate. I don't know how long it takes a clavicle and shoulder blade to heal, but I'm managing."

"Well then, congratulations. You did your job and found your suspects. Write up your report, and otherwise have a good rest. You can stay at the embassy until you receive orders from the White House."

Hardly had the ambassador finished his talking when a knock sounded at the door. "Yes? Come in?"

The corporal's head appeared at the edge of the door. "A telephone call, sir. From the Kremlin. Mr. Molotov, sir."

Harriman and Mia exchanged glances. "Thank you, Corporal. Would you put the call through?"

Mia stood up to leave and grant him some privacy, but he raised a hand to stop her. "No, please stay. This concerns you, I'm sure," he said, picking up the handset at the sound of the buzz.

After the initial polite exchanges, the ambassador's side of the conversation was succinct. "Yes, yes. Of course. I quite understand. Certainly. It will be my pleasure. Shall we say tomorrow at four o'clock? All right then. Good-bye."

The ambassador leaned back in his chair. "He knows and can't wait to come and discuss you."

"So, the ball is in your court."

"Yours, actually. Yours and Harry Hopkins's. Now that you're under the shelter of the embassy—" He drew out a pad and pencil from his desk drawer. After a moment of scribbling, he slid it toward her.

Your information could conceivably purge Mr. Molotov from the Kremlin, not to say from the earth. You are in a very strong bargaining position. Consider what you want from him, but don't go too far.

Mia nodded, thought for a moment, then said out loud, "I know what I want."

"Good, and in the meantime, I'm going to call Dr. Kuznetsov, a doctor who treats the staff on occasion. I want him to take a look at that cast. It seems awfully heavy, and since you've worn it for over a month, maybe he can replace it with something less dramatic."

Portly and with a full drooping mustache and thick hairy eyebrows, Dr. Kuznetsov reminded Mia of Friedrich Nietzsche, or at least of a sketch of him she'd seen. He examined Mia's cast, asked a few questions, then stood back smiling.

"You have to admit, if you give our military hospitals the supplies they need, they are extremely thorough. That cast would hold a horse's leg in place." He knocked on it for emphasis, the almost imperceptible thud suggesting a great deal of plaster had gone into its making. "You say you've worn this for a month?"

"More than that. And for that long I haven't had a good night's sleep."

"Well, I'm afraid you still won't after I remove it and immobilize your shoulder with a bandage. Quite the opposite. You'll feel some pain if you lean on it. But you'll have less weight to carry around, and you can put a shirt on. A big shirt, of course, using only one sleeve."

From his bag, he drew out a tiny circular saw attached to an electric wire and bent over to plug it into the wall. When he approached her, she eyed the little machine with suspicion.

"You're going to slice through the plaster with that? How do you know how deep to saw? I mean, there's me inside."

He chuckled softly, and she realized he probably heard the same protest from every patient about to lose a cast. "Don't worry. The radius of the blade is less than the thickness of the cast, and the bottom layer is fiber. Never slashed anyone yet. Now rest your elbow here on the back of this chair." With that, he stepped behind her and began with a vertical slice up the length of the plaster on her back.

It was nerve-racking to hear the buzz of the saw so close to her ear—and skin, and she couldn't help but flinch each time he forced it into the cast wall. Finally he cut away a portion of the rear support, and her arm dropped about an inch onto the chair back. She felt a painful tug on her shoulder muscles.

Docile and patient, she grimaced through the remaining slices, none of which produced any bloodshed. Finally he set his saw to the side. Then, gripping the edges of the plaster segments, he tugged them apart, tearing the final layer of gauze that covered her skin.

"Now you must hold very still while I put it into the right position and bandage it again."

With her arm still bent at the elbow and supported by the chair back, all she felt was the cold air across her newly exposed skin. The whole limb felt frail and weightless, and it itched, but she dared not scratch it.

He palpated the area around her clavicle gently, eliciting a grunt of pain from her, then stopped. "Now I'm going to move your arm down. Your stiff shoulder muscles won't like the new movement, but it will be all right."

With that he lowered her elbow gently to her side, then laid her forearm across her midsection. "Hold it here with your other hand while I bandage it," he ordered. The injured parts of her neck and back began to ache as he wrapped several rolls of bandage around her upper arm and shoulder. A third layer around her midriff and forearm fixed the arm in place.

"There you have it. Keep it wrapped for another week at least, ideally longer. Would you like a souvenir?" he asked, holding up a piece of the cast.

"No, thank you. The pain is souvenir enough."

"Very good." Leaving the plaster fragments for the embassy to dispose of, he packed up his circular saw and snapped his bag shut. After a handshake to her good hand, he strode from the room. She heard him exchange a few words with the ambassador and then the sound of the closing door.

As she drew on her shirt, Harriman appeared in the doorway. "Everything all right?"

"Yes, thank you. Um...he knew I'd been in a military hospital. What did you tell him about me?"

"Very little. I said you were a journalist and were injured while photographing a battle at the front. I don't think he believed me, but he knew that was all he would get from me. If his people tell him something else later, no matter."

"I suppose you're right. Anyhow, this feels better." She patted her arm. "I didn't want to confront Molotov looking like a scarecrow waiting for a crow. I can also almost wear a shirt now. See?" She buttoned the shirt under the bulge of her forearm. Her shoulder and neck were aching badly from the movement, but it felt good to be more or less dressed.

"So, have you decided what you're going to say to him? Molotov, I mean," Harriman asked.

"I'd like to tell him to go to hell, but don't worry. I won't."

The ambassador's expression suggested he felt the same way.

❖

At four o'clock precisely, a black limousine drew up in front of the Spaso House portico carrying the foreign minister. Mia watched from the window, recalling the way she herself had arrived two nights earlier, a fugitive in rags, and in the sidecar of a motorcycle. Now, the balance had shifted.

A driver climbed out and opened the car door for him. Molotov stepped out and marched to the door of the embassy. Mia backed away from the window to watch the door open from the inside. The guard was the same corporal who had admitted her, though this time, of course, he was more servile.

Ambassador Harriman shook hands with him, and only after the exchange of formalities did Molotov notice her standing off to the side.

"Ah, Miss Kramer. I am pleased to see you are alive and well. I trust your injury is not causing you much trouble." His smile was wooden.

"Thank you for asking, Foreign Minister. None of consequence. But I believe you have business with the ambassador. We can speak later."

With a slight tilt of the head, the foreign minister followed Harriman into his office, and the corporal shut the door behind them. Mia took a seat in one of the stiff ornamental chairs in the lobby. The official meeting, during which Molotov would stitch together some explanation of her disappearance, couldn't possibly last long.

So this is what *smug* feels like, she thought. To catch someone in a lie. In a cat-and-mouse game, to finally be the cat. It was a good feeling.

Scarcely fifteen minutes later, the door opened again, and the two men stepped out. Harriman gestured toward the front door and said the words she was waiting for. "I believe you and Miss Kramer have some business to discuss, and the air in the garden is quite fresh this time of year."

The corporal opened the door again, and Molotov marched expressionless through the doorway. Seeing the foreign minister emerge, the driver stepped out of the car again, but Molotov waved him back in. He was going for a walk.

Mia fell in step next to him, and they traced virtually the same path she had already walked with the ambassador the day before. Like a boxer waiting for the match to start, she considered her opponent.

She knew whom she was up against. Molotov had weathered the

revolution, Stalin's several purges, and four years of war—and he was as unpredictable as a cobra. But she had the weight of the White House on her side and the benefit of not being terrified of *her* head of state, while he was on his own. When they were halfway around the circle of the garden, he spoke first, and his voice was pure oil.

"I understand you were wounded at the front. Unnecessary, but courageous."

Mia was in no mood for small talk. She halted and faced him. "You ordered me killed."

He looked hurt. "I have no idea what you're talking about. I simply sent you on one of your own deliveries. If the Luftwaffe attacked you, that is one of the unfortunate hazards of being in the midst of a war."

"That fairy tale might have worked with Stalin, but not with me. Your own NKVD man told me what his job was. And he would have carried it out if we hadn't been shot down just at that moment. Yevgeny survived the crash, too, by the way, and was very brave. The Germans tortured him, but he gave nothing away, so they shot him."

Molotov snorted. "No one will believe that absurd tale now, since there's only you to tell it."

"The ambassador believes me. And Harry Hopkins will, too. More importantly, they will believe that I discovered who's responsible for the theft of so much Lend-Lease material. Not the big war materials, the jeeps and airplane parts, but the little things that you can conceal and then sell on the black market."

He jammed his fists in his coat pockets, and for a moment she feared he carried a gun. But it was just a gesture of frustration. "You stupid girl. Whatever story you invented to tell your ambassador will carry no weight. It's the hysterical imaginings of a secretary against the word and reputation of a foreign minister. I don't need to remind you that the most powerful men of this century are about to negotiate the fate of half the globe. Before the force of history, your tale of what you saw in a single visit to an arms factory will amount to the buzzing of a mosquito, an irritant and an embarrassment."

"Perhaps so, but you, too, will be an irritant and an embarrassment. All Stalin has to do is *suspect* you might be stealing, and he'll sweep you away. You of all people know how he disposes of men who are of no use to him. One telephone call from Harry Hopkins to put the idea in his head, and you'd be liquidated the same afternoon."

The foreign minister was silent and began walking again, slowly, obviously collecting his thoughts. He had called her a stupid girl, but it was he who had arrived unprepared.

He halted, clearly ready to deal. "We will explain the material losses as an error on our side. Then I can guarantee you safe passage home on an American plane. No flights over enemy territory. Medical assistance for your arm, an exit visa, and a friendly escort to the airport, together with your ambassador, if you wish. Just go home and leave us to conduct our business, which is outside your area of competence." He pivoted around as if to return to the embassy, the deal done.

She spoke to his back. "Oh, Mr. Molotov. You haven't been paying attention. You evidently missed the part about our informing Marshal Stalin about your indiscretion. I'll be the one who states the terms."

He stopped and turned, and his cold glance stunned her. It was the look of a man who had already once organized the starvation of a million peasants. If he could have shot her on the spot with no consequences to himself, he'd have done it in an instant. But he couldn't. Through his wireless glasses she could actually see him blink.

"What do you want?" he asked softly.

She took a breath.

"Everything you mentioned, and more. One, that you send for Senior Corporal Alexia Mazarova of the 109th Rifle Division and deliver her to Moscow. Two, that you provide whatever documentation is necessary to permit her to travel to the United States."

"To the United States?! What wild fantasies you have. In fact, we have already investigated the 109th Rifle Division, or what's left of it. Senior Corporal Alexia Mazarova was transferred to a penal battalion."

Mia could feel her face redden with rage. Penal battalion. A death sentence.

"Then you are about to fall as well. This discussion is over." She brushed past him to return to the embassy.

He let her go five steps, then called out. "Wait."

She halted and turned slowly toward him, now as coldhearted as he. She wanted nothing more at that moment than for his own tyrannical government to humiliate and then execute him.

"I can contact the head of the battalion. If she's still alive, I'll have her transferred back here. But only if you maintain complete silence and drop the whole investigation. Tell Mr. Hopkins it was bad bookkeeping. Tell him anything."

"Complete silence. That's what you'll get. But only so long as I am sure Corporal Mazarova is safe. If, at any moment, I learn that she has been killed, or imprisoned, or harmed in any way, your trashy little scandal will go first to President Roosevelt and then to *The New York Times*. I understand Marshal Stalin has *The New York Times* read to him every morning over his breakfast tray."

"Assuming I can arrange her transfer and subsequent exit, what do you plan to do with her?"

"That's none of your business. Until then I have the entire story written out with dates and names. I reside in the White House so can hand it personally to the president. As soon as Corporal Mazarova arrives here at the embassy, I will turn it over to you."

"That's a promise that only an extremely naïve person would accept. How can I trust that you won't simply write it again?"

"I don't know what kind of betrayals you are used to, but that is not my way. I actually keep my word. Your fall from grace, or liquidation, if it came to that, would be of no benefit to me."

"And Ambassador Harriman? Of what benefit could it be to him?"

"He knows only bits and pieces of the story, and as a diplomat trying to keep communication and goodwill between our governments, such a scandal would not benefit him either. In any case, he has left the entire matter in my hands."

He glanced away, and she could see his jaw moving slightly. It amused her to think he might be grinding his teeth. "All right. I will look into the status of Corporal Mazarova and send word tomorrow morning."

Dry leaves crackled under his feet as he marched away.

❖

Harriman joined her in the garden later. "I'm glad you're giving Molotov a taste of his own medicine, but do you have a master plan? If so, I need to know it."

"I'm afraid not. I've been playing this whole thing too much by ear, and I know that diplomats don't have that luxury."

"True. But diplomats are not usually kidnapped to be murdered for uncovering a scandal. So you have my complete sympathy. But when you spoke with Molotov, you made a deal not to expose him if he met your conditions. What were those conditions?"

"I'll give you some background. When I was shot at Pskov, a soldier who was also a personal friend saved my life by dragging me out of the line of fire. She had to leave her post to do it, and for that she was arrested for desertion. As a result, she was put in a penal battalion, where, as you know, the fatality rate is very high. They are sent out to walk through minefields, for example, to set off the mines before the other troops pass. That sort of thing. I said I'd hand over my report to him if he removed her from the penal battalion and had her brought to Moscow, and then here."

"Here? I can see wanting to save her, but why can't she go back to her own unit?"

"Because she also knows about Molotov's dirty deeds. And her association with me puts her in the same danger that I'm in. I think the only way to save her is to take her out of Russia."

"Out of Russia? You mean defect." He took a step back. "Miss Kramer, have you thought this out? What if she doesn't want to? And if she does, what can she do in the United States, a woman who speaks only Russian and has killed scores of men?"

"She can learn English, the same way millions of immigrants have done, and as for the body count, thousands of young American men are also going home from this war with the blood of dead Germans on their hands. Why would it be different for her?"

Harriman frowned slightly in what looked like agreement. Still, his question was a fair one.

"Of course, we have to ask her what she wants to do. But if she does defect, I can think of at least one job that would fit. When Major Pavlichenko was in Washington on her lecture tour, Georgetown University offered her a position teaching Russian. She turned it down, but Lorena Hickok told me they do have a Russian department and always need staff."

"Well, that's plausible. All of this would have to be done with extreme discretion, without embarrassment to either the White House or the Kremlin. And if it blows up, you're on your own."

"Ambassador, I won't be any *more* on my own than I was crashing on the battlefield in Belarus and stealing the identity of a dying soldier."

❖

As promised, the news arrived the next morning in a letter delivered by motorcycle currier. Corporal Mazarova was still alive, and orders had been sent for her immediate transfer to Moscow.

"Immediate" was a frustratingly indefinite term, and while she waited, Mia paced the corridors of the embassy like a specter. So many issues could not be resolved until she had spoken with Alexia herself. What if she had completely misjudged her? What if Alexia was bitter and blamed her arrest on Mia? The thought was excruciating. And *would* she defect? What if Mia's entire extortion scheme was for nothing, and Alexia remained a loyal Soviet patriot, prepared to die, even in a penal battalion, for the motherland?

She rubbed her forehead with her good hand, as if it could soothe her tormented conscience. But it simply allowed her anxiety to shift to another set of questions. If Alexia *did* want to defect, just how would they do that? On what plane? With whose permission? Mia herself had come to Russia on behalf of the White House, so the ambassador had the authority to put her on an American military plane home. But did that include a Soviet defector?

And, dear Lord, what would Alexia think of Washington? Mia loved to imagine the two of them curled up in her bed at the White House, but that was clearly a childish fantasy. In practical terms, a defector at the White House would present considerable embarrassment to a president.

She dropped onto her bed and hugged her pillow in despair. Jesus. What had she done?

CHAPTER TWENTY-THREE

When the call came, the caller was anonymous and merely announced that the soldier Alexia Mazarova had arrived in Moscow and could be fetched at the Kiyevsky train station. Presumably her release from the penal battalion did not include local transportation. But she was delivered alive, and in that respect, Molotov had kept his word.

"I'll send you with Robert to bring her back here," Harriman offered, and Mia gratefully accepted.

The October winds had already started, the gray sky portended snow, and when they arrived at the station, Alexia stood shivering at the entrance in a filthy uniform and padded field jacket. At least they'd left her the jacket. She carried no soldier's pack or weapon.

Her somber demeanor changed to joy when she saw the embassy car pull up and Mia step out. "I'd hoped it was you who got me out," she said as Mia pulled her into a one-armed embrace. "You're looking better than you did in the medical station at Pskov."

Mia stood back and studied her at arm's length for a moment. "I'm sure I do, but I have to say, *you* look terrible. We'll have to clean you up and get some hot food into your stomach. Then we have a lot to talk about." She laid her good arm across Alexia's back and guided her into the car.

"Hello, Corporal Mazarova," Robert said over his shoulder from the front seat. "Welcome back."

"Thank you," she said, and dropped back against the car seat, obviously still dazed. She turned to Mia. "No one explained what was happening or where they were taking me. They simply escorted me to a train and put me onto one of the freight cars. I rode for two days and nights, and twice, someone brought me food and water. When the train arrived in Moscow, somebody else escorted me off and told me to wait. I had no idea what was coming after that."

"The bastard." Mia snorted. "Releasing you was the condition I gave Molotov for not exposing his crimes to Stalin. He kept his end of the bargain—but only just. Nonetheless, I'll keep mine. But now I want to hear about what happened after your arrest. I was so terrified they'd execute you for desertion."

"Commissar Semenova would like to have, but Colonel Borodin didn't want the army to lose a good marksman and convinced the judges to reduce the sentence to six months on a penal battalion. Semenova was furious. She's just like Stalin. If you don't die at your post, you're not a good communist. But now tell me about what happened to you."

"Oh, it's long story. It seems I'm always trying to escape from ambulances and hospitals, and changing identities along the way. They fixed my collapsed lung and broken shoulder in Novgorod and then sent me to Botkin Hospital to finish recovering. I spent the whole time trying to come up with a way to get back to the embassy, and finally, believe it or not, Major Pavlichenko helped me. But no one must ever know that."

Alexia sighed. "So much secrecy. It's exhausting."

At that moment, the car pulled up in front of Spaso House.

The ambassador met them as they entered and greeted Alexia in his slightly awkward but adequate Russian. The perfect host, he offered her a guest room next to Mia's and an opportunity to bathe while her filthy uniform was run through the embassy laundry. During the hours the damp uniform hung over Mia's oil heater to dry, she wore Mia's clothes. They were a size small and made her look like Alice in Wonderland on the growth potion, but Mia knew it was a joke she couldn't share.

Two hours later, they joined Harriman in the dining room for a late lunch. The situation was awkward in the extreme, but Harriman, the consummate diplomat, merely said, "Let's all enjoy this lovely meal, without any political discussion. We'll have time for that later, perhaps on our evening walk." He swept his glance across the ceiling and around the room, and Alexia nodded understanding.

They ate potato and leek soup, chatting about Russian and American culinary traditions. Alexia remarked on the military diet and its recent enrichment with Spam. After a comfortable hour of small talk, the ambassador reiterated that the garden air was much fresher than inside and suggested they go for a stroll.

Mia threaded her good arm into the sleeve of her jacket, and Alexia buttoned it across the bandaged one. It was a tender, caring gesture, and for Mia, who thought of herself now as the protector, it felt odd.

Outside, the ambassador got immediately to the point. "It's clear to me that Miss Kramer's investigation, which was supposed to improve the Lend-Lease supply chain, has instead uncovered corruption at very high levels at the Kremlin. Unfortunately, revelation of this corruption would endanger negotiations between both our governments, so we must suppress the information."

"We're beyond the issue of corruption, Ambassador," Mia said, but Harriman raised a hand.

"Please let me finish. At the heart of the scandal is Mr. Molotov, who attempted to have Miss Kramer murdered and may still do so." He turned toward Alexia. "As the condition for her silence, Miss Kramer required that you be reprieved and brought back safely to Moscow. That leaves us here with the question of what we shall do with you."

"It's really up to you, Alexia," Mia said. "Molotov handed you over, but he wasn't happy about it. I think at this point, you have only two choices. You can declare your loyalty to country above all and go back to the battalion to finish your sentence, although you're already tainted by association with me, so you may still be in trouble. Or you can…well, I have to say it. You can defect."

"Defect." Alexia winced, as if tasting the word in all its bitterness. "I never would have considered it."

"I know. And I'm so sorry to have involved you in this whole mess. You were a good soldier and a loyal communist. I've taken that all away from you."

Alexia exhaled. "No. All you really took away was my political innocence. You made me suspicious. When we arrived near Warsaw, where the Poles were rising up against the Germans, we were ordered to stand down, to let the Germans wipe them out. Only then could we advance and defeat the Germans on our terms. That didn't seem right. Then I kept thinking of what Molotov did to you. So many things go on among our leaders that we don't know about, that we would hate if we did know. I love this land, would still fight and die for it, and I'm still a communist, but I feel no loyalty to Stalin and his men."

"Does that mean you're willing to defect?" Ambassador Harriman asked coldly.

"It means I understand my choice is to return to the field and probably die for a government I can't trust, or to betray it. Both make me terribly depressed."

Harriman offered no sympathy. "I'm sorry if it depresses you. But you must choose, because if you want to defect, we have to plan for you to do so, and, ironically, it must be done legally. That is, the embassy can't be part of an escape plan. We have to see to a discharge from active service and an exit visa. Only Molotov can issue those."

"What are my chances if I go back?"

"To the penal battalion? Even if you survive and return to a normal unit, you'd remain a threat to Molotov because of what you know, and I'm sure he wouldn't tolerate that. You'd be very easy to eliminate at the front."

Alexia seemed to slump. "Well then. I agree to go to America. I'm not sure what I'd do once I got there, though."

Mia felt her own disappointment growing. This was not what rescue was supposed to be like. "Please don't worry about that part. I have a friend, a journalist, who thinks you'd have a good chance to get a job teaching Russian. You said you were already a teacher before you enlisted, so that should be an easy transition."

Alexia resumed strolling, and the others kept pace with her. "Me, teaching in a school in America. I suppose that's no stranger than Mia being a sniper in the Red Army, is it?" She murmured quietly, as if to herself, "Father Zosima would certainly approve of that."

❖

Consummation, Mia thought. Such a powerful word, suggesting a long, passionate courtship, a great drama of reunion, and an ecstatic joining. The war had brought them no end of drama, in which the suffering and sacrifices were all terribly real, but when Mia looked at

Alexia across the table, it was rather with a sense of serenity that she knew they would belong to each other that night.

And because she knew, she didn't need to hurry. They shared a quiet evening with the ambassador and some of his staff, exchanging the small talk they'd all become adept at making under the Soviet bugs. The conversation was a back-and-forth in both Russian and English. Alexia listened when the others spoke English, sometimes seeming to catch a phrase, and other times looking quite bewildered. They would have time enough to deal with that, Mia thought.

When the cook offered a late-evening meal of sandwiches, Alexia ate ravenously, making up for the deprivations of the battlefield.

Around eleven, the ambassador slid his chair back and announced his day was over and that he would meet his guests again at breakfast. One of the staff invited them for a card game, but Mia begged off with the explanation of fatigue.

Their rooms were adjacent at the end of the corridor. Mia had planned to slip across the way into Alexia's room, but Alexia arrived first. She glided across the room to sit next to Mia on the bed and, without a word, took hold of her head and kissed her on the lips.

It was a simple, straightforward kiss, hard and full on her mouth, and though passive, Mia was quickly excited. Finally she broke the kiss and spoke softly into Alexia's ear. "They may have bugged this room as well. We must whisper everything."

"What should I whisper? That I've waited almost a year for you to kiss me again?"

With half-closed eyes, Mia brushed her lips over Alexia's cheeks, which smelled deliciously of the embassy's Ivory soap and reminded her of home. "I've waited, too. I even came back to Medved when the ambulance was destroyed, because of you. And finally we're together. Alone and safe."

"Yes, alone and safe," Alexia repeated. "So now what are you going to do to me?" She punctuated her question with another fillip of her tongue at the corner of Mia's mouth.

Mia responded with little half kisses, lingering only a second. "What would you like me to do?"

Alexia's hand crept up into Mia's hair, caressing her head, drawing her forward. "All those things you hinted at in that trench at Pskov, which made my heart pound so that I fired too soon."

Mia drew back. "It was *you* who fired first?"

"Yes, but I lost my concentration and missed him. Then the German fired toward the flash and hit you. It was my fault you were shot. I'm so sorry."

"But it was my fault for talking all that nonsense about kissing when we were supposed to be taking aim. And you left your post because of me, too."

"There was so much blood that I had to get you out of there. I didn't even mind so much being put under arrest for that, except they wouldn't tell me if you were dead or alive."

"I was frantic, too. I knew the penalty."

"Don't talk about it." Alexia's voice softened. "We're safe now, and I want you to live up to those promises."

"Promises? I don't recall making any promises."

"Oh, but you did. All that about 'I have better kisses.' Tender ones and searching ones. I want them all."

"And you shall have them." Mia's lips began exploring Alexia's face while she groped for the straining button on Alexia's shirt and undid it. Then the next one and the next until the young breasts emerged uncovered. She slid her palm across them, caressing their warmth, their innocence. She traced a line with her lips down Alexia's throat to kiss where her hand had lain and felt Alexia shiver with pleasure.

Alexia held Mia's head in her arms like an infant and murmured into her hair. "Do you remember your last words before the shooting started? You said, 'Feel me,' and I did. I truly did. And after they took me away, the memory kept me going through months on the penal battalion. If I'd fallen on the field, I'd have died as your lover."

"You were my lover. You are." Mia snickered softly. "Unfortunately those tender words got me a smashed shoulder, so I don't know if I can do it. I mean make love to you the way I want."

Alexia drew her back up next to her. "I've imagined for a year how you'd do it. Here. Let me help you." She unbuttoned Mia's shirt, exposing the gauze bandage that covered her shoulder, upper arm, and half her chest. Unperturbed, she knelt and kissed softly downward from throat to cleavage and finally over Mia's exposed breast.

The sensation was electric, and Mia realized that no lips had visited that breast for over a year, and none had ever visited it so lovingly. She held Alexia to her with her good arm, floating in the waves of pleasure that radiated down to swell her sex. But she didn't want to be the passive one. Not this time.

"Stand up," she commanded softly, urging Alexia up with her free arm until the pale young Russian stood between her knees. She opened the final button on the borrowed skirt, letting it fall to the floor. White skin, from breast to vulva, marked here and there by bruises, gave off the mixed aromas of arousal and Ivory soap.

She bent forward to kiss Alexia's belly, then let her lips trail down to the tangle of dark blond hair below.

"Is this what you mean?" she asked.

CHAPTER TWENTY-FOUR

October 1944

Some time just before dawn and without fully wakening, Mia sensed Alexia slip away. She murmured something inane and fell back into unconsciousness. Two hours later, the sound of someone passing in the corridor awakened her again. She sat up and peered through the one intact window not covered with plywood, and the bright overhead sun told her it was past eight. She had missed breakfast.

She dressed quickly and rushed down to the dining room. It was empty. Only the cook was present, collecting dishes and silverware.

"Oh, it's you, Miss Kramer. The ambassador said to tell you to stop by his office as soon as you were up."

Embarrassed, Mia nodded her thanks and hurried to the office on the floor above. She was doubly chagrined to discover the ambassador in conversation with Alexia, who had obviously been there some time. She wore her uniform again—torn, threadbare, and with all signs of rank removed...but clean.

"Sorry I'm late," Mia said, wincing. "I tried to hurry, but I can't dress very fast with this shoulder." She patted her upper arm, in case they had forgotten, then realized how pathetic the excuse sounded.

Harriman dismissed her apology with a light wave. "I've been thinking of how to manage what we discussed recently." He began with appropriate vagueness, for the benefit of their Soviet listeners. "We still have regular transports of Lend-Lease material to depots close to the front lines, but now most start from airfields farther west. A few fly overhead, carrying raw materials to Chelyabinsk and the factories beyond the Urals. Very few go out from Moscow except for ones we engage for diplomatic purposes. Which is to say, it's a system that's hard to modify."

Mia nodded slowly. He was saying it would not be easy and would be diplomatically costly. "But in view of the circumstances, could you make a case for special arrangements?"

"Possibly, in light of the fact that you were here representing the White House and now must return home. Besides—"

"Excuse me, Mr. Ambassador." Another young corporal, of which there seemed to be half a dozen, stepped into the dining room. "There's a call for you, from the Kremlin. Will you take it? It's Stalin."

"What? Of course." The ambassador's phone buzzed and he picked up the handset. "Good morning, Marshal Stalin."

Mia glanced at Alexia, then back at Harriman, trying to make out the subject of the conversation. But the ambassador said little beyond an occasional "Ah, I see," or "That's good news, then," and "I'm glad to hear it." But the deep frown that formed suggested it was not good news at all.

Finally he said, "Thank you for calling. I'll be happy to tell her. Good-bye, then." And when he hung up he rubbed his face.

"What's wrong? What did he say?" Mia asked.

Harriman gave a long exhalation. "Marshal Stalin called to thank you for your excellent work in identifying the thief of millions of rubles of American Lend-Lease goods. He promised to see that the culprit, Leonid Nazarov, and the factory foremen who worked under him would be appropriately punished for this act of treason."

Mia grimaced. "Molotov has found a scapegoat."

"Worse than that. He's taken half of the credit, saying he worked closely with you to discover the thieves. He's Stalin's new best friend. The marshal's last words before he hung up were, 'You see how important it is to have good men around you, to help you ferret out the bad ones.'"

"That means—" Mia tried to formulate their precarious new situation.

"That means," Harriman said abruptly, "that we must go for a walk in the garden."

"The garden. Yes, of course. I'll get a sweater."

She returned in a few moments wearing one and carrying Alexia's padded jacket, and the three of them filed outside.

As soon as they were ten feet away from the door, Mia summarized. "So, I assume that call from Stalin means Molotov has effectively eradicated any culpability he might have had."

"Exactly. You can bet that Nazarov and anyone else involved is already in isolation, with no one to talk to until execution. So you'll get no more concessions from Molotov for anything."

Alexia spoke up. "We're both in danger now, aren't we?"

Harriman shook his head. "He won't touch either of you while you're here at the embassy. Especially not with Churchill arriving in a few days."

Mia halted. "Winston Churchill's coming? That could offer us a chance to get out of Russia by air, couldn't it? When does he arrive?" She realized she'd asked three questions in a row, but only one needed answering.

"In four days. He'll be staying at the British Embassy across from the Kremlin, but we'll meet with him, of course. As for its being an opportunity, I don't know. I'm sure the prime minister would be happy to give *you* a lift back to England, but he might balk at taking a deserter. On the other hand, he hates communism, and I think he'd consider it a coup if he could get just one communist to defect. We won't know that until he answers our cable."

Mia had already done an about-face. "Let's send it, then."

"Fine. I'll call my code clerk to put it into code. You'll need to reduce the message to its basics."

"I can do that right now. 'Harry Hopkins assistant here with dodgy companion. Need quick exit. Can they hitch back to GB with you?' How does that sound?"

"Dodgy, eh? Well, that says it all."

❖

The prime minister's reply arrived within twenty-four hours, also in code, but the ambassador translated.

Dodgy are my favorite kind of people stop happy to assist if you arrange particulars.

And while they waited for his appearance, three days after receipt of the cable, the embassy buzzed with activity. Other cables came and went, and Harriman met with the British ambassador in Moscow. Mia was amazed at the running of the embassy, understaffed though it was, and was careful to stay out of the way. Her role as a representative of the White House was worn thin, and Alexia was an obvious liability.

But at the end of each day, the three preceding the prime minister's arrival and the three while he visited, Mia and Alexia enjoyed a sort of honeymoon, hampered only by one immobilized arm and the need to talk in bug-resistant whispers.

"I like this," Mia murmured into Alexia's neck on one of the nights after passion had run its course. "It's so much more exciting when it's secret, forbidden, and *silent*. So when I touch you here and here, and you get all excited, you can't make *any* sound."

Alexia giggled. "Just imagine if we did. The NKVD men listening to us would get very excited and then go home to their wives. 'Why, Boris,'" she mimicked. "'Why this sudden passion when you come home each night from work?'"

Mia snickered but then grew serious. "Darling, I need to ask you something very important."

"What's that?"

"You're really certain you want to come back with me? I know you agreed, but I also know you're a patriot, and it must be like a leap into empty space for you."

"It's absolutely a leap. And I don't really want to leave Russia. I still have a grandmother who doesn't know where I am or even if I'm alive. But Russia doesn't want me anymore. If Molotov didn't have me killed, all that's left is the Gulag, and when I came out of that, there'd be nothing much left at all. I think I'm forced to go, but at least I'll be with you."

"I love knowing you trust me so much, but there's so much about me you don't know. I'm afraid when you find out, you'll pull away."

"Tell me now and end the uncertainty. What could you possibly do that would make me love you less?"

Mia breathed for several long moments into Alexia's hair, then leaned back and glanced away.

"I...uh...I killed my father."

"What? How? For what reason?"

"Not with my hands, but with my words, by shaming him to death. I discovered that he'd seduced a woman who had been, briefly, my lover, and I called him a pig. He said, "We are both sinners, but I acted as a natural man while you are an abomination. I speak a father's curse on you for it."

Alexia covered Mia's hand with her own. "How awful. What did you answer?"

"I laughed and said I spat on his pathetic curse. His words, 'sinner, abomination, curse,' were all magic words from his silly scriptures and couldn't touch me. I could live with my 'sin,' but could he live with being a pitiful, hypocritical old fool? Our quarrel was overheard by neighbors, and that humiliation was enough to push him over the edge. Literally. He committed suicide by jumping from our roof."

Alexia lifted Mia's hand and brushed her lips over the back of it.

"Loyalty to the father, like to the homeland, runs deep in our souls, doesn't it? When we withdraw it, we suffer a great guilt."

Mia turned her hand and cupped Alexia's lovely Slavic face. "Yes. It's a Russian thing, I suppose. Even when they disappoint us."

"Before I was a soldier, I was a teacher, and I believe in seeing things as they are, not what we wish them to be or what tradition tells us they are. Right now, I love only you and the comrades who fought with me at the front. All the rest is shadows."

Mia could think of nothing to reply, and, like the Inquisitor's prisoner, she responded with a kiss.

Winston Churchill and his secretary were already in the banquet room enjoying wine and hors d'oeuvres when Mia and Alexia entered. Harriman waved them over to join the group.

"Mr. Prime Minister, may I introduce Mia Kramer? And this is Alexia Mazarova, of whom I wrote you recently."

Churchill offered his hand, the one that was not holding his wineglass and cigar. "Harry's assistant, eh? I believe I saw you lurking behind him once or twice in Tehran. So, Harry sent you to Moscow but didn't arrange for you to get home? And look at you. You've obviously been wounded in the line of duty. Shame on him."

Mia chuckled, studying his square and slightly puffy bulldog face.

"Mr. Hopkins shouldn't be ashamed. The mission took an unexpected turn, and he couldn't know that I needed to return home at this particular moment."

"Awfully nice chap, that Harry, but he should keep a better eye on you. No telling the things that can happen to a young lady alone in Moscow."

Churchill turned finally to Alexia. "And this is the dodgy companion." He stepped back, obviously scrutinizing her uniform. "I must say, you left out some important details, old fellow. I had no idea she'd…"

Harriman shushed him with a finger to his lips and a glance toward the ceiling.

Churchill nodded and changed course. "…that she'd be so attractive."

"So, Mr. Prime Minister, you are scheduled to depart tomorrow at noon. Do you foresee any obstacles to your departure…as discussed in your cable?"

Churchill puffed on his cigar. "No, we've made our plans and shall stick by them. Unfortunately, Mr. Stalin has invited me to a festive dinner this evening, and you know how that always ends." His mouth flattened out into a rubbery smile.

Mia translated his banter into Russian for Alexia's benefit, though she, too, seemed frustrated by the apparent small talk and by the impossibility of discussing the escape plan.

Harriman was doing his best. "Miss Kramer would like to attend the departure. I'll be giving a brief speech, about the promising future of Anglo-Soviet relations, and I expect you will have a few words to say yourself. Who will accompany our young lady?"

Churchill squinted for a moment, obviously trying to extrapolate from the remark the real information being requested, then seem to grasp it was merely a question of "How do we get the women past Soviet security?"

Again the prime minister puffed on his cigar, apparently formulating a coded reply. "Don't worry about it, old fellow. General Ismay has a charming adjutant, Captain something or other. I'll see to it that she's well taken care of."

Mia made a note of the information. She knew Ismay was a general in the prime minister's delegation, and apparently his adjutant, who was a captain, would be the one to guide them onto the field. The captain's name would probably emerge later in the dinner conversation. Things were moving along.

Mia and Alexia spent the rest of the luncheon following the group surrounding the prime minister and then eating a meal far superior to what they'd been given before. All of it was marked by superficial banter and political gossip. The escape plan the next day never came up again, nor did the aforementioned captain.

"I'm sorry. I have no idea what's going on," Alexia said when they were alone after the luncheon.

Mia bent toward her and whispered, "I think you aren't supposed to. It's all small talk and false leads to confuse anyone listening. I have confidence the ambassador will tell us what to do tomorrow."

"You trust your politicians?"

"This one I do."

The morning of the departure of the British delegation, Harriman suggested one last walk in the garden. Once they were some hundred feet from the door, he said, "Churchill's man is Captain David Laughlin. He'll meet our car upon arrival, and while the prime minister and I are giving our little speeches, he'll escort you to the airplane."

"Anything special we have to do?" Mia asked.

"Yes." He turned his attention to Alexia. "You must change out of that uniform and into some of Miss Kramer's clothes again. A Red Army soldier will never get past the guard. You must pass as one of the British delegation. A secretary, perhaps."

"Anything else?" Mia asked.

"Keep in mind that since Molotov has not provided an exit visa or official military discharge, what we're undertaking will be a grave offense to the Soviets. It is critical that the prime minister, or my office for that matter, not be compromised at this critical time, so if anything goes wrong, if you're stopped or recognized, we must disavow you."

It was an ominous warning, but the alternatives had run out. "I understand."

The driver brought the embassy car to a stop in front of the main terminal, and a young officer with a rather bland English face stepped toward them to open the rear door. As Mia struggled out, he offered his hand.

"Captain Laughlin?" she asked, shaking it. "Yes, ma'am," he said, repeating the gesture with Alexia. "I'll escort you to the prime minister's plane while he's addressing the public."

"Who are we going to say we are?" Mia still hadn't gotten the whole picture.

"You'll be yourself. But this young lady will be Catherine Dunn, one of the prime minister's secretaries." He handed over an envelope of papers.

"Cassrin Don." Unaccustomed to the "th," Alexia repeated the name awkwardly.

"However. If she's identified and blocked from entry, we will say the forgeries are Russian and that we do not know her. The prime minister is willing to appear taken advantage of but not complicit."

"Ah, yes. Deniability. I recognize that. Fine."

Ambassador Harriman checked his watch and instructed the captain. "It doesn't look like Churchill and entourage have arrived yet, but the Soviets are already on the field. It's best you get into position at the far end of the terminal. Stay within the crowd. When the prime minister's plane tests his propellers, you can escort the women out onto the field. The flight crew should be expecting them. In the meantime, I'll be seeing to protocol."

The ambassador turned his head at the sound of the military band. "That's the honor guard starting the ceremonies. I've got to go now. Mia, it's been a pleasure meeting you. Miss Mazarova, good luck to you."

"Thank you so much, Ambassador," Mia said. "I can't tell you how grateful I am that you could arrange this. I hope I haven't caused too many problems."

"That's quite all right. Sometimes one has to improvise. But please tell Harry he owes me one."

Alexia was succinct. "Thank you for everything," she said in Russian.

He shook hands with both of them and then was gone.

Captain Laughlin stepped into the lead, and they followed him silently. When they reached the end of the terminal, the crowd blocked their view of the field, but the distant sound of the British national anthem told them that Churchill had arrived.

"The Star-Spangled Banner" followed, and then the Soviet anthem, and Alexia looked pained. It was obviously not a good moment to hear patriotic music.

They edged forward and finally caught sight of the ceremonies. Mia could discern the main players: the tall, slender Anthony Eden; Molotov, looking nondescript; and the handsome, dark-haired Harriman standing next to white-haired Churchill.

Molotov stepped up to the microphone but was mercifully brief. Then Churchill addressed the crowd, and through the public speakers, she could hear his words. "The last two years have been ones of unbroken victory, the Russian Army has broken the spirit of the Wehrmacht, the final triumph will bring a better world for the majority of mankind." *A better world?* God, she hoped so.

The British delegation's B-24 bomber waiting out on the airfield tested its propellers, then taxied closer to the terminal to receive its passengers.

"Time to board," Captain Laughlin announced, and marched ahead of them onto the field.

They were within a dozen yards of the plane when two guards approached them. "No one is allowed on board yet," one of them said in Russian. Laughlin looked slightly perplexed. Alexia, who understood but dared not react, stared at the ground.

"We are authorized, and all of us have identification," Mia said in Russian.

All three presented their papers, and Mia hoped the trembling in her hand was not obvious. But after several tense moments, they were allowed to pass. When they reached the plane, the captain opened the hatch toward the rear of the fuselage. Hands reached out and helped lift her inside.

The interior of the refitted B-24 Liberator heavy bomber was cavernous, no doubt the result of the removal of all the weaponry. The bomb bay doors were closed, and a temporary floor had been laid over the metal walkway, a portion of which was still visible at the far end.

Some ten rows of passenger seats had been installed, and she chose the last two seats at the rear of the plane, hoping to draw as little attention as possible.

The other passengers were largely military personnel, heavily decorated officers with their adjutants. Mia made no effort to talk to them.

After some twenty nerve-racking minutes, the hatchway opened again, and the rest of the delegation boarded: first Captain Laughlin, then more military, and finally Churchill and Eden. The prime minister appeared grumpy as he took his seat at the front and buckled himself in.

The plane began to taxi, and, in spite of the movement of the plane, one of the younger officers marched up the aisle to hand the prime minister a short glass of whiskey. He accepted it with a sullen nod.

The lack of windows made it impossible to tell how far they were from the terminal, but for Mia every moment they taxied brought them farther away from danger. In another five minutes, they'd be in the sky and on their way to freedom.

But the plane suddenly stopped. Churchill peered over his shoulder and grumbled, "What the devil…?"

Obviously someone from the control tower had contacted the pilot, because one of the flight crew left his post, came back to the hatch, and opened it.

Two Soviet officers stepped in, and their royal-blue caps revealed them as NKVD. Beside her, Alexia stiffened.

The prime minister had gotten out of his seat, as well as Captain Laughlin, and both stood in the aisle near the entrance way. Marching past them, the NKVD men stopped in front of Alexia. "Alexia Vassilievna Mazarova. You will come with us."

Mia leapt up to confront them, but one of the men pushed her back down onto her seat. "No. You are required to leave." The senior officer laid his hand on his holster.

"I say, what's going on here?" Churchill gestured vaguely toward Mia with his whiskey glass.

The senior officer replied in English. "This one is Soviet citizen and deserter." With that, the junior officer lifted Alexia from her seat with one hand and urged her toward the hatch. She offered no resistance.

Mia glanced desperately toward the prime minister. "Sir…"

He took a step toward the senior NKVD officer. "Oh, dear. I had no idea we had a stowaway. So sorry, Major. Please extend my heartfelt apologies to your government for this unfortunate incident. I shall certainly have words with my flight crew about that." He stepped back and allowed the two men to escort Alexia through the hatchway and onto the tarmac.

Mia rose halfway up to follow, but Captain Laughlin laid a hand on her shoulder. "No. It's best if you sit down again."

Obeying the pressure of his hand, Mia fell back in her seat and watched with horror as the hatchway was sealed up again. Churchill turned away.

"Mr. Prime Minister, you promised. Why didn't you do anything?" she called, outrage displacing all sense of propriety.

He turned back toward her again. "Sorry, my dear, but you must keep some perspective. Our negotiations with the Kremlin have not gone well. You may have lost your little deserter, but we've lost Eastern Europe."

Holding his whiskey glass to his chest, he did an about-face and returned to his seat.

As soon as the prime minister was seated, the aircraft taxied onto the field. Moments later, they took off with a roar.

Stunned and broken, Mia laid her head in her hands.

CHAPTER TWENTY-FIVE

The trip to London, with a refueling stop in Stockholm, took place largely in daylight, but for Mia, it was the darkest night of her life. She sat the entire time with her head pressed against the bulkhead, bereft and crushed with guilt. She welcomed the constant ache in her still-bandaged shoulder because it distracted from the shame and regret that ate away at her.

Once or twice, a member of the British delegation ventured back to engage her, but she was monosyllabic, and each one, realizing she was a lost cause, retreated and left her in her misery.

Every image of every second of the arrest replayed itself in her memory in slow motion, like the still frames rotating inside a primitive zoetrope, recording the capture of the most precious thing in her life. And for the second time, she was responsible. Worse, only one outcome of this second arrest was likely. Alexia was a deserter, this time a genuine one, and would be executed.

The London arrival offered an end to the physical exhaustion of travel but not to the strain on her mind. She hadn't felt such bereavement since the death of her mother, but even then, she'd suffered no guilt. Now she could barely make herself walk.

As a courtesy to Harry Hopkins, she presumed, the prime minister provided overnight accommodations for her at the Clairidge Hotel, and someone from his office booked her on a commercial flight the next morning back to Washington. She stumbled through every step, damaged, uncommunicative.

Three days after her departure from Moscow, she arrived in Washington with much the same luggage as she had departed with, her

Lend-Lease documentation, now with an addendum in the form of the Molotov Report. She wore the clothing she'd left at the embassy—a wool skirt, cotton blouse, and blue sweater, with her bandaged arm folded inside—but now everything hung on her frame, which the battlefield and three days of not eating had rendered gaunt.

She took a taxi to the White House and forced herself along the path to the staff entrance. The security staff greeted her with genuine warmth, and that was comforting. Grateful, she nodded her thanks, though it took all her effort to climb the stairs to her tiny top-floor room. After almost seven months, it seemed to have shrunk in size and grown in dreariness. She washed at the corner sink and changed into the clothes she had left behind in the closet. Then she gathered the last of her forces and trudged down the stairs to report to Harry Hopkins.

"Oh, Miss Kramer, do come in," he said, opening the door to her. "Security called me to say you'd arrived." He gestured toward a chair. "We're so glad you're alive and safe. After you disappeared, we thought you'd become a fatality of war."

"Not a fatality, but nearly, though I was in the war. It's all in the report."

"Of course I want to know the whole story, and so do several others here. I suppose the first thing I should tell you is that the disagreeable woman who was blackmailing you last March hasn't been heard from again. Our plan, for you to temporarily leave the White House, was the right solution, though it was never intended to last so many months or to leave you injured. We may have protected the president, but your investigation, it seems, ended up being a wild-goose chase."

Her mouth twisted in an expression of irony. "And the goose got away, too."

"You're referring to Mr. Molotov, I presume. I got a cable from Mr. Harriman, in code, of course, explaining that Molotov was at the heart of the theft and that nothing could be done about him. He also mentioned that your life was endangered more than once, but I'll leave you to tell the details."

She let out a long breath and would have preferred not to talk about it at all, but clearly, reporting was her primary duty.

"Oh, where should I begin?" she said dully. "I uncovered major deficiencies at a factory where the foreign minister had assured me our deliveries had been received. I naïvely reported the discovery to

Mr. Molotov, or attempted to, not realizing he was part of it. Within minutes, he had me detained. With the flimsy excuse that I should attend a Lend-Lease delivery, he put me on a plane with two thugs who were supposed to dispose of me in the air."

"Oh, my Lord. It's like a bad novel. How did you escape them?"

"The Luftwaffe shot us down. I survived the crash and was rescued by a Soviet unit on the front line. Unfortunately, their commander reported my presence to STAVKA and planned to return me to Moscow, where of course Molotov would trap me again. But an air attack on the ambulance convoy enabled me to escape and join the local infantry division." She thought for a moment, then snorted. "Imagine that. Saved twice by the Luftwaffe."

His eyebrows seemed to rise to their maximum height. "You joined the Red Army!? Just like that!?"

"Yes, as a sniper," she said dully. The word had too many tragic associations for her to enjoy the shock value.

"A sniper. Well, this just gets better and better. And then?"

"Well, we fought all the way to Pskov, where I was wounded again, this time more severely."

"In the shoulder." He nodded toward the bandage.

"Yes, fractured clavicle and shoulder blade, and a collapsed lung. That meant I had to be carried with the other wounded back to Novgorod and eventually Moscow. I managed to get to the embassy, but then someone I had become close to was arrested for trying to save me, and when Molotov tracked me down, I...um...blackmailed him to have her released, with the threat of revealing his crime to Stalin."

"You blackmailed the Russian foreign minister!?" Hopkins's eyebrows had nowhere left to go, but his voice rose a note higher.

"I tried to. But he outmaneuvered me by telling Stalin that he and I together had uncovered the thief and that it was Nazarov, some lower-level guy in the group. At that point, my friend and I tried to leave Moscow with Mr. Churchill, but Molotov tracked us down and seized her from the plane. I was allowed, well, forced, actually, to go home."

Hopkins sat in silence blinking, for a few moments, while his eyebrows finally relaxed.

"I think you need to tell that to the president."

❖

"So that's what kept me away for so long." Mia had concluded her story once again.

Roosevelt screwed a Chesterfield into the front of his cigarette holder. "My Lord. What a tale!" he exclaimed. "Though I'm afraid there's nothing I can do to help, my dear. I can't even protest. At the moment, Molotov is number two at the Kremlin. Besides, the Russians have done far worse things than embezzle and threaten a diplomat, and we've had to overlook them." He lit the cigarette and took the first puff, then shrugged. "With the fate of Europe resting on our agreements with them at the next conference, we can't afford to antagonize them. No matter how horrendous the crime."

It all made terrible sense to Mia, who added morosely, "The prime minister's last words to me were "We've lost Eastern Europe.""

Roosevelt nodded somberly. "Yes, it appears we have." He moved on to other subjects. "That reminds me, Harry. Bring your Lend-Lease summaries with you to the meeting on Thursday. I've asked Cordell Hull to come, and we'll be talking primarily about the United Nations charter, but I want him to know what you've been doing."

"Yes, sir. It's on my calendar. I'll have the statistics ready."

Mia fell silent. It was obvious that the discussion of the creation of a United Nations far surpassed her personal tragedy in importance. It was a loss she would have to endure, as millions of people were enduring all over the war-torn world. The interview over, she and Hopkins withdrew.

As they strode along the corridor together, Mia tried to focus on foreign policy. "What did Mr. Roosevelt mean when he said 'far worse things than embezzlement'? Was he referring to Stalin's purges?"

They arrived at Hopkins's office and both sat down automatically, he at his desk and she in front of it. He lit a cigarette. "I'm not really at liberty to say. Not specifically, at least. It's something we don't want to fall into the hands of the newspapers, for just the reason the president said. We need the Kremlin's goodwill."

"Well, can you give me a general idea?"

He took a long drag on his cigarette, exhaled through his nose, and cleared his throat. "Something to do with opening a mass grave. In a forest in Poland. The Russians blame the Nazis, and the Nazis blame the Russians. Unfortunately, evidence suggests it was the Russians. But it's one of those things that history must bring to light. It won't be Mr. Roosevelt. He has a lot on his mind. Don't forget, over and above his negotiations with Stalin, he has an election coming up in ten days."

"That's right. All that time I was at the front, he was campaigning. Hmm. I'm beginning to see what Mr. Roosevelt and Mr. Stalin have in common. Of course one is a tyrant while the other's a good man and a pragmatist, but still, both look over the heads of the suffering masses at some future ideal. Machiavellian, come to think of it."

"It was ever thus." Hopkins tapped the ash off his cigarette. "Your time in Russia has made you philosophical."

"I was always philosophical. My time in Russia made me ruthless. Do you know I killed a man? Dozens, in fact, though I looked into the eyes of this one before I shot him in the face. The women I was with call that 'the sniper's kiss.'"

"I don't think that makes you ruthless. We in government don't pull triggers, but we kill thousands, millions, I suppose, by our actions or our agreements. It's a sobering thought. I wonder sometimes how we can call ourselves Christians."

"I don't. I scarcely did before, but now religion doesn't touch me at all. If you'll excuse me, I'll go finish my report." Without waiting for him to reply, she stood up and strode from the room.

The work was a therapy of sorts, and she was able to keep despair at a distance by composing, formulating, typing, until she had some ten pages of report. The numbers would follow the next day, and he cared less about those anyhow. At this late date, Hopkins no longer needed to justify the expenditures with Congress.

At six o'clock, she trudged up to her chilly room. It was a depressing kind of cold, not like the cold of the battlefield she'd shared with comrades. That she could endure, like the hunger and the pain.

"Oh, Alexia," she moaned out loud. In shame, perhaps, or from some strange urge for self-punishment, she unwrapped her bandage and let her arm fall to her side. The sudden tug on her fragile shoulder caused a sharp pain. Then she dropped onto the bed and fell asleep without supper.

The next morning she rose early and went down to the White House dining room. She forced down toast and coffee without tasting it, then trudged up to her cubicle to work. Mechanically, she collated the pages of her report, inserted the schedules, lists, and columns of numbers into their respective places, and took them to Hopkins's office.

She knocked and entered at his response and laid the report on his desk. Instead of acknowledging it, he picked up a yellow envelope at the side of his desk and handed it to her. "It's for you, from Ambassador Harriman. It arrived in code, so of course we had to read it in order to transcribe it for you. Interesting. Perhaps you will explain it to me."

Perplexed, Mia drew the paper from the envelope and unfolded it. Between the coded lines, which were gibberish, someone had glued in strips with the decoded message.

> *Contacted Ustinov who claimed innocent and proved it by saving A from execution stop sent to labor camp Vyatlag where he assures me she is alive stop.*

"You could start by telling me who A is, why she is in a labor camp, and how this is of interest to you."

She sat down, a flutter of emotions making it hard to order her thoughts. "In the embezzlement, at the bottom of the chain of authority was a man called Leonid Nazarov, who had oversight over a string of factories. Above him was the commissar of armaments, Dmitriy Ustinov, whom you know, and above him was Molotov. I had assumed all three were guilty, along with a pack of Nazarov's men who fenced the goods on the black market." She waved the cable. "This tells me I was partly wrong. I'm glad. Ustinov did seem like a decent man when we met him."

"Who is A, and what does she have to do with the diversion?"

"That's my friend Alexia, who was really an innocent bystander. In fact, she and her sniper friends saved my life on two occasions. She was put on a suicide battalion for leaving her post to carry me to the medical station. I thought I was saving her, but I'm afraid I condemned her by blackmailing Molotov into freeing her. In the end, when he couldn't get to me, he took *her*, and I was sure he would execute her. But apparently Ustinov intervened. Now I need to find out where Vyatlag is."

"I wouldn't hold out much hope for her if she's in the Gulag system. It's only a few notches above a suicide battalion," he said, coughing smoke into his fist.

"I know. You die from overwork after a year instead of immediately from a grenade. And she won't be released while Molotov is in power."

Hopkins shrugged. "I'm sorry about your friend. We all lose people we care for." He crushed out the last inch of cigarette in his ashtray, and a tiny part of her mind registered it as a waste of tobacco. But the rest of her was depressed by his cavalier attitude toward Alexia.

"Will you at least show the president the cable?" she asked. "Just so that he's aware. She saved my life and…well…that's all…"

"Of course. He needs to know about every communiqué that comes in from the Soviets. Anyhow, thank you for your report. I'll show him that as well. In the meantime, I've laid another assignment on your desk. Can you work on it first thing today?"

She was being dismissed, obviously, so she stood up. "Certainly. I'll start right away." With a faint wave of the hand that felt a bit like a civilian salute, she left his room for her cubicle.

Diligence was one of her strengths, and it served her well in this case, too. Manipulating numbers, categorizing objects by various criteria, calculating depreciations all required a mechanical part of her brain that allowed her to shut off her emotions.

She worked steadily until lunch, grabbed a fried baloney sandwich, and went back to work until five. With no desire to make small talk in the cafeteria and even less in retelling the story of her Russian adventure, she fetched another sandwich and a 7 Up for supper in her room. Then she moped. Still travel weary and lethargic, she dozed for a while, then woke later in the evening with her bedside reading lamp shining in her face. A knock at the door made her realize that was what had roused her in the first place.

Rubbing her face, she stood up and opened the door. Lorena Hickok stood in the corridor holding two bottles of Rheingold beer. "I heard this morning that you'd reappeared and was hoping to run into you in the cafeteria. You never showed, so I thought I'd celebrate your arrival personally. I hope you don't mind."

Mia stepped back, admitting the visitor. "Uh, have a seat." She pointed to the only chair in the room and sat down on the edge of her bed. "I had a lot of work to catch up on," she said dully. "After all those months, you can imagine how it piled up."

Lorena handed her one of the bottles. "Eleanor, I mean, Mrs.

Roosevelt and I feared you were missing in action." She sipped from the bottle, and Mia followed her example, odd as it felt. The beer tasted surprisingly good.

"I almost was. But that's another story. How are you?"

"I'm fine, thanks. Working hard for the Democratic Party in the election campaign, of course. We both are, even though his reelection seems a pretty sure thing. It's obvious how sick the president is, but who would be crazy enough to change administrations so close to the end of the war?"

"After all the negotiations, he's the only one who can bring it to a close. But I can see how all of that is wearing him down."

"It is, but my dear, you don't look so good either. What happened over there? I know you've told the story to Hopkins and to the president. Maybe you can summarize for me."

Mia took another swallow of the beer. She'd eaten so little in the last week, she feared it might make her sick. "Summary, eh? Let's see. Stalwart civil servant sent to Russia to uncover source of major diversion of Lend-Lease supplies into black market. Civil servant is successful but gets into trouble for it, arrested, escapes, joins Red Army, is saved from death by young woman sniper. Sniper arrested while I escape. She's sent to a penal battalion and later to the Gulag."

Her throat tightened and her voice rose in pitch. "And it's all my fault."

Lorena stared at her for a long moment, but it was a kind stare. "Is that all?" She tilted her head back and took a long drink from her bottle. "Well, I always thought you were the kind of woman who took control of events. But the loss of your friend explains that new stoop you have, like you're carrying a great weight."

Mia imitated her, feeling a slight light-headedness after the third swallow. "Well, I also had a broken clavicle and scapula, and just today took off the bandage. It stoops all by itself."

"Even so. Something in your face looks like bereavement."

"You're very discerning. I made several good friends among the women snipers, and most of them were lost. Except the most important one, and she's in the Gulag. Because of me."

"You loved her, didn't you?"

"Don't talk about her in the past." Mia felt tears welling up and pressed her lips together to keep them from trembling. She took a breath.

"I told Mr. Hopkins about her, but he only offered some platitude like 'we all lose people we care for.' I might have been talking to a wall."

"You mustn't be so hard on him. He just lost one of his sons. In the Pacific. He never talks about it, though."

"Oh, I didn't know. Then he's stronger than I am." The beer was making her reckless, but she didn't care. "I'm choking with guilt, and I can't bear it. If she hadn't become involved with me, she'd still be with her friends at the front." The pooling tears flowed over onto her cheeks, and she sniffed noisily.

Lorena bent forward across the small space between them and laid a plump hand on her good shoulder. "I understand more than you know. I mean about loving someone."

"Do you?" Mia was certain Lorena was hinting at Eleanor Roosevelt, but she dared not ask.

Lorena nodded somberly. "Loving someone doesn't do anything to change the world, but it changes you. Being a person who loves, that makes you somehow a superior being. I don't believe in God, but if there is a divinity in *us*, that has something to do with our capacity to love. I'm sure that's not much comfort to you."

She finished her beer and added, "Do you have any idea where she is?"

"Somewhere in Vyatlag. I don't even know what that means. Only that bastard Molotov knows exactly where she is. He's the one who sent her there."

"Molotov? The one with the gun and the sausage in his suitcase?"

"Yeah. I caught him stealing Lend-Lease supplies, presumably to sell for profit on the black market. His revenge, since he can't kill me, is to arrest the woman I love."

"But she's alive? You're sure she's alive?"

"At least so far. Mr. Hopkins showed me a cable from Ambassador Harriman today that said so. He's going to pass it on to the president. That's all I know."

Lorena glanced down at her bottle that was now empty. "I'm sorry, deeply sorry for your bereavement." She stood up and stepped toward the door.

As Mia stood up as well, Lorena turned and embraced her. Mia found it awkward being pressed against Lorena's plump breasts but appreciated the sincerity.

Lorena let go and stepped through the doorway. "If you don't mind, I'll tell your story to Eleanor," she said over her shoulder.

"Thank you, for the beer and the sentiment," Mia said, gently closing the door behind her. Then she let go and had another good, long cry.

CHAPTER TWENTY-SIX

Franklin Delano Roosevelt's reelection in November 1944 was probably the least celebrated presidential victory in American history. Though it was for an unprecedented fourth term, most appreciated that victory came primarily from the understanding that a nation at war could not change its commander in chief.

The Allies were winning the war, but after the euphoria of taking Paris and marching along the Champs-Élysées in August, they met with an iron-hard Wehrmacht and had to wring every town and village from them.

The president and his advisors, including Hopkins, spent a great deal of time in the Map Room tracing the slow advance of their troops, and when Mia asked Hopkins about the Eastern Front, she was disappointed by the paucity of new information.

It was mid-December. Where was the Red Army? Newspaper reports showed it was poised to cross the Vistula and enter Germany itself. In the south, it was sweeping across Bulgaria and Hungary, edging toward Budapest. Where was the 109th Rifle Division, or the 62nd Armored Division that had absorbed them? Were Kalya and Klavdia still alive? And Galina, the medic?

Hopkins's voice broke her reverie. "Our men are held up here in the Ardennes," he said, punching the map on his desk. "The Jerries are mounting a terrific offensive, and it doesn't help that it's the worst winter in years. Our guys aren't used to that much snow."

Snow, she thought. Did the Americans use snipers in white camouflage? She didn't think so. Maybe that was part of their problem. They didn't really understand winter, and now it was killing them.

Victory seemed both inevitable and distant. And there was more ominous talk, just a word or two, that something big was going on. Some great weapon that scientists were developing in the deserts of southwestern United States. Something more terrible than the flamethrower and mustard gas.

She excused herself and returned to work, for the Lend-Lease shipments continued, though she wondered with each list and manifest how much was still being stolen.

Christmas came and went, leaving no impression on her. No pastor came to read Dostoyevsky to them, and while she herself gained back her weight, both the president and his closest advisor looked ever more gaunt.

And scarcely had Roosevelt been sworn in on January 20 when, a few days later, news came from the Eastern Front that the Soviets had come upon a horror near the town of Oświęcim. A few days later she heard the name in German: Auschwitz. Were Kalya and Klavdia among the liberators?

All the while she wondered if Alexia was still alive. She *willed* her to be alive, however cruel the labor. Against all reason, she yearned to return to Russia to be closer to her, perhaps to find a way to contact her.

And so her heart leapt when Hopkins called her into his office and said the word "Yalta."

Yalta, resort city on the south coast of the Crimean peninsula that had been liberated from the Germans the previous year. Yalta was once again Russian.

"So, do you feel up to going back? It's only a week away. February 4 to 11. I know you had some bad experiences in Russia, but I do need a Russian-speaking assistant, and no one else in the White House is qualified."

"Oh, yes," she said, perhaps a bit too quickly, then added, "So, Molotov will be there."

"As the foreign minister, yes, of course. But we won't let him kidnap you this time. Given what you've told me, I think he'll be more afraid of you. He has to always worry about your exposing him."

Mia shook her head. "No. He knows I won't do that. He has a hostage. My sniper friend. You saw the cable, so you know what he holds over me."

"I see. Something of a Mexican standoff, isn't it? I wish we could do something, but we can't."

"The president has already made that clear," she said somberly.

"All right, then. Start packing. We're going back to Russia."

❖

February 1944

Mia hadn't seen so much military brass since Tehran. The British delegation arrived on the same day as the Americans at Saki airport, and she lost count of the officers with stripes along their forearms and "salad" on their caps. Churchill was accompanied by an army field marshal, an admiral, and an RAF marshal, but she didn't know any of their names. In addition to his civilian advisors, most notably Harry Hopkins, Roosevelt was supported by an army chief of staff and a fleet admiral. All the military jackets were heavy with medals, though in the competition of who had more decorations, badges, and ribbons, the Russians won by a landslide.

A convoy of vehicles carried them into Yalta, where the main street was lined with Soviet soldiers standing in the melting snow. Lacking military rank or political status, Mia rode in a sort of bus near the end of the convoy. She sat behind the driver, and when he discovered she spoke Russian, he cheerfully provided some of the history of the Livadia Palace, where the Americans would be housed.

"The summer vacation house of the tsar, you know. Nicolas and Aleksandra and all the children. They went to Italy, you see, and liked what they saw, and when they came back, they said, 'We have too much of that Russian architecture. Let's make a Renaissance palace.' So they hired the architect Krasnov, and he made one for them in 1911."

"Very interesting," Mia said politely, but he wasn't finished.

He rattled off a series of names of tsarinas, tsarevnas, tsarevitches, grand dukes, and duchesses who had resided there, but they all seemed to be variations of Nicolas or Aleksandr, so she lost interest. Mercifully, the bus pulled up at the entrance of the palace, terminating the narration.

It was an impressive façade, she had to admit, and thoroughly un-Russian. Snow-white granite, with an arched portico of marble and a

Florentine tower, it could have been an Italian villa inhabited by some Renaissance prince.

Arriving toward the end of the convoy, she had to wait until the primary guests were escorted to their rooms. Then a butler of some sort invited her and the other lesser luminaries to follow him. Her room, she learned, was on the same floor but some distance away from Hopkins's room.

She asked where the Soviets were housed and was told they hadn't arrived yet. But some time that afternoon, Stalin and his bodyguards, traveling by armored train, would be received at the Yusupov Palace. So many palaces, built in the face of vast nineteenth-century Russian poverty. She shook her head.

The first morning was taken up by the plenary session, involving hundreds of participants from the British and American delegations alone.

Mia glanced around and noticed, as she had in Tehran, a paucity of women, only a few secretaries and briefcase holders like herself. Among the Russians, a few women stood as palace guards, without any say in the conference, though hundreds of thousands of them had died and were dying on the front lines.

She sat directly behind Hopkins, taking notes. Numerous note-takers were evident, but Hopkins liked that she didn't depend on the official interpreter for what the Russians said. She could draw her own nuances and discuss them with him later when she had transcribed her notes.

The first session addressed in general terms the locations of the allied armies and their expected victory within the next month, or two months at the outside. No one made any mention of the frightening new American weapon that was being whispered about. Just as ominous, both Stalin and the foreign minister, Molotov, were taking a hard line regarding the expected sphere of Soviet influence after the war, and she recalled Churchill's remark about losing Eastern Europe.

On the second day, the sessions addressed the final assault on Germany, clarified the Soviet commitment to fight Japan and organize the UN, and identified lesser postwar issues.

The morning of the last day, Hopkins met her at breakfast, and it was clear he was disturbed. "The Soviets aren't letting anyone in to the meetings today. The talks are apparently 'sensitive' and only between the heads of state. The president has insisted on having me there, but no one else is allowed."

"And the issues of the previous three days were not sensitive?"

"Ridiculous, isn't it? But the Soviets get to make the rules here. Please stay in the palace. I'll look for you as soon as I come out and dictate everything I remember while it's still fresh in my mind."

"Yes, sir. I'll walk around for an hour and then wait in my room."

Churchill arrived, striding alongside Roosevelt, wheeled by his doctor. But at the door, the doctor was turned away, and Hopkins replaced him pushing the wheelchair.

Relieved at having a free morning, she wandered through the palace like a common sightseer. It was as lavish as she expected a tsarist palace to be, but after strolling through three or four staterooms, all differently decorated, she became disgusted with the opulence. The excess of grandeur and ornament had no doubt contributed to the downfall of the Romanovs in the first place.

She traced her way back to her room and opened the novel she had brought along. *Crime and Punishment* hadn't been a good choice, and just as she was growing bored, a knock sounded at the door.

One of the palace guards stood there, a handsome lad in a spotless uniform. "Miss Kramer, you have visitor," he said in bad English, and she replied in Russian.

"Visitor? That's impossible."

In Russian he said, "It is very possible. She asked for you by name. I think it's the famous sniper."

"Sniper?" She was stunned. "Where is she?"

"In the entry hall. You can follow me there."

Tossing her tedious book aside, she hurried after him, her heart racing. As she paced alongside the guard, a dialogue ran though her head.

Could it be Alexia? Impossible. She's in a labor camp. But maybe Molotov changed his mind. Why would he do that? The war is almost over, and he has nothing to worry about. The Molotov I met does not do favors. But miracles happen. No, they don't.

When they passed through the wide double doors to the entry hall, the sniper stood up, and it was not a miracle.

Swallowing her disappointment, Mia met her with a warm handshake. "Major Pavlichenko, how nice to see you again. Um…what brings you to Yalta?"

"A little vacation. I've been training snipers without rest for six months at Saratov but developed some back problems, so my commander has granted me a few days' rest in a warm place." She smiled. "I know the Crimea. I was one of those who liberated Sebastopol." She tilted her head westward in the general direction of that city.

"So, you went out for a short walk and ended up here in Yalta. And how did you manage to get past security? The hotel is supposed to be blocked off."

Pavlichenko chuckled. "I assure you, it is. It so happens that I am a friend of one of the generals accompanying Marshal Stalin. He invited me to visit him, but then I learned that Mr. Hopkins was here and remembered you were his assistant." She held out her hand. "Glad to see you made it back home."

"Thanks to you. I would have expressed my gratitude for your motorcycle intervention sooner but assumed any message to you would have been compromising."

"Very perceptive. So, how's the shoulder?" They strolled slowly along the ornate corridor but paid little attention to it.

"Much better, thank you, though I don't think I could aim a rifle again."

"Aim a…? Oh, yes, I forgot. You were with a sniper unit for a while. You are quite an amazing woman."

"Not as amazing as you, Major. Or the women I fought with in the 109th."

"I understand. One develops real loyalties to one's comrades. It's wrenching to the soul when they fall in battle."

"I lost much of my unit, though one of them…" She hesitated, not knowing if she dared to ask yet another lifesaving favor.

Pavlichenko waited, eyebrows raised. "One of them…?"

"Alexia Vassilievna Mazarova," she blurted. "She saved my life. I was shot, and she left her post to carry me to a medical station. For that they arrested her. First she was in a penal battalion, and then she was transferred to a camp in Vyatlag for attempted desertion."

Pavlichenko frowned. "I believe I met her somewhere on the front. But a labor camp is an unusual punishment for a desertion."

"Well, it's a long and complicated story. I was wondering, could you help me get a letter to her? Just a brief message so she knows someone cares about her?"

Pavlichenko shook her head. "Some camps allow letters and parcels, and some do not. Unfortunately, if the authorities say no communication, I have no more ability to penetrate that wall than you do. All I can do is advise you to take heart. The war will be over soon. Our troops are already in Germany. Afterward, your government can make an appeal through the Central Committee to contact her, maybe even to shorten her sentence." Pavlichenko offered simultaneously a smile of encouragement and a shrug.

They continued down the corridor for a few minutes without speaking. "Do you remember our conversation about Dostoyevsky when we first met?" Mia asked.

Pavlichenko clasped her hands behind her back as they paced. "Yes, though I still can't fathom why he interests you."

"Well, one of his characters makes a virtue of submission, of insisting that a person should offer love, a kiss, as it were, to the world no matter what evil is visited upon him."

The major laughed in a sudden burst of derision. "Well, with 309 dead Germans behind me, you can imagine my opinion of submission."

"But what about submission to the state? How is that different?"

"Submission to the state is done in the belief that the state is the collective will of the people. Dostoyevsky's submission involves only the individual, a privilege of the comfortable intellectual who cares about his personal salvation more than for the suffering masses."

She glanced down at her watch. "Oh, it's twelve o'clock. I promised General Kruglov to meet him for lunch. It has been a pleasure to talk with you again, Miss Kramer, and I hope you find your friend, Alexia Vassilievna."

They embraced lightly, and Mia hurried back to her room, arriving only a few minutes before Hopkins knocked at her door.

"Good that you're in. Can you take some dictation right now? I want to set it all down before I forget." He was already inside and seated on the one chair in the room.

"Of course." She readied her fountain pen and notebook.

"The long delay of the Western allies in entering Europe has allowed the Soviets…" So he recounted for some fifteen minutes, but soon his voice grew hoarse. His almost-transparent skin and blue lips revealed how much the talks had taken out of him, and he seemed to be at the end of his strength.

"Please type that up as soon as you can, with carbon copies," he said, coughing into his handkerchief. "I'm going to have a rest now. The president will have a private conversation with Stalin at two o'clock this afternoon in the blue suite, before the final press photos. I'd like you to be there, as a standby, in case the president needs another interpreter or messenger."

"Yes, of course," she said anxiously as he slouched toward the door and let himself out.

Mia arrived at the Blue Suite just before four, but as she feared, Hopkins had not made it. President Roosevelt greeted her as his assistant brought him down the corridor, but reaching the suite, he dismissed the man and rolled himself inside. Stalin was already inside with the single interpreter who was allowed.

What was so critical, she wondered, that excluded Churchill and all the president's military staff and advisors? Could it have something to do with the mysterious Great Weapon the US was developing and everyone was whispering about?

Whatever the subject, the president emerged after an hour, and the leaders and their entourages collected before the main portal of the palace.

The three heads of state sat together much the same as they had done at Tehran, only this time they wore winter clothing. As the press snapped away and their flashbulbs popped, various officers wandered in and out of the frame behind them.

Mia knew most of the names of those in the American and British entourages, fewer in the Russian group, but had no trouble recognizing Molotov. He studiously avoided looking in her direction, but it no longer mattered; the power they once had over each other was gone.

What concerned her was that Stalin, in his military greatcoat, seemed gleeful, while Churchill glowered, and President Roosevelt huddled haggard and frail inside his cape.

All the while she watched the three leaders posing for the press, the thought of Alexia haunted her. What was life like in a Russian labor camp in the dead of winter?

CHAPTER TWENTY-SEVEN

November 1944

Alexia stepped down from the prison train at the Vyatlag station and stood with the other new prisoners. Numb and docile, she still had not come to terms with her conviction for treason and the court's sentence of death. It had scarcely made a difference when the leader of the troika had "by the generosity of the state" commuted the sentence to twenty-five years at hard labor.

Treason. Twenty-five years. Enemy of the people. She struggled to understand the downward spiral that had begun with a decision to leave the honor guard and fight actively for the homeland. Was Father Zosima right, that violence begets violence?

Vyatlag, colony 14, was assigned to forestry, and learning that, she was at first relieved. But now she saw she should not have been. It was bitter cold, and the colony where she would be put to work consisted of a row of wooden buildings, too few buildings to house all the prisoners. Where were they? And what were the strange-looking mounds in the field behind the buildings?

Soldiers led her to the nearest building, and she hoped it would be their barracks. But it was merely an administrative center where she had to wait to be registered. Then she followed the line leading to another large room, where male guards ordered her to strip. They sniggered at the naked women as they handed them the bundle of their prison clothing: underwear, padded trousers and jacket, and felt boots. In the room beyond, they were allowed to dress.

As she slowly warmed in her padded clothing, rough hands shoved her toward one of a row of chairs. Men with razors and buckets of water stood behind them and shaved the newly arrived prisoners completely. "To keep away lice," someone said, dragging the razor along her scalp. Afterward, someone handed her a ushanka for her bare head, similar to the one she'd worn at the front. But on this one, the flap across the forehead displayed the same number that was painted on her jacket, G 235.

The entry procedure ended in a double lineup, with women on one side and men on the other. A guard counted off twenty and led them onto the field with the strange hillocks. Smoke wafted from most of them through a narrow pipe at the center, and she realized with horror they were in fact hovels, covered holes in the ground where people lived.

"This is your *zemlyanka*," the guard said, shoving Alexia toward one of them. The canvas door opened, and a bony woman drew her into the dark interior and urged her onto a wide wooden plank. When her eyes grew accustomed to the dim light of a kerosene lantern, she could see the walls were packed soil with narrow logs pressed against it to keep it from falling in. Overhead, a mass of saplings, branches and twigs, made up the roof, with dirt and snow packed into it to create a solid mass. Off to one side was a barrel of what she presumed to be water, and at the center, with a metal pipe leading through the roof, was an iron stove. She could see it was burning, but in the frigid November air, she felt none of the heat where she sat. In spite of the cold, the entire hovel stank of mold, urine, and sweat.

"Didn't expect that, did you?" the woman who had guided her in said. "Well, you better get used to it. You're a *zek* now, and every place else you'll be is going to be worse." She took off her winter hat and scratched her scalp. Her head was covered with short, oily brown hair, obviously several weeks of growth after a head-shave.

"A 'zek'? What's that?" Alexia asked.

"Short for *zaklyuchennyi*, prisoner," a second woman explained. She had slightly longer hair, jet-black, and a flat Asiatic face. "By the way, I'm Nina. That's Olha." She pointed with her chin. "And this one here is Sophia." She poked her neighbor with her elbow.

Alexia managed a weak smile at all three women. "This is where I'm supposed to sleep?" She patted the plank they sat on.

"Yeah, and this is your blanket." Olha poked something filthy and brown rolled up against the wall. "It's got lice.

"We've all got lice," she added more cheerfully, "but at least they let us bathe once a week and they wash our clothes. It's important to stay clean and not let yourself go. Do you smoke?"

"Uh, no," Alexia replied, puzzled.

"Good. Most of us don't. But we still get a tobacco ration. Not much, less than the men, but if you save it, you can exchange it with someone for the things you'll need."

"What am I going to need?" Looking around, she realized it was a stupid question.

Nina said the obvious. "Everything." Then, "So, what's your name? What were you before?"

"Alexia, from Arkhangelsk. I was a soldier. Rifleman." She saw no reason to elaborate.

"Ah. I was a farm girl in Kurgan," Nina said. "The wife of a kulak."

"Me, a seamstress in Smolensk," Sophia added.

Eyes turned to Olha, who simply said, "None of your business."

"So what happens next?" Alexia asked, facing the others.

"You learn the rules next." Sophia sat down beside her. "Don't go near the barbed wire. The guards on the watchtowers are allowed to shoot you then. Do your share of the work so your brigade gets done on time, but learn the ways to not work too hard. Don't go out to the latrine alone. A good way to get raped."

A siren rang in the cold air, startling Alexia. "What's that?"

"Supper," one of the women at the back of the dugout called out, rushing toward the canvas door.

"C'mon. We want to make sure we get there while the food's still hot." Nina nudged Alexia by the elbow out of the dugout, and they jogged together toward the mess yard.

They lined up before a low window where a hand shoved forward a bowl of something thick. It was kasha, though of a cruder sort than Alexia had eaten at the front. She gave her number and was also handed a slice of black bread in the dimensions for which she qualified. As a new arrival, that was for only 500 grams.

She moved quickly away to stand with two of the women whose

names she knew. Both ate with spoons, though she had none. "How do I eat this?" she asked.

"For now, just drink it or use your fingers. You'll have to buy a spoon from someone, and a bowl, too, if you can. They don't have enough, so sometimes you have to wait until someone finishes eating and turns in their bowl. If you have your own bowl, you're served first."

Alexia ate, observing the others, calculating how to survive. Spoons, bowls, lice. At least the trivia of daily existence let her forget for a moment the greater tragedy. They finished in silence, and Alexia handed in her bowl, for which later arriving prisoners already waited.

Another siren sounded, and they lined up in the mess yard to be counted. The November day had been short, and it was already dark when they returned to their earthen shelter. Someone added the last log to the inadequate stove, extinguished the single smoky kerosene lantern, and the dugout was dark, save for the dull orange visible in the stove vents. She dropped back onto her bed plank and rolled up in her filthy blanket. *Oh, Mia. I could endure all of this if you were here.* But Mia was at home in the US now. How long before she would forget her Russian sniper and their kiss? She was too weak and tired to cry, and dropped into sleep as into a bottomless pit.

The now-familiar siren awakened her. They'd slept in their work clothes so needed only to stand up, use the latrine, and report for roll call. It was still full night outside. Another lineup for what was obviously the same kasha reheated for breakfast, and then they fell in for work assignments.

The system appeared straightforward. Each task required a brigade, and since almost no paper was available, a wide wooden plank on the wall of the dining hut displayed the list of brigades, their members—shown by numbers, and their tasks. Alexia was on woodcutting brigade three. Fortunately, Nina, Sophia, and the five other women from her dugout were its members. The brigadier who led them was a man who, according to Nina, lived in a wooden hut rather than a dugout. The obvious question was, how did he manage that?

The zeks lined up in rows of five, and at the next siren, the gate opened and they began the daily march out. It had begun to snow lightly, and Alexia was glad for the felt valenki she wore in place of shoes. Only her hands were red with the cold, and she blew on them.

It was already well below zero. Could she make it through the day without frostbite?

When they reached the work site, the brigade leader pointed out the stand of slender trees at the bottom of a gully that had to be felled and trimmed for transport. The quota for the brigade that day was thirty trees. She was aghast. She saw no sign of chainsaws. Nor could she see any motor vehicle to collect or transport logs. Ten women were going to have to do it all by hand, and she had no gloves.

"Comrade Brigadier," she said, turning to the leader whose name she did not yet know. "I see the other women have gloves, but none were issued to me."

"Gloves are special. You have to buy them."

"Buy them with what, Comrade Brigadier?"

He leered at her, and she took a step back, horrified at the implication. To her relief, Nina stepped forward. "I paid you in tobacco, Ivan. Why can't she do the same?"

Ivan wrinkled his nose at missing an opportunity and conceded. "Yeah, sure. Twenty grams of tobacco." He produced a pair of tattered gloves from the pouch he carried and held them up. "Now, where's the tobacco?"

"Come on, Ivan. You know she won't get her ration until the end of the week. I'll give you ten grams tonight, the last of my supply, and she'll give you the other ten when she gets it."

He spat to the side. "All right. Fine. Now stop gabbing and start working. We have to make the quota or no one gets full rations, and if you get me in trouble, someone will have to pay." He handed out the axes and dragging chains and indicated the trees to be cut.

They worked in two-woman teams, and Alexia saw immediately that most were experienced at bringing down a tree efficiently. First the lower notch, in the direction the tree would fall, then the higher cut on the opposite side. Nina showed her how to chop at a forty-five-degree angle and leave enough uncut wood for the tree to stand until they could step out of the way. After thirty minutes of hard swinging, they stepped back as the tree leaned forward, groaned, and finally crashed. It was satisfying, but by then, Alexia's arms and shoulders ached.

The felling was only part of the task. They also had to strip away the limbs, which required another half an hour of small chops, and then it took an equal amount of time to drag the trunk chained to hooks over their shoulders to a pile in a central area. Alexia did the calculation. If each tree took roughly an hour and a half to finish, and they made up only four teams, they would need some eleven and a half hours of hard, unbroken labor to reach their quota of thirty trees. It was possible only if they were willing to kill themselves doing it, and it would be impossible to do a second time.

After Alexia and Nina had felled, stripped, and stacked their third tree, and it seemed she could no longer walk or stand up straight, she dropped to her knees. "I can't keep up this pace, and I don't think anyone can. I don't understand how you manage your quota each day."

Nina clapped sawdust and snow from her gloves. "In the camps, you can either reach your quota or give the illusion of reaching it. Wait until twelve o'clock, when Ivan reports back to administration and we're allowed to rest for fifteen minutes."

"If you say so," Alexia said, limping awkwardly toward the next tree.

At noon, as promised, Ivan disappeared, obviously confident that his brigade would continue working. "All right…NOW," Sonia ordered. At that moment, she and the other women sprinted to the other side of the gully, where several piles of logs already lay from previous jobs. In teams of two, they hauled five cut logs over to their side, trimmed off the ends to make the cuts appear fresh, and loaded them onto their own pile for that day's quota. Now, instead of the thirteen trunks they'd finished since early in the morning, they had eighteen. That meant they had another twelve to do, and at four every hour and a half—every two hours, given breathing time between each one—they'd finish by sunset.

The women's energy flagged as the day wore on, but they still managed to drag the last log in by twilight. They marched back to the camp in darkness, and having met their quota, they were entitled to full rations. This consisted of a bowl of *balanda*, a watery soup made from spoiled cabbage, potatoes, and fish heads, and 700 grams of black bread.

Alexia devoured her food, again spoonless. It tasted dreadful, but she didn't care and would gladly have eaten more. Instead, the siren sounded again for final roll call, and they lined up in their rows of five to be counted. Olha was right. After that, the plank bed and lice-ridden blanket in their hole in the ground seemed a relief.

"That trick of stealing those logs, if you do that every day, I can't believe Ivan doesn't catch on," she said to Sonia, who stood at the stove with her blanket.

Sonia picked off a couple of lice from the blanket and crushed them between her nails. "We don't take so many that it's obvious. And there must be eight or ten piles lying around the forest. Once the trees are piled up and counted, no one bothers to count again. Even if Ivan figured out what we do, all he really cares is that he can report at the end of the day that his brigade made its quota. And we always do."

"Doesn't anyone at the top of the chain count them at the end and realize they're far short of what the camp says it has?"

"You'd think so, wouldn't you? But each person at every level lies to his supervisor, who then lies to *his* supervisor, and so it goes. As long as it looks right on the books, the whole system moves along."

Alexia rolled up in her blanket and thought of Mia, who had investigated exactly that kind of fraud and almost been murdered for it. What would she think of the economy of the Gulag?

"Mia," she murmured to herself as she slipped off into unconsciousness, "don't forget me."

❖

Alexia endured four weeks of the woodcutting regime, paid her tobacco debt to both Ivan and Nina, but could feel herself weakening. She had always been trim, but now she was wiry, and soon, she feared, she would look like Olha.

She learned the tricks of survival: to save a scrap of bread from supper to eat just before going to bed, since it was hard to fall asleep hungry, to sleep with her hat pulled low and covering her ears, to trade tobacco for essential items as soon as possible.

With her fourth issue of tobacco, she "bought" a crudely carved wooden spoon and, with the next four rations after that, a wooden bowl. The latter meant she no longer had to wait for one to be handed in and rinsed. But the food, whether kasha or balanda, seemed to make no dent in her constant hunger.

After a few weeks of working, stealing, and sleeping alongside the other women, she began to see them as family. And then she woke up one morning to a cluster of green branches, from one of their cut trees, on the one rickety table in the dugout. On its top a length of wire had been bent into something vaguely resembling a star.

"What's this?" she asked. "Don't you get enough of trees on the job every day?"

Sonia sat up on her bed plank and wrapped her blanket around her shoulders. "You haven't been paying attention to the calendar, my dear. It's Christmas."

"Christmas! We're celebrating Christmas?" Alexia laughed.

Nina laughed with her. "I know no one believes in that nonsense anymore. I certainly don't. And of course we have nothing to make the 'holy supper' with. But I love the rituals, the singing, the specialness of it. I like to have a day when we're supposed to show our love for people."

Sonia grew somber. "The last time I saw my husband and daughter was at Christmas four years ago. For my mother, who never gave up the faith, we had a special festive dinner at home. My husband was so kind. He brought a fur hat for my mother and a snow-maiden doll for our daughter, and we were all so happy. Two days later he was arrested, and two months after that, I was, too. My family has no idea where I am."

Alexia took her hand. "Yes, I spent a lot of nice Christmases with my babushka and Father Zosima. And…the best one of all with my dearest friend, Mia. We went to a Mass together, two nonbelievers, but being there in that beautiful place with her…well, that made it holy for me."

Nina slid off her plank and came, wrapped in her blanket, to sit next to Alexia. "What was she like, your Mia?"

Alexia hesitated. Then she blurted out, "She's lovely. An American who somehow ended up with us on the Eastern Front. Can you imagine? Someone who would give up a comfortable life in the West to fight beside us?"

"What happened to her?" Sonia asked.

"We were trying to return to America together, with some English diplomats, but the NKVD arrested me and pulled me off the plane. I suppose she continued on."

"To America? Ooh. That sounds exciting." Nina threw an arm across her back. "I bet she hasn't forgotten, just like you haven't. Look. I have a proposal, that I tell you all the wonderful things about my

Timor, the man of my life, and you tell me all the things about Mia. Sonia can talk about her husband. I'm sure even grumpy old Olha has someone to talk about. Every night we'll tell a little bit, and that way, it's like they're still with us."

"Yes. I like that idea."

The siren sounded, and they got to their feet to start the new workday.

Alexia stood shivering with the other women in the yard. They'd already had their miserable little portions of soup and root tea for breakfast, and now they were waiting for all the work crews to fall into their lines of five to be counted. If the count went well, it took only fifteen minutes. If the yard leader miscounted, or someone was missing, it could take an hour, and they still had the same work quota to meet.

At five thirty in the morning, the winter sky was still pitch-black but crystal clear and full of stars. Stamping back and forth to keep off the chill, Alexia gazed up at them. Idly, she wondered if she could spot the one constellation Mia had shown her how to recognize, that of Orion.

A shiver of pleasure went through her when she saw them, the three stars of Orion's belt, and above and below them, the stars that made up his shoulders, feet, and shield.

She almost wept, as if recognizing an old friend who had looked down on her and Mia on Christmas night only a year ago. That night, that wondrous night, when Mia had rambled on about "millions of stars, millions and millions and millions" and then had kissed her. For a brief moment, she sensed a connection between herself and Mia, and the stars, proof of the existence only of themselves. *They have no interest in comforting us, and yet we are comforted. As by the sunrise.*

Through the month of January, it became clear to Alexia that the only ones who survived were those who had friends and could cheat the system with them. But even then, sheer luck or the lack of it could save or kill. As a "twenty-fiver" she was not allowed letters or packages from home, but perhaps to add to her torment, some invisible authority passed through a message letting her know her grandmother had died. No details, just that she was gone. Dear Babushka, with her forbidden icons and a celibate priest for a "husband." Alexia's fervent wish was that she died in peace, in her sleep, believing her grandchild still served at the front.

In February, the weather worsened radically. Merciful Soviet law required that work be suspended at temperatures below minus twenty-five degrees, and on the first such day, the brigades were exempted from labor. Instead, they were required to attend a lecture entitled "The Ideals of the People's State" given by the district commissar of education.

While they waited outside the administration hut, which she had passed through upon arrival, she studied the newspaper posted on the wall. It was the only one available to the camp, since any others that arrived were quickly torn into cigarette papers. But this one was sacrosanct, and though it was a week old, it gave some news of the war. Budapest had been liberated, and even better, the Red Army had taken Warsaw and crossed into Germany.

She wondered whether Kalya and Klavdia were still alive. A smaller article mentioned that the Arctic convoys were now arriving without casualties, though their cargoes continued to show deficiencies at several destinations. Alexia snorted bitterly. Apparently Molotov and his cronies still had their hands in the supply line.

Finally her brigade and four others were called in, and in the warm air of the crowded room, she took off her ushanka and ran her hand over her head. Her fingers slid over the short, boyish growth that scarcely warmed her but made her feel like a person again. Without a mirror, she could only wonder what it looked like.

The lecture was hardly different from what she'd heard in her Komsomol days and in military training. The sheer repetition of the "heroic revolution of the working class" theme already rendered it boring, but now, to an audience of "enemies of the people" who labored until they died, it was absurd. She marveled that any of the prisoners could believe a single word of it.

The next day, the temperature warmed considerably, and the brigade returned to the taiga, though the team's usual log-borrowing was temporarily thwarted by the lunchtime appearance of the commissar. Alexia thought at first he was there to inspect them, and shuddered at the thought, but was pleased to see that he merely wanted to hunt rabbits.

Alexia's group had already slowly edged toward a desirable pile of previously cut logs when they heard the first gunshot. Alexia glanced up to see the commissar aiming at a rabbit. His cursing and the continued flight of the creature showed he'd missed.

He fired a second time, but the rifle jammed. He cursed again and raised the rifle to his shoulder as if to shoot a third time.

"Stop!" she shouted at the top of her lungs, startling him. He lowered the rifle and glanced toward her, clearly perturbed.

She dropped her ax and ran toward him, both hands held out in front of her. "The bullet's jammed in the barrel. If you fire again, it'll explode."

"Oh," he said, staring down at the rifle as if it were something alien. "Damn. I should have remembered that, but this isn't the rifle I usually shoot. The commandant lent it to me, one of the old infantry rifles."

"It's a Mosin-Nagant, the kind we all used on the Front. Would the commissar like me to break it down and remove the jammed cartridge?"

"You can do that out here, without tools?"

"Yes, Comrade Commissar." She took a chance calling him that. As an enemy of the people she was technically forbidden to call someone comrade. "But it must be in a sheltered place. Over there, perhaps, under the large fir."

He nodded, and they hiked to the tree, which had a ring of soil at the base untouched by snow. Taking the gun from his hands, she first opened the bolt and pried out the cartridge shell that was in place behind the jam, then slid the whole bolt back off the body of the gun. "The beauty of the Mosin Nagant is that you can use the bayonet as a tool," she said, clicking it off the end of the nozzle. She removed the two barrel bands and lifted the hand guard off the top of the barrel. Then she drew out the cleaning rod and laid it aside. Using the flat tip of the bayonet, she undid the screws at the front and the rear of the magazine chamber. Pressing out the magazine chamber allowed her to lift the entire barrel and slide in the cleaning rod to tap out the slug.

Triumphant, she held up the delinquent plug of metal. "It looks like the cartridge had almost no powder in it. Just enough to shove it halfway up the barrel."

"Sabotage, I'm sure," he muttered.

She ignored the accusation, which almost certainly was justified, and in as short a time as she had dismantled the rifle, she reassembled it. "Sorry it took so long, but it's hard with gloves," she said, handing it up to him.

The commissar hefted the gun, as if it now weighed less. "How do you know so much about this rifle? You were a soldier?"

"Yes, Comrade Commissar. A sniper in the 109th Rifle Division. Thirty-two recorded kills."

"Oh, well done. Does the commandant know he has a sharpshooter in his camp?"

"I'm certain he doesn't, Comrade Commissar."

"Well, well," he said, ambiguously. "Thank you for…uh…saving my head. Now you'd better get back to work." He ambled away, his newly cleaned Mosin-Nagant cradled in his arms.

Fortuitously, Ivan joined him, and they marched back to camp together for the midday report. As soon as they were out of sight, Alexia called out, "Now," and the women scrambled toward the nearest log pile to transfer the logs that would allow them to make their quota and earn their full ration one more day.

At supper, while Alexia wiped out her bowl with the last of her bread, one of the guards called out her number. "To the commandant's office," he ordered. With an anxious glance at her friends, she followed him.

Upon entering the commandant's office, however, she saw the commissar was present also, and the recalcitrant Mosin-Nagant lay across the commandant's desk.

"So, I hear you're a hotshot marksman with thirty-two dead Germans under your belt," the commandant said, snickering. "And that you can dismantle one of these things in the blink of an eye."

"Yes, Commandant."

"A shame it's a skill you can't use in a labor camp. What did you do before you learned to shoot?"

"I was a teacher, Commandant. In Arkhangelsk."

"In Arkhangelsk?" He seemed astonished. "What school?"

"Primary school number 12. Unfortunately, it was destroyed in an air raid in September of last year."

The commandant shook his head in disbelief. "I know that school. My son went there the year before." His face softened and lost the harsh authority of his office.

For a moment, Alexia forgot too she was a prisoner. "I was probably one of his teachers. What was his name?"

"Mikhail Ivanovitch."

"I remember him. A shy boy who liked to draw horses."

"Yes. That was him." The commandant seemed deeply touched, as if recognizing for the first time that his prisoners were his countrymen and neighbors. He scratched his jaw.

"Well, I think the camp can find a better job for a schoolteacher than felling trees. How good are you at typing?"

"Superb, sir. Almost as good as shooting."

"All right, then. I can't do anything about your housing. The barracks are full to bursting with criminals, and putting a political in there would cause you more grief than comfort. But at least I can put you to work where you'll be indoors for the rest of the winter. Report to the administration tomorrow after the morning count."

❖

Thus was Alexia saved from starvation. The hours as an administration typist were just as long, her food ration slightly less than before, but she labored sitting, in a warm room, while the others marched out into the icy forest every morning. She felt guilty returning each night to the dugout to face the other physically depleted women, but on the rare occasions when extra bread appeared mysteriously on her desk from some benefactor, she took it back to her comrades. It was the least she could do.

Nina and Sonia had become expert at shifting logs from one pile to another wherever they were assigned and always exceeded their quota. The brigadier Ivan was either very stupid, or very kind, for he never said a word.

And every ten days, their turn came for the bathhouse, a noisy, poorly heated shed that offered little comfort other than a brief respite from the lice. The camp issue of soap was small, evil-smelling, and had to be used for hair and body. Fortunately, they could dump their lice-ridden rags into a pile to be boiled and disinfected by the laundry workers. Then for fifteen minutes, they huddled together in the tepid warmth of the washroom, scrubbing each other's backs and hair, and joked that now at least the lice would be clean.

March and April passed, and the sub-zero temperatures gave way to warm, drenching rains, but there were no deaths among the women. Life in the underground zemlyanka continued to be squalid, and now the mildew smell was permanent, but Alexia lost no more weight, only her previous convictions. Over the months of her sentence, political doubt had hardened into cold cynicism. And after living intimately with her friends in a hole in the ground, she sensed they felt the same.

One night, they even dared to talk, to say things that on the outside would have gotten them a doubled sentence.

Nina began the treasonous discussion. "Did you see the new banners in the camp? *Patriots working for the glory of Communism.*" She laughed. "I wish they'd make up their minds. Either we're patriot brothers and sisters, celebrating the victory of Leninism, or we're enemies being brutalized for *not* celebrating it. You can't be celebrating and at the same time have a gun to your head."

A vague idea that had haunted Alexia now coalesced in her mind. "That's true not just of the Gulag, but of Soviet society in general."

It was a vast leap in thought, and Sonia and Nina, and the others within earshot, waited for her to elaborate.

"Even on the outside, how can we celebrate the glory if, even in our own homes and jobs, we live in fear? And what exactly are we supposed to glorify? Our shops are empty, and not just because of the war. The collective farms don't produce enough food, factory workers labor fourteen hours a day on patched-up machinery, and everyone at every level, even in the Kremlin, is corrupt." Her voice dropped in volume, as if she spoke only to herself, but the words were incendiary.

"I've begun to think sometimes the entire Soviet experiment has failed and no one has the courage to admit it."

"That's treason you're talking," a small voice said from the other side of the dugout. It was Olha. Ominously, no one contradicted her.

In the deadly silence that followed, one of the women extinguished the kerosene lantern. Alexia knew she'd sealed her fate. But what more could they do to her? She already faced twenty-five years at labor, and the one person she desperately loved was lost to her forever.

She rolled up in her blanket and stared into the darkness. Let them execute her now for treason. She no longer cared.

❖

The next morning, she awoke full of regret. She had said reckless things the night before and realized, in fact, she *did* care. Not especially for herself—since twenty-five years was as good as life—but for her mates. If any one of the women denounced her, the other women would be held guilty, too, for agreeing with her. Even if their sentences were not doubled, at the very least, the group would be broken up and the prisoners sent to other camps or colonies. Everyone would have to start over, building a new support network to trick the system and survive.

She reported for work in the administration office but was nervous all day. And at the end of her ten-hour shift, her worse fears were realized. Prisoner G 235 was summoned to the commandant.

She cursed Olha, who had obviously denounced her.

Calming herself, she tried to formulate some sort of half lie to protect the innocent ones. Something about having a fever and saying deranged things she should not be held responsible for, and that the others had only humored her out of kindness. Would he believe it?

She knocked, and at his reply, she stepped inside, her ushanka in her hand. She saluted unnecessarily—her imprisonment was not military—but she wanted to remind him she'd been a good soldier.

"I have no idea what's going on here, but it's my duty to follow orders," he said.

"Yes, Commandant," she replied, dry-mouthed. He was about to pass sentence, all because she couldn't keep her mouth shut. She rocked slightly, almost physically sick, and her hands began to tremble.

"Orders have come to transfer you to Moscow. Leave behind whatever possessions you might have. You won't need them. A truck will pick you up after supper."

CHAPTER TWENTY-EIGHT

Throughout March 1945, the war news from Europe was largely good. Finland had declared war on Germany, while the Allies had crossed the Rhine at Remagen and plowed through Cologne and then Mainz. The Germans were evacuating Danzig before the imminent attack by the Red Army and were clearly in the throes of defeat. However, for reasons known only to the president and General Eisenhower, the Western Allies had deliberately slowed their advance to allow the Red Army to take Berlin. Mia thought it might have been a final concession to the Soviets, who had demonstrably done most of the fighting and dying in the European war.

Lend-Lease continued, and Mia carried on with the drudgery of her job. Then, at the beginning of April, a call came from Security that she had a visitor. A woman. She had few female friends in Washington so was filled with dread. It could be only one person.

"Grushenka," she said coldly, as she caught sight of the visitor waiting at the ground-floor guard station. She marched another ten paces toward her. "I thought we'd gotten rid of you."

"Don't be like that," Grushenka said mournfully, linking her arm with Mia's. "Shall we go to your room, or is there someplace nearby where we can talk?"

With no intention of letting this blackmailing harridan into her private quarters, Mia led her toward a ground-floor storage room. She motioned toward two folding chairs, and they sat down facing one another.

In spite of her bitterness, Mia had to admit Grushenka was still a beauty, at least in a superficial sense. But she looked worn out. She wondered if Alexia looked the same way now, after months at hard labor. No, she decided. Grushenka was not battle-and-labor hardened, but sullen and tight-faced, like a gambler who'd finally lost too much. Mia was certain Alexia would never be broken like that.

The brief thought of Alexia made her impatient. "Why have you come? You know I won't give you a cent." She crossed her arms, creating yet another barrier between them.

"I don't want money," Grushenka said. "I want your forgiveness."

"For turning my home into a sewer?"

Grushenka looked pained at the vulgar remark, and Mia regretted making it. "You know," she said. "I'm not even interested anymore. I've faced so much bigger tragedy since you were here. So…yes. Because I don't care, I forgive you."

Grushenka clasped her hands in front of her lips as if praying. "I'm glad, because I'm not the same person any longer. I've left Pavel, and I'm much happier on my own. I came because I wanted to clear the air between us."

"Well, it's cleared. So you can go now." Mia stood up. She did not want to hear about Grushenka's fanatical husband or her relationship with him.

Grushenka remained seated. "Please, don't be so brutal, although I suppose I deserve it. Give me a few more moments. I have things to tell you. About your father."

"My father? That's a subject best left untouched, don't you think?"

"It's about his death." The prayer-hands became fists, as if they held something valuable.

Mia turned to leave. "It was suicide. Period."

Grushenka grasped her wrist and drew her back down onto her chair. "Listen to me. Please. Yes, Fyodor went to his death by his own choice, but Pavel drove him to it."

Mia pulled her hand away. "What do you mean, 'drove him to it'?"

Finally holding Mia's attention, Grushenka leaned back in her chair. "What I'm trying to say is that my husband was the villain here. You know, your father was a pious man."

"Pious? I thought of him more as sanctimonious. And only on his sober days."

"Well, it started out as piety. Surely you remember. But when your mother died, he thought it was a punishment of some sort. He began drinking and wavered between doubt and outrage. Sometimes he doubted that God existed, and sometimes he was simply outraged that the God he still believed in, *needed* to believe in, would punish him in such a way."

"I already know that about him. But millions of people lose loved ones and don't fall apart."

"Yes, but the punishment continued. He chased women, as you know, but more and more, he became impotent."

Mia covered her ears. "Grushenka! I *do not* want to know about that."

"You have to know the whole story. It didn't happen at first, but when it did, he just prayed harder. It didn't help. I broke off our relationship and made the mistake of confessing to Pavel—my own sort of contrition, I suppose. But Pavel used the information as a weapon and humiliated Fyodor further. He told him he could never satisfy a woman, not even his wife. And to pour salt into the wound, he even lied and said he'd slept with your mother, many years ago."

"My mother? A ridiculous, disgusting lie."

"Of course it was. But Fyodor was in such a state, he believed it, and it was the last humiliation. It broke him to think he couldn't satisfy his wife or his lover, that he'd disappointed you, and, ultimately, God. So he jumped."

Mia stared into space for a moment. "Well, Pavel Smerdjakov's lies were only the first blows. I added to them, so in the end, we both are guilty."

Grushenka took Mia's hand in both of hers. "You see, it was a sewer we all made for ourselves. But now, just like you, I want to be clean of it. The first step was to leave my husband, and the second one was to confess to you."

She stood up. "And now, I'll leave you in peace." She took a step, then halted. Her voice became gentle. "How foolish of me. I haven't even asked how you are these days. You look exhausted. Are you happy? I truly hope I didn't ruin everything for you."

Mia was caught off guard by the sincerity, and she shrugged vaguely. "Happy enough. I like it here. Well, who wouldn't like living in the White House? And my job is meaningful."

Then the words seemed to slip out. "But I met someone in Russia. You wouldn't believe it. A soldier. She looked a bit like you."

Grushenka sat down again and bent toward her. "Really? What a compliment. I'm touched. So what happened? Was she killed in battle?"

"No. It's a long story, but she got into trouble because of me, and she's in a labor camp now. I haven't given up hope that I can get her out once the war's over."

"Oh, I hope so, for your sake. You deserve it. You've always had such noble purposes." She brushed a strand of hair out of Mia's face in a gesture full of warmth and devoid of flirtation.

"I certainly don't qualify as noble, but my boss, Harry Hopkins, certainly is, and his boss, the president, is one of the noblest men around. He raises all of us."

"Lucky you. That's a rare thing. They should make a monument to a man like that."

"They are. Well, not a monument. A painting, in fact. I've asked to visit the sitting, and the president agreed. He's been very frail since he got back from Yalta, and for that matter, so has Mr. Hopkins."

"Well, I'll let you go and do that." Grushenka brushed the back of her fingers across Mia's cheek. "I'm really glad I came today. I needed to have this conversation."

"I'm glad, too. Take care of yourself." Mia walked her back to the guard station, gave her a quick embrace, and watched, bemused, as Grushenka disappeared behind the closing door.

The visit had, in fact, lifted her spirits. The mystery of her father's death had been solved, and the bitterness she'd felt toward him had evaporated.

It was good to talk openly to someone about Alexia, she thought. And then the irony struck. Grushenka's blackmail had been the cause of her final trip to Moscow and the whole misadventure that followed: Molotov's attempt on her life, her involvement with the snipers, her dragging Alexia into the political mire, Alexia's condemnation. The solace she'd felt talking to Grushenka did nothing to alleviate Alexia's misery. Only the end of the war could do that…maybe.

And when *would* the war end? She craved it like a swimmer seeing the thinnest line of shore in the distance. The tension was wearing them all down. Hopkins was in the hospital again trying to absorb food with half a stomach, and the president, too, was ghostlike. His portrait painter would have to add color that he no longer had in his face.

She hurried upstairs to the Private Meeting Room, where the sitting had already gone on for half an hour, and slipped in just ahead of Thomas, who was about to serve him lunch. Roosevelt's assistant, Edwin Watson, stood inconspicuously in the background. The artist Elizabeth Shoumatoff had already sketched an excellent though slightly idealized representation of the president's face, leaving out the frighteningly dark circles under his eyes and his sunken cheeks.

Roosevelt glanced up as Mia entered and smiled. "Hello, Miss Kramer. Nice to see you."

"Please don't let me disturb you, Mr. President." Mia hurried to take a seat.

"It's no disturbance at all. By the way, I've been meaning to thank you for your service in Russia. You must feel a certain futility since we were not able to act on your information."

"Not at all, sir. I understand that state matters must take precedence over individual ones."

"Sometimes I wonder," Roosevelt mused. "States are as transitory as we are. They only change more slowly. With individuals, you bring your ethics, your understanding of things to the conversation, and the result is immediate. Not so with states. Even those of us at the helm can only move them so far and so fast, and we have no way of knowing the ramifications of each decision, a year, a decade, a century later. It's exhausting to think of it."

"Yes, sir. It must be."

"Do you believe in God, my dear?"

Mia hesitated. "Uh…no sir. Not in the usual way. I see the absolute only in the movement of the stars. Not astrology, of course. I mean in the galaxy and beyond. But I don't think any benevolent divinity is looking after us."

"The stars, eh? A nice thought. Beautiful, over our heads through all the centuries, but indifferent. Leaving us to make all the decisions, take all the responsibility."

"Yes sir, but I find that somewhat comforting. No matter what we do, they go on."

"Perhaps so. Anyhow, I've been wanting to tell you that I did my best for you, but unfortunately…" Suddenly he grimaced. "Oh, I've got a terrific pain in the back of my head," he said through clenched teeth. He went rigid for a moment, then slumped, his head lolling to one side.

Both Thomas and Watson rushed to him, catching him as he toppled from his chair, and together they carried him into the adjoining bedroom.

Mia snatched up the office phone and told Security to locate Howard Bruenn, the president's doctor-in-residence. Within moments, he arrived and rushed into the bedroom.

Mia stood at first helplessly with the artist, wondering what was the appropriate thing to do. Watson would inform the First Lady, but then Mia remembered that one other very important person needed to know.

She took up the phone again and asked the switchboard to connect her with the hospital. While she waited for Harry Hopkins to come to the phone, Dr. Bruenn emerged from the bedroom and closed the door behind him.

"I'm sorry to tell you. The president is dead."

CHAPTER TWENTY-NINE

Two days later, the body of Franklin Delano Roosevelt was borne on a gun carriage from the hospital back to the White House before a sea of mourning Americans. Mia stood on the White House steps with the other staff as six uniformed pallbearers slow-walked the flag-covered casket up the stairs. The president had not wanted a state funeral, and so his casket lay only briefly in the White House to be visited by close friends and by Congress, then was transported by train to Hyde Park for burial.

The world war had been so cataclysmic and the president's leadership so central that his sudden passing seemed a nasty trick of fate. Now, while a bland Missouri hat maker was stepping into the shoes of a giant back in the White House, Mia rode on the train with Roosevelt's close friends and family.

She stared brooding out the window at the early spring countryside, then felt someone sit down next to her.

Lorena Hickok laid a hand on her forearm. "We haven't spoken in a while, and I've neglected you terribly. I'm sorry. I just want you to know I did my best for you."

"How very strange. That's exactly what the president said, just minutes before he died. But I have no idea what that means."

"He said that too? I'm sure he was referring to the cable that came after you returned from Moscow. About your friend. Eleanor asked the president if he had any influence on Stalin for such things. He was sympathetic but didn't hold out much hope. Obviously, he either never brought it up or Stalin said no. Bigger issues to deal with, I suppose."

Mia cringed at the idea that five people in the White House, including the president, knew about her love for a Russian sniper. "I thank all of you for your concern, but that was completely unnecessary. It was my personal sorrow."

"Yes, dear. I know. But we take care of our own. And now I've got to go take care of Eleanor." She patted Mia's hand one more time and continued down the aisle of the train.

Mia slumped back in her seat, both embarrassed and touched, and with an additional reason to mourn the passing of Franklin Delano Roosevelt.

❖

April continued with one momentous event following the other. Within ten days of the funeral and the swearing in of Harry Truman, the Western Allies and the Red Army met on the Elbe. The Third Reich was on its knees. Five days after that, Adolf Hitler committed suicide, and it became headless. Seven days later, its remaining military leadership surrendered unconditionally.

Truman, who had been vice president only eighty-three days and had played no part in Roosevelt's negotiations, turned his attention to the continuing war in the Pacific. Yet more—much more—needed to be done about Europe. On May 20, 1945, Harry Hopkins called Mia into his office one more time.

She sat down without invitation. They'd long ago done away with formalities, and she felt sure he was about to terminate her job anyhow.

"So, now that President Truman has shut down Lend-Lease to the Soviets, we'll be closing this office, I suppose," she said, making it easier for him.

Hopkins tapped off the millionth ash of his millionth cigarette and smiled ambiguously. "Not quite yet. It's true that Truman ended the program officially on May 11, but Stalin was so angry, it looked like it would affect postwar talks. So I've got to go over there and work out a compromise. An extension, with limited provisions, at least through the summer."

Mia nodded. Where was this leading?

His smile widened. "You ready for one more round with Uncle Joe?"

"Me? Meet with Joseph Stalin?" She was speechless.

"Yep. Six meetings, starting on May 26. Harriman's also coming, to discuss China, Japan, the Control Council for Germany, Poland, the United Nations, all that kind of thing."

Mia stared into space for a moment. Return to Moscow, where she'd suffered the greatest joys and worst torments of her life? Where the woman she loved might be within reach, but also the man who wanted to kill her?

"Ready when you are."

❖

Hopkins, with Mia at his side taking notes, labored through the six meetings, placating Stalin. It seemed to her they'd given up a lot, but they still needed Stalin's goodwill to work on the United Nations, to continue against the Japanese, to plan the agenda for the reconstruction of Germany.

She dared not bring up the subject of Alexia and the Gulag, had no idea even of how to approach it with Hopkins. Against the magnitude of the negotiations, it seemed presumptuous, not to say ludicrous, to plead for the life of a single woman.

The meetings she attended were tense, and she sensed the waning of goodwill of both Hopkins and Harriman in the face of Stalin's demands—demands they would have to meet.

But after the final session, with typical Russian bonhomie, Stalin slapped Hopkins on the back and announced a victory dinner in the Catherine the Great Ballroom.

The banquet was pure Russian and included the entire Politburo, the top echelon of military leaders and commissars, and Moscow's inventory of ambassadors of other countries. For Hopkins, who had already said in private that he was "on leave from death," it was obviously a test of endurance.

Mia was glad the fighting was over and that Hopkins had wrung at least a few concessions from Stalin, but her personal bereavement remained unchanged. Molotov made no eye contact with her during the evening, but she sensed his cold presence. He was being lionized by the great dictator and applauded by the entire company, and she hated him for it.

She drank with restraint, as Hopkins did, though out of bitterness rather than sickness. By the end of the evening, which was in fact nearly morning, she and Hopkins were two of the very few people in the Catherine the Great Hall still sober.

As the guests began to stagger away, she saw that Hopkins was in a conversation with Ustinov and showed no sign of leaving. Catching his eye, she signaled that she would meet him later at the embassy car outside and left the hall.

The victory banquet would be the last hurrah before the return to Washington to face multiple terminations. Harry Hopkins would retire from White House service, Lend-Lease contracts would expire, and she would soon have to find other employment. The Kremlin visits would simply be memories colored forever by the images of a stunning Kremlin guard she'd fallen in love with. She regretted bitterly that she had no photo of her and nothing she could use but her name to track her down one day.

For that matter, she'd have to memorize Moscow and the Kremlin as well. Would she be allowed to explore the Kremlin Palace a little before their departure?

The adjoining great halls were open, and she crept as inconspicuously as possible from one to the other. She could not help but be both appalled at the extravagance of the tsars and impressed by their art.

"So, *you* are the one," a rough voice said behind her. She froze, as if caught in a crime, wondering who had snagged her. Chagrined, she turned around.

Joseph Stalin stood in the doorway smoking his pipe.

Mia was confused. "'The one,' sir?"

"Yes, the one who helped my foreign minister Molotov uncover the corruption in the factories. That we punished severely and without hesitation."

Mia forced a smile. "Yes, sir. That was me."

"And you were also the object of a certain remark President Roosevelt made to me. On behalf of his wife, he said." The dictator puffed a moment on his pipe and blew the smoke out of the side of his mouth.

She was puzzled. What had she to do with President Roosevelt or the First Lady? He continued puffing on his pipe as he strolled past the ornate walls and furniture without bothering to look at them, like someone's uncle who'd been talked into visiting an art gallery he didn't care about.

"A good man, your President Roosevelt. This Truman fellow, I don't think he's made of the same stuff."

"It's hard to say, sir. He's only just started."

Stalin shrugged. "Maybe. But I was fond of Mr. Roosevelt. He always wanted to talk 'man to man,' as if no one else was in the room but us."

"He valued the personal touch."

"Yes, the personal. It's easy to forget the personal when you're conducting a war. You get used to moving armies around, issuing orders that will cost thousands of lives—those of your people or the enemy, sometimes both."

Mia thought of the endless purges.

"Did you know, we lost about a million people in Stalingrad alone? But it couldn't be otherwise. Stalingrad had to be held, even if it took a million dead to hold it. If I had thought about the suffering of any one soldier and held back, we'd have lost the city and perhaps the war."

Where was he going with this? Why wax philosophical to her, a foreigner and a capitalist? He had no idea she'd been one of those soldiers he didn't care about.

"You have to harden your heart, ignore loyalties, the urges of friendship, and concentrate on annihilating the enemy at whatever cost. Ultimately, a father knows what is best for his children, and they must obey."

She cringed inwardly, at the same outrageous words she'd heard her father say. She was also aware of how he could bend and twist the word "enemy" and strike at the heart of the people he was ostensibly defending. Curiously, she was not afraid of him.

"And yet, Marshal Stalin, doesn't the personal intrude now and again? After all, we're not automatons, not even a field marshal moving armies. We're flesh and blood, and we love." She realized with a shock that she was arguing with Joseph Stalin and fell silent.

He seemed not to notice her insolence and puffed again, blowing smoke again from the side of his mouth. "Yes, I remember love. It was a very long time ago. A dangerous indulgence."

Finally he took the pipe from between his teeth. "In any case, the 'personal' is not really my style. I'm not in the habit of granting personal favors, least of all to foreigners." He pointed the mouthpiece of his pipe at her, as if to hold her attention. "But this was a man I admired."

"He asked you for a favor, sir?" She hoped he'd get to the point soon.

"Yes, and it is also curious that this favor was identical to the one requested by Major Pavlichenko. I might almost think it was a conspiracy." He chortled, and she wished she could shout, "What the hell are you talking about?!"

"But a great man has died before he could see the fruits of his labors." Stalin walked another few paces, looking everywhere but at her. "So, out of respect for his memory, I will grant this one request, strange as it is. Good evening to you." With a brief nod in her direction, the dictator of the Soviet Union exited the room, letting the fifteen-foot door close behind him.

She stood, speechless, still at the center of the great chamber, a bundle of confusion in a dark dress in the midst of splendor.

The creak of another door opening drew her attention. Molotov stood in the entrance of the neighboring stateroom and beckoned her.

Molotov, her archenemy. Yet in the wake of Stalin's little speech, he seemed harmless. She crept cautiously toward him, and as she reached the door, he stepped aside, revealing another person seated on a chair behind him. Mia entered, incredulous.

Alexia stood up. She wore a fresh uniform, though it was stripped of insignia, medals, and rank. Her face was thin, not yet gaunt, though lack of facial fat accentuated the muscle around her mouth. Her hair was shorter than it had been, and not shaped, as if it had grown untended. Her gray eyes shone as she smiled weakly, then glanced anxiously at the foreign minister.

"By order of the boss," Molotov said dismissively, as if her release meant nothing to him. He slapped an envelope into her hand. "Here's her exit visa. Now get her out of the country and out of my sight."

"Just like that? She's free?" Mia stammered, taking the first steps toward Alexia.

Molotov's face grew hard. "On this condition. Not *one* word. Not the slightest hint to the press about our arrangement and its history. And if you believe you can break this agreement once you are in your own country, let me disabuse you. We have men in Washington who will be watching, reading your newspapers. If this story appears, something very bad will happen to you. Immediately."

She was certain his threat was real. "Do Mr. Hopkins and Mr. Harriman know about this?"

"I presume the boss is telling them now. What they do about it is no problem of mine. Her name is removed from the military records. Just take her out of here."

He did an about-face and strode from the hall.

CHAPTER THIRTY

Five days later, Mia and Alexia stood together among the spring blossoms in the Rose Garden.

"So this is the White House," Alexia said. "I hadn't expected it to be so simple."

"Compared with your tsarist palaces, I suppose it is. But then, we didn't have five hundred years of autocracy flaunting its wealth."

"Your head of state is now…?"

"Harry Truman. Much less scary than yours. He's less inclined to execute people who disagree with him. I wish I could have brought you back to more stability, but everything changed all at once. The war in Europe ended, Mr. Roosevelt died, and my job has almost finished. I'm at loose ends myself." She touched Alexia's hand lightly, not daring to hold it. "But I'm sure it's much worse for you."

"Yes. I feel like I've leapt a great chasm and that I'm still in mid-leap."

Mia turned to face her directly, smiling at the new hairstyle. "Are you having any regrets yet?"

"Many of them. That I was not kinder to the friends I lost. That I wasn't present when my grandmother died. That I wasted so much time as a Kremlin ornament rather than as a soldier. But no regrets about coming home with you, my dear Demetria. None at all."

Mia began strolling again. "Well, the US is not paradise. We have our own problems. Negroes still don't enjoy the 'freedom' we're all supposed to have, and people like you and I must still live in secret."

"But at least we don't have to fear labor camps or execution," Alexia said.

"No. No execution. And can you feel it? That both our countries are changing? Perhaps one day, before we're too old, we can return to a kinder Russia without Stalin, and locate Kalya and Klavdia."

"Yes. That's something to look forward to."

"In the meantime, you have a job at Georgetown, thanks to Miss Hickok, and we have a sunny room in a boardinghouse until we can get our own apartment. I still have to tie up the loose ends of Lend-Lease for Mr. Hopkins, so I'm employed for another month. After that, we have our whole lives to do what we want."

"And you're still allowed in the White House?"

Mia laughed. "Don't worry. Mr. Truman has given me all the time I need to transfer my records to Mr. Hopkins's Washington office and move my belongings from my room."

"So we can sleep there tonight? That's good. I want to be able to say one day that we made love in the White House."

Mia snickered lewdly at the thought. "We'll have to do it quietly, you know."

Alexia brushed one shoulder against her. "We can be quiet. We're snipers, remember?"

POSTSCRIPT

World War II: September 1939 (invasion of Poland) to September 1945 (surrender of Japan.) The US supplied its allies with war material from August 1941 but sent troops initially to Asia in 1942. The first frontal assault on occupied Europe was not until June 1944, and the Soviet Union, by far, suffered the most casualties. Wikipedia estimates: USA: 420,000, England: 451,000, France: 600,000, China: 15–20 million, Soviet Union: 27 million. Recognition of Soviet casualties and victory in Berlin makes it all the more disturbing that many Americans today do not know that Russia was an ally and believe that the US won the war.

Women in Soviet Military: Women began in the usual support roles: administration, industry, medicine, traffic control, communication, laundry, political education, partisans bands. Due more to the dire threat posed by the German invasion in 1941 than to the Communist policy of egalitarianism, women were gradually accepted into active combat. By the middle of the war, they were fighter pilots, tank commanders, machine gunners, artillery and anti-aircraft gunners, and snipers. Soviet policy remained ambivalent, however. Although some 800,000 women served actively in battle, women were not allowed to march in the Moscow Victory Parade, and after the war they were pressured to return to the roles of wife and mother.

Central Women's School of Sniper Training: Between 1943 and 1945, the school at Vishniaki graduated seven classes totaling more than

1,000 female snipers and 407 sniper-instructors. The most conservative estimate is that female snipers eliminated more than 18,000 fascists, equivalent to an entire division.

Stalin (Joseph Vissarionovich Dzhughashvili) 1878 –1953: Supreme ruler of the Soviet Union from the mid-1920s until 1953. Though he oversaw the Soviet victory over Nazi Germany, he did it at the cost of millions of his people, a ruthless "not one step backward" frontline policy, and the abandonment of Russian POWs. He deeply resented the delayed entry of the Western Allies into Europe while Russians were dying by the millions, but the advance of the Red Army to Germany without the aid of allies meant communist domination of virtually all of Eastern Europe after the war.

STAVKA (Russian Ставка): Soviet High Command, a term taken over from tsarist times. It consisted of Stalin, his defense minister, chief of staff, foreign minister, several marshals, a commissar, and an admiral. It also established "permanent counselors" of more marshals and heads of air force and police. Membership shifted throughout the war as people fell in and out of favor.

Vyacheslav Molotov (1890–1986): As Stalin's "right-hand man" and foreign minister, he played a prominent role in all negotiations with the Western Allies during and after the war. Infamously, he was the chief negotiator of the Nazi-Soviet nonaggression pact until the Germans violated it by invading the Soviet Union in 1941. He also held the title of first deputy premier from 1942 to 1957, when he was dismissed by Khrushchev. While he apparently *did* visit the White House with a hidden loaf of bread and loaded pistol, he did NOT siphon off Lend-Lease supplies to the black market or kidnap an American investigator.

NKVD: The People's Commissariat for Internal Affairs was the principal law-enforcement agency of the Soviet Union. It consisted of regular, traffic, and military police; firefighters; and border guards. As a state security force, the NKVD managed the Gulag system (see below) and conducted deportations, espionage operations, and political assassinations. Its responsibilities were later subdivided into specialized groups, of which the best known is the KGB.

Lyudmila Pavlichenko: Celebrated Soviet sniper, with a tally of 309 recorded Germans killed. She was invited to the White House by the Roosevelts in November 1942, then toured several American cities and Toronto to encourage American entry into the war. She made her "you have been hiding behind my back" speech in Chicago. She survived the war and worked as a researcher at the Soviet Navy headquarters. The film *Battle for Sebastopol*, released in February 2016, supposedly is based on her life, with a purely fictional romance interjected.

The Mosin Nagant: The sturdy workhorse of the riflemen, which could be dismantled with its bayonet as the only tool. A special scope was added to the Mosin for use by snipers.

Gulag: Acronym for "main administration of the camps." A vast network of forced labor camps established in 1918 and greatly expanded during the Stalinist era. Camp inmates were criminals at all levels, political opponents, and anyone who fell afoul of somebody important. The camps, with their free labor, played a valuable role in production and also served as an important means of political repression. Sentences were arbitrary and severe, while conditions ranged from rigorous to deadly, particularly in the Siberian camps. (Aleksandr Solzhenitsyn made them famous in the West in 1973 with the publication of *The Gulag Archipelago*.)

Franklin Delano Roosevelt (January 1882–April 1945): Arguably America's most liberal twentieth-century president and the only one elected to a fourth term. After creating the New Deal programs to relieve the Depression of the 1930s, he led the USA in war in the 1940s. With US public opinion against fighting on foreign soil, he provided diplomatic and financial support first to China and Britain, then to the Soviets and dozens of other countries through his Lend-Lease program (see below). When the Pearl Harbor attack forced military engagement, he worked closely with Winston Churchill and Joseph

Stalin, and depended greatly on Harry Hopkins to manage diplomacy with them in his absence. He died of a cerebral hemorrhage one month before the end of the war (and eighteen days before Adolf Hitler).

Harry Hopkins and Lend-Lease: Social worker and charity leader, Hopkins became a trusted advisor to FDR while the latter was governor of New York. In the 1930s, the new president then entrusted him with creating and directing various relief programs in the New Deal. When the war began, Hopkins was a key policy-maker for the Lend-Lease program that manufactured and shipped some fifty billion dollars in war material to Free France, Britain, China, the USSR, and other allies until 1945. From May 1940, he lived intermittently at the White House for some three and a half years, becoming Roosevelt's de facto secretary of state in negotiations with Churchill and Stalin regarding the war and the formation of the United Nations. A suspected cancer caused the removal of most of his stomach, which, for the rest of his life, made him gaunt and sickly, and he died nine months after FDR of cirrhosis and malnutrition.

The Tehran Plot: Soviet Intelligence uncovered a plot (called Operation Longjump) by the Waffen-SS to capture or kill Stalin, Churchill, and Roosevelt at the Tehran Conference. The plot was subsequently aborted. Nonetheless, it caused Roosevelt to house his delegation in a part of the Soviet embassy in Tehran. While Western intelligence was skeptical of the story, Soviet intelligence—and later public opinion—was convinced of its authenticity. It has been the subject of several books and documentaries.

Eleanor Roosevelt and Lorena Hickok: Due to the increasing visibility and legitimacy of lesbian relationships, the friendship between Eleanor and Lorena is now accepted by most historians as romantic. Whether or not they actually slept together, Eleanor's more than two thousand letters to Lorena were unmistakably love letters, revealing that their affection was constant and passionate. From January 1941 until January 1945, Hickok slept in a guest room on the uppermost floor of the White House, while she kept a nominal address at the Mayflower

Hotel in DC. After FDR's death, she lived in a cottage on the Roosevelt estate in Hyde Park until she died in 1968.

Dostoyevsky and the Grand Inquisitor: Characters and themes from the novel *The Brothers Karamazov* haunt the novel. While Dostoyevsky was obsessed with God, and the average Soviet soldier was certainly not, there are significant emotional parallels. The Bolsheviks rejected Orthodox Christianity only to replace it with the secular "religion" of obedience to the Communist State, and thus perpetuated the same tension—between obedience to oppressive authority and its overthrow. Dostoyevsky's novel revolves around a patricide, an obvious symbol of throwing off authority, and one could argue that desertion and defection from the Soviet State amounted to political patricide. Joseph Stalin stands in well for Dostoyevsky's Grand Inquisitor, who claims to be a realist and the savior of men from the agony of too much freedom. Both are tyrants. But Dostoyevsky's antidote, the all-conquering kiss—in the context of a world war—rings childish and pathetic. However, as the novel suggests, there are kisses, and *kisses*. Some can kill you and some can make you free.

About the Author

Retired university professor, opera manager, editor, Justine Saracen has written eleven historical thrillers that span the ages, from Ancient Egypt (*The 100th Generation*) through the Italian Renaissance (*Sistine Heresy*), to World War II; on opera (*Mephisto Aria*) religion (*Sarah, Son of God, Beloved Gomorrah*), and mountain gorillas (*Dian's Ghost*).

Recently, she's focused on World War II, starting with *Tyger, Tyger, Burning Bright*, which traces the lives of spies, terrorists, and queers in Nazi Germany; *Waiting for the Violins*, about the French and Belgian resistance; *The Witch of Stalingrad*, on the life of Soviet fighter pilot, Lilya Litviak; and *The Sniper's Kiss*, about female Soviet snipers, with shades of Dostoyevsky lurking in the background.

While her novels have won numerous Golden Crown and Rainbow prizes through the years, in February 2016, she was awarded the high-profile Alice B Readers' medal for her entire body of work.

Justine, who speaks German and French, lives in Brussels, from whence she travels widely for research and scuba diving.

Books Available From Bold Strokes Books

The Sniper's Kiss by Justine Saracen. The power of a kiss: it can swell your heart with splendor, declare abject submission, and sometimes blow your brains out. (978-1-62639-839-9)

Divided Nation, United Hearts by Yolanda Wallace. In a nation torn in two by a most uncivil war, can love conquer the divide? (978-1-62639-847-4)

Fury's Bridge by Brey Willows. What if your life depended on someone who didn't believe in your existence? (978-1-62639-841-2)

Lightning Strikes by Cass Sellars. When Parker Duncan and Sydney Hyatt's one-night stand turns to more, both women must fight demons past and present to cling to the relationship neither of them thought she wanted. (978-1-62639-956-3)

Love in Disaster by Charlotte Greene. A professor and a celebrity chef are drawn together by chance, but can their attraction survive a natural disaster? (978-1-62639-885-6)

Secret Hearts by Radclyffe. Can two women from different worlds find common ground while fighting their secret desires? (978-1-62639-932-7)

Sins of Our Fathers by A. Rose Mathieu. Solving gruesome murder cases is only one of Elizabeth Campbell's challenges; another is her growing attraction to the female detective who is hell-bent on keeping her client in prison. (978-1-62639-873-3)

Troop 18 by Jessica L. Webb. Charged with uncovering the destructive secret that a troop of RCMP cadets has been hiding, Andy must put aside her worries about Kate and uncover the conspiracy before it's too late. (978-1-62639-934-1)

Worthy of Trust and Confidence by Kara A. McLeod. FBI Special Agent Ryan O'Connor is about to discover the hard way that when you can only handle one type of answer to a question, it really is better not to ask. (978-1-62639-889-4)

Amounting to Nothing by Karis Walsh. When mounted police officer Billie Mitchell steps in to save beautiful murder witness Merissa Karr, worlds collide on the rough city streets of Tacoma, Washington. (978-1-62639-728-6)

Becoming You by Michelle Grubb. Airlie Porter has a secret. A deep, dark, destructive secret that threatens to engulf her if she can't find the courage to face who she really is and who she really wants to be with. (978-1-62639-811-5)

Birthright by Missouri Vaun. When spies bring news that a swordswoman imprisoned in a neighboring kingdom bears the Royal mark, Princess Kathryn sets out to rescue Aiden, true heir to the Belstaff throne. (978-1-62639-485-8)

Crescent City Confidential by Aurora Rey. When romance and danger are in the air, writer Sam Torres learns the Big Easy is anything but. (978-1-62639-764-4)

Love Down Under by MJ Williamz. Wylie loves Amarina, but if Amarina isn't out, can their relationship last? (978-1-62639-726-2)

Privacy Glass by Missouri Vaun. Things heat up when Nash Wiley commandeers a limo and her best friend for a late drive out to the beach: Champagne on ice, seat belts optional, and privacy glass a must. (978-1-62639-705-7)

The Impasse by Franci McMahon. A horse-packing excursion into the Montana Wilderness becomes an adventure of terrifying proportions for Miles and ten women on an outfitter-led trip. (978-1-62639-781-1)

The Right Kind of Wrong by PJ Trebelhorn. Bartender Quinn Burke is happy with her life as a playgirl until she realizes she can't fight her feelings any longer for her best friend, bookstore owner Grace Everett. (978-1-62639-771-2)